I0635712

Thing were so perfect—and then this has to happen…

"I can't marry you, Jim." She started crying, slowly at first and then profusely. She buried her head in her pillow and sobbed uncontrollably.

"I don't understand," he said in disbelief. "What do you mean?"

When she had stopped crying, she spoke again. "I just can't live on a farm. I want to live in Dallas or Houston or maybe even San Antonio. I don't want to dry up and wither away out in the middle of nowhere.

"But that's crazy, Laura. No two people have ever been as right for each other as we are. What can it possibly matter where we live? You have to know that I love you."

"I know," she said. "And I love you too. I just wish you could see things my way. You have so much going for you. You could play baseball or start your own business. Why do you have to be so obsessed with that farm?"

He talked to her and tried to reason with her but to no avail. Her mind was made up and there was no changing it, and it left him heartsick. The blow had stunned him down to his foundation. How could he not see this coming? How could this girl, this woman, he loved with all his heart have turned out to be so shallow? Even if he changed his mind now and consented to what she wanted, it would not be the same. It would never be the same again.

Thing were so perfect—and then this has to happen...

"I can't marry you, Jim." She started crying, slowly at first and then profusely. She buried her head in her pillow and sobbed uncontrollably.

"I don't understand," he said in disbelief. "What do you mean?"

When she had stopped crying, she spoke again. "I just can't live on a farm. I want to live in Dallas or Houston or maybe even San Antonio. I don't want to dry up and wither away out in the middle of nowhere.

"But that's crazy, Laura. No two people have ever been as right for each other as we are. What can it possibly matter where we live? You have to know that I love you."

"I know," she said. "And I love you too. I just wish you could see things my way. You have so much going for you. You could play baseball or start your own business. Why do you have to be so obsessed with that farm?"

He talked to her and tried to reason with her but to no avail. Her mind was made up and there was no changing it, and it left him heartsick. The blow had stunned him down to his foundation. How could he not see this coming? How could this girl, this woman, he loved with all his heart have turned out to be so shallow? Even if he changed his mind now and consented to what she wanted, it would not be the same. It would never be the same again.

Texas dairy farmer, Alton Kemper, has a life changing experience following the death of his son James, a soldier in World War II, when he decides he has to live again for his grandson. Alton's grandson, Jimmy, grows up in the shadow of his bigger-than-life grandfather, learning what is it means to be a man of honor. While in college, Jimmy suffers a broken heart and, as a result, joins the army, becoming a helicopter pilot, and is sent to Vietnam. Though he fears for Jimmy's safety, Alton understands his grandson's desire to serve his country. Jimmy promises to come back and run the farm for his grandfather after the war. But Alton dies before Jimmy returns, making Jimmy all the more determined to be the best man that he can be as a tribute to his beloved grandfather. But life presents many challenges, and the Kemper family must endure not only hardship, but loss…

KUDOS for *The House Wren*

In *The House Wren* by Jack Sprouse, Alton Kemper is a dairy farmer, taking over for his wife's father when the old man dies. Alton and his wife Mary lose their son Jim in World War II, but his grandson Jimmy inherits the farm when Alton dies. The story follows Jimmy and his family through their trials and tribulations as they struggle to raise their children and be honorable men and women. Like most of Sprouse's stories, this one is moving and poignant, both a family saga and a heart-warming romance. ~ *Taylor Jones, The Review Team of Taylor Jones & Regan Murphy*

The House Wren by Jack Sprouse is the story of the Kemper family, Texas dairy farmers and entrepreneurs. Alton's son Jim dies in World War II, but his grandson Jimmy, who is five at the time, gives him something to live for and brings him out of his depression. When Jimmy goes to college, he falls in love, but the girl doesn't want to be a farmer's wife, and she breaks up with him. This sends him into a deep depression and he leaves college and goes to war in Vietnam. Alton dies while Jimmy is in Vietnam, and Jimmy is devastated. The story then follows Jimmy and his children through their lives, loves, and losses as they carve a niche for the family in the history of Texas. Like Sprouse's other works, *The House Wren* has multiple plot lines all woven together into a cohesive whole. While it is a saga of an important Texas family, it is also the story of each individual family member seeking love and a meaning to life, trying to outshine or outdo his or her siblings, but most of all, trying to be upstanding and honorable human being so as not to disappoint their father and grandfather—poignant and heartwarming. ~ *Regan Murphy, The Review Team of Taylor Jones & Regan Murphy*

The House Wren

A Novel

Jack Sprouse

A Black Opal Books Publication

GENRE: FAMILY SAGA

This is a work of fiction. Names, places, characters and incidents are either the product of the author's imagination or are used fictitiously, and any resemblance to any actual persons, living or dead, businesses, organizations, events or locales is entirely coincidental. All trademarks, service marks, registered trademarks, and registered service marks are the property of their respective owners and are used herein for identification purposes only. The publisher does not have any control over or assume any responsibility for author or third-party websites or their contents.

THE HOUSE WREN
Copyright © 2018 by Jack Sprouse
Cover Design by Cheyenne Middleton
All cover art copyright © 2018
All Rights Reserved
Print ISBN: 978-1-644370-37-7

First Publication: NOVEMBER 2018

Published by Black Opal Books **http://www.blackopalbooks.com**

*This book is dedicated to
my grandson, Kai Sensabaugh*

Prologue

Alton Kemper

1918:

Twenty-six-year-old Alton Kemper wiped the sweat from his forehead and cursed at nothing in particular. While many of the young men around Coleman County were joining the army to go to France to fight the Germans, Alton was working on a dairy farm and had not been drafted. His boss, Leonard Bartley, had encouraged him not to enlist because he needed Alton on the farm. He'd promised more pay and bonuses if he'd stay on, but none of that had been forthcoming. Alton grew more and more disgruntled as the days turned into weeks and then into months. He felt he would never get out of this place.

Bartley hired several migrant workers who had wandered onto the farm looking for any work available. He used them for two weeks and then when payday rolled around, the County Constable showed up and arrested them before they got their money. The men were trying to talk to the constable in what broken English they knew. Alton could only assume they were trying to explain that they had not been paid yet, but their efforts fell on deaf ears.

He confronted Bartley about it. "You cheated those men, Leonard, you know you did. You had that set up with the lawman to come and pick those men up so you wouldn't have to pay them. That's a sorry way to do a man."

"It's none of your concern, Kemper," Bartley said. "You need to mind your own business and let me handle mine."

Leonard Bartley was twenty years older than Alton, and a few inches shorter, so Alton had no intention of doing him any harm. But the man was arrogant and seemingly without conscience. He sneered at Alton through a mouthful of gapped and broken teeth. His graying beard and deep set dark eyes were menacing, but not as menacing as the pistol he always carried in his right front coveralls pocket. "You get your ass back to work or I'll fire you."

"You won't have to fire me," Alton said, "I quit. I've had enough of your lies and sorry ways. Just get my pay and I'll be off your property."

"You don't have much coming," Bartley said. "You've got room and board coming out of it."

"I know exactly how much I got coming, just get it, and I'll be on my way."

"I don't think I owe you anything, mister, you just go on and get out of here before I get mad." The man patted his right pocket where he kept his gun and again sneered at Alton.

Alton rushed Bartley, suddenly, before the man could react, and he knocked him to the ground. He then took the pistol out of Leonard's pocket, unloaded it, and threw it into the water tank under the windmill. He was on top of the man beating him on his face and head when the man's wife came out of the house, screaming and crying. "Don't kill him, please don't kill him."

"I'm not going to kill him," Alton told her. "I just want my pay and I'm leaving."

"How much does he owe you?"

"He owes me four dollars minus a dollar for room and board, so three dollars."

She went into the house and came out with a five-dollar bill. "Here Alton, take this, I'm sorry for the trouble my husband caused you."

"Thank you, ma'am," he said. "You're too good for that man."

Alton never forgot the look on those men's faces when they realized they had worked for two weeks and were not going to be paid for their labor. Seeing the injustice of such an act, Alton Kemper made himself a promise that he would never cheat another human being as long as he lived. White, Black, Brown, or whatever color they might be, he would never again look at the face of a man who'd had his labor, the work of his hands, stolen from him by another man. Food taken from the mouths of his children must surely be a terrible thing to happen to a man. If he had any means of preventing such inhumanity, Alton would do so. Hell, if there be such a place, must have a special place for men who do such things, he believed.

Alton got his bag, with everything he owned in the world in it, walked to the highway, and started trying to thumb a ride. He wanted to get as far away as he could from the Bartley farm, for fear that Bartley might call the law on him. Alton nervously looked both ways down the road, not caring which way a vehicle might be going, as long as it would take him out of Coleman County. He spotted a Model T truck coming toward him.

The truck slowed down as it approached him then pulled over and stopped. The man motioned for Alton to get in, and he did. "Where you headed, pal?" the man asked him.

"Anywhere but here," Alton replied. "Where are you going?"

"I'm headed over to Comanche, been delivering some stuff for my pa. We live just outside Comanche. My pa owns a hardware and lumber yard in town. I'm Homer Sudbury, what's your name?"

"I'm Alton Kemper. I grew up around Brady, Texas. No work around there that pays a decent wage. I was working for a man named Leonard Bartley near here. He made a lot of promises he didn't keep, never meant to keep, I expect. One thing led to another and I ended up beating the hell out of him and drawing my pay. Now don't get me wrong, I didn't beat him up just because I wanted to, I beat him up because he wasn't going to pay me. His wife paid me so I stopped beating the hell out of him."

"Sounds to me like the man needed to have the hell beat out of him," Homer said.

"No man ever needed it more."

"So, what kind of work do you do, Alton?"

"My ol' man owned a dairy farm outside of Brady. I worked for him until I was seventeen. He beat up my ma one too many times, so I took a tire iron to him. He spent some time in the hospital, and I helped my ma sell the farm before he got out. I signed his name to the deed for the new owner and gave the money to my ma. She went back to her family in Indiana."

"Sounds like you've had a hard time of it, Alton. Why don't you come stay a while with us? My pa won't mind, he'll be glad to have you. We can give you some work in the lumberyard and give you room and board."

"That's mighty generous," Alton said. "I appreciate it. I'm a hard worker."

"I figured you for a good hand. I kinda run the store for Pa so I'll fix a place for you there. There's a café across the street where you can eat. We have a contract with them to provide two meals a day for our hired hands. The food's tolerable and there's plenty of it."

Alton nodded, thinking he'd finally got a break.

Homer took Alton to a room in the back of the hardware store. There was a single bed, a small chest-of-drawers, a bath tub, and clothes stand but no closet. "It's not much, Alton," Homer said. I'll fix it up a bit. Pa used to sleep here ever so often when he worked really late. Like I said, it's not much."

"It's fine, Homer, I'm obliged to you."

"The Wander Inn café is just across the street. You can eat breakfast and lunch there on us. You're on your own for supper. The name is a takeoff on the first owner, Wanda Burton. She died a couple of years ago and the new owners didn't bother to change the name."

"Thank you," Alton said. "And tell your pa I said thanks, too."

Alton started to work the very next day. The work was not hard, just fast-paced because the store had a lot of business. It was the only hardware, mercantile, and lumberyard for many towns around.

The food was not as good as Mrs. Bartley's was, but the company was a lot more congenial. Alton filled nail orders, climbed ladders to retrieve goods or tools from the higher shelves, and helped load lumber onto customer's trucks. The days were busy and went by quickly but nights were lonely and boring. He turned in early but often could not sleep. He spent a lot of time at night in the café across the street, just drinking coffee, and occasionally eating a piece of pie. Sometimes he'd walk around the town and talk to whoever might be standing around.

Alton soon became fairly well known around town He impressed many folks as being a congenial man who was best not riled up. Homer Sudbury discovered one afternoon the peril of getting on the wrong side of Alton Kemper.

Two brothers, Burt and Billy Crenshaw, came into the store to return a hand cranked drill and bit they had purchased two weeks earlier. The tool had been used and appeared to have been left out in the rain.

They wanted their money back. Homer refused to return their money, claiming they had damaged the drill. The two were not happy and threatened Homer with a beating.

Alton heard and saw what was going on and came over to observe.

"Who the hell are you?" Billy Crenshaw asked him, looking hard at Alton.

"I work for Homer," Alton said.

"Well, if you want to be able to keep working, you better mind your own business," he replied.

"This *is* my business." Alton said.

The man moved toward Alton and poked his index finger into Alton's chest. He ended up on the floor, the receiver of a punch from Kemper's right hand. Before he could get up, Alton pummeled the other brother with a series of punches. Both men got up and ran out the door yelling something about getting even with Alton as they left, leaving the drill lying on the counter.

"Damn, Alton," Homer said. "I sure am glad I gave you a ride." They both laughed. "Thanks for helping me out."

"It was my pleasure, Homer. I hate obnoxious assholes like that."

"I do too. Those guys are nothing but trouble. They're always drunk and disorderly. They're just good for nothings but you better keep an eye out for them. They might come back one night to get even."

"I will," Alton said.

"Hey, Alton, why don't you come out to the house this Sunday for dinner?" I can pick you up in time for church and then we'll go to the house. Mother is a real good cook."

"I'd like that," Alton replied. "I'm not much for church but I guess it won't hurt me. I don't have any Sunday clothes, though."

"It's a country church, hell, nobody dresses up. Most of the folks who go there don't have a pot to piss in."

Alton was ready at eight a.m. when Homer arrived to pick him up.

They drove out the north side of Comanche to a small white wood frame building. Other folks were starting to arrive. There were quite a few, Alton noticed, at least thirty-five people or so. Homer's folks were standing outside waiting for them.

Homer's dad was a tall and lanky man, clean shaven with a full head of gray hair. He reached out and shook Alton's hand. "I am happy to make your acquaintance, Alton. I've heard good things about you from my son Homer."

"I've heard good things about you too, Mister Sudbury—from Homer, too"

"Now none of that," he said, "you call me George. This is my wife, Emma."

"I'm happy to meet you, ma'am." Alton said. She reached out her hand and Alton shook it. Her handshake was so soft that he was afraid he'd hurt her.

As they entered the church, Alton noticed a sign by the front door.

MOUNT PLEASANT BAPTIST CHURCH

Organized under a brush arbor, with 21 charter members,

Oct. 16, 1892. First pastor, F. M. Herring, and E. M. Moore, Jesse Cunningham and C. C. McCurdy composed the Presbytery. Will Dewitt gave land, Nov. 26, 1892, on which the first building was dedicated, May 1893. Tabernacle was built in 1906 and present church, 1913. The charter members were The Revs. and Mmes. Frank Herring and Jim Fagan, Messrs. and Mmes. Will Dewitt, Jake Hodges, John Cameron, Dave Coker, Alfred Loftis and J. A. Payne, also Mrs. E. B. Farmer, Beckie Leech, Green West, Cordelia McNutt, Z. K. Smith.

Before the preaching began, they sang several songs out of the Baptist Hymnal. Then a young girl went to the front of the church and sang a song called Beulah Land. Alton had never heard such a voice before. The girl was pretty, but not overpoweringly so, and slightly plump and she kept looking at Alton over her shoulder from the front row of pews. There was an older man sitting with her, Alton assumed he was her father.

Alton had not been to church in years, not since his mother used to take him when he was a boy. The sermon was pretty much like he remembered from his childhood. There was a lot of talk about Jesus and hell and loving your neighbor. Neighbors were not always easy to love, Alton knew, but the Sudburys were good people, he could tell that right away.

The Sunday dinner was just about what he expected, fried chicken and mashed potatoes and cream gravy, some vegetables—squash, green beans—biscuits and Iced tea.

"This is the best meal I've had in years, Mrs. Sudbury, maybe the best meal I've *ever* had," Alton said.

"That's quite a compliment, Mister Kemper, but you call me Emma."

"I will, ma'am, if you'll not call me Mister Kemper, my name is Alton."

"It's a deal," she said.

On the ride back to town, Alton asked Homer about the girl who sang the song.

"That's Mary McCarthy," Homer told him, "And her father James McCarthy. James has a farm just east of the church a couple of miles. He's a good man but he's had a hard time. His wife died a few years back and now it's just him and his daughter. Mary is twenty-two and never been kissed, as near as I can tell."

"I'd like to change that," Alton said.

"I figured that might be where you were going with that. I can have them come to dinner next week after church and you can meet her. That's if you want me to."

"Yes," Alton replied quickly, "I'd like that very much. You mean you'd do that?"

"My folks are good friends with the McCarthys, we have them over quite often. Count on it next Sunday."

"I don't know what to say, Homer, thank you. I'll do some extra work around the store to make it up to you."

"No need for that," Homer said, "you do plenty of work. You're the best hand we ever had."

Mary McCarthy was a pleasant girl but, to Alton, she seemed very lonely. She rarely left the farm except to go to town with her father. She smiled at Alton across the Sudburys' dinner table, and he smiled back. "I really enjoyed your sing-ing, Mary," he told her. "You sing like an angel."

"Thank you, Alton," James McCarthy interjected before his daughter could respond. "I think so too. Mary sings all the time around the house. It's about the only entertainment I have since my wife died. She was a singer too."

Mary was embarrassed and started blushing. She kept steal-ing looks at Alton, a fact that was not lost on either Alton or Mary's father. She liked him, Alton could tell. He asked James if he could take Mary for a walk around the Sudbury property, and James agreed. Homer Sudbury assured him that he, Alton, had no ill intentions toward James' daughter. He explained Alton's circumstances to James and told him that Alton was a good man, a diamond in a coal bin was the way Homer put it.

The woods behind the Sudbury home led down to the creek. Mary said she liked to walk along the creek so they wandered down to the water's edge and Alton picked up some stones and threw them into the creek. She was nervous, not really knowing this man she was with. He was a very quiet man, although Emma Sudbury had told her how he had fought to save her son from a beating. She knew he was not timid, but he seemed withdrawn to her. "What are you thinking, Alton?" she asked him.

"I'm thinking how lucky I am," he said. "Two months ago, I was out of a job, broke, and didn't know where I was going to sleep at night, and now I have a good job, a place to stay, a little money in the bank, and here I am walking along Duncan Creek with you, the prettiest girl I've ever seen."

She almost swooned but managed not to show it. "Oh, come on, you flatterer, surely you've seen prettier girls than me."

"Maybe so," he said, "but they weren't pretty on the inside too. Listen, Mary, I like you. I liked you the first time I saw you looking over your shoulder at me in church. And when I heard you sing, well, that was it." He clutched at his heart, dramatically, and fell to the ground while she giggled at him.

"Well, I see that my mysterious man is also very charming. What do you do for an encore, Mister Kemper?"

He seemed to be deep in thought, putting his hand up to his head to emphasize that he was contemplating her question. She continued her giggling.

Suddenly, a water moccasin came slithering out of the grass headed for the creek. It was not attacking but its path would have taken it right between Mary's legs.

He yelled, "Watch out," and grabbed her around the waist. Swinging her around out of the path of the snake, he set her down but kept his arms around her. She saw the snake and was terrified but turned her face back toward his. He kissed her and she did not draw back but returned his passion with her own.

They kissed for what seemed to Alton a very long time. Finally, he stopped and they just looked at each other. "I promised your father this wouldn't happen," he said. "I hope you can keep a secret."

"I don't believe that just happened," she said, "so until I'm convinced it, did I'm not going to tell anyone."

"Oh, it happened, Mary," he assured her, and pulled her to him again and down to the ground. They were on their knees, locked in each other's arms. They kissed again, stopping momentarily only to breath and then continued. She was hungry for a man, Alton knew. His need made him lay her down on the ground.

"I can't go all the way, Alton," she told him while trying get her breath, "not here, not yet."

"I know, Mary, I don't expect that. I'm sorry, I'm really sorry. I didn't mean to disrespect you. Can I call on you sometime?"

"Yes, Alton, I would love for you to call on me. I'll be disappointed if you do not."

"Thank you, Mary," he said sheepishly, "I promise you this won't happen again."

"Well, in that case, don't bother calling on me," she said, giggling.

"Okay," he said, smiling, "I can't promise you this won't happen again."

As they were walking back to the Sudbury house, Alton noticed that Mary had gotten some mud on her dress when he laid her down on the ground. "How are we going to explain the mud on your dress, Mary?" He asked her.

"Watch me," she said, and when they got back to the house she told her father. "Daddy, I almost got bit by a water moccasin, but Alton grabbed me and pulled me out of the way. We almost fell in the creek. I think I ruined my dress."

"You'll survive the dress," her father said. "A snake bite could have cost me more than a dress. I'm obliged to you, Alton."

"Wasn't that big a deal, Mister McCarthy," Alton responded. He looked at Mary who was smiling at him.

Mary began picking Alton up for church every Sunday, saving Homer the trouble, and it wasn't very long before Alton was having dinner at the McCarthy's place. He offered to do some work for Mary's father but James wouldn't hear of it. Instead, Alton helped Mary do the dishes and clean up the house. James finally relented. "Okay, Alton, you win, you can help me slop the pigs and milk the cows. I can't stand to see a man washing dishes."

One Sunday, after dinner, James McCarthy asked Alton to take a walk around the farm with him. "I want to talk to you about something."

"Yes, sir," Alton said, "what can I do for you?"

"Alton, I'm twice your age, and I'm not in the best of health. I'm not yet blind, although a blind man can see that Mary loves you. You're all she talks about. I mean she won't shut up about you. I don't know how you feel about her, but I do have some idea. In any case, I'd like to offer you a deal."

"I love her too, Mister McCarthy. I never loved anyone until I met Mary."

"I'd allowed you might say that, real love is hard to hide. But here's my deal. I'm going to ask you to come here and work for me. I'll talk to the Sudburys, if that's a problem for you. I'll match the pay, and you can stay in the room across the breezeway.

"Would you be opposed to me asking Mary to marry me?"

"No, Alton, I wouldn't," James said "I'd be honored to have you for a son-in-law."

"What if Mary turns me down?"

"That's a risk I'm willing to take, Alton." They both laughed out loud at that.

"Now all I have to do is ask her, any suggestions?

"Just ask her," James said. "Now I recall that you said your dad had a dairy farm and that you liked working with cows. Well, I will turn this farm into a dairy farm, if you want me to. I don't know much about dairy farming, but you can teach me. I'll put this place in yours and Mary's name so that, when I croak, it will belong to you two.

"What's croak mean, Mister McCarthy?"

"That's a term for dying that my ol' man used to use."

"Croak, okay," Alton said.

⁊⁊⁊

The wedding was held at Mount Pleasant, and James McCarthy loaned them his car to go on their honeymoon. They spent the weekend in Brownwood, and Alton was back at the farm Sunday night to get some sleep before the next work day on Monday.

Mary moved her things to the room across the breezeway.

Homer Sudbury told James that he saw this coming the first time he saw Alton and Mary trying not to look at each other that first day in church.

James bought ten cows and more milking equipment, buckets, and another separator. They still had to do the work by hand. He couldn't afford milking machines yet. Alton told him that would come in time. Alton was up before dawn every morning and worked as late as the work required. "I've never seen a man work so hard, Mary," James told his daughter. "He is driven to get things done."

"You gave him a chance, Daddy. You gave him hope and a reason to work."

"No, you did that, daughter. A good woman can turn a man around. Alton was never a bad man, he just got down on his luck."

೮∕ාℰ∕ා

In July of 1922, a baby boy was born to Mary and Alton Kemper. He was fat and healthy. They named him James, after Mary's father. McCarthy was a good grandfather, and he spoiled the boy terribly, but neither Mary nor Alton complained. They were happy to have a son and each other. Alton began considering the possibilities of the farm he had almost inherited. As long as his strength held out, he knew he could make the place financially viable. James wanted to continue growing watermelons and peanuts, rather than make the farm exclusively a dairy. He wanted another means of making money, just in case.

A year later, Mary discovered she was pregnant again.

"A girl this time," Alton said, a girl just like you, Mary."

But it was not to be. Mary miscarried a month later. She cried for days, and Alton tried hard to be strong for her. Both he and James were heartbroken over it, but they went on about their business.

Just before Christmas, 1925, James McCarthy passed away. The loss hit Mary hard, and Alton was hurt more than she would ever know. James had been like a father to him. He'd given Alton both his daughter and his farm. Alton just could not comprehend these kinds of people, so trusting and so giving. He thought, surely, he must have been singled out to have a blessed life. But now it was just him and Mary and the baby James. The work had to go on.

Alton rolled up his sleeves, kissed his wife and son, and went out to work their dairy farm.

Chapter 1

The Beginning

1947:

The August sun hanging in the clear blue Texas sky seemed not the least bit inclined to continue its afternoon trek westward. Those fortunate men and beasts who could afford the luxury had long since sought shelter and shade from the heat. This caused no grief however to the mighty sun who was content, as was his nature, to vent his fury on all who remained out of doors.

Allie Kemper thought that summer must surely be a curse visited only on Texas. It seemed, to Allie, that a blanket had been spread across the length and breadth of Comanche County, a hot sticky wool blanket that covered the land and threatened to stifle life itself. She wiped the perspiration from her forehead and peered out through the kitchen window of the little wood-frame farmhouse that had been her home for the last seven years. Cloth curtains, adorned with little yellow flowers, framed the window. Gathered at the sides, to permit entry to any errant breeze that might present itself, they allowed the clinking sound of the dishes Allie was washing to drift out through the window and steal gently across the east pasture. It was the only sound that could be heard in the still hot air, save that of an old box turtle plopping into the shallow water over on Duncan Creek.

Moving one of the curtains slightly, allowed Allie to see her father-in-law Alton Kemper. He was sitting on a little wooden bench propped against the smokehouse. She studied

him momentarily, hoping he would not catch her staring at
him. He was tired, she knew, bone tired, not just tired from the
day's work but tired down to his soul. Alton was tired of life,
she guessed.

She watched the hard, handsome face, now weathered and
beaten by time and stress. The graying hair made him look
older than his fifty-five years. Were it not for his excellent
physical condition which had been tempered by a life of
steady work, he could easily have been mistaken for a man
with at least ten extra years. Still, Allie thought, her father-in-
law was a better man than most men twenty years younger
than he was. He was troubled though, so troubled. It hurt her
to see him this way. She took a dish from the soapy water,
rinsed it and laid it on the draining towel, and then moved one
of the curtains slightly so he would not see her through the
window. Wiping a tear from her eye, she brushed her hair back
off her forehead. He was so different from the man he once
had been.

The curtains started to dance in a sudden breeze and the
windmill cranked up again with that infernal rattling that drove
her crazy. The breeze was welcome, though, truly a welcome
relief, and Allie leaned her head back and opened the front of
her dress to enjoy the rushing air coming in through the window.

⋐⋑⋐⋑

Alton reached for the butcher knife on the table next to
him, cut a slice of watermelon, and bit into it. It was still cool
from the icebox. He took in seeds and all and separated them
inside his mouth then spat each one out with a little thumping
noise into the dry dust at his feet. He was watching a wren at
work building a nest in the eave of the house just where the
roof came down to meet the porch overhang. Alton had torn
down the nest once, but now the little bird was back and
seemed intent on moving in. Soon, if the male wren could entice his ladylove to move in as well and lay her eggs, then the
farm would be alive with the noisy little creatures. This time,

Alton had decided to leave the bird alone. His energy was gone, and he had other struggles to deal with, too many other things to worry about. There was no time anymore to pick a fight with a little house wren that seemed more determined to take up residence in Alton's home than Alton was to kick him out. If the bird could live with a hard-nosed old man, then Alton figured he could tolerate the bird and his new family.

The sudden gust of wind that blew in the kitchen window, so softly caressing the lovely face of Allie Kemper and starting the windmill to rattling, was a mixed blessing to the old man. It cooled him momentarily, but now the windmill was singing a song that grated on his ears. One of the vanes had worked loose over a week ago, and Alton still had not climbed up there to fix it. The rattling noise of the loose vane was another reminder that he had fallen down on the job. His wife's gentle chiding, although well intentioned, only made him feel worse. Nothing made him feel worse, though, than the hurt look that had become a permanent fixture on the face of his daughter-in-law. Nothing topped that.

The old days were gone now, and he longed to have them back—those days so long ago when he had that special fire in his breast, that fire and that determination so prevalent in the young, so wasted on the young, that made him want to attack the world and make his mark on it. He'd wanted so badly to make something of this old place. He would have too if it hadn't been for the war. That damned war that had taken his son and had left his daughter-in-law and grandson without a husband and father. Now, if Alton didn't get off his backside and go to work, the farm was going to fall into disrepair before too long.

The watermelon tasted good, and he took another slice. Some clouds were forming off in the Northwest, promising rain. "Good," he said out loud, casting an accusing glance at the still blue sky, "about damned time." Then his face softened a little. "We could use some rain."

One day his strength would return—he knew it would—and more importantly his "want to." Then he would get back on his feet. They said hope springs eternal, or something like that. Anyway, soon he would get the dairy started up again. Then everything would be okay. Lord, he wasn't that old yet. He wasn't old enough to have just given up the way he had.

Shade from the big twin oak next to the smoke house provided some relief from the heat, but it did nothing to discourage the bothersome gnats that buzzed continually around his head. Slapping at them was futile. Cursing did not seem to help either, although it sometimes made him feel better. A man could learn to live with the dust and the heat, but no one ever got used to the damned gnats.

Reaching into his back pocket, he pulled out a handkerchief and wiped the sweat from his face. The wind died down momentarily, robbing him of what little bit of cool breeze he'd had but mercifully stopping the rattling noise of the windmill. Out of the corner of his eye, he noticed some movement behind the big oak. A small hand holding a toy pistol was protruding slightly from behind the tree. The hand was at the end of a little arm that was in turn attached to a young towhead about five years old. The boy's head was peeking out warily, just far enough to permit one eye to watch the old man. It quickly withdrew from time to time when he thought he had been noticed. A closer examination revealed a pair of bright blue eyes under an abundant crop of white-blonde hair. They were piercing sky blue eyes that adorned the handsome little face in perfect order and arrangement. Mischievously, they observed the man from a safe distance as the boy, wanting to move closer but not daring to, sought attention that was not being offered.

Sounds of imaginary gunfire began to emanate from the boy's mouth and were aimed, along with the toy pistol, at the graying head of the man trying to eat his watermelon in peace.

"Don't point that gun at me," Alton said quietly.

His request went unnoticed and, using all the patience, he could muster, he tolerated the assault a little longer. There was a time he recalled when it was accepted that you did not point a gun at a man, not even in fun. You only pointed a gun when you intended to use it. Kids were taught this rule early on, and it was never questioned. It still made him uncomfortable to look at the wrong side of a gun, even a toy. He was a throw-back perhaps. Maybe he *was* too old. He didn't know, but he still didn't like it. He never would."

"Boy," he said, his voice rising slightly, "how many times have I told you not to point guns at people?"

The boy seemed not to hear, and the imaginary gunfight continued. The man cut a fresh piece of melon and motioned to the figure behind the tree.

"You want some?" he asked him.

Slowly the youngster eased out from behind his cover and moved toward the man. A quick jerk sent the piece of wet red fruit flying through the air and the nuisance, now exposed, caught it full in his astonished little face. Instantly regretting his action, the man tried to reach for the boy who was now crying as loud as he could, but the tyke turned and ran.

The sudden appearance of the man's daughter-in-law told him that he had gone too far this time. She was angry, spitting mad. From her workplace at the kitchen window she had witnessed the entire scene. Her son's screams brought her out of the house just in time to see him running across the pasture toward the south woods as fast as his five-year-old legs would carry him. She spun on her heels and turned on the man who, now sorry for what he had done, was sitting there limp, waiting for the dressing down he knew was coming.

"Why did you do that, Dad?" she yelled at him.

"I told him over and over—" he started, but she wouldn't let him talk.

"He's just a little boy. He's not a man that you can talk to like a man or treat like a man. He's just a boy."

"He has to learn," he said defensively. "How is he ever going to learn if someone doesn't teach him?" He was wrong and he knew it, but it was not his way to admit it. He could not defend his actions to himself, much less, to the boy's mother. This was an argument he was not going to win. "I was just trying to teach him the right way to act," he said. "It'll save him a lot of grief when he grows up. I was just trying to teach him a lesson."

"No, you weren't, you were just being mean. That's the

wrong way to go about it anyway. Why can't you have some feelings for people? I swear, Dad. You treated James the same way. He hated you for it." She was crying now and the sudden look of anguish on the old man's face made her wish she had not said what she had.

"What do you mean?" he shot back. "James didn't hate me. Why did you say that?"

The man's hard exterior almost cracked and, for a brief moment, Allie thought he was going to cry too, but he quickly corrected himself and stood there staring at her as if he was lost. He struggled for words but none would come.

She wiped the tears from her eyes, unable to meet his gaze. Words uttered in anger, she thought, always hurt the most. He turned to walk away and she followed along after him, hoping to erase what had happened.

"I'm sorry, I didn't mean it, but James is dead and we can't change that. I wish it were not so too but it is. You don't have to be strong forever. Can't you just accept it and stop keeping it all inside you like you do? "Please," she said, still crying. "Go find Jimmy before he gets hurt or lost."

"I can't accept it. They took my son away and got him killed, and now everyone says I should just accept it and go on like nothing ever happened. I'll never accept that."

"They didn't take him away, Dad," she said. "He volunteered. He wanted to go. You know how he felt about it."

"It's okay for you, you have a life ahead of you without him—I don't."

"We've been through this before," she said, turning to go back in the house. "You know that's not fair."

He shrugged his shoulders and started out across the pasture to retrieve his grandson. Knowing she was right did not ease his pain. He had wanted his son to wait as long as he could before he went into the service. God knows he was needed on the farm. He would have been a lot more help to the country if he had stayed at home and helped Alton produce milk and food for the war effort. James would have none of that. Whatever it was that drives a man, to join the army and go off to war, to leave wife and child and his folks when he is so badly needed at home, Alton would never know.

James had wanted to sign up right away after the Japs bombed Pearl Harbor, but Allie talked him out of it because she was pregnant. They had rested easy for a while but then in late December of '42, barely six months after little Jimmy was born, James's mind was set, and he enlisted in the army. He'd seemed almost afraid the war would end before he got there. James and Allie waited four years to have a baby and then off James went just that easily.

After James's boot camp leave, they drove him to the bus station in Brownwood to go to Dallas for his shipping out orders. The last time Alton saw his son, James was hanging out of the bus window, waving goodbye to them all. Allie held Jimmy up so James could see him, not knowing it would be the last time he would ever see any of them. He had been full of that self-confidence and strength of purpose often found in young men, especially young American men headed for war. He was smiling broadly and then he was gone, gone to do his sacred duty, gone to save the world for democracy. Now he was buried somewhere in France, right alongside thousands of other people's sons who just like James, went off to do their duty.

The town held a memorial service after the news came about James's death. James had "made the ultimate sacrifice," the man said. He had paid the greatest price that anyone could pay. Because of James and many other boys just like him, millions of people in Europe would now be free and America would be safe. Alton sat and listened while Allie and his wife Mary cried. They meant well. Alton knew that, but speeches were cheap and easy to come by. Sons were not. He'd only had one and now that one son was gone and Europe still was not much better off.

Alton Kemper didn't much care who was free or who wasn't free in Europe. Those people fought all the time anyway. Nobody he knew could even tell the difference in a Kraut, or a Frenchie, or even a Pollock for that matter, without maybe getting real close and listening to them talk. Some could maybe if they heard them talk, but he couldn't. Now the war was over and everybody was all friendly again, acting like nothing had ever happened.

He'd heard on the radio that America was now stronger than ever. That was good, he guessed. That was fine for America, but the Kemper family sure as hell wasn't as strong as it once was. The war had cost him a lot more than it had cost America. America had lots of sons. He'd only had one. Somewhere now, out there on his farm, a little boy was hiding, hiding from his grandfather.

"What a sorry state of affairs," Alton said out loud.

He walked the length of the creek that ran through his property, expecting to find Jimmy sitting on the bank. The water was not deep in the creek but the bottom was treacherous in places with many sinkholes, almost like quicksand, that could trap and hold small animals or a child. Once he'd pulled two pigs out of one of the sinkholes after James left the gate to the pen open and the pigs ran off. It was funny now, twenty years later, but he'd really tanned James's hide for it. He wished now that he had not done it.

A search of the south woods—which really didn't deserve to be called woods, for it was just a stand of trees about two acres in area which Alton liked to identify thusly—did not turn up the boy. Crossing the peanut field, he checked the water tank where his son used to sit for hours on end, just daydreaming. It was quiet and still, except for the buzzing of gnats and flies that were always in abundance. Alton was dumbfounded now, more annoyed than concerned, that the boy would run off like that.

Ruined my afternoon break, he was thinking. There were few places on the farm with which Alton was not familiar so he really was not worried about finding Jimmy, but now with the wind picking up again and rain threatening, he was starting to feel some sense of urgency.

When he got back to the house, the women were starting to fret. His wife suggested he go for the sheriff, but he said no. He would make another pass around the farm.

"I'll find him," he assured them. "He's just a boy. He couldn't go far."

His daughter-in-law's eyes met his, and he stared at her, wanting to apologize but not knowing how.

"It's okay, Dad," she said to him. "I know you didn't mean it."

"Thank you, Allie," he said. "Don't worry about Jimmy, I'll find him."

He turned and shuffled off toward the barn, expecting to find the young man there. He had hurt Allie, and he knew it, and she, as always, had forgiven him again. Allie was the one person he most of all didn't want to hurt. She had stayed with them on the farm after James was killed at Normandy. She had stayed and let Jimmy spend his first few years with them. When most women would have been out husband hunting Allie had stayed. She had endured the last three years of his downfall with a stubborn inner strength he'd never realized she had in earlier days. Allie had practically supported them— practically, hell, she had supported them, when he almost lost the dairy and the farm as well. What a blessing his daughter-in-law had been to him and Mary. More a daughter than a daughter-in-law, she came into their lives unexpectedly and had remained with them when no one else would have, especially with her own family trying to tear her away as they had done. Guilt came over him as he paused at the door of the barn to catch his breath. He was having a little trouble breathing. "Just worried about Jimmy," he said out loud. He pulled his handkerchief out of his overalls again and wiped his forehead. He was sweating much more than usual now. The barn was empty except for the cows.

"Where's Jimmy, girls?" he asked them. He smiled as a couple of them actually turned to look, as if trying to help. "Nobody seen him?"

He called the boy's name several times but there was no answer. "He might be in the loft," he said, talking to the cows again, but as he started up the ladder a sharp pain suddenly shot through his left arm, and he decided against that. Jimmy wouldn't be in the loft. His mother never let him play there for

fear he might fall. Anyway, if he were there, wouldn't he answer when his grandfather called him?

When another search of the farm failed to uncover the
boy's whereabouts, the man was no longer just annoyed. Now
he was scared. A feeling like a cloud of doom came over him,
and he began to imagine all sorts of things that could have
happened. Jimmy could have left the farm and just kept going
and now could be lost, or worse. He could have stumbled upon
a snake and been bitten. He might be lying somewhere now,
dying. God, how could Alton go back to the house and tell
them that? All this trouble because he didn't want the boy to
point a toy gun at him. That was just how his old man would
have handled it—tough old bastard always had to be tough.
Alton hadn't turned out any better than his old man.

He had never been afraid of much in his life, neither man
nor beast, and only mildly timid in the presence of God Al-
mighty, being the strong-willed man that he was. But the fear
that gripped him now was foreign and confusing to him. Sweat
broke out on his forehead again, cold sweat this time, and he
again wiped it off as he began to grow nauseous. He yelled
Jimmy's name louder and louder with no response.

"Where is he?" he cried aloud, his voice heard only by the
wind and the rain that was now starting to fall.

Suddenly, his left arm became numb and then began to tin-
gle as if a thousand needlepoints were sticking into it. He felt a
tightening in his chest, a dull constricting pain, like a belt being cinched around him that held him powerless and unable to
move. He struggled, trying to cradle his left arm in the right
one and shook uncontrollably, falling first to one knee and
then the other. The pain doubled him over, forcing his face
into the dirt. Again, he tried to move but his stricken body
would not obey.

By now, Alton was certain he was going to die. He had
never prayed much. Prayer didn't come easy to him—for
women and kids, he always said. Anyway, Mary had always
taken care of that business. She must have prayed an awful lot
to have been able to tolerate him all these years they had been
married. After word came about James, she began to pray

more than ever. She prayed and he just sat and let everything go to the dogs.

It seemed a mite hypocritical to start praying now. He could not ask God for his own sorry life, not now, not after so many years of neglecting Him. God would see through that right away. But for the boy, though, for the boy he would do anything. God, he thought, his grandson was still out there somewhere, maybe hurt, maybe dead, by now, for all he knew. If something had happened to Jimmy, Alton hoped he would die. He couldn't face life if something happened to Jimmy and it was his fault.

The pain was almost unbearable now, and he cried out as loudly as he could with all the strength he could gather up but his voice was only a faint whisper drowned out by the wind and the slowly increasing rain that was now pelting the back of his head.

"Oh God," he said, "I've been a mean and selfish man all my life. I never gave you much thought. I never gave much thought to anyone but myself. I never took the time. If you let me die now, I know I deserve it but please, God, let the boy be okay. Let Jimmy be okay. Give me enough time to find him safe and make up for the way I've been, for the way I treated his daddy. God he's only five years old. They took his daddy. He needs me. Oh, Lord, I need him. I need them all."

He wasn't sure how long he'd been there on the ground, it seemed like forever, but after a while the pain started to ease up and after a while longer he sensed the feeling returning to his arm. His body began to relax as the intensity of the constriction in his chest lessened somewhat, and he found he could breathe a little easier now. For a moment, just for a moment, he felt like he might not die after all. Precious minutes longer, he lay there soaked now and starting to get a chill, a chill—in August. The women must be terrified. Thinking again, his mind racing now, first Jimmy gone and now him. *Much to do, much to do, got to find the boy.* Struggling, he managed to get to his knees and, in doing so, he thrust his face into the now driving rain and let the rain fall unabated into his eyes and mouth. "Thank You, Lord," he said, stretching out his arms and turning his palms upward in an act of total contrition. "Thank you, Lord, thank you for my life."

He sat there in the rain until the pain was completely gone then got to his feet, certain now that he was okay. He might go see Doc Ramsey next week about this if he could do it without anyone knowing. He didn't want the family to know. They would make a fuss.

Through Alton's rain-blurred vision the barn appeared in the distance. The loft door was open. It shouldn't be open. He hadn't checked the loft, too out of breath, and Jimmy didn't answer when Alton called him. Jimmy must be in the loft—no he would have answered, unless he was scared. But how could he be scared of his grandfather? How could he be so scared that he would hide from his own grandfather? It was impossible to think like a five-year-old.

Alton started for the barn, half walking and half running, the urgency of the moment almost overwhelming him as his heart raced faster and faster with each step he took. He got to the barn and struggled up the ladder to the loft. In the loft, he found the boy lying in the hay. He had apparently circled the entire farm, somehow managing to evade his older pursuer and then sought refuge in the barn.

Climbing into the loft, he had lain down between two bales of hay and had fallen asleep. He still slept soundly, the sleep of the innocent, not knowing that his grandfather was standing over him weeping unashamedly. Alton was free now of all the bitterness and anger that had plagued him the past three years since his son's death. He was grateful to God, grateful for this second chance at life. His big shoulders shook as he continued sobbing, his tears mixing with the rain that was still running off his head. Alton didn't want to wake the boy. He wanted to just stand and watch him for a while, and he would have done it, except for the women. He knew the women would be frantic. He had to let them know that Jimmy was okay.

The loft door offered an unobstructed view over the smoke house to the back porch of the house. He could see his wife and daughter-in-law standing on the porch wringing their hands and looking in all directions—terrified, he knew. Cradling Jimmy in his arms, he lifted him up and held him in the doorway so they could see that he was safe.

Mother and grandmother spotted them at the same time and both jumped up and down and hugged each other happily, the way women do. He waved his hand, and they acknowledged it then turned to go back in the house. He could see Allie wiping the tears from her face as she looked back over her shoulder at him.

"They'll be along when the rain lets up," she said.

As Alton was laying him down again, Jimmy awoke with a look of terror on his face. He tried to get away but his grandfather was quicker and held him tightly. It's okay, Jimmy," he said. "It's okay. It's Grandpa. You've been asleep. Why are you scared? There's nothing to be afraid of."

"I thought you were going to spank me," Jimmy said, whimpering. "I thought you were mad at me."

"Spank you, I've never spanked you. Why would I do that?"

"For pointing the gun at you, I thought you were mad at me. You yelled at me."

The man was overwhelmed with the love he felt for his young grandson. He brushed the hair out of the boy's eyes and watched him for a moment. In his mind, he had gone back in time thirty years and was sitting here with his son James. He was getting a second chance, a chance to make up for all the misery he had caused his family in the past three years and, more importantly, a chance to be a real part of another young man's life. He could not remember ever having such deep feelings before in his life, and it had been years since he had felt so wonderful. God had used this small boy to save an old man's life.

"I'll never spank you, Jimmy, never, Come here." Alton took the little boy in his arms and held him against his chest for a minute or two. "I love you, Jimmy," he said. "I'll always love you. I'm sorry for scaring you like I did."

A smile beamed across Jimmy's little face and he looked up at the man. "I love you too, Grandpa," he said.

"Look here, Jimmy I want to give you something. You

know that someday this farm will be yours. I don't care what you do with it—you can sell it if you want to, that doesn't matter. I know you don't know what I'm talking about. You will one day, but I want to give you something now." Alton reached into the bib of his overalls and pulled out his pocket watch, a shiny gold Bulova. He looked at it for a moment. He loved that watch. He fingers traced the little designs around the outer edge of each side. "You see this watch, Jimmy?" he asked him.

"Uh huh," the boy said, nodding his head.

"This is one of the finest watches ever made. It's a railroad watch and—"

"Did you work on the railroad?"

"No, I just got this watch. I'm going to give it to your mom to keep for you. Okay?"

"You're all wet, Grandpa," Jimmy said, pointing at the man's soaked clothing.

"What? Oh, yeah, I know, your mom says so too sometimes, I was looking for you in the rain."

"I know, I saw you at the tank. I was watching the snake doctors, and I hid from you and snuck back to the barn."

"Okay, that's okay, but now do you understand what I've been saying? You'll have to wait until I croak to get the farm, but I want you to have my watch now. You can play with it in the house and, when you're old enough, you can carry it with you. How does that sound?" There was no response from the boy and he seemed to be deep in thought. "You understand, Jimmy?" Alton said again.

"What's "croak" mean, Grandpa?"

"I mean when I die, Jimmy, when I go on to Heaven."

A wellspring seemed to open up inside the boy and his little blue eyes filled with tears. "I don't want you to die, Grandpa, I love you." He jumped into the man's arms and clung to his neck for all he was worth.

"I'm not going to die, boy, not now, not for a very long time. We've got too much to do now."

They sat there for some time, hugging and laughing and ruffling each other's hair, each throwing mock punches at the other like imaginary boxers.

"Listen," the man said, pointing at the roof of the barn. "The rain has stopped. I'll bet Grandma has some hot biscuits and sugar syrup ready, whatta you bet?"

"Yeah," Jimmy said. "I bet so too."

"Okay, up you go on my back. Put your arms around my neck and hold on. We're going down the ladder."

The clouds were drawing back, and brilliant beams of sunlight filtered down in all directions as if bringing a very special blessing to the Kemper farm. Alton believed that the sky was as blue as he had ever seen it. The wind had died down and the windmill was again quiet. He would climb up there tomorrow, for sure, and fix it. A lot of things needed fixing around this place, and he was going to see to that too. It was a beautiful day. Any day it rained in this country was a good day, but today was especially so.

They stopped at the edge of the house to look in on the wren and found him quite at home and content just sitting there waiting for the weather to clear up so he could return to his labors. Alton was glad now that the little bird had returned. He was happy now to share his home with him, and he looked forward to having all the other wrens around that he knew would soon follow. He held Jimmy up so the boy could get a closer look.

"He's our neighbor, Jimmy," Alton said, "and our friend. Wrens only live where there is lots of love, and this one has picked us to live with. We have been blessed this day." Then he carried his grandson into the house to get some of Grandma's biscuits and sugar syrup, stealing a look back over his shoulder at the clearing blue sky. "It was a beautiful day," he thought.

Yes, sir, it had really turned out to be a beautiful day.

Chapter 2

Allie

1940-1949:

She mostly wore sundresses—brightly colored sundresses that graced her figure in the most wonderful way, and permitted her light silky brown hair to fall ever so gently upon olive toned shoulders, shoulders that appeared to be perpetually tanned. Adorning her nose, a line of freckles, barely visible except in bright sunlight, gave her a tomboyish look. She observed the world around her through the most amazing green eyes, eyes that could draw a second glance from both men and women alike.

She became aware of her good looks early in her life. She learned about the magic in her eyes. She found that when she looked at men a certain way, a little longer than they expected, they would usually divert their eyes away from hers. She enjoyed the play. She enjoyed making men feel uncomfortable. Those eyes and her slightly parted and pouting lips always had the same results. She got her way. Little girl games, used first against her father, then uncles and such, then any other unsuspecting males who might come around, Allie had practiced and honed to perfection by the time she had reached her womanhood.

Allison Matthews (Allie) was the prettiest girl in Comanche county. There were few who would disagree that she was the prettiest girl for many counties around. At eighteen she was strikingly beautiful, and she knew it. Boys her own age were intimidated by her good looks and most were not capable of carrying on a conversation with her. She gained tremendous pleasure from the numbing power she found that she wielded over the young male animal. Even older men often became embarrassingly silly in her presence.

When Allie fell in love with James Kemper, no one was more surprised than James himself. He had not felt himself worthy of her, she, being from a well-to-do family and beautiful as she was and he, being the son of a farmer. He tried to not pay much visible attention to this flirtatious girl who commanded so much adoration from the other boys. He had noticed her, of course, and like all the other boys, he had feelings for her, secret longings, deep down inside where no one could see. Many nights, he lay awake in his bed, thinking of her, dreaming about her. But beautiful rich girls did not marry farmers. James knew that, and he hated his own life because of it, but he hated his father most of all for it was his father that James blamed for the family's station in this world. Fate had placed Allie Matthews out of his reach. He held no illusions concerning her, for he dared not hope that she would ever be his.

His life changed forever one Saturday afternoon when he ran into her at the Majestic Theater in town. She was with Trenton Hargrove, an older boy who worked for Allie's father, George Matthews. George had taken a liking to Trenton and was grooming him for what George called big things in his business.

Allie was with Trenton, but she didn't act like she was with him in the better sense of the term. He appeared to be more or less tagging along. James suspected that Trenton had been sent by Mister Matthews to watch over the man's capricious daughter.

"Hello, James," Allie yelled when she spotted him. "Come and sit with Trenton and me."

James was taken aback but, nevertheless, did as she had commanded. It was strange and wonderful to James, to be sitting next to her in the dimly lit movie house. Some friends from school spotted them and waved. James saw them looking back at the unlikely trio, obviously speculating about what was going on.

She played coyly between the two boys, talking at first to one and then to the other. Both sat there dutifully, grateful just to be in her company, neither seemed to resent the presence of the other. For the moment, there was enough of Allie's attention to go around. When she took James's hand and held it in hers, he thought for a moment that he was going to pass out. But he kept his head and his composure and managed to act like it was no big deal. He tried to act as if he were accustomed to going to the movies with the prettiest girl in town. He would never understand, for the life of him, why girls did the things they sometimes did. But he didn't care. It didn't matter why to James now. He was in love with Allie Matthews, and it wasn't long before everyone in town knew it. She started meeting him at the theater on Saturdays, and she no longer let Trenton tag along. A year later, they were still an item in Comanche.

The country was in the grips of the great depression. The 1930s had brought hardship on many folks in the county, but the Kempers had not fared too badly, considering. Alton Kemper had worked hard all his life. He stayed on his land and made it work for him. The small dairy didn't produce much, not like the larger dairies, but it was enough, and the watermelon and peanut crops added to his income and helped him make ends meet. He had even managed to accumulate a small savings account, a rarity for that day and time. It was hard work and prayers He had always said that he worked hard and his wife prayed.

Alton was determined that his son James would have every opportunity in life that Alton had not had. He wanted his boy to go to college. He wanted James to take over the running of the farm one day. To do that the right way, he needed an education. He wanted him to study agriculture and business. With the proper business know how, father and son could turn the farm into a prosperous concern. Alton was convinced of that. He knew James did not want to be a farmer. He couldn't blame him for that, but a gentleman farmer? Well, that was a different matter. Alton had always hoped he could make the farm into something that James would want to be a part of. That way, he would always have his family intact and at home. Alton had plans to buy some adjacent property so they could expand the operation. He hoped that somehow James would come to love the land as much as he did.

Alton denied, even to himself, that there was an underlying mood of resentment between the two, the depths of which neither of them fully understood. Years later, Alton would fondly recall the day James brought Allie Matthews home to meet them. James's mother Mary fell in love with her right away, and the feeling seemed to be mutual. She was invited to stay for dinner and quickly accepted. Both Alton and Mary were a bit surprised at James's catch. Not that their son was not a handsome boy, he was, but—and they would never say it to him—this girl was more than they had expected.

At the dinner table, Allie studied the older man at some length. He was as hard as nails, but he had a soft core, she decided, one that he did not allow anyone to see. She felt an attraction to him but was not sure why. It was respectful, but she was attracted to him just the same. He was a handsome man, for an older man. Although rough-cut and haggard, from years of hard work, he was actually more handsome than his son. She figured him to be in his late forties. He was, in fact, forty-five at the time.

She tried her female game on the elder Kemper. In time, Alton, would come to believe that Allies flirtations were not as much devious as they were attempts to gain attention. She was looking for something. He didn't think she knew herself what it was, that she tried to use her gender to obtain.

Nevertheless, on this night, she watched him across the table and captured his attention. As she gently stroked her long brown hair, she pushed one side behind her ear and, tilting her head slightly, she looked at him seductively through those captivating green eyes. She was surprised, almost miffed, when he did not seem at all disarmed by her. She was not accustomed to rejection, even passive rejection. Alton was amused at her transparent play.

"Can I pass you something, Allie?" he asked her.

"No, no thank you, Mister Kemper, I'm fine." She turned her eyes away from his, but something had happened that she would not be aware of until years later.

Alton Kemper was smitten with this lovely creature, half woman-half child, who had come home with his son but was now sitting at his dinner table toying with him, a man over twice her age. It was love at first sight, he would confide to her many years later. But it was not lustful. It was not a sexual attraction. She seemed to him to be more in need of a father than she did a man. He felt tenderness for her, and he sensed vulnerability in her that he expected she hid, knowingly or not, by her flirtations. If he could have had a daughter, if he could have designed the daughter of his heart, Allie Matthews was what she would have been. A quiet bond slowly formed between the man and this mysterious girl, who had suddenly come into their lives. It was a bond that neither would ever fully understand.

After dinner, James took Allie for a walk along Duncan Creek. The wind had died down and it was calm and pleasant out. She bounced slightly as she walked along with her hands clasped behind her back. They didn't speak for some time, then she broke the silence. "Your folks are nice, I like them both."

"My mother is nice. My father is…well, my father."

"That's mean, James. I thought he was very nice."

"He can be a hard man when he wants to be. I don't like him very much."

"James Kemper, don't you dare say that. You're talking about your father."

"You don't know him like I do, Allie. And you are a fine one to talk to me about my father, you don't have much respect for your father. How is that different from the way I do?"

"I don't want to talk about my father," she said, looking away from him.

"Why not, Allie?" he said. "I met him. He doesn't seem like such a bad guy."

"No, no," she said loudly, putting her hands over her ears and shaking her head dramatically.

"Okay, okay," he said. "I'm sorry, Allie. I won't mention it again."

"Please don't, James, I don't want to talk about him"

"Let me ask you something," he said, changing the subject.

"Okay," she said, looking at him curiously.

"That time at the movies, when you held my hand, I didn't think you even knew I was alive. Why did you do that?"

"I was trying to make Trenton jealous. Daddy wants me marry Trenton because he's Daddy's best salesman. He thinks Trenton has a great future. Besides, you're the only boy that doesn't trip over his tongue when you talk to me. I noticed you a lot in school. You just never realized. You're so serious. That's why I took your hand."

"That wasn't very nice to do that to Trenton. Everyone knew he was in love with you. Probably still is."

"I know, and I didn't mean any harm. He's a nice guy. He's never gotten out of line or anything. He's respectful, but I could never love Trenton because I love you."

James swallowed hard, not sure if he had heard her correctly. He had hoped that she might one day share his feelings, but they had never actually talked about that. He stared at her, not sure what to say next, and she gave him that same seductive look she had given his father at the dinner table.

"And you love me too, don't you?" she said.

"Yes," he said, "yes I do. From the minute, I first saw you, I loved you. I do love you, I do love you, Allie—" He would have continued fumbling around for more words, but she interrupted him.

"You've made your point," she said, laughing at his sudden ineptness.

He drew himself up straightly and turned to face her.

"Are you going to preach or salute the flag?" she said.

"Will you marry me Allie? He said, holding his breath.

She smiled devilishly and made him wait for, what seemed to him, an eternity. "Of course, I'll marry you James," she said finally. "I was beginning to think you weren't going to ask me."

"I wanted to," he said, "but I was afraid to. I was afraid you would say no."

"Why ever would I do that?" she asked him playfully. "Let's go tell your parents," she said taking his hand and pulling him toward the house.

George Matthews was not happy about the coming union but reluctantly gave Allie his blessing He asked only that she complete her second year of college so she could help him in the office. If she were not going to marry Trenton Hargrove, then he wanted her to be able to support herself, not being so sure that this farm boy would be able to take care of her properly. Allie agreed, and she and James were married a year later in the summer of 1938. Her father's hope that she would meet someone else while in college had not been realized, and he ultimately accepted the marriage.

The wedding was held at the First Baptist Church in town with May Ellen Matthews handling all the arrangements. The Kempers invited a few friends, and the Matthews invited a few hundred. The reception was moved away from the church so the guests could dance. Dancing was a mortal sin in the Baptist denomination. When Allie asked Alton Kemper for her first dance, he gently reminded her that that was a father's duty. She wrinkled up her nose and said okay, but Alton noticed that she did not dance with her father. He found his son and asked him if George Matthews was hard on his kids.

"I don't know," James said. "He must be because Allie wants nothing to do with him. The two boys are just stupid, I think, and Allie says they fight a lot with their father."

Later, Alton hugged her and told how happy he was to have her for his daughter-in-law.

"Thanks Dad," she said and danced away to enjoy her moment.

James and Allie rented a house in town. James drove out to the farm every morning to work, and Allie went to the Leather factory where she managed the office for her father. Old George just quit coming in to the office, and Allie could only speculate about where he went and what he did all day long. Rumor had it he was seeing a woman in Brownwood, but that was none of her business. Her mother didn't seem to mind as long as George kept her in spending money.

Allie suspected that her parents had not had a proper marriage for quite some time.

She was happy, truly happy. James was a good husband, not strong willed like his father but not as prone to losses of temper either. He never raised his voice to her when many men would have. He almost always let her have her way. Whether out of his all-consuming love for her or just from a desire not to have confrontation, James was a doting and dutiful husband. Some said he probably still could not believe she had married him.

"He thinks he'll wake up one day and find himself back on the farm married to some woman with no teeth," a friend said once, and James laughed along with everyone else.

Trenton eventually married a woman from over in Mills County and moved to Dallas to open a sales office for George Matthews. He had proven extremely capable in Matthews's leather-goods business. Trenton had introduced a new line of boots and hats that had almost doubled the company's income the past year, and George had virtually turned the business over to him, incurring the utter wrath and dissatisfaction of his own two sons, John and Luke, and his wife, May Ellen, as well. But George didn't care. Business was business, he always said, and if Trenton could make him more money than his two half-witted sons, then, by God, Trenton would run the business.

Late in the year of 1940, Mary Kemper took sick, and Allie stayed at farm to take care of her and to cook for her father-in-law. When Mary's illness lingered on, Allie suggested they move to the farm to live. James didn't like the idea but, at his wife's insistence, he reluctantly agreed, and the move was made back to the country. Allie took a leave of absence from the office, much to the displeasure of her father, and took over the Kemper household chores with a purpose. She cared for Mary Kemper like a dutiful daughter would do, and Alton was pleased to have her around. There was always a noticeable change in the atmosphere when Allie was around, he often remarked, a noticeably pleasant change.

In time, Mary's health improved, and she was back on her feet. Things slowly got back too normal, and James wanted to move back to town, but Allie objected. She liked it in the country, and she wanted to stay at the farm. Unable to sway her, he gave in. He was angry but he had never been able to stay mad at Allie for very long at a time.

Alton sat by the radio constantly now, listening for news from the war in Europe. "It's just a matter of time," he said, nodding his head with a knowing authority. "It won't be long before were in it."

"Do you think Roosevelt will really let us go to war?" James asked.

"Roosevelt—" Alton pronounced it Rewzavelt. "—wants a war. He wants to help the Limeys out."

"But shouldn't we help them, Dad? Don't you think the Germans have to be stopped? I mean, it's not right what they're doing, is it?"

"No, no it's not, but we saved the bastards once already, twenty years ago."

Mary asked him to watch his language, and he nodded his agreement to do so.

Allie said, "Isn't Kemper a German name, Dad?"

"The name is English, young lady," he said, smiling at her. "But I'm not. You mind your manners."

She smiled at his remarks. "Sorry, Dad," she said.

The evening talk around the dinner table continued to turn more and more toward the possibility of war. When Roosevelt was reelected in late 1940, Alton was more certain than ever that America would get into the fight.

After the 1938 recession, the economy had started to recover, and, by now, was booming, due to orders from European countries for arms and war equipment. The Kempers were doing better than ever. James had come to accept his station in life and his relationship with his father had improved to the point that he actually enjoyed being around the *old man* and, in spite of an occasional spat, he and Allie were happy. The family's financial situation improved considerably through 1941. The dairy was booming, right along with the rest of the country. James had landed the contract to provide milk for the schools in several counties, and that really brought in a lot of extra money. Alton didn't like billing people for his product and waiting a month for the money. He would have preferred cash on delivery, but as James explained, that was the way people did business now.

"If we're going to be gentlemen farmers, Dad, then we must adapt to the ways of the world."

Alton adapted, but it still made him uncomfortable to have people owe him money. He guessed he was just old fashioned, but he never knew when somebody might go broke and not pay him.

It was on a cold day in December while Alton and James were working on the smokehouse they heard a car racing up the road with the horn honking happily. A closer look told them it was Allie's car, but she was driving erratically and laying on the horn. They looked at each other in astonishment and, when she turned up the driveway and slid to a stop at the house, they both ran to see what was wrong.

"I'm pregnant," she said, smiling broadly then laughing loudly. "I'm going to have a baby."

James whooped and grabbed her, spinning her around wildly then holding her off the ground while he kissed her passionately.

"Easy, boy," Alton said. "The girl just said she was going to have a baby."

"It's okay, I'm three months along. I've suspected for a while but I went to the doctor today and he confirmed it. I'm so happy, James."

Mary came out of the house and joined in the celebration. "Allie's going to have a—"

"A grandson, yes, Mary, I heard." Alton wanted the baby to be a boy but the idea of having a granddaughter was very nice too, especially if she turned out looking like her mother. Alton wondered if this world was ready for another Allie Kemper. He wasn't so sure of that.

Sundays were quiet on the farm. With Alton mostly doing only what was essential to tend the cows, the cows did not know one day from another. The radio came on in the house, telling him that the others had returned from church. He could hear it, but he couldn't actually hear it. Someone in the house turned up the volume, and the ominous tone in the announcer's voice made Alton stop his work and go to check it out. Half way to the house, he saw Allie on the back porch, her hands covering her face, crying. A chill ran down his spine, and the hair stood up on the back of his neck.

"What's wrong, honey?" He was almost afraid to ask.

"The Japanese have bombed Pearl Harbor," she said.

The United States of America was at war, another war they had not wanted. It would be a long and bitter struggle, with no certainty at the moment of the final outcome. Alton knew their lives would soon change. Even as they listened that evening to what few details were available, the call was going out for manpower. He knew they would want his boy.

James Earl Kemper Jr. came into the world and into the lives of James and Allie Kemper on June 24, 1942. He was the most beautiful baby ever born, his paternal grandparents agreed. Allie's folks shared that appraisal of the young man but were prevented from saying so by the fact that they had other grandchildren. But, to the Kempers, he had no equal. Alton observed that the boy's eyes were Kemper blue. He would have bet money that any child of Allie's would have inherited those wonderful green eyes, but this was not the case. James Kemper was as happy as any new father could be, and he proved to be a good parent just as Alton had expected he would But, every day, more and more, he could see that far off look in his son's eyes. Alton knew what it meant. All across America, and across Comanche County, young men were going off to war.

James Kemper felt it was his duty to go to. He was almost hoping he would get drafted, so he would not have to fight with Allie and his folks about joining up. If he were drafted, they wouldn't be able to talk him out of it. He had acquiesced to Allie's pleading that he not go before the baby was born, but now Jimmy was here and...well, a man had his duty to do. He could not have other men going off to in his place. Not if he still wanted to call himself a man.

Before 1943, married men with children were not usually drafted, so it was unlikely that James would be called up. There was another way out, Alton knew, one that he would not dare suggest to his son. A farm worker could get a deferment if his father went to the draft board and requested it. This policy caused hard feelings between some families that used it to keep single sons from being called up, and other families who did not. Alton Kemper would not have felt good about using that method of keeping James at home. It left a bad taste in his mouth, and he knew James would not allow it.

"I'm going to join the army," James announced one evening at supper.

There was no talking him out of it, though Allie and his mother tried. And Alton was not so sure now that it was not best that he do what he perceived as his duty. A man certainly could not live with himself if he did not. Some counties in Texas were sending men to the Pacific, while others dispatched them to the European Theater. James wanted to fight the Germans, and he wanted to go to Europe, so in December he went down to Gillespie County where his uncle, Mary's brother, Joe Olson, lived, and there, he enlisted.

Around the Kemper household, the mood was almost as if someone had died. They hardly spoke at all, as if words were painful. Letters came regularly. James was happy with army life *It isn't so bad after boot camp.*" He didn't know where he was going. *They never tell us anything,* he wrote. *"We just do what we're told, no questions asked, but, after all, there is a war on and the army knows what's best.*

Early spring of 1944, Allie got another letter. James was in England. A lot of the letter was cut out, the work of the army censors, but from what she could tell, he was having a good time. He'd had to learn to drive on the wrong side of the road and now drank tea instead of coffee. *The British are the brav-*

est people on earth, he'd written to her. *They've been at war for so long, they've been bombed mercilessly, and yet they just keep on fighting.* He was convinced, he told her, that this was indeed a noble cause and that he had done the right thing. He was supposed to be here. There was history being made, and he was going to be part of it.

The radio brought the news daily, and the newspapers ran story after story of the war in Europe. A new front would be opened soon. The invasion of fortress Europe was imminent.

When he heard the reports about the Normandy invasion, Alton said a prayer for his son. Out of character for him, he knew. It was not a prayer to rival his wife's daily devotions but, nevertheless, it was a prayer. Some things were too much for a man to handle by himself. He knew the Man upstairs would make allowance for one man's human failings. He believed they had this understanding between them.

The abbreviated Kemper family, their wonderful daughter-in-law and grandson blessing their lives daily, set about the daily routine of their lives. Each of them masked their fear for the wellbeing of the one who was away at war.

But life went on for those who didn't go to war, and Allie was a great help to Mary in the house. She tried to learn how to milk the cows, but Alton gave up eventually because the city girl was much too squeamish for such tasks. "Maybe you're more suited for killing chickens, Allie," he told her. He saw the look on her face and said, "Well, maybe not—no, forget that."

Life turned in a moment sometimes. It turned for the Kempers late in June of 1944. Allie was in the kitchen when she heard the sound of a car coming up the drive. She didn't recognize the car, but she knew the driver, it was Kinnie Sullivan, a friend of Alton's who lived in town. "Why would Kinnie Sullivan come to the farm?" she wondered. Alton saw him when he went to town, but Kinnie never came to the farm. He was looking for Alton and, spotting him in the field, headed toward him. In his hand was an envelope of some kind. It looked like a telegram.

"Mary," Allie said, "Mary, come here a minute."

Her mother-in-law came in from the living room and followed her eyes out to the field where the two men were now talking. "What is it?" she asked.

"I don't know," Allie said "It's Kinnie Sullivan, from town."

She heard a crash behind her and turned to see Mary lying on the kitchen floor. She had fainted. In an instant, Allie knew that James was dead. The full weight of that would fall on her later, but now her feelings were for her mother-in-law and for the man standing out there trying to come to terms with it. She watched Kinnie place his hand on her father-in-law's back just for a moment. Then they shook hands, and Kinnie left. Alton stood for a while with his head lowered and then turned and started for the house.

ℯↄℯↄ

The coming years were alternating periods of sadness and joy on the Kemper farm. Little Jimmy grew into a fine-looking boy, learned to walk and talk and follow his grandfather around the farm. Alton practically worshipped the boy but eventually grew more and more despondent over the loss of his son James. He withdrew inside himself and began to have long periods of inactivity and non-communication. The farm began to suffer from his lack of attention to it. He even started to grow apart from his grandson.

For four years, after James was killed, Allie stayed on the Kemper farm, much to her parent's dismay. They wanted her to move back into town and start a new life, but she remained adamant and refused to consider it. The farm had become her home, and Alton and Mary Kemper, her family. George Matthews had to accept that he could not compete with the elder Kemper for the affections of his daughter. As painful as it was, he still refrained from criticizing the other man, for Allie had let him know that she would not tolerate it.

Allie tried to encourage her father-in-law but to little avail. Occasionally, after one of her talks with him, he would find some renewed strength, but it always failed him when he was alone in the field and was not able to come to grips with his life as it had turned out.

He was at the end of his rope the day his grandson peered at him from behind the big oak and pointed his toy gun at him and providence intervened in their lives.

Now, Allie watched from the kitchen window as the older man climbed up the windmill toting a bag of tools to fix the loose blades. Jimmy started to climb up the wood ladder that was used to reach the metal ladder higher up, but Alton made him go back down. Allie could barely hear the conversation, something about Alton needing someone on the ground to cover for him. Jimmy climbed back down and watched the work from the ground.

Her father-in-law was a new man. Since Jimmy had disappeared that time, and Alton found him in the barn, they had been as close as any two people could be. They had become father and son for all anybody knew. She didn't know what had happened that day—it didn't matter what—only that something had happened. Mary said her husband had a religious experience, and Allie guessed it might be so. In any case, he had become the man he was when she first met him, and she was glad about that.

Allie continued to work at her father's business. They had done quite well, and George paid her handsomely. In the years following James's death and the end of the war, she had helped the Kempers out with their living expenses, as well as supporting herself and Jimmy. She worried so much that they might lose the farm because of Alton's despondency but then the change came and all was well on the Kemper farm. Now that her father-in-law was back on his feet, she had seriously started to think about her future.

"You're such a beautiful girl, her mother would say, "you deserve more than life on a farm."

"For years," Allie said, "I needed the Kempers. Then they needed me. Now, Mother, maybe you're right. Maybe I should look ahead, not just for me but for Jimmy too, but I'll never leave them, not completely, not ever."

"I know you have always been close to James's family, and

I never resented that, not like your father. God knows I wouldn't try to come between you and them, but I never understood it. I don't mind telling you, I never understood."

Allie thought about that. She thought a lot about it. This man who had wanted to die after his son's death was now so devoted to his grandson and her, that he had almost become a young man again. A twenty-year age difference, and she could have loved him in a completely different way. Probably could have anyway if he would have allowed it, though she knew he wouldn't.

There were no gray areas with Alton Kemper, only black and white. There was no foolishness in him that she had ever detected. Other than a quick temper and a bent toward occasional use of profanity, he had no vices. They were a serious bunch, these Kempers. Even little Jimmy went after things with a sense of purpose, obviously developed from listening to and watching his grandfather. One thing remained for Allie, something she knew she could always count on, something constant in a world of variables. It was this—when Alton put his arms around her and hugged her, she was his daughter. Perhaps he thought of her as the daughter he'd never had, the girl that Mary had lost in childbirth, and the reason they never had more children. She didn't know. But his arm would never *accidentally* brush against her breast, as some others did, and his hand never slipped down her back lower than it should have. No, no matter how far she might go away from here, she would never, ever really leave.

Trenton Hargrove began coming more and more often to the factory in Comanche, although it was not really necessary that he do so. Everyone knew he was coming to see Allie. Since his wife had died the past winter, he had devoted almost all his time to the business. They had no children, and Allie suspected that the house he had bought in Dallas was truly a lonely place for a man alone. He asked her to lunch one day, and she accepted. It was obvious that he still loved her. The glow that came over a man's face when he was in love was unmistakable on Trenton. They began having lunch whenever he was in town, and on one occasion, he asked her right out to marry him. She wasn't ready for it, although she knew it would just be a matter of time before he did, and she looked a little surprised.

"You don't have to answer now, Allie," he said. "Just tell me that you'll think about it. You know I've always loved you. I never stopped. Just think about it, will you?"

"I will, Trenton," she said. "Thank you."

Saturday was a big day in Comanche, as it was in most country towns. Farmers came and set up on the square and sold their fruits and vegetables to the townspeople who passed among them looking for bargains. Men sat around in small groups playing dominoes or checkers or just passing the time of day and it seemed that every kid in the county came to town to the picture show.

Alton started taking his grandson to town on Saturday. They ate ice cream, went to the movie sometimes, and just walked around the square meeting and talking to people, Alton being content to play the proud grandfather. Jimmy was a handsome boy and the older man liked to show him off. A quiet boy who studied people intently, the youngest Kemper never played with other children, spending his time on the farm as he did. His maternal grandparents constantly troubled Allie about moving to town for this reason, so he could be with kids his own age, but she figured he would be starting to school soon, and then he would have other kids around to play with. In the meantime, he spent most of his time with Grandpa and seemed more than happy with this arrangement.

From the corner of the square, where a small group of men had gathered, Alton saw a raised hand motioning to him to come on over. It was Homer Sudbury, his old friend from way back, who was attached to the hand.

"Hey, Alton," he said. "Introduce us to your grandson."

Several of the men were kicked back in chairs enjoying the conversation, and the sunshine, some occasionally leaning forward to spit tobacco juice into the street and then pushing back onto the hind legs of the chairs on which they were sitting.

Alton joined in and made the rounds, having Jimmy shake

hands with each as they, in turn, ruffled his sandy-blond hair and told Alton what a fine boy he was.

"Yes, sir," Sudbury said. "That's a fine-looking boy."

Jimmy took it all in, not terribly impressed with them, but he drew back when his hand was taken by a scruffy-looking man named Leland Trumble who was standing on the curb near Alton.

"So, this is Allie's boy," he slurred, full of the liquor from the flask that was protruding from his rear pocket. "How is your pretty little mother doin', boy?"

An ill-bred man in his late thirties, Leland had never amounted to much. He worked as a handy man and picked up whatever work he could from the local businesses. He stayed drunk most of the time and rarely bathed. He fancied himself tough, and he was imposing at six-one and a hundred and seventy-five pounds. He pushed his weight around, bullying smaller men—all the more when he had been drinking.

Homer looked around at the other men and winked, knowing that this was one time that Leland should keep his mouth shut but suspecting that he was either too drunk, or too stupid, to know it. The look on Alton's face, Homer had seen before, back in the old days, when men fought each other more than they did now, and it was no less frightening than it had been then. Homer had never been on the receiving end of his old friend's temper, a fact for which he was thankful, and any prudent man would have taken the warning. But Trumble was not a prudent man.

"Hey, Kemper," he said, a grin breaking across his sharp, pinched face, "I hear ol' Trenton Hargrove is beatin' out your time wit—"

Leland's sentence was cut short by Alton's big right hand as it smashed against his jaw. He landed on his back in the street, out cold before he hit the ground. A chorus of laughs arose from the men in the group, and Homer slapped his knee.

Jimmy hid behind his grandfather's leg and held on, waiting to see what would happen next.

"When that sonofabitch wakes up, you tell him if he wants any more, he knows where to find me," Alton said.

"He won't want any more, Alton," Homer said. After Alton and Jimmy left, Homer turned to the others. "You've just seen a lesson on the perils of talking dirty about Allie Kemper when her father-in-law is around. That poor dumb bastard got the crash course," he said, pointing to Trumble's still prone body lying in the street.

Homer told them about the time Alton beat the hell out of the Crenshaw brothers to save him from an ass kicking. "Alton Kemper is not a man you want to be on the wrong side of."

Later at the farm, Allie stopped her son as he was headed out the door. "Did you have fun in town?" she asked him.

"Yeah," he said, impatient to go outside.

"What did you and Grandpa do all day?"

"Grandpa beat up a man and then we went to the show." With that he was out the door, leaving her wondering what had actually happened. She found Alton at the barn and, approaching him, eyed him suspiciously. "Dad, what happened in town today?"

"Nothing much, same old thing," he said. "Jimmy and I went to the movies."

"Did you have trouble with somebody?"

"Oh, that, that was nothing," he said, avoiding her eyes.

"It was about me, wasn't it?" she said. "Tell me the truth."

"Yes," he said, nodding, "yes it was, Allie, but it wasn't anything you've done. It was just somebody who needed some manners taught to him."

"There's been some talk, I suppose," she said. "You know how people are. I've been seeing Trenton Hargrove, just for lunch when he's in town. His wife died last year, you know."

"Honey, you don't have to explain to me," Alton said. "You've never done anything to be ashamed of. I could never be ashamed of you. You've been a blessing to us ever since the day James brought you home. Trenton is a good man, from what I hear. It wasn't him that was doing any loose talk."

"Yes, he is a good man, Dad." She studied a minute and then said, "He's asked me to marry him. but I didn't say one way or the other. I wanted to talk to you and Mary first."

"Well, I think you should at least think about it. My gosh,

you're only thirty and, God knows, Allie, you're as pretty as you ever were. This is no place to while away the rest of your life. You've been as respectful a wife to my son as anyone could ever expect. You have a life ahead of you, and you deserve that much."

"I'm so glad you feel that way," she said, smiling at him. "I was afraid you'd be mad."

"Now why would I be mad? I want you to be happy. I'll be sad to see you and Jimmy leave, but you won't be that far away." It had not occurred to him that Trenton would be taking them to Dallas. Of course it hadn't, Alton didn't know the extent of Trenton's involvement with George Matthews's business. When he realized they would be leaving, he was distraught for a while but Allie reassured him.

"I'll come every other weekend," she promised. "And Jimmy can spend every summer on the farm.''

The Matthews, elated, wanted her to have a big wedding but Allie refused. "No matter that it's the second marriage for both," her mother said. "She deserves it."

She would finally be leaving that dreadful farm where she was dying on the vine, so to speak. Her father was beside himself that they would now be shed of the Kempers, whom he had never liked, though he had not told them so in all the time his daughter had been with them.

Allie wanted the wedding to take place at Mt. Pleasant Baptist Church, a few miles from the Kemper farm, and Trenton agreed, not really caring. He was marrying his Allie, and that was all that mattered.

"I won't be bothered with a lot of hoopla," Allie said, "no shower, no reception, no giving away, none of those things." She had done that already and would not do it again." She could not ask Alton to give her away, for his strong sense of decorum would have forced him to tell her "That's a father's duty."

After the wedding, Alton nodded to George and May Ellen Matthews. They were acting a little distant, he thought, but then they had never been very friendly. He spoke a while with Allie's new husband. He was a nice fellow, as Allie had said, not as tall as James had been and certainly not as good look-ing—a little ugly, in fact, Alton decided. But he would be good to her. Alton was sure of that, and he would be good to Jimmy too. The pain that ran through his mind, when it dawned on him that she would no longer be his daughter-in-law, was almost unbearable. Then Allie came over and put her arms around his neck and kissed his cheek and said.

"Nothing has changed, Dad. Nothing will ever change."

They watched as Allie and Jimmy got into Trenton's Nash 600, and he pulled it out of the church parking lot and headed down the road toward town. In a moment, they were out of sight. Trenton had sent a truck for their belongings, so they would not be coming back. Alton's neck was still wet from the tears his grandson had left there when they hugged for, what must have seemed to both, the very last time.

"Nothing has changed," he mumbled to himself.

Maybe not, but it sure as hell didn't feel like nothing had changed.

Chapter 3

Arlington

1949-1958:

"Look, Jimmy." Trenton said, pointing to the flying red horse on top of The Magnolia Building. "Look at that." Jimmy stood up in the back seat and peered at the big sign, not knowing what it was but knowing that it was just one more wonderful thing to see in this strange place.

Dallas of the late forties was a city on an upward spiral, the war had brought tremendous growth to the area. Thousands of people worked in federal offices in Dallas helping to coordinate defense related activities. North American Aviation, in Grand Prairie, alone employed as many as thirty thousand workers turning out B-24 bombers and P-51 Mustangs. By the end of the decade the population had risen to 400,000.

Having spent his first few years in a country town of less than 4,000 people, Jimmy Kemper could not comprehend a city so big. It was truly an adventure and his mind was full of wonder about this new place, how different it was from his grandpa's farm. His mother told him that everything would be new and exciting in Dallas, and Mother had never lied to him before. So with that promise, he had climbed into the car of this man, who was nice enough to him but not nearly as much fun as Grandpa, and now he was here.

"What is that?" Jimmy asked.

Trenton told him about the flying red horse and how it was a prominent landmark in Dallas.

"When you see that red horse, Jimmy, you know you're in Dallas."

The Hargrove family would not actually live in Dallas, however. Trenton sold his house in Dallas after his wife died and rented a house in Arlington, desiring to get out of the city and live in the country. The family would live in the rented house for the time being and perhaps look for a new home later. The country that Trenton Hargrove had sought would soon disappear and Arlington would become one of the fastest growing cities in the country by the Mid-1950s.

Allie discovered that it was an exciting time to be living and raising a family in the Dallas area. It seemed that the entire post-war world was gathering around them, preparing to embark on a bold and exciting mission, and the Hargrove family had been invited along for the ride.

By 1952, with the arrivals of a daughter, Sarah Beth, in 1950, and a son, whom they named Trent, in 1951—they called him Trent to distinguish him from his father, Trenton—he family was in need of a bigger house. Trenton decided to buy them a home in a housing development.

"Happiness Homes?" Jimmy read off the sign as they turned onto Forrestal Drive and into their new neighborhood.

"Here it is," Trenton said, "Nine-thirteen Forrestal Drive, our new home, what do you think of it?"

"I like it," Jimmy said. "Do I get my own room?"

"Yes, you do," Allie answered. "And Sarah will have her own room. It's a three bedroom, so when the baby is older he will share your room with you, is that okay?"

"Sure," Jimmy said. "How much did it cost?"

"What, you mean the house?" Allie asked. "Why do you want to know that?"

"I like to know what things cost."

"The house cost nine thousand, nine hundred, and ninety-five dollars," Trenton said.

"Why didn't they just say ten thousand dollars?"

"That's an old trick, Jimmy. Ninety-nine ninety-five sounds less than ten thousand dollars."

"But it's only five dollars. Did you pay for it all or do you have to make payments?"

"We put a hundred dollars down, and we'll pay sixty-seven-fifty a month for thirty years. Unless, of course, I can manage to pay it off sooner. We bought it on the GI Bill. I was in the navy during the war, you know, and a serviceman can buy a house real easy on the GI Bill."

They drove slowly by the house but did not stop. Some workers were still putting the finishing touches on it.

"It should be ready to move into next week," Trenton said.

"That's twenty-four thousand dollars," Jimmy said. "That's a lot of money for a ten-thousand-dollar house."

"You've certainly got a head for numbers, Jimmy," Trenton said. "And you're right, that is a lot of money, but unless a person can come up with the full amount, he has to finance. I didn't have the money to buy the house outright, so I put down a hundred dollars, and now we have our own home. It's still much better than renting, don't you think?"

"Yes, I guess it is," Jimmy said, but he filed that information away in his head. He didn't think he would ever pay twenty-four thousand dollars for something worth only ten thousand dollars. Paying that much didn't make sense to him.

Allie Hargrove loved her children—practically worshipped them, all three of them—but the bond between her and her older son was stronger than most people ever knew. She had determined early in Jimmy's life that he would be more than just an ordinary boy. She had kept her word to Alton, and took Jimmy regularly, at least once a month, to stay at the farm, and he spent most summers there, foregoing all the activities that were available to him in the city, to be with his grandfather. Allie could see the love between the two of them, that look in the older man's eyes when he saw them coming up the drive to the farmhouse. And she knew she would never be able to destroy that relationship, even if she had wanted to, which she certainly did not. She molded her son, spent hours with him, teaching him how to conduct himself in one given situation or another. She never wanted him to be intimidated by a living soul, and she sought to prevent that by teaching him simple concepts.

"You are as good as any human being alive," she told him. "You are not better than anyone. But you must act better than others. You must be reserved and aloof. Treat everyone with respect, the way Grandpa and your stepfather do, until they show you that they are not deserving of respect. And when they show you that they are not deserving of respect, then get away from them and leave them alone."

"Grandpa said if people don't treat you with respect, then you should kick their ass."

"You shouldn't talk that way, Jimmy," she said. "What your grandfather was trying to tell you is that there are times when you may have to fight, but you must try to avoid it as much as you can. Grandpa didn't mean for you to go around fighting all the time." She taught him to soften his speech. "You are not a hick, and you don't want people thinking you are."

It was not enough for Allie that her son learned proper grammar, he had done that, for Jimmy was an excellent, almost a straight A, student, but she insisted that he use it in his everyday speech. "It's not he or she 'don't know' something. It is, he or she 'doesn't know.' And you don't say 'duddin' know. You say doesn't." She drilled it into him day after day until it became natural to him.

She corrected him when he said tuck, instead of took, or clawset instead of closet. Allie was convinced that the nature of the Texas accent, even when spoken by an intelligent person, could make the person sound less intelligent than he or she actually was and could make a marginally intelligent person sound like a moron, especially if he tended to exaggerate the speech pattern. This was no degradation of Texans. They were, Allie believed, on average, as intelligent as any other people and wiser than most to the ways of the world. But Allie Hargrove meant to ensure that all her children would be well mannered and able to communicate on any level of the social spectrum.

Allie had a vision that most mothers did not have. She had

looked far down the road and saw a time when her son would walk among the rich and famous. He would move in political and cultural circles of prominence and importance. Most folks would have thought her insane had she even hinted that she believed it would happen. If Jimmy Kemper were not ready when that time came, it was not going to be his mother's fault.

Her husband watched in amazement at the way Allie successfully shaped the lives and personalities of her children.

"You're like a sculptor slowly forming a piece of rock into a great work of art," he often told her.

Early one afternoon, Allie got a call from the principal at South Side Elementary School, where Jimmy attended the fifth grade. Mister Ward wanted to see her about Jimmy, some problem with Jimmy's behavior.

She thought it strange, for Jimmy had never caused trouble in school, and she was anxious to find out what the trouble might be. At the school, the secretary showed Allie into the office. There was a gruff-looking, red-faced man named Mister Ward, sitting hunched over his desk looking down, but he appeared to be ready for a confrontation. Allie's first assessment of him was that he looked extremely uncomfortable. He continued to look down until he heard the tap of Allie's high heels on his tile floor.

His entire demeanor changed, and his face softened when he saw the beautiful, brown-haired woman with the riveting green eyes approaching his desk. He jumped to his feet and held the chair as she sat down.

He stammered a little at first as he made a clumsy attempt to sit back down in his own chair without taking his eyes off Allie. Shuffling some papers on his desk, he started to tell her the problem with her son.

"Jimmy has become a discipline problem in one of his classes, Mrs. Hargrove. Mister Whitehead, our American History teacher, has told me that Jimmy cursed at him."

"I find that hard to believe, Mister Ward," Allie said. "Jimmy has never done anything like that before. What did he say?"

"Mister Whitehead said he was correcting another boy for not being prepared for the lesson and Jimmy came to the boy's defense, so to speak, and cursed him out."

"I don't understand," Allie said "What did Jimmy say?"

"He told Mister Whitehead that he talked like he had a mouth full of s-h-i-t," the principal said, spelling the offensive word for her. "Except Jimmy did not spell the word. You understand my position, don't you?"

"Yes, yes of course." Allie said. "I must apologize, Mister Ward. You see, Jimmy spends a lot of time with his grandfather and that expression is one that Mister Kemper uses a lot. You must understand, he's an older man, and he's a little rough cut. He is a good man but just rough mannered. He doesn't mean anything by it, and I know he shouldn't talk that way in front of Jimmy, but it's just his way. I will speak to Jimmy about it."

"Good," he said. "I wouldn't want to suspend Jimmy from school. I know he's a good boy."

When Jimmy came in from school that afternoon the first thing he saw was his mother's finger in his face, demanding an explanation for his actions.

"What do you mean cursing out a teacher?" she asked. "I didn't raise you that way."

"What did they tell you?"

"Never mind what they told me. You tell me what you did."

"Okay, okay. Calm down and I will. Mister Whitehead called on stuttering Steve, that's Steve Proxmire, to read, and he knows Steve gets nervous when he tries to read out loud. He laughed at Steve when he started stuttering and then yelled at him. The more he yelled, the more Steve stuttered. Then all the other kids started laughing. I told him to stop, and he said it wasn't my business, told me he'd send me to the principal if I didn't shut up. Well, Mister Whitehead is from Georgia, or someplace, and he talks funny. You know, like that revival preacher that came that time. He talked funny too, remember, Grandpa said he talked like he had a mouth full of shit."

"Jimmy, you can't be cursing in school. I don't care what the reason is. I want you to promise me that you will never do that again."

"Okay, Mother, I promise. I'm sorry. I won't do anything to cause you any more trouble. I just didn't think he should talk to Steve that way."

"You're right, son," Allie said "And I'm proud of you for standing up for your friend, but—"

"He's not my friend. Steve is just a boy in class."

"Okay, you stood up for what you thought was right, and I'm proud of you for that, but please don't curse out any more teachers." She hugged him and kissed his forehead.

He was almost as tall as she was—ten years old and almost as tall as his mother. His blond hair had slowly turned brown over the past few years, and his bright blue eyes had taken on a kind of smoky look to them. His eyes seemed to be more and more penetrating each time she looked at them. They had life in them, a zest for life, and determination, burning determination that would not, could not, accept an injustice. One could look into Jimmy's eyes and see brilliance there. He was alert, and bright, and quicker with a response than anyone Allie had ever known.

"I won't, Mother," he said again, "I promise."

"I will go and talk to Mister Ward again and tell him your side of the story. He may not do anything about it, but at least he will know the truth."

"Thanks, Mother," Jimmy said.

It was dry and hot. Summer in Texas was brutal, almost always dry and hot. And if not dry and hot then steamy and hot, interrupted occasionally by fast moving afternoon thunder storms that sometimes turned violent and could spawn tornados. At twelve years old, Jimmy and his friends seemed impervious to the stifling heat that drove older people indoors. They played baseball and rode their bicycles up and down water tower hill. Summer was a wonderful time for a twelve-year-old boy in 1954.

Dewey Lowe, one of Jimmy's friends from South Side Elementary, had whittled out a small wooden pistol to which were attached a pair of clothespins—one on the barrel and the other on the handle. The clothespins were tightly wrapped with tape to hold them in place. Using a strong rubber band as a propellant, the device would hold a large kitchen match. When the rear clothespin was released with the thumb, the *gun* would sling the match about ten feet, striking it as it did.

The boys took turns shooting the weapon and setting fire to clumps of dry and dusty, yellow grass and weeds. Once a good blaze had started, they would rush in and stomp out the fire before it could get out of control. It was an exhilarating game, a flirtation with danger that they could not get from baseball or bicycles. It offered a few moments of unparalleled excitement.

Near the local water tower there was a large open field that bordered on a line of houses on one side. Dewey set a fire in some weeds as Jimmy and two other friends named Cecil Gillespie and Bud Harlow, prepared to move in to stamp it out when it *caught good*. The flames leaped into the sky and then jumped to some nearby clumps which started to blaze also. "Now," Dewey yelled, and the others rushed in and started stomping on the quickly spreading flames.

Jimmy wasn't sure at just what point he knew they were not going to be able to put out the fire, but the others must have realized it at the same time, for panic suddenly gripped the four boys.

"Oh, shit," Dewey screamed, "whatta' we do, whatta' we do, Jimmy? We can't stop it."

"We have to stop it," Jimmy said. "Keep fighting it."

He took off his shirt and slapped at the fire with a frenzy but with little effect. Reality was thrust upon them in an instant. Jimmy was thinking that this was going to be one of those learning experiences his mother always spoke of. He almost laughed in his panic but was glad he didn't. If he got out of it alive, it would be a learning experience.

Cecil and Bud were crying and their pale, tightly drawn faces, would probably have been comical to a casual bystander, as they frantically jumped up and down on the flames that were now completely out of control. But Jimmy saw no humor in the game now. It was like watching a movie. Everything seemed to be moving in slow motion. He looked around for Dewey and didn't see him. He caught a glimpse of the boy going over water tower hill.

"Damn," he said, to himself. "I knew he couldn't be trusted."

Cecil and Bud continued their dance, out of step with each other, atop the flames.

"It's no use, we can't stop it," Cecil yelled, now in a shrill panic. "It's burning toward that house. It's going to catch that house on fire. Let's get the hell out of here."

"No," Jimmy said, "we can't leave." But the two boys had already abandoned their posts and were scattering in opposite directions. "Oh god," Jimmy muttered. "What should I do now?"

The fire burned over to the wooden fence behind a house and set the fence ablaze. The owner of the house was trying to put out the fire with his garden hose. Jimmy could hear the sound of a fire truck's siren off in the distance heading toward them. He ran back up the hill and found Dewey hiding behind one of the water tower's concrete supports. Together they watched as the firemen put out the fire.

"Well," Jimmy said. "I guess that's over. Way to hang in there, Dewey, you jerk."

"Whatta' you mean jerk? There was nothing more we could do. I didn't see any reason to hang around and get in trouble."

"You don't run out on your friends," Jimmy said. "Never run out on your friends."

Dewey shrugged. The lesson was lost on him.

The wind that had so quickly whipped the fire to a frenzy had also signaled the arrival of an afternoon rainstorm. It began to come down in torrents now, wiping out any remaining threat that the fire may have offered. Jim and his unreliable friend lay where they were, getting thoroughly soaked, watching as the fireman determine that all danger had passed. The two breathed a sigh of relief as the fire trucks pulled away from the scene of the crime.

They agreed to keep quiet about the incident. No one saw

them, and if they did, it was easy, they knew, for older people to get kids mixed up. They could make a clean break and not get in any trouble, Dewey suggested. The other two were found, and they also agreed to keep their mouths shut.

If I can put this past my mother, Jim thought. *Everything will be okay.*

೧೨೧

"Burn it in here, Jimmy," Trenton said, punching his fist into the catcher's glove.

Jimmy eyed the glove, imagining himself in a major league game. He started his wind up then let the ball fly toward his waiting stepfather. Snap, the ball slammed in hard.

"Ow!" Trenton yelled. "You've really got a good pitching arm, Jimmy. I never saw a twelve-year-old throw as hard as you do. Accurate, too, you've got good control. You should be playing on a little league team."

"Maybe," Jimmy said, thinking it would prevent him from making his regular trips to the farm. "It takes a lot of time, though."

"It's just that it's a shame not to use your talent. You really are a natural." Trenton loved baseball. He'd played when he was a boy, and he had tried to instill in his stepson his love for the game. He had taught Jimmy the rudiments of the game, and the boy took to it easily. "A natural talent," Trenton said.

Jimmy stopped throwing the ball and began playing with his little brother, Trent. Trent was four years old and full of mischief. The boy was headed for the street, and Jimmy intercepted him and put him up on his shoulders. "No, you don't," he said. "Get Sarah and play in the back yard."

"Jimmy's like a mother hen with those two," Trenton said, as Allie drove into the driveway and got out of the car with her arms full of groceries.

"I know," she said, "you'd think they were his kids. Hello, Jimmy," she yelled to him and noticed that he did not look at her. Trenton took the bags from her and went into the house with them. Allie went to the back yard to where Jimmy was wrestling with his younger siblings.

"I talked to Mister Ward today about the incident at school, and he said he would look into it. He said if what you said is true, then he would take some sort of disciplinary action against Mister Whitehead. I assured him that you were telling the truth so let's see what happens. Okay?"

"Sure, Mother," Jimmy said, still not looking at her. "Thanks."

Later that evening, Allie knocked on her son's door, went in, and sat down on the bed next to him. "What's bothering you?" she asked him. "You've got something on your mind."

"Nothing," he said, "no I don't."

"Come on, Jimmy. Do you think I just met you yesterday? I'm your mother. I know when something is bothering you." His mother had the same uncanny ability to read people that Alton Kemper possessed. Both Alton and Allie seemed to be able to immediately, upon meeting a stranger, judge the character of the person—their quality as a human being or the lack thereof. Jimmy could not fool her into believing that he was not troubled.

He told her about the grass fire, the fire trucks, and the fence that had burned. It was one of the hardest things he had ever had to do. It was not so much because he feared punishment as it was he hated that she might be disappointed in him. He could not fathom how she knew. She was a busy woman, with two other children to look after and a house to keep. Jim was amazed that she could be so tuned into his life that she knew that something was bothering him when he was doing everything he could to keep it from her.

What an amazing woman his mother was, an incredible woman, Jim believed, not just beautiful, but smart, and blessed with a sense of honor, or more correctly decency that touched all she came in contact with.

"What do you think we should do about it?" she asked him.

"Well, there wasn't much damage," he said. "The man probably has insurance. The other guys aren't going to help pay for anything. We could just let it go. It will never happen again, I promise."

"So, is that what you want to do, just let it drop?" Her marvelous green eyes stared at him, awaiting his answer.

Jim was no match for his mother in the field of polemics, for she did not engage in argument as a debater might, but rather appealed to common sense and right and wrong, using logic against which Jim had no sufficient defense.

She drove him to the neighborhood where the boys had started the fire.

He showed her the man's house. "That one there," Jimmy said, pointing, "no, the next one."

Allie pulled up to the curb and got out of the car. She made Jimmy go with her to the door of the house. She introduced herself to the man and told him they lived several streets over. "My son was one of the boys who set the fire that burned your fence. I'd like to pay for any damage that might have occurred."

"Well, ma'am," the man said, "there really wasn't that much damage. It was not as bad as it looked. I put up some new boards and repainted the fence. It needed painting anyway. I wouldn't worry about it. It was nice of you to come and offer. We didn't even know how the fire got started."

"Thank you," Allie told the man. "I wanted my son to do what was right."

Jimmy breathed easier as he got back in the car.

"Don't you ever do anything like that again," was all she said to him. But that, along with her menacing finger in his face, was sufficient. He never did.

And he never forgot what she had given him that day, the best gift of all. She had given him her sense of honor and decency and the desire to always do what was right regardless of the consequences.

She had taught him that God always knew what he was doing even if no one else did. He would keep his mother's gift with him all the days of his life.

കൗ

At sixteen, Jimmy decided he had outgrown, Jimmy. He started introducing himself as Jim Kemper and correcting anyone who called him by his boyhood name. His mother and his grandparents ignored him. Only his stepfather Trenton respected his wishes, and Jim was happy about that.

At five feet, eight inches, he would grow another three inches by the time he got out of high school. His brown hair had turned a darker brown, and his smoky blue eyes grew more intense with each passing year. His eyes revealed a soft demeanor and deep brilliance that resided behind them. Jim's eyes were mesmerizing, some said. He spoke in a soft easy manner with an accent that was more Southern than Texan, his mother noted. She didn't know why that happened. It just did.

He rarely raised his voice to anyone. This gave him the appearance of being in control in any situation. He exhibited wisdom beyond his years, wisdom learned at the side of his grandfather. The elder Kemper's social and analytical skills Jim had slowly absorbed over the years. His ability to keep himself in check, and not given to emotional outbursts, he received from his mother.

But what made his mother most proud of her son was his relationship with her two other children. Jim loved his brother and sister with an intense, passionate, and protective love. They clung to him, almost worshipfully, and he to them. There was a strong bond between them that was never troubled by jealousy or sibling rivalry.

Chapter 4

Los Mohados

1958-1963:

W hy do they work so hard, Grandpa, for no more money than they make?" Jim nodded toward the three Mexican laborers who were busy chopping weeds out of the Kemper's peanut fields.

"I don't know, Jimmy." Alton looked up and stared at the men for a moment. "They are damned hard workers, sure as hell a lot better than most everyone around here." He shrugged and went back to adjusting the milking machine on the cow he was tending.

"Quenton Potts says they steal a lot. Is that true?"

"Some do, I'm sure," Alton responded. "I never had any of them steal from me."

"Why did you go through Potts to hire these three?"

"None came by offering to work like they usually do," he said. "I hire some of them every year when they show up. Quenton knows a man named Joe Garcia who brings them here. He says Garcia takes care of the paperwork and collects from the workers for transporting them."

"How much do you pay them?"

"They ask for fifty cents an hour. Don't seem like much but I guess it is to them. I can't afford much more. I pay Quenton seventy-five cents an hour for them because he provides them. He makes a quarter an hour off each one for his trouble."

The sun was beating down unmercifully and yet the migrant workers maintained their pace. Up and down the rows they went, chopping the weeds out of the ground and tossing them aside with the hoes. Alton had Jim take them water and some sandwiches that Mary Kemper made. He talked to the men in his broken high school Spanish. They seemed to understand him but he couldn't pick up much of what they said in response. He guessed it was because he had learned proper Spanish and the men spoke street Spanish. Same as with English he figured.

Quenton Potts showed up about three that afternoon and collected from Alton for the week's work. "Let's see, Alton," he said, his shifty eyes darting back and forth from the older man to the boy, and back again. "Six days at ten hours a day for three men. That's a hunnert and eighty hours at seventy-five cents an hour. That comes to a hunnert and thirty-five dollars."

"You gonna' charge them men for sleeping in your barn and for making them sandwiches every day?"

Alton stared hard at the man and Quenton chuckled nervously. "No, I guess not," he said. "I allowed you wouldn't. Don't see why not. You spoil them and you won't make any friends."

"I've got enough friends," Alton said. "Don't worry about what I give them."

"I can see that you do, Mister Kemper." Quenton turned and headed for his car and Alton called to him. "You going to pay those men, Quenton?" He said.

"Oh, oh, yeah, I'm going to get my hat" Quenton rummaged around in his car for a moment and then walked back to where Alton and Jim were waiting. "I must have left it at home," he said. "I'll go pay the meskins now."

"Watch that sonofabitch, Jim," Alton said. "I don't trust him."

Quenton walked down to where the three men were working and talked to them for a few minutes. He waited until both Kempers went back into the barn and then he went to his car and drove off.

About four p.m., the three laborers knocked off work for the day and came up to the farmhouse. They were trying to talk to Alton, but he held up his hand and told them to hold on a minute. He called his grandson. "Jim, come here and see what they want."

"*Que tienes, amigo*," Jim said, asking him what was on his mind.

The small weathered man took off his hat when he spoke to Jim. "*El otro hombre dijo que tu nos pagara*," he said.

"What's he saying, Jim," Alton broke in.

"The best I can figure, Grandpa, is that Potts told them we were going to pay them. He didn't give them any money."

"That dirty sonofabitch. He didn't pay these men. He's trying to cheat them and me too."

That moment a car turned off the road and was coming up the driveway. Alton recognized the driver and the car. It was the local constable, Grady Rowen. Grady was, in Alton's opinion, not much better than Quenton Potts. He noticed that Joe Garcia was sitting in the passenger seat.

"What the hell is going on, Grady?" Alton asked, when the man got out of his car.

"We got a report of some wetbacks working here, Mister Kemper. I've arrested this man here," Grady said, gesturing with his thumb back toward Joe Garcia who had gotten out of the car and was leaning against it.

"He doesn't look too damned arrested to me," Alton said. "What are you trying to pull?"

"Not trying to pull anything. There are illegals working all over the county. We gotta' crack down on 'em."

"You're a liar, Grady, and you know it. You and Quenton are trying to cheat these men out of their pay, and I'll not stand for it."

"Nobody is trying to cheat anybody out of anything, Mister Kemper," Grady said. "It's just that the law—"

Alton wouldn't let him finish. "To hell with the law," he said. "And to hell with you too, Grady, you're a poor excuse for the law. I'm going to pay these men what they have coming and then I'm going to find Quenton Potts and get my money back from him."

"I don't know where Quenton is now. He may be in the next county."

Alton pointed at Joe Garcia. "This man knows where he is." He looked at the greasy little man with contempt. "Where is Potts?" Alton asked him.

"*No hablo ingles, senor.*"

"Yeah, I bet you don't," Alton said. "Jim," Alton nodded toward Garcia.

Jim asked the man in Spanish. "*Donde esta Quenton Potts.*"

"*No se, senor,*" Garcia said, but would not look at Jim.

"*Si, tu sabes a donde está el, diga me ahora o mi abuelo te luchara,*" Jim told him. "He knows where Quenton is Grandpa. I told him if he didn't tell us, he'd have to fight you."

The man agreed to go with Alton to where Potts was staying.

Alton went into the house, got his pistol, and motioned for Garcia to get into Alton's car. "You stay here, Grady," he told the man, "until I get back. Jim, tell the workers to wait here for an hour, I'll pay them for the wait. If I'm not back in an hour, get some money from your grandmother and give them their pay. If this man tries to leave, I want you to whip his ass."

"Yes, sir," Jim said. As he turned to face Grady, he clinched his fists.

Grady raised his hands up in front of him. "That won't be necessary, Mr. Kemper," he said, as he watched the younger boy who, although he was only a kid, showed absolutely no fear of the older man. "I'll wait here until you get back."

Alton was back in about a half an hour with all of his money. He had made Quenton Potts give him all of it. Quenton protested that he had a cut coming, and the older man just stared at him with contempt.

"Give me all the money back, Potts," Alton told him, "or you'll get a cut you don't want. You're a sorry bastard, Potts, for trying to cheat those men out their hard-earned money. You know they have families."

Quenton started to speak. "Aw, hell Kemper, I wuz gonna—"

The next thing he knew, he was looking up at blue sky. His head was ringing and his eyes were out of focus. Joe Garcia laughed at his partner lying there on the ground.

"I guess he knocked you on your ass, huh, Potts?" Joe said.

"I thought you didn't speak English," Alton said, heading for his car.

"I speak a little, Mister Kemper. Sorry for the trouble."

"If I see either of you people anywhere near my property, I'll shoot you," Alton said, not looking back.

He got into his car and drove back to the farm. He paid the three workers all the money he had retrieved from Quenton Potts, more than they were expecting, and then drove them over to Mills County out of the jurisdiction of Grady Rowan. Jim went along to try to explain to the men why they had to get out of the county. They did not seem concerned much about it. They had undoubtedly known trouble before.

At supper, Alton was telling Mary how tough her grandson had been earlier that day. "Grady Rowan almost pissed his pants when Jimmy turned on him with his fists clenched," he said, laughing. He was enjoying the events of the day much more now than he had when they were taking place. "I sure am proud of that boy, Mary."

"You shouldn't encourage him to fight, Alton," she said. "He could get hurt."

"Not by that little weasel, he couldn't. Jimmy's tough. He don't take sass from no one."

She scolded him for his language, and he apologized but kept on talking about how tough his grandson was. Jim listened with growing excitement, feeling full of himself. He enjoyed his grandfather's praise, no, he loved it. He lived his life for his grandfather. Nothing could be better than having that old man proud of him. He would have fought Grady Rowan if it had been necessary. He was scared, a little scared, but not too scared to act. He almost wished that he could have hit the older man. *Grandpa would have got a kick out of that*, he thought.

The summer of '58 came and went, and Jim had grown, both physically and emotionally. He loved his time at the farm. As much as he loved his grandfather as a boy, he didn't think he could ever love the old man any more than he did at this point in his life. Rough cut and foul mouthed as he was capable of being on occasion, Alton Kemper had a code of conduct that was admired by all who knew him. Even those who hated him, like Quenton Potts, knew that Alton was an honest man.

Jim told his grandfather how proud he was of him for being fair with the three migrant workers, giving them more money than he had to, and all.

"Gotta' look at myself in the mirror," Alton said. "There's no honor in cheating people, Jimmy. Money just isn't that important. Sometimes you have to be more than fair to be rightly fair. You must learn to read people. It's no secret. Just watch them. Someone won't look you in the eye, you know they're shifty. You know they're lying right away but those are the easy ones. Some are more polished. They know they have to look you in the eye so you won't know they're lying too. But that kind is easy too. They'll look at you too long, like they're making themselves look at you. They're liars too, just more practiced liars than most."

"How do you know so much about people, Grandpa?" Jim asked.

"I learned from living, son, just from living, living and watching and listening, listening more than talking. You're a smart boy, Jim," Alton continued, "a lot smarter than I am. And you got a good head on your shoulders. You have the Kemper magic. We Kempers have always been able to tell a 'no account' from someone with value, right away. My father could do it, worthless ass that he was, so could yours. My guess is you will be better than any of us."

"I hope so, Grandpa. Sometimes it seems easy to see right through a person but other times I just don't know. I watch how you deal with people and I try to be the same way."

"Keep this in mind. Some folks think they are better than others. You'll run into people in your life who think they are better than you. And, you'll run into others who think they are not as good as you. Either way, you must show them by your actions that they are both wrong. The true mark of an intelligent man is that he can talk with anybody on their level, not just on his. You remember what I tell you, son. You'll have need of this as you get older."

"I will, Grandpa," Jim said.

School would be starting soon and, although he would miss his time at the farm, Jim was looking forward to the coming year. He was gaining his independence. He was a boy no longer. Slowly but certainly he was becoming a man. His grandfather had treated him as a man this summer. He had put his trust in Jim and treated him as a man. The incident with Grady Rowan was more telling than he had first perceived. As he thought about it, he came to realize what had actually happened. His grandfather had not been playing a game, trying to make Jim feel big, as Jim had first assumed. No, Grandpa would not have taken a chance like that. If he had not really believed that Jim could have handled the older man, Alton would not have told him to confront Grady.

The exuberance Jim felt was almost more than he could contain but he kept his 'face' on, in hopes that his grandfather would think that he had as much confidence in himself as the old man had in him.

On Friday, they went to the bank in town so Jim could draw out the money he had made over the summer. Alton paid him a dollar an hour. He also got room and board, of course, and considering his grandmother's cooking he would probably have been willing to work for nothing. The wage was more than Alton would have had to pay another laborer and both grandson and grandfather were happy with the arrangement. Allie came to get him on Saturday. He had saved almost $600.00. He told his mother he was going to buy a car.

Chapter 5

The Trophy

The handsome white-tail ambled slowly down the wash, moving from one side of the little stream to the other, seemingly unconcerned about the world around it. It was a beautiful animal, a big buck with four, maybe five, points on each antler, a nice rack.

Jim watched as the deer came to within a hundred yards of him. His mouth grew dry and his breathing quickened as the creature continued toward him. His fingers nervously stroked the barrel of the Winchester and his right leg began to tremble involuntarily.

Seventy-five yards, now fifty, the deer came closer. Soon he would be able to hit it with a stick. He slowly raised the rifle from his knees and lowered it gently down on the rock in front of him, resting it on his left hand as his right hand moved to the trigger.

Stealing a quick glance to guide his shaking fingers he drew a deadly bead on the still unsuspecting quarry.

Can't miss at this distance, he thought, squinting down the rifle's sight at the animal's heart. This is what he had come for. This was the reason Robert had planned this trip. One moment in time, alone in the quiet Texas back country, just him and the deer. Another rite of passage would soon be behind him.

He would slowly pull the trigger, and he would forever be a man.

❦❦

"When are they picking you up, Jimmy?" Allie yelled as Jim ran through the house into his room.

"Anytime now, Mother," he answered, barely audible from inside his closet. "Where's my sleeping bag?" he yelled. He was tossing things out into the room as he searched for the missing bag. "It was here the other day."

"In the laundry," his mother said. "I washed it for you. Take some extra socks and clothes." She heard a car pull up in the driveway and the horn honking. It was Robert Cunningham. She knew his sound by now. *Rich kid, with too much time on his hands*, she was thinking. Allie did not like her son's friend. He was so different from Jimmy, more irresponsible.

She couldn't understand why they had been friends for so long but that was Jimmy's choice. "Robert is here," she yelled.

"Damn!" she heard him say.

"Watch your mouth, Jimmy, your sister is home."

"Sorry, Mother," he said, still rummaging around in his closet for missing items. His sister Sarah, upon hearing her mother's admonition to her older brother immediately came into his room.

She was bright eyed and pretty, beautiful being a more appropriate adjective, with long brown hair, like her mother. She was walking on her tiptoes. "Where are you going?" she asked

"Hunting," he said, trying to ignore her.

"Hunting What?"

"Deer hunting."

"You're going to kill them," she said, matter-of-factly.

"If we're lucky we are," he said.

She wrinkled up her nose and stared at the tip of it, causing her eyes to cross. "Why?" she asked.

"Why what?"

"Why are you going to kill the deer? They don't hurt anyone." Her eyes remained crossed and she continued looking at the end of her nose.

"I don't know," he said, "we just do. Don't cross your eyes, they might stick like that."

"Emily Harper says that's just a myth. Eyes won't stay crossed like that. That's no answer, we just do. Why do you want to shoot a deer? They don't hurt anyone."

He stopped and looked at her. She was waiting for an answer. "Emily Harper doesn't know everything, you know," he said, as Robert started laying on the horn again. "Damn," he said. "I wish he'd stop that."

"Mother told you to stop cursing."

"I'm sorry," he said. Putting his arm around her, he kissed her on the top of her head. "Go get my sleeping bag for me, will you?"

"Okay," she said, and skipped out of the room to retrieve the bag.

"Don't forget these," his mother said, handing him a large bag, as he entered the kitchen.

"What's this?"

"Apples, baking apples, you know, with cinnamon and sugar like I fix them for you."

"Oh, yeah, thanks, Mother, the guys love these. I'll be back Sunday night. We're staying at Grandpa's tonight, don't worry about me."

"Be careful," she yelled, as he ran out the door.

Robert was holding the trunk open. Jim threw his things in, and they both jumped into the car. Robert jammed the gearshift into reverse, and the car squealed back out of the driveway then sped off down the street. "You got everything?" he asked.

"I hope so. I threw everything together as fast as I could. Where are we picking Bill up, at his job?"

"Yeah," Robert said. "Dave Ingles is coming along too, if he shows up that is."

Robert swung the car into the drive-in where Bill McCarthy worked. They could see Bill through the window of the store cleaning up. Robert honked the horn to get his friend's attention and pointed to his watch. Bill held up all ten fingers indicating that he would be finished in ten minutes. He then pointed to the curb where Dave Ingles was sitting cross legged, looking down and dejected.

"Hey Dave," Robert yelled, motioning for him to come over. "Get in. Where's your stuff?"

"At home," he said. "My old lady locked me out again. I'll have to climb in the window." Dave got into the back seat. "What did you bring to eat?"

"We haven't even left yet and he's hungry," Robert said. "I brought some steaks and pork chops, and Jim brought some stuff, and those apples his mom always makes."

"Good deal," Dave said and slid down in the seat.

Bill came out shortly. He was carrying his pack and rifle with him. Some heads turned to observe the boy walking across drive-in parking lot with the deer rifle in his hand.

"Old dead eye," Robert said. "Best shot in Texas."

"Hey, guys, how's it going?" Bill said, as he climbed into the back seat. "Move your stilts, Dave."

Dave struggled to get his six-foot, two-inch frame out of the way.

At Dave's house, he instructed Robert to pull up quietly in the alley that ran behind the house. "I don't want old lady Morgan, next door, to see me," he said. He got out, went around to the side of the house, and started prying open a window.

"What's going on?" Jim asked.

"Dave's mother is a clean freak," Robert said, "a real idiot, according to Dave. She keeps the house spotless. They don't even wear shoes in the house, and well, you know how Dave is." They both nodded. "She locks him out and won't give him a key. He's not allowed in the house unless she or his sister is home."

"What about his dad?" Jim asked.

"Gone," Robert said.

"Gone, you mean dead?"

"No, just gone, ran off with another woman. Can you blame him? Every time the poor guy farted, Dave's mother would have the place fumigated."

Dave was coming out the back door with his things. He had strapped a brown leather holster, holding a .38 Special, around his waist.

"Dave was born a hundred years too late," Jim said.

"Really," the others agreed.

"He couldn't hit the side of a barn," Robert said, "but he thinks he's a cowboy."

Dave neared the car, as a window opened up in the house next door and the wrinkled, angry face of the next-door neighbor, Mrs. Morgan, appeared. Jim noted that the woman was still wearing curlers in her hair, at three-thirty in the afternoon.

"Dave," she yelled at him. "You know your mother don't allow you to go in that house when she's not there."

Dave did not look at her, and she yelled again. He still did not look but he stuck up his middle finger at her, causing the woman to gasp loudly and close the window.

"Old bitch," he said, as he got back into the car.

Robert pressed down hard on the accelerator and the big Pontiac surged ahead to seventy-five, increasing speed as he held his foot to the floor. Jim watched from the passenger's seat as the speedometer reached eighty-five and then ninety and still Robert did not let off the gas. The car ate up the highway. The lines in the road rushed up, as if they were inspecting the vehicle, and then dashed madly under and behind it. An oncoming car met them just as the speedometer topped one hundred mph and the other driver, caught by surprise, veered off the road and skid to a stop in the bar ditch.

"He's okay," Robert said, looking in the rear-view mirror.

"How do you know?" Jim said. "What if that guy calls the cops?"

"Are you serious? We could be in Mexico by the time he gets to a phone."

"What if he got your tag number?"

"We're doin' a hundred. That guy's lucky if he even saw what kind of car we're in."

"Maybe," Jim said, "but slow down. If you're going to kill us, at least wait until after the weekend when I bag my deer."

"C'mon, Jim, you scared of a little speed?"

"I am when you're driving. You could kill us all, and the two sleeping beauties in the back would never even know what happened."

Robert was showing off again. Jim had seen the look of terror on his friend's face when they met the other car and knew that Robert was more afraid of his own driving than Jim was.

"Just slow this thing down. You've impressed me enough today."

"Okay, okay," Robert said, glad to have an excuse to slow down without losing face, "if you insist." He let off the gas and the car backed down to sixty.

Robert was a showoff, a braggart, and overbearing. He and Jim had been friends for six years, and Jim still wasn't sure just why. They were so different, like night and day, according to Allie Hargrove. Jim's mother did not like Robert, and she didn't make any bones about it. His folks were good people, down to earth, she said, and Robert did not appreciate them. He was too loud and too arrogant, not at all like her son Jimmy. But Jim saw something in his friend that others did not see, some hidden quality, perhaps, he wasn't sure. Bill McCarthy hung around with him because Bill liked to hunt and Robert's dad was a hunter. The elder Cunningham always took Bill along on hunting trips. There seemed to be a common bond between them that was independent of Bill's friendship with Robert. Mister Cunningham described Bill McCarthy as "my cold-eyed little killer."

At five feet six, Bill was shorter than the other boys but he deferred to no one. He handled a rifle like a marine and never flinched when it came time to pull the trigger. Even Jim Kemper, who was generally considered the leader of the group because of his level head and possession of wisdom beyond his age, held the dark eyed, sullen boy, in the highest regard, although they were never as close as Jim and Robert.

"Bill never gets close to anyone," Robert had once told Jim. "He's a loner. He likes my dad, 'though," he added.

Dave Ingles, on the other hand, hung around with anyone who would tolerate him, and Bill had sort of taken him under his wing.

The Cunninghams were well off, quite well off, much more so than the Hargroves, although Jim's stepfather, Trenton, had provided a good living for his family. Robert's parents had been a local success story in Abilene, where Robert had spent the first ten years of his life. Inheriting half interest in an oil field service company from an uncle who had died, both elder Cunninghams had worked very hard. Robert's mother managed the office and his father ran the field operations. And together they built the business into a profitable concern. They eventually bought out the other stockholders and moved the company to Dallas because, as Mrs. Cunningham often explained, "Nobody lives in Abilene, Texas, if they have an option."

Jim did not know for sure just how much money Robert's family really had but it was rumored to be in the millions. *A lot of money*, he thought. He couldn't imagine having that much money. The Cunninghams had always been gracious to Jim. They were self-made people and not the least bit pretentious. He had stayed at their house many times, and it always seemed to Jim to be very pleasant. That changed only when Robert and his dad came together in the same room. It was then the tension mounted. There was an undertone of animosity between father and son, a deep conflict that neither allowed to surface completely. It disturbed the otherwise congenial atmosphere of the Cunningham home.

കൗകൗ

"I was just blowing out the engine a little," Robert was saying. "My old man never gets it over fifty."

"What, what's that?" Jim had lost his train of thought and suddenly realized that Robert had not stopped talking the entire time he had been thinking.

"He drives worse than my mother," Robert added.

"No he doesn't," Jim said. "I've ridden with your mother. Nobody drives worse than your mother. Good cook, bad driver."

Robert laughed out loud. "Right you are," he said, amused that one of his friends would make such an affable remark about one of his parents. His friends all liked Robert's folks. This was a source of amusement as well as irritation to him.

He thought his parents were not much more than a nuisance, an ever-present intrusion into his daily life. "We're coming into Comanche now," he told Jim, "how do I get to your grandfather's place?"

"Turn right at the square, that's Austin Street, then to Wright, w-r-i-g-h-t, not right," he said, holding up his right hand, "then left to Mt. Pleasant Church Road. I'll show you where to turn."

The others were waking up now and stirring around in the back. "Where are we?" Dave asked.

"Comanche," Robert said. "We're spending the night at the Kemper farm."

Dave was stretching and rubbing his eyes, trying to wake up. "Well, E-I, fuckin' Oh!" he said.

"Watch it, dipshit," Robert said, seeing the look in Jim's eye. "Kemper will kick your ass for making fun of his family."

"I'm sorry," Dave said. "I was just kidding."

"Nothin' more important to Kemper than family," Robert said ominously.

Jim's grandmother had prepared a feast for the boys. Dave's eyes almost popped out of his head when he looked over the table that was completely covered with ham and pork chops and mashed potatoes, corn, squash, and okra. Through the steam rising off the table he could see two pies cooling on the stove. "I never saw so much food," he said, "not for just one meal."

"It's a special occasion," Mary Kemper said, her plumpish frame moving quickly around the table as she tended to the boy's needs. "It's not often Jimmy brings his friends home to see us."

Robert held up his clean, empty plate for Mary to see. "Didn't care for it, Mrs. K," he said.

I can see you didn't, Robert, maybe the second plate will be better."

Robert laughed as he spooned a second helping of mashed potatoes.

"Slow down, Dave," Bill said, "you're eating like a convict."

"Now, leave him alone," Mary said. "I like to see a hungry man eat all he wants."

Dave looked up and smiled at her, then went back to eating.

After dark, the boys set up camp in the south woods and built a fire. Alton Kemper joined them later and, to his grandson's delight, made a big hit with the other boys. He told them stories about the old days and bits and pieces of Texas history. "There was a time," he said, "when it took a tough and tenacious people to settle this land we're sitting in right now. This country can be as harsh as it is beautiful. The weather was the biggest problem they faced, I suppose, then the snakes and other dangerous critters. And if that wasn't enough to give a man heartburn, then he had to fight the damned Indians."

"I'm an Indian fighter," Dave said. "I mean I would have been an Indian fighter if I'd lived back then. I should have lived in the old west.

"You'd have been the first one shot," Robert said.

"That's right," Bill agreed. "It wasn't fun and games. It wasn't like in the movies, and you're not John Wayne."

"Indians weren't pushovers," Alton said. "They were tough, all right, but they weren't the noble savages that people say they were either."

"Wasn't an Indian's word his bond, Mister Kemper?" Robert asked. "I heard that an Indian could be trusted if he gave his word."

"He could as long as you kept a Colt 45 to his head. But then that's how it is with most people, I think."

Robert said he would have wanted no part of the old west. "They didn't have cars," he explained. "I couldn't live without a car. Bill here would have been right at home back then. He could have been a buffalo hunter. Jim too, Jim's as tough as they come, but I don't know about Dave. I think Dave would have been with Custer."

"Those 'good old days,'" Alton said, "were never as good as people like to believe. They are just inventions of old men's memories. It was a hard life back then. The only thing good about the old days was that I was young then. When I was eighteen, like you boys are now, I had my life in front of me. As a man gets older, he runs out of future, so he starts looking back. People around here like to fancy themselves as pioneers, but it's not so. They sit in their air-conditioned houses and watch television and pretend they are in kinship with the early settlers. We even have Old Settlers Day every year, but the old settlers are long gone."

"You sound like my dad," Bill said. "He says people now days are soft."

"Most are," Alton agreed. "But it's not their fault so much as it is that life has just changed so much. Things are easier now and that's not necessarily bad, not really. People don't change though. People never change. There are good folks and there are bad wherever you go. If you're smart and watch people close enough, you can pick out the good ones from the bad."

When he had left for the night, Jim showed the others the Winchester 30/30 that Alton had given him. It was a magic gun according to Jim. He had seen his grandfather shoot a chicken hawk in mid-air with it from at least a hundred yards away.

"No scope," he said, "Grandpa never uses a scope. He's just like Bill."

Jim was still amazed at that marvelous shot. He told them the story. The hawk was perched on a telephone pole and flew off just as Alton took aim. Jim remembered wincing and closing his eyes, thinking that the shot was surely lost then he heard the crack of the 30/30 and looked up just in time to see the hawk fall out of the sky and crash to Earth.

"Lucky shot," his grandfather said, but Jim knew better.

"I never saw anybody shoot a bird in mid-air with a rifle," Dave said, a look of disbelief on his face.

"It could be done," Bill said. "If you had a bead on him before he flew and tracked him just right, it wouldn't be too hard a shot. It's just hand eye coordination, that's all it is."

"Yeah," Robert said, "and what do you know anyway, Dave? You couldn't hit a chicken, much less a chicken hawk."

They pitched two tents. Bill and Dave slept in one and Jim and Robert in the other.

"Can I ask you a question?" Robert said, just as Jim was about to drop off to sleep. He didn't wait for an answer. "Your grandmother said that you didn't bring friends home very often."

"I don't very often," Jim said "It's kind of out of the way, and you guys are always playing baseball or chasing girls."

"No, that's not what I meant. She called this your home. You've always lived in Arlington, as long as I've known you, but she called this your home."

"This is my home," Jim said. "Arlington is where I live but this farm is my home. I couldn't have asked for a better stepfather than Trenton Hargrove but my grandparents are my home. Where ever they are, that's where my home is."

When Allie Kemper remarried, she made her father-in-law a promise that she would never take his grandson away from him. Allie Hargrove had kept that promise. Jim spent many weekends, and every summer, at the farm. It was the reason he had never gotten involved in after school activities. Although his stepfather had encouraged him to play baseball Jim did not do so, preferring to keep his free time free so he could spend it with his grandfather.

The next morning before dawn the boys were awakened by the clanging of cow bells. Jim could hear the shuffling of many hooves near the tent. Robert sat up with a start. "What was that?" he yelled, poking his head quickly out of the tent flap.

"My grandfather's cows," Jim said. "Relax, they won't hurt you."

"What do they want?"

"Nothing," he said, chuckling, "they don't want anything, they're just nosy. Cows are very curious creatures."

"There's someone out here," Robert said.

In the pre-dawn, light Jim could make out the lanky form of Alton's right hand man. "It's Danny Carlisle. He works for my grandfather. Hello, Danny."

"Mornin', Jim, Mary said to tell you boys that she'd have breakfast ready in about a half hour."

The mention of breakfast was sufficient to roust the boys out of their beds and get them heading toward the house.

"This is good, Mrs. K," Robert said. "What is it?"

"It's sugar syrup, Robert. I make it by boiling sugar in water until it thickens. It's cheap molasses. Do you like it?"

"Yes, ma'am," he said, "everything is good."

"Where did you say you were going hunting?" Alton asked Robert.

"My father has an oil lease south of Abilene. We hunt on the lease. That is, we go and blow holes in nature's woodland creatures."

Alton studied the boy for a moment. "You don't like to hunt?"

"Oh, sure, Mister Kemper, my old man has been taking me hunting since I was a kid. My brother Randy is the real killer in the family, though. Randy shot his first deer when he was twelve. We still have the head hanging on the wall at home. My dad is real proud of Randy because he went to West Point. Now he's a captain in the regular army."

"Well, hunting isn't much of a sport," Alton said, "at least not for the animals. But if you don't do it for fun, I mean if a man hunts for food, then there is nothing wrong with it. A man shouldn't kill just to prove he can kill something. I don't think that's right."

"Bill always gets a deer, but he doesn't kill for the trophy. He takes the deer home and his dad makes sausage and stuff out of it."

"That's good," Alton said, nodding at him. "That's the way it should be. That's why God created them, for man's food, not to be killed for sport."

They all nodded agreement, except for Dave. He was busy reaching for another biscuit.

After breakfast, they broke camp and loaded the car. Each boy thanked the Kempers for their hospitality. Jim waited until the others were in the car and then talked with his grandfather.

"I appreciate everything, Grandpa. I hope we weren't any trouble."

"Of course, not, Jimmy," Alton said. "Your friends are always welcome here, you know that."

"They get a little loud and unruly sometimes, Robert more so than the others. Mother doesn't like him. She thinks I shouldn't hang around with him so much."

"They're good boys, especially Robert," Alton said. "He's got a good heart. You can see it in his eyes. He's troubled, that's for sure, but underneath all the bullshit, I believe he's got a good heart. Your mother can't read people the way we Kemper men can."

"Thanks Grandpa," Jim said and hugged Alton. "I'll see you soon."

"Ten more miles," Robert announced, "ten more miles to the campsite."

"Good," Dave said, "but I gotta' go to the bathroom before we set up camp."

"I hate to tell you this, Dave, but there are no bathrooms out here. You'll have to wait till we get home, and when did you ever help setting up camp? Move your ugly head, I can't see in the mirror."

"This whole country is one big bathroom. What do you mean I don't help set up camp? I always help, and since when do you look in the rear-view mirror? You don't watch what's in front of you, much less what's in back."

"He's got you there," Jim said, giving Dave a thumbs-up, and they all laughed.

Robert eased off the gas as the car approached a gravel road that was guarded by a metal gate. "Somebody get the gate." he said.

Jim and Dave jumped out, opened the gate, and waited as Robert drove through, then closed it, and got back in. Robert jammed his foot down on the gas and the big car fishtailed down the road, throwing up a cloud of dust and gravel as it went.

The campsite was just a clearing in a mesquite thicket, but it was a good campsite, with a permanent fire pit. A circle of logs had been placed around the outer perimeter of the camp, to define it, and another around the fire pit itself for people to sit on. The Cunninghams came here often, and Bill with them, so the camp had a well-used look about it. Several spots had been cleared of rocks and leveled with sand for tent pads.

Dave went to the car, retrieved his .38 Special, and strapped it around his waist. "I'm goin' to kill something," he said, walked off a short way from the others, and started blasting away at some imaginary foe.

"Don't shoot in that direction," Robert yelled at him, pointing toward the area where the lease operator's house was located. "Old man Nichols won't appreciate you shooting holes in his house or killing his sheep. He hates kids anyway so try not to be so barbaric."

Dave looked dumbfounded, not understanding the need for restraint in all this open country, but nevertheless, as always, he complied with Robert's order and turned and started firing in another direction.

"Who put all this wood here?" Jim asked, pointing to a neatly stacked pile by the fire pit.

There was at least a full cord of wood. Some smaller logs had been chopped into kindling and it was stacked next to the larger pile.

"Old man Nichols did that," Robert said. "He always fixes things up before we come."

"I thought you said he didn't like kids."

"He doesn't, but he likes my dad. They go way back."

Jim suggested they go and thank the man, grateful that they would not have to gather firewood.

"I already did," Robert said. "I called him before we came."

Dave had tired of his game and was returning to camp. The others had pitched the tents and had a roaring fire going. He backed up to the fire and warmed himself as his friends busied themselves with other campsite duties.

"It's gettin' colder," he said. "This fire feels good."

"It won't feel so good when you catch your pants on fire," Bill told him, seeing Dave's backside smoking.

"Ow!" Dave yelled as the heat reached his skin. "I'm on fire."

He slapped at his rear end in an effort to relieve the pain, as the others rolled with laughter. His efforts did not help so he finally just took off his pants and stood there in the cold rubbing the affected area until it had cooled sufficiently.

"There goes your fire safety merit badge, Dave," Robert said. "Put your pants on before you freeze."

Dave found his pants and felt the seat to be sure it was safe to put them on again and then sheepishly complied. "What's for supper?" he asked. "I'm starved."

"What's new?" Bill said.

Robert was pulling stuff out of the cooler. "We've got steaks, pork chops, and some baking potatoes, and Jim brought some chicken and those famous apples his mom makes."

They placed all the food, wrapped in tin foil, down into the coals and let the meat stew in its own juice. The apples that Jim's mother had learned to prepare from Mary Kemper were always a big hit. The apples were first cored and then packed with cinnamon-sugar and butter. Baked in coals from a campfire, and eaten out in the cold country air, the taste had no equal.

The four boys ate ravenously, with their hands, "like field hands," Jim said. Bill said he hadn't realized how hungry he was until he started eating.

"Yeah, me too," Dave said. "Why is that?"

"Just one of those things, I guess."

Robert raised his hand authoritatively. "Your stomach is inactive and all the gastric juices just lie there dormant until you put in some food and once they go to work they don't know when to quit."

"Well, there you go," Bill said. "Professor Cunningham has cleared that up. Thank you, Professor Cunningham. Thank the professor, Dave."

"Why? He just made that shit up."

"It sounded good, didn't it?"

Dave started tossing bones over his shoulder, and Robert yelled at him.

"Pick up your scraps, Dave. How many times do I have to tell you? Don't throw food around the campsite. It'll attract animals."

"Animals got to eat too, don't they?" Dave replied.

"Okay, leave 'em there but after we turn in I'm going to pick up all your scraps and put them around your tent so the coyotes won't have too much trouble finding them when they come around tonight."

"Oh," Dave said. He understood that and went off to pick up the leftover food scraps for proper disposal.

The sun was sinking slowly behind a line of low, finger-shaped hills that were called mountains, although they were far from being mountains, not real mountains like in Colorado. They were more like rounded mesas dotted with scrub brush and mesquite trees. Night fell quickly as the sun disappeared completely in the west.

Jim left the others talking and wandered off away from the camp until he was out of earshot. This was beautiful country, he'd always thought so. It was harsh country, as his grandfather had said, and unforgiving to the unprepared, but exciting and even fulfilling to those who gave it the proper respect. The sky was endlessly deep—a dark blue, almost black—and the stars were brighter than he had ever seen them. He spotted two constellations, one of the dippers—he wasn't sure if it was the big one or the little one—and another but he couldn't remember its name. Closing his eyes, Jim listened intently to the sounds of the night. The wind, the gentle, searching wind that rarely stopped blowing, sifted through the mesquite thicket, caressing each limb and spine in a lover's embrace, and sang an eerie song of seduction that numbed the senses. He felt that he understood now how a man could become "one" with the land, how a man could love the land so much. He had felt this many times on his grandfather's farm but never like this. He had never seen the night like this before.

The rhythmic, metallic heartbeat of a pump-jack some-where out in the dark captured his attention and he listened a while longer. This was the real heartbeat of the land, the oil pump. The oil pump was the heartbeat of Texas. It had made

Texas wealthy and arrogant. It had made Robert's family rich as well and brought a better standard of living to most people in the state, but it had also left a legacy, and Jim was not sure the affluence it had offered was worth it. The pumps scarred the landscape, making it ugly and foreboding.

"Dollar Bills," Robert called them. "They're not pumping oil, they're pumping dollar bills."

True enough, Jim agreed, but those dollar bills always seemed to go into someone else's pocket, not his.

The yelp of a coyote not too far away disturbed his thoughts. Jim remembered that he had not brought a weapon with him. He also remembered that his grandfather had once told him that it was much easier to be one with the land if you kept a rifle at your side. Jim hoped he would not have to confront a coyote this far away from camp.

He heard gunfire coming from the direction of the campsite. *Dave*, he thought. The others must have heard the coyote, and Dave had opened up on him. It was time to head back.

The sun was just beginning to intrude through the tent flap when Jim awoke to the sound of a rifle shot. The single report, perhaps a half a mile off, told him that Bill McCarthy was at work playing his deadly game. Robert was still asleep and Jim kicked his friend's foot to awaken him.

"Robert, get up," he yelled. "The others are in the field already, let's go."

"Go ahead," Robert mumbled, barely audible. "I'd rather sleep. They don't need my help killing critters." And he buried his head in his pillow.

Jim had not heard. He stopped long enough to get his rifle and was headed in the direction of the gunfire.

Not far from camp he found Bill and Dave squatting beside a huge deer that was lying lifeless on the rocks of the little stream where it had come to drink. It was shot cleanly through the heart. The two boys were studying the kill. Bill as usual remained serious while Dave was beaming like a Cheshire cat, as if he had shot the deer himself. He spotted Jim and waved. "Look at my deer," he yelled.

"You shot him? I don't believe it," Jim said.

"Nah, Bill did it. I was just foolin' around. I never saw any-thing like it. He never misses. Nothin' is safe in the woods with this guy. He was five hundred yards away."

"Five hundred yards, come on," Jim said, looking at Bill who was shaking his head.

"It wasn't that far," he said. "It was an easy shot."

"For you maybe," Dave said. "Nobody I know can shoot like that."

Jim looked at the deer. Once a magnificent animal, its tongue protruded from the side of its mouth and the teeth were clenched down hard on it. Eyes that only a few moments be-fore had warily searched for signs of danger were now dull and blank and searched for nothing. Life blood seeped out of the wound, ran in little rivulets across the rocks, and mixed with water in the stream.

Poor creature, Jim thought. *He'd had the chance misfor-tune of wandering into the flawless sights of young William McCarthy, sharpshooter nonpareil in these parts.* Bill was a cold-eyed little killer, as Robert's dad had so admiringly re-ferred to him, with adoration. He'd be a national treasure if the country ever went to war again.

"Help us string him up, Jim, so I can field dress him," Bill said.

Jim helped them drag the deer to a tree that would support the weight, then he and Dave lifted the animal up while Bill secured the rope to the hind legs. Then Bill went to work im-mediately with his knife. He had been so confident of his own abilities that he had brought all the equipment needed to per-form this task.

Jim noticed that he had forgotten to bring his own field dress kit. "I'm going upstream to look for another one," he said, not wanting to watch the butchering. "If you hear shoot-ing, come and help me out."

They said they would, and he left them to their business. *Heck of a pair*, he thought, pondering the strange relationship between the two—Dave Ingles, of whom it was said he could not tell the truth with a gun to his head, and Bill McCarthy, who would not lie, even at the risk of hurting someone's feelings. Yet they seemed to be good friends, strange pair indeed.

About three miles upstream, Jim decided to stop and rest for a while. He sat down behind a large rock, rested his rifle across his knees, and waited quietly for about fifteen or twenty minutes.

He was thinking about heading back to camp and had started to get to his feet when a faint noise somewhere up ahead caught his attention. It sounded like an animal moving slowly through the brush. He cupped his hand behind his ear trying to make out where it was coming from. The sound grew louder as some unknown creature, moving through the brush, came closer.

Jim eased farther down behind the rock and listened intently with nervous excitement, fighting with his own emotions to remain calm. Then he saw the deer. Taking slow deliberate aim, he drew on the trigger, ever so slightly, a little more, then still a little more. His hand began to shake, and he loosened his grip momentarily then drew up again. Again his hand betrayed him and then his leg started shaking involuntarily. It seemed as if he were losing complete control of his whole body. He struggled to be still.

The deer lifted its head, seemingly unconcerned, and stared directly into Jim's eyes. Animal and boy remained transfixed on each other for what seemed, to Jim, an eternity. He felt as if the big brown eyes were looking into his very soul, and then they were suddenly frozen by the terror of impending doom. Still they stared at him, almost pleadingly, as if unable to turn away.

A deer can't think like a man, Jim thought. *It can't look a man in the eye and beg for its life. They just don't do that. It's just an animal.* He lowered the rifle and continued looking into the eyes of the creature he had been so intent on killing. If he could just stay calm, the deer would not run away. He could still do this. Quickly, he raised the weapon again and tried to pull the trigger but his finger would not obey the ambiguous signals his brain was sending.

He couldn't do it. He couldn't shoot the deer. "Grandpa was right," he said out loud. "Kill only out of necessity and only when absolutely unavoidable."

As if suddenly aware that he had been given a reprieve, the deer bolted, turned in mid-air, and was gone as quickly as if he'd never been there. Jim sat there limp, not sure how he felt about what had just happened. He heard his trophy crashing through the brush, now well out of harm's way, back in its own domain. He had heard about people getting buck fever. They said it happened all the time, but he never thought it would happen to him. He took some comfort in knowing that, at least the others wouldn't know. He could just say he never saw a deer. It was a small lie. Grandpa wouldn't approve, but Grandpa didn't have to face Jim's three friends and tell them he had failed at something that they seemed to take for granted. He guessed he could live with such a small bit of deception. He got to his feet and started to turn when he noticed some movement out of the corner of his eye.

"You okay, Jim?" It was Robert. He was standing there watching him. He must have gotten out of bed after all and had followed along after. He had seen everything, surely. Jim tried to speak but his mouth was dry and no words would come out. "I must have scared him off," Robert said. "I'm so clumsy. I'm sorry man."

Jim finally found his voice. "You didn't scare him off, Robert, I did. I couldn't shoot him."

Robert's face took on the look of one much older and wiser than his eighteen years, and he spoke to Jim as one would speak to a younger brother.

"Listen, Jim, I know you think that most of what I say is hog wash and I don't take things serious enough, but I'm telling you straight now. Killing something just to be doing it is nothing to be proud of and not being able to kill is nothing to be ashamed of. I never wanted to kill a deer. My old man made me do it. I shot one in the face so he couldn't hang another trophy on the wall. I didn't want to walk in every day and see a deer head, my deer head, hanging in the den next to the one my brother Randy shot. He never took me hunting again after that."

Jim had never seen this side of his friend. Underneath all the posturing and bragging, when his defenses were down, Robert was a different person. There were feelings and compassion in him that Jim had never imagined existed.

"Why didn't you just refuse to shoot them?" Jim could simply not visualize his grandfather, or his stepfather ever faulting him for failing to do something. They just weren't like that. "Why didn't you just tell him you didn't want to hunt? If he insisted, then you could have shot high or wide or something like that."

"He knew if I missed it would be on purpose, and he would not allow that. My old man could never accept that one of his sons could not pull the trigger on a deer, or anything else for that matter. That would show weakness, and he could not tolerate weakness. He's a self-made man, you know, so I shot the deer in the face to make sure he didn't have it mounted. It was easier that way, not for the deer of course, but for me, it was. I know it wasn't right. I guess you could say it was a lack of personal fortitude on my part I just didn't have the balls to tell him no. Mind you now, I don't have a problem with others who hunt for sport, that's their decision to make, and if I had to kill an animal to feed my family, then I'd do it, but I just can't do it for fun."

"I understand," Jim said. "I guess I'm the same way. I didn't know it until today but I guess I feel the same way."

A sad look came over Robert's face momentarily, a look Jim had never seen before, and then in an instant it was gone and the old Robert had returned. He squared himself and adopted his usual demeanor. "I don't think we need to share this moment of soul searching with the unrefined, old buddy, if you know what I mean. We don't want to destroy any images today."

"Thank you," Jim said, "thank you, Robert."

They shook hands. Jim didn't know why they shook hands, it just seemed appropriate, like sealing their new relationship, he guessed. Now he reckoned he knew what the glue was that had held their friendship together all these years.

Jim would take home a trophy today but it would not be one to hang on the wall. It would be a trophy that he would keep in his memory and in his heart for the rest of his life.

Back in camp, Robert relived the incident for the others, telling and lamenting about how he had stumbled upon the scene and ruined Jim's shot for him. Jim, he said, had exercised tremendous self-control by not shooting at the fleeing deer, perhaps wounding it, and leaving it to crawl off and die in agony.

Jim listened quietly, saying nothing, now more concerned about Robert's lying than he was about what Bill's and Dave's reaction would have been to his inability to shoot the deer. The old Robert had indeed returned. That night as the car roared down the highway, with Bill McCarthy's deer tied to the fender, Jim sat in the passenger's seat and smiled to himself about the day's events.

Some years later, when things that take place in the life of an eighteen-year-old boy tend to lose their perceived gravity, Jim would tell the others what had really happened on that fateful hunting trip. They would laugh, and he would laugh too, and he would discover that their friendship was not at all diminished by the revelation. Even more so, he would not forget the friend who had so zealously guarded his feelings and his boyhood honor.

Robert pressed down on the accelerator and the fence posts beside the road shot by with ever increasing speed. Jim folded his jacket and placed it between his head and the car window, to keep the vibration from making his nose itch, and drifted off to sleep

Chapter 6

Cleve

The bus was crowded, almost fully loaded, and hot, extremely hot. Jim wished they would leave the station so the air conditioner would start up. Some of the people on the bus were fanning themselves with magazines while others shifted back and forth in their seats trying to cool off. A small child ran down the aisle with the mother close behind. Jim took a seat by the window so he could watch the scenery and maybe get some sleep on the way. He wished his car had not broken down. He hated riding the bus, but Trenton had promised him that it would be fixed by the time Jim returned from Austin, and his stepfather always did what he said he would. The car would be ready when he started to college in September at the University in Austin.

Across the aisle sat a pretty girl about Jim's age, she smiled at him when he boarded the bus, and he thought for a moment about sitting next to her but decided against it. He still had some trouble initiating contact with girls he didn't know, when he didn't have a good reason to do so. He didn't think he was bashful. Maybe it was just the fear of rejection, although he was rarely rejected by girls. They were always telling him how cute he was. It was nice, he guessed. Better than being told he was ugly but sometimes it was tiresome. Girls, as wonderful as they were, could be nuisances sometimes.

What might at first seem to be an opportunity to meet a pretty girl could turn into five-hour bus ride with a shallow, boring person who didn't know when to stop talking. So, with that in mind, he had let the moment pass. He glanced at her again and she was staring at him and still smiling. Again, he thought about moving into the empty seat next to her but the driver came aboard and was getting ready to depart. The driver started to close the door and then opened it to allow a late arriving passenger to get on.

"Hurry up," he said. "We're running late."

Struggling up the bus steps was a tired, stooped, old black man. Jim figured him for sixty-five years old, maybe seventy. It was hard to tell with older people, especially if they had worked hard all their lives. He always had trouble guessing their ages.

The old man held out his ticket. The driver took it without looking up and immediately started the bus in motion, forcing the man to steady himself on a seat back before moving down the aisle to find a seat. Jim saw that there were only three seats open on the entire bus—one next to an overdressed spinster in a sun hat and high heels and the other two next to him and the pretty girl across the aisle. The spinster placed the magazine, with which she had been fanning herself, on the empty seat next to her. She gave the old man a hateful look that told him not to sit down. He stood between the seats containing the two young white kids, not sure what to do, still supporting himself on the seat backs as the bus rocked back and forth, going down the road. It was not appropriate in the white society of 1960 for a colored man to sit down next to a young white girl, and the old man did not dare to do that, so he continued to stand there, looking around.

"This seat isn't taken," Jim said. "You can sit here."

"Thank you, sir," he said and sat down. He placed his small bag between his legs on the floor and leaned back. "Mighty hot today, mighty hot."

"Yes, sir, it is," Jim responded. "But it'll cool off now with the air conditioner on."

"You don't have to call me sir. I'm a colored man. My name is Cleveland Green, Cleve, call me Cleve."

"My folks taught me to speak respectfully to my elders," Jim said. "I don't recall them saying that meant only white people. I talk like that to everyone."

"Your folks mus' be good people," Cleve said. "Yes, sir, that's good when folks teach they kids right. So many kids these days, white and colored, don't talk respectful. They go around yeahin' and nawin' and don't say sir or ma'am or nothin' like that. Makes me mad sometime."

Jim watched the old man. He'd not had much dealing with Negroes. There weren't very many where he lived and the ones who were there kept mainly to themselves. He had not been raised to be prejudiced. He'd not been raised to have much of an opinion at all about them. He guessed that was a form of prejudice. But not really, not like the people who called them niggers. No one in his family ever called them niggers, not even Grandpa, who didn't like most people, white or otherwise.

Now, sitting next to this old colored man, Jim started to think about how he really felt down inside about it all. There had to be something wrong with a society that an old man, even though he was colored, was afraid to sit down next to an eighteen-year-old white boy on a bus without first getting permission. The old man had paid the same price for his ticket as everyone else. Wasn't he as entitled to a seat as anyone else? And yet, he'd stood there waiting for Jim to tell him that it was okay for him to sit down.

Cleve was a slightly built man, about five feet nine, maybe, shorter than Jim and not nearly as heavy, probably no more than a hundred and thirty pounds, Jim figured, for his Khaki pants and shirt hung loosely on his body. Time and hard work had left him with a permanent stoop in his walk. Jim had noticed the bent posture when Cleve got on the bus. His hair was graying, and the little round glasses he wore, gave him a studious look. Educated, Jim thought, although Cleve would tell him later that he had not gone past the fifth grade in school.

I lives in Gonzales, Texas," the old man said. "You heard of Gonzales?"

Jim nodded. "I'm not sure where it is though."

"Jus' east of San Antone. Been there ten years now. Grew up in Luziana, New Awlins."

"I always wanted to go to New Orleans. I plan to one day."

"Nice town, too big tho. My boy graduated from college and left so I left too. I likes it jus' fine in Gonzales. My sister lived there till she died. I moved there back in 1950, cause she lived there with her family. Tha's when my boy went to Dallas."

"What does he do?" Jim asked him.

"He's a pharmacist there in Dallas. First one in my family to go to college. You a college man?"

"Yes, sir," Jim said. "I mean I will be this September."

The old man was chuckling. "There you go again," he said, "callin' me sir."

"I'm sorry," Jim said and laughed. "I mean I'm not sorry, I told you I just talk that way. It's the way I was raised."

"Tha's okay. But we talkin' man to man now. No need fo' none of that."

"That's true," Jim said. "Yes, I'm going to Austin now to see about signing up at UT for next semester."

"Man, cain't get too much education. Some of 'em are educated idiots, if you know what I mean," he said, winking at Jim, who nodded, knowingly, and smiled.

"But that don't make no matter. Man, still cain't get too much education. My boy went to Dillard University, tha's in New Awlins. Fo' years there and then to pharmacy school at Xavier. Tha's in New Awlins too. When he got his license, they offered him this job in Dallas. NAACP. folks helped him find it. They good people. Some of 'em ain't, I guess, they's good and bad. I don't know how you feel about them folks."

"Well, I don't fault anybody for trying to better themselves. Seems to me that's what America is all about, or should be at least."

"Tha's right. Man should always try to better hisself, nothin' wrong with that. What are you takin' up at the university?"

"Business," Jim said. "I didn't really want to go to college but my mother insisted."

Cleve nodded his head up and down several times.

"My stepfather too", Jim continued. "He probably had more to do with me going to college than anyone else. You see, I want to take over my grandfather's farm one day, and Grandpa wants me to, but they all thought I should get a college degree first. I didn't see the need to waste the time but they all insisted. I thought about going to A and M and studying agriculture. But it's a Dairy farm, and Trenton, that's my stepfather, said I needed to know about running a business if I was going to manage a dairy farm. He agreed I might not need a degree but he said I needed the knowledge. He talked me into going to Texas for at least two years. I promised him I'd stay at least two years." Jim thought about it a few seconds. "I'll probably go the whole four years," he said. "My stepfather is paying good money so I owe it to him to do my best."

"Your stepfather sounds like a real good man," Cleve said.

"He is," Jim replied, "a real good man."

"An' what happened to your daddy?"

"Killed in the war, killed at Normandy."

Cleve shook his head slowly and curled his lips together. "Tha's too bad," he said, "too bad. Many a good man died in that war, white and colored, fo' that matter. It's mighty good, tho, that you got a good stepfather. He's been good to your mama?"

"Yes, yes, he has. He's been good to all of us. I have a little sister and brother, half sister and brother actually, but we're real close. Trenton has been like a real father to me. I never knew my dad but Trenton knew him, and he told me what a fine man my real dad was. He never tried to take his place or anything like that. He's just been sort of like a good friend all my life."

"You a lucky boy," Cleve said, "lucky boy indeed. Now don't get down there to college and start chasing girls and forget to study. You got a girl friend?"

"No not really, no one special." The girl across the aisle had been listening to them talking, and she glanced at Jim.

"I don't have a girlfriend," he repeated, raising his voice so she'd be sure to hear.

"Well, you got plenty of time fo' that. Women comes and goes but one day you'll meet one that won't let you go. Women are a blessin' an' a curse at the same time. Three things a woman cain't stand—not knowin' where her man is, not knowin' what he's doin', and not knowin' who he's with. They cain't stand that. They get mean sometime, but you cain't hit 'em. Man cain't hit a woman, not an call hisself no man, he cain't. Bes' jus' get out of they way when they gets mad, cause you cain't talk to 'em. I had a good wife. Married fo'ty years. She died in 'fifty-seven."

The bus pulled into Waco, and Jim got up to go into the station for a Coke. "You want a drink, Cleve?" he asked the older man. "I'm going to get a Coke."

The old man said he believed he would have a Coke too. The spinster gave them a hateful look, but Jim pretended not to notice and walked on down the aisle to the door of the bus. He returned in a few minutes with three cokes and handed one to the pretty girl across the way.

"You looked like you could use a Coke," he said to her.

She gushed, said, "thank you," and flashed her eyes at him. He wished for a moment that he had sat with her when he got on the bus, but he wouldn't leave the old man now for anything.

Cleve winked at him after Jim sat back down. "You a ladies' man, you ain't foolin' me none. Yes, sir, you a ladies' man."

Jim smiled at that. "What did you do for a living, Cleve?" Jim asked him.

"I worked in the plasterin' trade. All my life, seems like. Cos' they don't do much of that no more. They use sheetrock now, mainly, drywall, they call it. Not much call for plaster no more. I worked all up an' down River Road, from New Awlins to Baton Rouge. Some of the finest old plantation homes you ever saw, both sides of the Mississippi."

"What did you do, remodel them?"

"Tha's right, we fixed them up. They's some fine places down there. One place, I remember, in St. Francisville. It was haunted. Place called the Myrtles Plantation. They said a long time ago someone killed some kids in the school room, back of the main house, and the ghosts were still there. I don't know if tha's so or not. I didn't see any. I didn't stay in one spot too long neither, I don't mind tellin' you." He laughed out loud and slapped his knee. Jim laughed too and said he didn't blame Cleve. "You know, they still had bullet holes in that house from the Civil War," Cleve continued. "Tha's what they said, anyway. I think somebody done shot those holes in that house on purpose sose they could say that. You know how folks is."

Jim nodded, wondering what it would be like to be as old as Cleve. He'd seen a lot of history, that was true, but Jim suspected that Cleve had seen great events come and go, mostly unaware of what was happening around him. Cleve had lived through both wars, and the depression, but Jim probably knew more about those periods of time, from a historical viewpoint, than the old man did. Most people, he'd discovered, related great world events by how those events affected them personally. Cleve talked about the depression as just one more hardship in a life of hardship. It had not been a worldwide cataclysmic event to the Green family of New Orleans.

"Weren't a whole lot different after the depression came than it was befo'." He said. "Rich folks did okay, jus' like they did befo', and po' folks had to scrape and scrub fo' a livin', jus' like befo'. Nothin' much changed. Cose' now when the war come then things got better. Lots'a business came then. Aw, everybody went around pretendin' like they's all concerned about the war, an' some was I guess, specially them with sons in the war, but mos'ly they was jus' happy that things was gettin' better."

"Were you in the war, Cleve?" Jim asked.

"No, sir, I was too old. I tried to sign up after Pearl Harbor happened but I was fo'ty nine and they wouldn't take me. Fo' the best, I guess, I wouldn't a' been much good a' runnin' around tryin' to keep up with those young'uns. My boys went though, both my boys. Henry, tha's the one in Dallas, he came out okay but Alvin—" The old man's voice cracked and he choked on his words for a moment. Jim wished he hadn't asked him about the war. "Alvin, he didn't come back from the war. Nawth Africa, tha's where my boy died."

"I'm sorry," Jim said.

"Tha's okay. Alvin died fo' what he believed in. He always
believed that things would one day get better fo' the colored
man. They will one day. I believes that. Some colored folks go
aroun' sayin' we shouldn't fight fo' the United States cause
we don't get treated right. Tha's foolishness, I say. My boys
said so too. Alvin would a' went to school too if he hadn't got
killed. Jus' like Henry did. Henry went to school on the GI
Bill and he got hisself an education. Now he makes a good
livin' fo' his wife and kids. Helps me out a lot too. I'm grateful fo' that. No, this country been good to me. I always had a
job and made a decent livin' If a man don't mind workin', he
can make a livin'. Always a place fo' a man that don't mind
workin'. Now my gran'baby, she's 'bout your age, she's goin'
to college, an' my grandson next year. Tha's somethin' a man
can be proud of. Don't make no never mind I never went to
school, not more'n the fifth grade, that is, but my grand
chillen' goin' to college. Yessir, the good Lawd's been very
fair with me. Mighty fair indeed."

Jim studied the old man, trying to decide if what he was
saying was real or just for the benefit of his young white traveling companion. He had heard others say that colored people
sometimes said what they thought white folks wanted to hear
and not what they really felt. A means of getting by with as
little confrontation as possible. He could understand that. But
Cleve was real, he decided. He said what he really believed.
Had he been full of hatred for white people, as some Negroes
were, Jim didn't believe Cleve would have even started talking
to him in the first place. He was a simple man who spoke with
simple wisdom. He had managed to survive in a segregated,
racist society without giving into hate. A victory, in itself, for
the human spirit. Jim could see, in this old man, although he
would never meet them, a family of hard working, decent people, a family that had overcome great odds to make a better
life for themselves. Discrimination, intolerance, and systemat-
ic exclusion had not kept them from prospering. They had not
thrown up their hands, saying the deck was stacked against
them, and relegated themselves to a life of mediocrity.

This was what America was all about, what all Americans should be like. He'd heard bigots talk about how the Negro would not try to better himself. How he had accepted his lot and lived poorly because he was satisfied with being inferior. The bigots said that slavery was not a bad system. They said, giving an example, that Negroes were given housing and food, and all their needs were met, and they virtually had no worries to speak of when they were slaves. They were always quick to point out, however, that they would not choose the life style for themselves, but for the Negro, they didn't see why it was so bad. The Green family were "uppity niggers," to the bigot. A family that had actually done what others of their race were so often derided for not doing. *There is something wrong in this country*, Jim thought, *something terribly wrong*.

Cleve had fallen asleep and the bus was pulling into the station in Austin. Jim got his things together without waking him. He thought about stepping over the sleeping man without disturbing his slumber but he couldn't leave without telling him goodbye, so he shook Cleve gently and the old man woke up. He was still a little groggy and seemed unsure of where he was but he brightened up when Jim spoke.

"Cleve, this is my stop. I'm getting off now. I just wanted to say so long."

"Why, thank you, young man," Cleve said. "I sure did enjoy talkin' to you. Lands sake, where are my manners? I never did even ask you your name."

"It's Jim, sir, and don't say anything about the sir," he said, "Jim Kemper from Arlington, and I enjoyed the talk too. Thank you."

"No need to thank me. You just go on and get that there education like your family wants you to and you'll do fine. I know you will. An' if you ever get to Gonzales look me up. I'm in the phone book."

"I will," Jim said, and he took one last look at the girl in the opposite seat. She smiled and waved to him, and he winked at her then got off the bus.

Cleve waved to him as the bus pulled out, then Jim heard an angry voice behind him, and he turned to see the spinster in the sun hat and high heels standing there.

"It's people like you that cause the nigger trouble," she said, with venom in her eyes.

"What?" Jim said, taken by surprise. "What are you talking about?"

"You people that go treating them like they're as good as we are. Soon they start thinking it themselves, and then they get out of hand. No decent God-fearing white woman will be safe when that happens."

"Lady, you're nuts," Jim said, waving her off with his hand, and he turned to leave but she grabbed his shoulder.

"You're a nigger lover. That's what you are. You'll see, one day when they take over, you'll see what you've done."

Jim thought about telling her to go to hell but he knew he should not do that. He wrenched his shoulder loose from her grip and just looked at her disgustedly. "Shame on you," he said, borrowing a line from his grandmother. "You should be ashamed of yourself. Jesus sees everything you do." He turned and walked away, chuckling to himself over the shocked look on the woman's face. "She's lucky," he said to himself. "I could have used one of Grandpa's lines on her."

He would meet many people in his lifetime. Some, he would know for years, and once they were gone, would not think about again. Others, like Cleve, he would know only a short while, and would never see again, but would never forget. Cleve would remain in Jim's memory forever. A brief encounter that would leave an indelible mark on him. He hoped that one day people would seek him out for his honesty and his simple wisdom. For a gentleness of spirit and optimism they perceived in him everywhere he went, he hoped to be remembered for the same qualities he had seen in an old colored man who had done Jim the honor of sitting next to him on a bus.

Chapter 7

Austin

1960-1963:

Robert Cunningham was the first to notice the change in his best friend. He stared at him mischievously across the sixth period study hall table.

"What?" Jim said, glancing at him but not returning Robert's stare.

"You know what," Robert said. "You were out with Cassie Woodard last night. How did it go?"

"It went just fine. No big deal." Jim still would not look at his friend.

"That's it?" Robert said. "It went just fine, nothing else?"

"What else is there?" Jim said, knowing Robert would not drop the subject.

"Methinks, ol' buddy, that you have glow about you that was not present in your demeanor yesterday. Methinks that it is entirely possible that the fair Cassie may have gone down for the count with my good friend James Kemper. Am I correct in my assumption?"

"Just don't tell anybody. I don't want to be known as someone who blabs that sort of thing around."

"I won't tell a soul," Robert said. "I won't have to. Cassie told the other girls on the cheerleading squad, and now it's all over Arlington High School."

"Shit," Jim said. He threw up his hands in mock frustration. "Now why would she do that?"

"Because, my naïve friend, it seems, according to my information, that at least half the girls on the squad are in a life-and-death competition over who can lay you first. Looks to me like Cassie Woodard won the first round."

"That's crazy," Jim said. "Just doesn't make any sense. I'm not sure I like that. That should be a private thing. What should I do now?"

"Only one thing you can do now, Kemper," Robert said. He sat up in his seat and narrowed his eyes at Jim. "You owe it to me and every other guy in the school to do every girl on the squad."

℮ℴℰℴ

McKinney Avenue in Dallas was a popular spot in the early 60s. The street was dotted with coffee houses and hangouts that attracted kids from around the area. Some of them went to The Cellar in Fort Worth but Jim liked McKinney Avenue because it had atmosphere. Much of the atmosphere Jim enjoyed so much came in the likeness of a five-foot-four, raspy-voiced beauty named Angelette Cuvier. She was French, or at least she had taken a French name for her act. Angelette was a singer at The Rubaiyat on McKinney Avenue.

The Rubaiyat was one of many coffee houses that dotted the street in those days. There was no legal drinking but a good variety of non-alcoholic exotic drinks and lots of cigarette smoke. People went there to pretend they were beatniks and for the entertainment which was often quite good.

Angie, as she was often called much to her dismay, had fallen for Jim Kemper the first time she saw him. At seventeen, he carried himself with more confidence than men much older. She was not bothered by the fact that she was twenty-six and that he was still in high school. One night after her show, she invited him to her apartment in The Arts District and the two of them began a love affair that had lasted three months.

Now this situation with Cassie Woodard had him confused. He had not told Robert or his other friends about the woman from McKinney Avenue. It had just seemed best to not do that. There was some honor in that, he guessed, because there were times when he really did want to brag about it. Now this cheer-leader was telling everyone how great he was in the sack. He hardly thought the encounter warranted rave reviews. It had been sort of a clumsy affair in the front seat of his car, parked at White Rock Lake in Dallas. The earth had not moved for him, and he couldn't help but believe that Cassie was exagger-ating the whole thing for the benefit of her friends.

It was flattering, he thought, very flattering indeed. Some-times he felt like he could walk on air. Sometimes he felt like he could have any girl he wanted. All he had to do was just snap his fingers, and they would be his. He tried to study but kept thinking about Angie. Angie was not as pretty as most of the girls he knew in school. In fact, Jim sometimes thought she was a little strange looking. Her nose was just slightly too big and she had an overbite. Somehow the two minor flaws made her sexy. She exuded sex from every pore. Jim became aroused just by looking at her. And her voice. When she opened her mouth to sing, men would melt right where they sat. He figured it was fortunate that half the guys in the place were homosexuals, or else he would have been in a lot of fist fights with other men who wanted to get their hands on Angie.

Coach Neal came by and reminded Jim about baseball practice. The coach had taken a personal interest in Jim be-cause he was the best pitcher in the city, according to the coach, with a real promising future in the Big Leagues, if he would play four years in College. Jim didn't think he was that good. He certainly didn't have the passion for baseball that he knew he would have to have to play professional ball. Never-theless, the man had encouraged him greatly, so had his step-father Trenton. Trenton had always been his biggest fan and promoter. Trenton Knew that Jim could make it to the Big Leagues if he really wanted too.

It was his stepfather who had convinced him to go to col-lege. He made Jim promise to go at least two years just to see how he liked it. Trenton insisted on paying all the costs. He wanted Jim to concentrate on his studies and not have to hold a part-time job. If he got a baseball scholarship later, that would be okay, but it would be okay too if he didn't. Trenton advised him to get a business degree. It would help him later if he decided to take over the farm from his grandfather.

Jim gratefully accepted his stepfather's offer. It seemed that his grandfather had been in on Trenton's attempt to talk him into going to college because it was all that Alton talked about lately.

Jim was sitting by himself in study hall when he heard someone approaching the table.

"Hi, Jim, what are you studying?"

Jim looked up. It was Laura Speelman, one of the girls from the cheerleading squad. She sat down across from him.

"Economics," he said. "You know, supply and demand, recession, depression. It's not very interesting, tho. I like history better, but I don't think history is as important as economics. What do you think?"

"Well, I guess it depends on what you plan to do in life. You are going to college, aren't you, Jim?"

Jim nodded. "UT in the fall," he said.

Laura looked at him seductively. A hint of a smile crossed her lips, and she toyed with her long brown hair. "I'm going to Texas too," she said. "My daddy owns an apartment building in Austin. I'm going to have my own apartment. Maybe you can come and see me sometime."

Jim straightened up and pushed his chair back slightly. He clasped his hands together behind his head, trying to appear more in control than he was, and looked back into the enchanting brown eyes of the girl who had just shown him a glimpse of the future.

"Maybe I will, Laura," he said. "Maybe I will."

They stared deeply into each other's eyes for what seemed like an eternity to Jim. He was certain that she could hear his heart beating. She smiled broadly once and then resumed her coy demeanor. "By the way, Jim," she said, finally. "I had no part of that Cassie Woodard thing."

Jim closed his eyes and covered his face with his hands, which drew another smile from Laura.

"I didn't think you did," he said. "I was just a little embarrassed by it all."

"No need to be," she said, smiling again, "just because half the girls in the school are in love with you."

"Only half?" he said, with a look of mock disbelief on his face.

"That's just the ones who know you," she said, and laughed. She slid a piece of paper across the table to him. It was her address in Austin. "I'll let you know my phone number when I get one."

She stood up to leave, reached out her hand, and brushed his hair out of his eyes. Her touch was soft, very soft, and alluring. He enjoyed her touch, more than he would have imagined. What a surprise this afternoon had brought him. Life took some strange twists sometimes. This surely was one of those times. It caught him flat footed, unprepared, but pleasantly surprised. He would spend much time in thought and anticipation of the next time he felt her touch again.

∽∾

Austin, Texas, was the most fascinating place Jim had ever seen. A beautiful city on rolling hills situated on both banks of the Colorado River. It was to be his home for the next four years.

He took to the city right away. He loved the activity, the constant motion. Everybody seemed to be in a hurry to get somewhere else. Thousands of students at the university clamored to take care of all the last-minute arranging of schedules. They rushed in and out of the stores and shops along Guadalupe Street that ran next to the campus on the west side. Nobody seemed to talk to anyone else. *Too busy*, Jim guessed. They offered hurried apologies when bumping into another student but not much else. He was certain the pace would slow down once classes started.

It took him a week to get registered. On his counselor's advice, he carried a sixteen-hour workload. Jim wanted to take more but it would have required more of his weekend time and he wanted to spend weekends either at home or at the farm.

A room in a house on Nueces Street became his home. The house was owned by a widow named Gutterman and was a few blocks north of the campus just off Guadalupe.

There were two other rooms which were also rented to students. His room had a single bed, a small refrigerator, a private bathroom, and a desk.

The house rules were simple: No Drinking. No Smoking. No loud music or other activity and, of course, No Girls.

Jim consented to all her rules and endured stories about Mrs. Gutterman's grandson who had graduated from the university some years before and was now a lawyer in Houston.

Jim's classes turned out not to be the drudgery he had expected but rather interesting and enjoyable. He dedicated himself to getting everything he could out of his lessons, not only because he felt that he owed it to Trenton, for paying for his tuition, but also because he really wanted to amount to something someday.

He wanted them all to be proud of him, his mother and stepfather and his grandparents. He would stay in school. He would get his degree and go back and help his grandfather make the farm a successful enterprise.

It all came fairly easy to him, the economics, the English grammar and the business administration courses. The following years would require accounting, marketing, business management, and good old history, which he loved. It was hard work at times, but he was up for it. Nobody in his family had ever gone to college, not even Trenton. He was the first. He would do his best to see that every Kemper who came after him would have the same opportunity.

A call from his mother, reminding him that he had not come home for two weekends, convinced him to do that very thing. He got home around seven on Friday evening, along with his laundry.

"I guess you expect me to wash your clothes for you?" his mother said.

"No, Mother, I told Sarah I would pay her to do them for me."

Allie looked hurt. "So, you don't need your mother any-more?" she teased him. "Okay, okay, I know when I'm not needed."

"You're the only woman I've ever needed, Mother," he said, taking her in his arms. "Some of them I like and some of them I want, but you are the only one I need."

"You always know the right thing to say, handsome. I will help your sister with your laundry."

Jim smiled, thanked her, then kissed her on the cheek. "I'll probably stay at Robert's house tonight," he said. "But I'll be home all day tomorrow, okay?"

"See that you are. I miss you. Your brother and sister miss you too." Allie wasn't sure she believed that her son was spending the night with Robert Cunningham or not, but she didn't question him. She wasn't sure she wanted to know what he did when he was away from home. Every mother worried about her children and Allie was no different, but her son was growing up and was no longer under her control. He would do what he would do and all she could do was pray that he didn't get hurt in the process.

When Jim walked into the Rubaiyat, Angie came running over to him and kissed him passionately right in front of everyone in the place. It no longer embarrassed him. He had gotten used to her quixotic behavior and her flair for drama. "Why have you been away from me so long, Jim?" she said, raising the back of her hand to her forehead pretending that she might faint. "I need to see you."

"I needed to see you too," he told her. "School takes up more of my time than I thought it would. I just can't get home every weekend. I came as soon as I could."

"I'm off at eleven," she said. "We'll go to my place."

At her apartment, Angie went into the bathroom and came out without her clothes on.

"See anything you like?" she asked him, turning around so he could see her body.

Jim was almost tongue tied. He stood there drinking in her beauty, caressing her with his eyes, every inch of her creamy white body, from her soft, succulent neck to her breasts, and, finally, to those magnificent legs. "Turn around again," he said.

"No," she squealed.

She ran, jumped into his arms, and wrapped her legs around him. He fell backward onto the couch. They kissed like people ate who had not had food for a week. It was Angie's affair, and Jim felt like he was just along for the ride. They made love twice, and he awoke at six the next morning, still exhausted. He took a shower and got dressed while Angie scrambled him some eggs.

"I'm going to New York," she yelled to him from the kitchen.

"New York, why?"

"I'm going to sing in a nightclub there," she said, watching the bedroom door for his reaction.

"I don't understand," he said "Why New York? When did this happen?"

"Last week. A man came into the place who owns a club in New York. He wants me to come and perform in it. The pay is good, and it's a chance to do something with my career. He's going to pay my way and get me a place to live."

"Sounds like bullshit to me," Jim told her. "You sure he isn't just after your pants?"

"I knew you would say that. But no, it's not like that. He says he really wants to help me with my singing."

"Like I said, it sounds flaky, so what about us?"

"Oh, Jim, I won't ever stop caring about you. But you're in college now, and you won't want me forever. I'm just a roll in the hay for you. You know it's true. You don't ever want to marry me, do you Jim?"

"I'm not sure I want to marry anyone, Angie," he said. "I haven't really thought about it. I just don't want you to fall for a line of crap from some guy and get hurt. I can't tell you what to do, but I hope it works out for you. I do love to hear you sing."

"Thank you. I wanted for us to have a last night together. It meant a lot to me."

"So, last night was your going-away gift to me?"

"No," she said, "It was my going away gift to me. Did you enjoy yourself?"

"It was a lot better than getting a sweater," he said.

She laughed and threw a towel at him.

Jim was philosophical about Angie's leaving. He never expected it to last very long with her. She was a free spirit and too unpredictable for him. It was just a fluke that they had ever gotten together in the first place. He wasn't sure if he would ever see her again. He wasn't sure if he wanted to ever see her again. She would have caused him trouble at some point in time. He was sure of that. He kissed her and left her apartment.

He spent the weekend at home in Arlington. He paid his sister Sarah for doing his laundry and thanked her.

"*De nada, mi hermano*," she said. "It was my pleasure, big brother."

"I see you are working on your Spanish," he replied "Good, keep it up. It will pay off one day."

"My friend Aliana is helping me. She speaks Spanish—"

"That's because she is Spanish," Allie interrupted.

"No, she's a Mexican," Sarah corrected her, "But she's not from Mexico."

"Where is she from?" Jim asked.

"I'm not sure, someplace besides Mexico."

"Then she may not be a Mexican," Jim explained. "She may be some other nationality like Guatemalan or Salvadoran.

"No, she says she's a Mexican, but she's not from Mexico."

"Then she must be from Texas," he said teasingly.

"She didn't say Texas," Sarah said, wrinkling her brow. "She said she was from Corpus Christi."

"That's in Texas, honey, and Texas is in the United States, unless you're talking to Grandpa, so Aliana is a Texan."

"No, she's a Mexican."

Jim explained how a person could be a Mexican and also a Texan as well as an American. When he finished, he was convinced that his sister understood what he was trying to tell her. He enjoyed talking to the precocious ten-year old. Sarah and nine-year-old Trent practically worshipped their older brother.

They clung to him and followed him everywhere he went in the house, asking him questions about anything they could think of. He always tried to provide satisfactory answers, no matter how unimportant the subject might seem to him.

Allie was thankful for the relationship her children shared. Many older brothers had no time for younger siblings. They were mostly interested in themselves and their friends. Younger brothers and sisters were often a nuisance, an affliction that had to be endured.

This was not the case with Jim and Sarah and Trent Jr. Jim loved them as much as Allie did. He treated them more like his own children than he did as brother and sister.

Sunday evening, he put his clothes in his car and told everyone goodbye. He kissed the two younger ones and his mother and talked with his stepfather for a few minutes before he was ready to head back to Austin.

"I almost forgot," his mother said, as he was leaving "Some girl called for you. Said her name was Laura. She gave me a phone number to give to you. Who is she?"

"She's a girl from school, high school," he said. "She said she might be at UT this year."

"I haven't heard you talk about her. Is she one of your…you know…"

"No, she's just a friend, Mother. She helped me once with my economics homework."

"She didn't sound like just a friend, Jimmy," Allie said. "If you know what I mean."

He didn't answer her as he went out the door. She called to him as he walked to his car. "Be careful," she yelled.

Business administration turned out to be Jim's favorite class. They explored every aspect of running a successful business. Methods of receiving and storing inventory, keeping up with taxes, advertising, and many other things that Jim never realized he would need to know to manage a business. His grandfather never seemed to know any of the stuff that Jim was now learning and yet he had made a living off the dairy for most of his life. It seemed simple enough. Buy the feed and the equipment and milk the cows, process the milk and sell it, but there had to be more to it than that. Grandpa and Danny Carlisle had always talked about packaging the milk themselves and selling it rather taking it to a bigger dairy or a distributor. They just needed financing to make that happen. Jim decided he would make it his first order of business to establish the Kemper dairy as its own milk company. There was potential there on that little plot of ground. He knew it, just as Grandpa had always said. He would make it work. But now there was so much to learn.

He needed to know how to finance great projects, how to find investors, and how to spot, once in a lifetime, opportunities. The class was made more enjoyable by the instructor, a lanky, sort of sloppily dressed man, with a permanent cowlick on the back of his head, whose name was Barnhart, Nelson Barnhart. He always looked, to Jim, like he had just crawled out of bed. The man had taught at Harvard, years before, and that was his claim to fame. He talked constantly about The Yard and his classes there. Jim sometimes wanted to ask him why he didn't go back to Harvard, but he didn't. In Jim's opinion, the man was nonetheless brilliant for his proclivity to live in the past.

Barnhart really knew his stuff, Jim thought. He didn't know if the man had ever actually put any of his theories and teachings into practice but Jim believed that he would take away enough information from Barnhart's class to really help him later on. He came to have some respect for the quirky professor with the goofy hair and strange ways.

Professor Barnhart had been heavily involved in an anti-segregation movement, at the school, that had achieved some spectacular results. The city of Austin was far more liberal than most of the state, but that fact did not diminish his accomplishments. The university desegregated in 1956, and there was a growing trend now to desegregate restaurants and other businesses in the city.

The professor crowed about all that had been achieved in the name of civil rights. He was proud of the role he had played in the movement and he constantly reminded his students of it.

Jim endured it because he had come to like the man, but he was not a crusader. He had no causes as yet, other than to get an education and to make something of himself. He sympathized with the plight of the colored man. He remembered his talk with the old man on the bus the past summer. He believed that they were just like white folks. Some were good and some were not. You just had to pick out the good ones and leave the bad ones alone. Same way he did with everyone. Still, the segregation issue was a force that would have to be dealt with at some point in time. He didn't see how the United States could go on much longer with a segregated society. The concept was distasteful. It made him feel guilty sometimes and he had never done anything to discriminate against anyone.

Jim recalled the time when he was nine years old that Trenton took him with him to the bus station in Dallas to pick up some things that his grandfather Matthews had sent from the leather factory in Comanche. There were two drinking fountains in the station. One of them read *White* and the other read *Colored*. Trenton laughed out loud when Jim said he wanted to wait until someone used the one marked *Colored* because he wanted to see what color the water was.

The professor had made it no secret that he had applied to return to Harvard in a teaching capacity. Jim wondered why the man left in the first place, considering that it was such a passion of his to be at Harvard. Jim didn't give it much more thought than that, and he never asked Barnhart about it.

Jim sat staring at the piece of paper his mother had handed to him as he was leaving home to come back to Austin. He looked at the name, *Laura*. A hundred things were running through his mind at the same time. He wanted to call her right away but didn't. He wasn't sure if he should. He remembered the way she looked at him that time back in school, the way she smiled then brushed his hair and touched his cheek. He thought for a long time that she might just be toying with him. He never really expected her to call. Her family was rich, very rich, and his was not. They didn't fit, that was a fact. They were miles apart on the social scale. No way could it work out for them.

And yet here he was staring at her name and number. She had called him. Perhaps she was still toying with him. He wasn't sure. He'd thought about taking a shot at getting in her pants, and decided on that course of action. The problem with that, however, was that he wasn't sure if that was all he wanted from her. He remembered the feeling of warmth he felt as she walked away after giving him her address. He wasn't really looking for another easy time with a girl.

The voice on the other end of the phone was soft and inviting.

For a brief moment, he wasn't sure if he had the right number. "Is this Laura?" he asked.

"Yes, it is," she answered. "Who's this?"

"This is Jim Kemper."

"Jim, I was afraid you wouldn't call. I left my number two weeks ago. Your mother was very nice on the phone."

"I just went home this past weekend. My mother gave me your number. I'm sorry, I would have called you. How've you been?"

"I've been just wonderful, Jim. I'm all settled in my apartment. I have two friends staying with me. They're at the university too, no one you know," she said and laughed slyly. He knew what she meant. "Don't you just love Austin, Jim? Isn't it just the most marvelous place in the world?"

"Yes," he agreed. "Austin is a great town."

"I want to see you, Jim. Can we go somewhere?"

They made small talk for a half hour or so. She played to him over the phone line, her voice drawing him and holding him spellbound. She wanted him to pick her up at her place. She insisted on seeing him that night. He did not argue that it was a study night. He didn't care. When he hung up the phone, he sat for a moment. He was almost weak. *Strange*, he thought. He had not even touched her yet and already he knew that he was in over his head.

The apartment was very nice. Situated in a rather exclusive section of west Austin called Tarrytown, it was just about what he expected for a college girl whose father was rich. Now he would see how the other half lived, he was thinking, as he rang the buzzer to Laura's apartment.

She opened the door and let him in then took his hand and held it in hers. He'd half expected her to kiss him but she didn't. Laura's two roommates were standing in the living room, obviously there to examine him. They looked at each other and then at Laura.

"So, this is the secret you've been keeping," one of them said. "You didn't tell us he was so pretty, Laura."

"No, silly," Laura said, "he's mine. I've been saving him all for myself."

She made the necessary introductions, and the two room-mates dutifully vanished to the other bedroom they shared. Laura was still holding Jim's hand. "So, what do you think of my place?" She asked him.

"It's beautiful," he said, "really. I like it."

Her bedroom, she explained, was furnished and arranged just like her bedroom at home. There were stuffed animals of every shape and size and breed covering her bed. It looked like a little girl's room, he thought, a bit immature for grown-up college girl, but nevertheless, there it was.

He was not surprised by it all. It just seemed like Laura to him. He was having trouble taking his eyes off her. He had either forgotten or had never realized how beautiful she was. Soft brown hair fell gently to her shoulders and flipped out slightly. She had the most beautiful brown eyes he'd ever seen. He remembered those eyes that had held his attention back in school at home but now they seemed to offer so much more. As he talked with her, he would look away from time to time and look back to find her staring at him.

"Where do you want to go?"

"Any place is fine. I know it's a school night." I want you to take me to Threadgill's this weekend. They have folk music and a great time. You don't have any plans for the weekend, do you?"

"If I did, I don't remember what they were."

She smiled broadly at him.

Jim suggested a pizza place he knew of near his room. It was called The Rome Inn. It wasn't too loud, he explained, and had really good food. She consented and Jim drove to the place.

He was almost embarrassed to take her out in his '52 Ford. He had to remind himself that he was not yet the man of means that he intended to become one day. If she had paid any attention to his car, she did not let on.

At dinner, he was absorbed in the conversation and eye play between them. He crossed his eyes and mugged at her and she threw an olive at him. When he got out of his chair and retrieved the olive from the floor then put it in his mouth and ate it, she covered her face with both hands and giggled like a small girl. What struck him the most about the entire event was just how comfortable it felt to be with her, how natural, how right it was to be with her.

He pulled his car into the parking lot at her apartment and turned off the engine. He turned slightly toward her and put his arm up on the seat back. "I really had a good time," he said. "I can't tell you how much I enjoyed it."

She said nothing but slid herself across the seat next to him and wrapped his arm around her. Their lips met, but it was not the hot, desperate kisses of teenagers that he was used to. They kissed as if they had known each other forever. He kissed her cheeks and her forehead. Then her nose and then her eyes and then her lips again, not hurriedly but slowly and gently as if she belonged to him and he knew it. He couldn't help but think that Laura kissed like Angie did, not like girl but like a woman. But he quickly put Angie out of his mind.

"Now," she whispered in his ear. "Aren't you glad you called me?"

"Yes," he said. "I am. Aren't you glad you gave my mother your number for me?"

෧෨෧

The next few weeks flew by for Jim. He was keeping up with his class work, despite the distraction offered by his new love. They went to Threadgill's a lot because Laura loved folk music. Jim did not share her love for the music, but he loved being with her so he endured. It was a small price to pay, he guessed.

They had been an item for a little over two months, and Jim knew he was hopelessly in love with her. One Saturday night, early in December, they sat talking in his car in the parking lot at her apartment. Laura was leaned back against the passenger side door with her feet in his lap.

"I need to tell you something," he said.

She looked at him, sort of bemused. "You're not going to dump me, are you?"

He looked at her for a few seconds. "No," he said finally. "Why would you think that?

"It's just that you seem so serious."

"No, no, that's not what it is."

"Well, then what is it?"

"Well, it's just that—it's uh…"

She started giggling and rubbing his cheek with her toe. "Well, are you going to tell me or not?"

"I love you," he said.

"I love you too. I've loved you since our junior year."

"I didn't know, I had no idea. Why didn't you tell me?"

"It's not that easy for a girl. I guess I just loved you from afar." She flipped her hand into the air melodramatically. "I mean, you could have had any girl you wanted."

"You didn't seem to have any trouble that time in study hall," he said. "What was that all about?"

"It was the end of the school year. I knew you were going away to college. I was afraid I would never see you again. I just mustered up all my courage and went for it."

"I guess you're right."

"About what?"

"I guess I can have any girl I want. I've got you, and you're the only one I want."

"Oh, you go right for the heart, don't you? Now, what was it you wanted to tell me?"

"Oh," he said, "I just did. I wanted to tell you that I love you."

"Oh, that. Well, I love you too."

"You said that."

"I know," she said, smiling, "ever since high school."

He took her hand and pulled her over to him. "Come here, I need to kiss you before I go."

They kissed for a few minutes, and she looked up at him. "Don't go, Jim. My roommates are gone for the weekend."

Life, up until now, had not prepared him for this moment. Perhaps this moment would prepare him for the rest of his life. He didn't know. He wasn't sure of much at this particular moment in time.

They came together in her bed, with her stuffed animals thrown off onto the floor. He was lost in this lovely creature that had become his and his alone. Like their kissing had been, they did not make love with the fierce determination and desperation of teenagers. Jim savored every moment she shared with him. It was her first time, he knew. She knew that she was not his first and was thankful for it.

When it was over they lay in each other's arms, still breathing heavily. He held her for what seemed an eternity to him. He caressed her back, ran his fingers through her soft brown hair, and kissed her on her forehead. "I do love you, Laura," he repeated several times.

"I heard you the first time," she said, laughing, as she kissed his hand. "I love you too, Jim."

Jim was offered, and accepted, a scholarship to play baseball for the university. He had not wanted to invest the time but his reputation had preceded him somewhat, thanks to Coach Neal at Arlington High. Jim also felt that he owed it to Trenton to take the free tuition and books that would be provided. He would play for the school, despite the fact that it would limit his time and shorten his summers. Trenton said that he would have preferred to pay Jim's tuition because it was just something he wanted to do, but he was elated that his stepson was playing baseball. Trenton seemed to be playing vicariously through Jim. He continued to give him money for living expenses and other things that he figured Jim would need.

Jim knew he was a good baseball player, but the truth was he did not have the passion and drive to be truly great. There were some great standouts and All Americans on the Texas teams for which he played. Chuck Knutson was in the outfield in '61 and Pat Rigby at Second Base in '62. Two others, Bill Bethea at Shortstop and Butch Thompson at First Base probably, many agreed, prevented him from making the All-American team in '63 but Jim was not troubled by it. His career would not be in baseball. He was content to play mainly just for the scholarship money. Nevertheless, he was the best pitcher on the team and was much admired and respected by the coaching staff.

Laura attended every home game. She always managed to sit in the stands behind home plate. At times when he was in a tight spot, two runners on and no outs or some other dire situation, he would look up into the stands and see her staring at him. It didn't always mean he would win but it always helped him to keep his perspective.

Their second year, Robert Cunningham came down for a visit. He was attending SMU at his family's request. He brought his father's boat and they all went out on Lake Travis. He also brought a girl from school with him, a girl named Celeste, not overly attractive but congenial enough, Jim decided. It was a fun time for all of them. Jim invited them both to stay the weekend.

He wanted to go to San Antonio to the River Walk. It was decided that Celeste could spend the night with Laura, and Robert would bunk with Jim. Jim would clear it with Mrs. Gutterman.

They had dinner on the river and, after dinner, they walked and talked about old times and about the future. Robert would join his father's firm. He had decided that the old man was not that bad after all. Jim agreed and mentioned that he had told him that quite a long time ago.

"I have a confession to make, old buddy," Robert told him.

"Oh yeah, what's that? Jim said.

"I never realized in high school that Laura Speelman was so damned pretty."

"Tell you the truth, neither did I. It's amazing, isn't it? I passed her in the hallway, I don't know how many times and never noticed her. Now, I can't imagine my life without her."

"You better make a lot of money, Jimbo," Robert added. "Laura ain't no farm girl."

"I think she will be okay with it."

"I sure hope so," Robert said and shrugged his shoulders.

Laura took Jim's hand and led him up one of the many footbridges that span the San Antonio River. They looked over the side at their reflections in the water.

"Isn't this the most beautiful place in the world, Jim?" she said. "Let's live in San Antonio when we get married."

"So, you are going to marry me, after all?"

"If you'll have me," she said, coyly.

"If I'll have you? I can't imagine marrying anyone but you. But you know I have a business. I'm going to take over for my grandfather when I graduate. You know that. We've talked about it before."

"I know," she said. "But I thought you might change your mind about being a farmer after you graduate. I mean, you'll have a business degree. We can do anything we want to. You could work for my father."

"I don't want to work for your father. I want to work with my grandfather. Besides, Laura, we're not sodbusters. I mean it's not like I'll be plowing behind a couple of mules."

They let the subject drop. She started kissing him and only stopped when Robert and Celeste began making whooping noises from down on the riverbank.

In October of Jim's third year at UT, he took Laura to meet his grandparents. They planned to spend the weekend there, in separate bedrooms of course, so she could get to know the elder Kempers. They arrived just in time for dinner so Laura was treated to a real country fare. The meeting was easy, and Laura was very charming.

Mary Kemper liked her right off. Alton reserved his opinion until he could get to know her a little better. He noticed that the girl seemed to be totally infatuated with his grandson, and very little else. He tried to engage her in conversation but stopped when he found that she was not overly responsive.

"Oh, I almost forgot," Alton said. "You two kids come with me. I want to show you something." They followed him to the barn where he swung open the double doors.

Sitting inside was a brand new 1963 Pontiac Tempest.

"Grandpa," Jim said. "You finally bought a new car. Congratulations. I've been telling you for years to get rid of that old Buick and get a new car."

"That's just what I did, Jim. I traded in the Buick for this little beauty. But it's not for me, Grandson, it's for you."

"What?" Jim stammered. "You can't do that Grandpa. It's too much. I can't let you do that."

"I already did it," he said. "And of course, you can. Just consider it an early graduation gift. A college man can't be driving around in a '52 Ford. You'll look spiffy in this thing. Besides, what would an old man like me need with this car?"

Laura squealed and squeezed Jim's arm. "Oh, Mr. Kemper, it's beautiful," she said. "That's the nicest thing anybody could have done."

"But what about you, what are you going to drive?" Jim asked.

"I'll take your car and you can leave in your new one tomorrow. Take it for a spin."

"I don't know what to say. It doesn't feel right me driving off in a new car and you taking my throw away."

"Nonsense," Alton said. "This will make me a lot happier than it makes you. I guarantee it."

"I don't see how that is possible."

"You will one day, Jim, one day when you have kids."

Jim hugged the old man and fought hard to keep the tears out of his eyes. "Thank you, Grandpa," he said. "I'm going to take Laura for a drive in it."

He drove by the Comanche Leather Works factory that was owned by George Matthews, Jim's maternal grandfather. Laura did not seem to be impressed by anything he showed her.

"You said there are only about 4,000 people in this town?"

"I don't want to live here because of this town, Laura. I want to take over my grandfather's business. We've had an understanding since I was five years old. We've always known that one day I would come back here and run the place for him. It's what he's dedicated his life to, building a successful business for me. I can't let him down. I don't want to let him down."

"I know, that's all noble enough, and I do understand how you feel but it's just so isolated."

"I don't need to go to the symphony, Laura. I don't need a social calendar. I don't care what all the right people are wearing to the ball this year. I don't need any of that stuff. What I do need is you. You are all I need, and this farm. We can be happy here. This is something I have to do. But it won't mean anything without you. I will take you to San Antonio, or Dallas, or Houston...hell, I'll take you to New York, if you want, and anytime you want to go. Just trust me on this. It will work out for us.

They drove in silence for a while longer and then went back to the farm. The next day they drove back to Arlington. Jim dropped Laura off at her parent's house and went home to show the car to his mother and Trenton.

Wednesday nights were always jumping in Austin. Threadgill's had a regular Hootenanny with any variety of local bands playing blues and bluegrass, and sometimes country music. Hippies and rednecks came together in relative peace for the one night and everyone enjoyed the music and the cold beer. Laura loved the place and Jim took her there every week. It was too loud for quiet talks so they mostly just sat and stared at each other and listened to the music.

One night would be their last time there. As Jim pulled into the parking lot, he noticed a ruckus of some kind going on around another car. Three men were trying to pull another man out of his car. They were reaching into the car in an attempt to drag him through the driver's side window. Jim thought he recognized the man in the car and after a second look he realized it was his business administration professor, Mister Barnhart, who was embroiled in the ruckus. "Stay in the car," he told Laura and rushed over to see what the trouble was.

"Leave him alone," Jim yelled at the men, as he rounded the front of the professor's car.

"Mind you own damned business, boy," one of the men shot back. "We're going to teach this nigger lover a lesson he won't forget."

Jim waded into the three of them with his fists flying. He knocked one down and was pummeling a second one before he ever received a punch. The fist to his jaw stunned him and he fell back momentarily then regained his senses. All three men were up and coming at him and he just started throwing punches as fast as he could.

The professor managed to get out of his car and grab one of the men, the biggest one, from the back, and they went to the ground. Barnhart held a death grip on the man and would not let go, as Jim beat the other two so quickly that they ran for their truck and drove off, leaving their friend on the ground, still struggling with the teacher.

Jim took the man by his shirt collar and held him tight. "This is over," he said. "Get up and get out of here." The man complied, and Jim helped Mister Barnhart to his feet. "What caused this, Professor?" Jim asked him.

"I guess the signs on my car made them mad. They tried to run me off the road, so I pulled in here, thinking they wouldn't follow me into the parking lot.

Barnhart had some anti-segregation signs in his windows. It was as simple as that. The rednecks saw his signs and decided to beat him up, something Jim would expect in other parts of Texas but never in Austin.

"Thanks, Mister Kemper," Barnhart said, and shook Jim's hand. The professor always called his students by their last name.

"You might want to reconsider having those signs on your car," Jim said. "There are people like that all over. It might not be safe."

"It's a price we pay for social justice, Jim. I couldn't live with myself if I gave up the struggle."

"I understand," Jim said. "But maybe you could be a little more discreet. You know, join protests in large crowds. Don't try to rub their noses in it. All you'll end up doing is getting hurt."

"I know, I know, and you might not be around next time." They both laughed at that. "Don't think this business counts as extra credit, Mister Kemper," he said.

"I wouldn't dream of it, Professor," Jim said. "You be careful."

He spent the night at Laura's apartment. She doctored his scraped knuckles and kissed them. "That was the weirdest thing I've ever seen," she said. "You may have saved Mister Barnhart's life."

"More likely, he saved mine."

"What do you mean?"

"He took down the big guy. I couldn't have whipped all three of them."

Late one evening in February of 1963, Jim received a phone call in his room. It was his stepfather Trenton. His voice was low and his mood was somber. "I've got hard news, Jim," he said. "Your friend, Robert was killed in a car wreck somewhere in North Texas. His dad called and asked us to notify you."

Jim was shaken but managed to control the impulse to break down. He was just numbed by the message and by Trenton's subdued tone. "Do you know when the funeral is?" he asked.

"There are no plans as yet," Trenton said. "They said they would let us know when there is some news. I will call you."

Jim thanked him and hung up. He sat down on the side of his bed and hung his head. "Sonofabitch," he thought. "The damned fool drove like an idiot."

It was just a matter of time, he guessed. Those North Texas roads were infamous for black ice. Robert was probably flying along and hit some ice. What a waste, his one good friend in the world, and now he was gone.

Laura accompanied him to Robert's funeral. Allie and Trenton came by to pay their respects to the family as well.

There were a few old friends from high school. Some seemed surprised to see the two of them together. He guessed that most of the kids from school did not know that he and Laura had been together for almost three years now. It was noticeable to many that Jim and Laura interacted with each other more like they were married than as a steady couple. There seemed to be no doubt to most of their former classmates that the two were *doing it,* as one of them later observed.

Jim noticed two boys standing in the corner, more or less keeping out of the way.

One was tall and lanky and the other, much shorter, wore Marine khakis. It was Dave Ingles and Bill McCarthy. He had not seen them since high school.

"Too damned bad about Robert," Dave Ingles said, as Jim came over to where they were standing.

"Yes, it is," Jim replied. "How have you guys been? I see you joined the Marines, Bill."

They talked for a while, just small talk. He told them about his going to UT and Bill told him about the Marines. Neither had changed much. Dave finally moved out of his mother's house to an apartment where he could come and go as he pleased. Dave's mother eventually remarried but that husband left too after about six months.

Jim told them about the time he had gotten buck fever and was unable to shoot the deer and how Robert had kept the secret all this time.

"Nothing to be ashamed of," Bill McCarthy said.

"Hell no, Jim," Dave agreed. "I probably wouldn't a' been able to shoot the bastard either. All I ever kill is cans and bottles."

They laughed and shook hands. Again, they were really sorry about Robert. They both knew what good friends he and Jim had been. The two boys went over to speak for a moment to Robert's parents and then left.

The loss of his friend had hit him hard, but Jim went on. He was a little surprised that he had been able to recover so quickly. Robert was a good friend but Grandpa had always said that friends come and go. Some die, he said, and some just go away. Still, it hurt him when he thought about it. It had to be much tougher on Robert's parents. His mother had not taken her son's death very well.

Jim spent the weekend with Laura in her apartment because her roommates were gone. They made love, desperately this time and several more times during the two days off from classes. He could not get enough of her, and it seemed to him that it was the same way with her. He told her he loved her, but she did not respond right away. Finally, she said that she loved him too and always would. But then she said something that hit him like a kick in the groin.

"I can't marry you, Jim." She started crying, slowly at first and then profusely. She buried her head in her pillow and sobbed uncontrollably.

"I don't understand," he said in disbelief. "What do you mean?"

When she had stopped crying, she spoke again. "I just can't live on a farm. I want to live in Dallas or Houston or maybe even San Antonio. I don't want to dry up and wither away out in the middle of nowhere.

"But that's crazy, Laura. No two people have ever been as right for each other as we are. What can it possibly matter where we live? You have to know that I love you."

"I know," she said. "And I love you too. I just wish you could see things my way. You have so much going for you. You could play baseball or start your own business. Why do you have to be so obsessed with that farm?"

He talked to her and tried to reason with her but to no avail. Her mind was made up and there was no changing it, and it left him heartsick. The blow had stunned him down to his foundation. How could he not see this coming? How could this girl, this woman, he loved with all his heart have turned out to be so shallow? Even if he changed his mind now and consented to what she wanted, it would not be the same. It would never be the same again.

He left Laura's apartment and went to his place. He sat on his bed for over an hour, too stunned to move. Nothing in his future mattered anymore, not college, not baseball, not even the farm. He couldn't imagine that anything in his life would ever hurt him this much again.

Jim went to the farm the following weekend. He told his grandfather that he was going to drop out of school for a while. He hadn't changed his long-term plans, but he just needed to get away long enough to get a grip on his life. He had come to terms with the breakup with Laura. It hurt to lose her, but it hurt him more to know that a person can change so quickly. Things he had taken for granted he would never take for granted again. He would never blindly trust another person again, as long as he lived. Alton was upset about his leaving college, but he could see that the boy had experienced a severe blow, not only to his ego but to his very soul as well.

The old man was devastated when Jim told him he had decided to go into the army. He couldn't believe it. It just seemed so illogical to him for Jim to throw away his future like that. "I'm not throwing it away, Grandpa. I'm just putting it on hold for a while. I spent the past week looking into it. I can go to flight school and be a helicopter pilot. They'll make me a warrant officer.

"You can stay in school and become an officer if you want a military career. You just need one more year," Alton argued but Jim's mind was set.

"I don't want a military career. And I don't want to spend another year in school right now," Jim said. "When I get out, I'll come back here and finish my degree at Tarleton in Stephenville. I can take night classes."

The old man could see that his grandson was adamant about his decision and there was nothing that anyone could say to change his mind. "Okay, Jimmy, you do what you have to do," he said. "You know I have always trusted your judgment. If you feel this is what you must do, everything will be here for you when you're ready to come home."

"Thanks, Grandpa. I was hoping you would understand."

"I don't understand, and I don't agree. But I love you, son, and whatever you think is best for you is okay by me."

Chapter 8

Mattie

Jim applied for helicopter flight school prior to his induction. He passed every test the army gave him, and he was accepted. He was inducted in Dallas in June of 1963 and sent to Boot Camp first at Fort Polk, Louisiana. A hellhole, he discovered, with no equal. The heat was stifling and the bugs and gnats could almost drive a man insane

Fort Polk was established in 1941 and named in honor of the Right Reverend Leonidas Polk, the first Episcopal Bishop of the Diocese of Louisiana, and a Confederate General. Since then Fort Polk had adapted to service during every U.S. military crisis.

Thousands of soldiers learned the basics of combat here during the World War II, Louisiana maneuvers. Afterward, the post was opened and closed for the Korean War and for large-scale exercises Sage Brush and King Cole.

The Berlin Crisis prompted the post's reactivation in 1961, and Fort Polk became an infantry training center in 1962, one year before Jim Kemper arrived there. The training was hard but he survived it. Even with his baseball training, he was in poor shape, physically.

By the time, he left Polk, he would be as hard as nails, able to run a marathon if he wanted. The weeks dragged slowly by but eventually came to an end.

He was transferred to Fort Wolters in Mineral Wells, Texas, not too far from both Arlington and the farm. Life wouldn't be so bad here, he thought, with visits home on the weekends and the excitement of learning the helicopter business. He explained to Alton that one day the dairy might be big enough to need a helicopter, and Jim would be able to ferry them around.

"You'll not get me in one of those damned things," Alton said, emphatically.

Fort Wolters was originally established as Camp Wolters in 1925. It was four miles east of Mineral Wells in Parker and Palo Pinto counties. It was named for Brigadier General Jacob F. Wolters, commander of the Fifty-Sixth Brigade of the National Guard, and designated as a summer training camp for his units. The base covered 2,300 acres until World War II when the city of Mineral Wells provided land to increase the Camp's area to 7,500 acres. The camp became an important infantry-replacement center with a troop capacity that reached almost 25,000. Camp Wolters was deactivated after the war.

In 1951, the camp was reopened for the use of the US Air Force. It became known as Wolters Air Force Base and housed the newly formed Aviation Engineer Force. In September of 1956, the base became the US Army Primary Helicopter Center. The name was changed to Fort Wolters the same month that Jim Kemper arrived there.

The first class reported for training on November 26, 1956, and consisted of thirty-four warrant officer candidates and one chief warrant officer. The class graduated on April 27, 1957. All training was done at the Main Heliport and four stage fields. These facilities grew to three heliports—Main, Downing and Dempsey— and twenty-five stage fields.

The first seven stage fields were given western names while the rest were named after towns in Vietnam to get the students used to the names. The fields were laid out, directionally, the same as the actual towns were located in Vietnam. They had names like Stage Fields Bronco, Pinto, Ramrod, Mustang, and Sundance. Vietnam names included An Khe, Vung Tau, Tuy Hoa, Cam Ranh, Hue, Chu Lai, Soc Trang, My Tho, Bien Hoa, and Vinh Long.

During the Vietnam era, the United States Army had a need to train large numbers of helicopter pilots. They had already made a decision that pilots should be officers. But training only officers as pilots would be expensive and because of the requirements placed on officers to meet command time, operations time, and educational requirements, the army felt that this would not prove to be cost effective. Aviation warrant officers were needed.

For this reason, army command decided to expand the warrant officer ranks. This would allow them to have officers in charge of the aircraft, but with lower salary costs, and training would be specific to aviation only, with cross training to fit the needs of ground units.

The ground commanders, to which the aviation units were assigned, forced aviation units to adhere to strict ground rules for appearance and discipline. This helped to keep aviation units part of the army structure.

Jim was assigned bunk in a cubicle in a barracks with fifty-nine other candidates.

There were fifteen cubicles with two beds in each one. Twenty of the would-be pilots would wash out during the five months of flight training at Fort Wolters and another twenty at advanced training in Fort Rucker, Alabama. Only the very best would become army aviators. The pressure on each man to do his very best was tremendous. Washing out meant going to the infantry and, in all likelihood, being sent to a rifle company headed for Vietnam.

The man in the bunk next to Jim was a stocky man about five foot nine and a little heavier than Jim. He had a full head of thick black hair and eyes so brown they looked black to Jim. He was powerfully built, like a weightlifter, and carried himself like a Prizefighter. He immediately introduced himself to his new bunkmate.

"Where you from, guy?" he asked Jim.

"Dallas," Jim said. "Actually, Arlington, but that's right near Dallas. Name is James Kemper. I go by Jim."

"Csaba's my name," the man said. "Edward Csaba. But don't call me Edward if you want to stay friends very long. I go by Eddie."

Jim laughed. "I'll keep that in mind, Eddie. Where are you from?"

"Philadelphia," he said. "That's in Pennsylvania."

"I've heard of it. Pretty nice town, isn't it?"

"Nah, it's a shit hole. Why do you think I joined the army?"

Jim laughed out loud. "How long have you been in the army?

"Couple of years," Csaba said. "I was in Germany last winter, freezing my ass off, of course. One time they had some helicopters pick us up off maneuvers and I sat in the back watching those pilots. They were dressed real pretty, and they stayed warm all the time. I told myself it was time for a career change. I applied for helicopter flight training and passed all the tests and interviews. I was thinking I'd go right then and pack my bags and get the hell out of the cold but they told me they would let me know. I never heard a word for months so I put it out of my mind. Then last week, bingo, they told me to get my shit together, that I was going to Texas. So here I am. I'm going to be an officer and a gentleman. Well, at least a warrant officer, but I don't think they'll ever make a gentleman out of me.

"Yeah, me neither," Jim said.

They quickly became friends. It was a partnership that worked, despite their differences. Jim, the quiet, unassuming one, the strong silent type. The one who never did anything half-assed, according to Eddie, and Eddie himself, the self-described strong, loud type who was always looking for a short cut.

The two men spent a month of pre-flight training. They began learning the volumes of information they would have to know to safely and successfully fly an army helicopter. They were taught about lift and drag and the aerodynamics of rotary flight. They learned how to distinguish a low frequency vibration from a high frequency vibration. The training was intense, but Jim found it to be interesting and fun. He kept his mind totally focused on the business at hand. At Fort Polk, he thought about Laura every night after lights out. He would drift off to sleep with her on his mind. He kept a picture of her in his locker and sometimes at night he would get out of bed and look at the picture in the faint glow of a small penlight he had. Now he noticed that she rarely crossed his mind. He guessed it was because he was so absorbed in what he was doing. He knew it was not because he loved her any less.

Eddie Csaba was Hungarian. Rather, he was of Hungarian extraction, but in name only, he was quick to point out. His grandparents had come over from Budapest early in their marriage and had settled in Philadelphia. They were quickly assimilated into the American culture. Eddie didn't speak a word of Hungarian and didn't want to, he said. He was an American. He didn't call himself a Hungarian American. He was simply an American. Jim figured that, because of the Csaba's national origin, they were probably prouder of being Americans than many of those who could trace their lineage back to the revolution.

There was no doubt in Jim's mind that Eddie would be a big hit with Alton Kemper. Both were so down to earth. Despite Eddie's boisterous manner, he possessed good common sense. This trait was immediately noted by Jim's grandfather when they visited the farm on a three-day pass from Fort Wolters. The three of them sat talking for hours. The Yankee and the old man did indeed hit it off right away.

"Now mind you," Alton said. "I never claimed that Yankees were not just as good as Texans. I just never met too many Yankees. But I've met an awful lot of Texans and many of them I wouldn't let in my yard."

Eddie laughed and rolled off his chair onto the ground. "Mr. Kemper," he said. "You don't know what it means to me for you to call me a Yankee. I'm so used to being referred to as a Hungarian in Philly. They're big on ethnic origins there, to be called a Yankee means that I am an American. That's very important to me."

"I don't know what else we'd call you," Alton said. "Hell, we all came from somewhere else. I knew you came from good stock when I saw you drive up with my grandson. He wouldn't be friends with you if you weren't a good man."

"Yes, sir," Eddie said. "And the same goes for Jim. He's good people. We're going to Fort Rucker, Alabama, next week, Mr. Kemper, for advanced flight training. Don't worry about this guy here." He pointed to Jim with his thumb. "Anybody tries to mess with him, they got to go through me first."

"I can see he's in good hands," Alton said. "I appreciate that, Eddie. Be sure and come back here anytime you can. You're always welcome"

Eddie Csaba was no less fond of Mary Kemper's cooking than every friend Jim had ever brought home. After a hardy breakfast, he bid his goodbye to his new friend's grandparents and promised to come back to see them soon.

At Fort Rucker, the training intensified. They were introduced to the Bell Model 205 UH-1D helicopter. This aircraft was just now being deployed to Vietnam in ever increasing numbers. The UH-1D had a longer fuselage than previous models, increased rotor diameter, increased range, and a more powerful Lycoming T53-L-11 1100 SHP engine, with growth potential to the Lycoming T53-L-13 1400 SHP engine.

A distinguishing characteristic was the larger cargo doors, with twin cabin windows, on each side. The UH-1D was expected originally to carry up to ten troops, with a crew of four. It was discovered later that with the humidity and intense heat of Vietnam the actual load capability was closer to seven fully loaded Americans. It would still, however, carry the optimum number of the smaller and lighter Vietnamese soldiers.

It had a range of 293 miles and a speed of 127 mph. The *Hueys* could be armed with M-60D door guns, quad M-60C's on the M-6 aircraft armament subsystem, 20mm cannon, 2.75-inch rocket launchers, 40mm grenade launcher in M5 helicopter chin-turret, and up to six NATO Standard AGM-22B (formerly SS-11B) wire-guided anti-tank missiles on the M11 or M22 guided missile launcher. The UH-1D could also be armed with M60D 7.62mm or M213 .50 Cal. P cradle-mounted door guns on the M59 armament subsystem.

They learned advanced tactics and maneuvers. They practiced quick insertion of troops under hostile conditions and into contested terrain. There was no doubt in the mind of any U.S. Army Aviator in the military atmosphere of 1963 and 1964 that their enlistment would involve a tour of duty in Vietnam. But this was not ominous in their minds, it was exhilarating. Men in their early twenties think they are bullet proof and that they will not die in combat. It always happens to someone else.

When Jim and Csaba finished their training at Fort Rucker they were *Aces*. They could fly a Huey as skillfully as they could drive a car. Confidence in their newly acquired skills eventually reached the point of arrogance. They walked with a swagger that was common to the army aviators of that time. Jim never again second guessed his decision to drop out of school to join the army as he had done in boot camp and in his early days at Fort Wolters. No, this is where he belonged, he knew. This was his destiny. What he did for the next few years would influence the rest of his life. On his last leave before duty assignment he went home and then to visit his grandparents. He told Alton how happy he was to be doing what he was doing. His grandfather, noting his grandson's new sense of self-confidence, agreed that it had turned out to be the best thing for him.

Both Jim and Eddie were kept at Fort Rucker as instructors. They were that good and their superiors wanted to project that skill to new recruits. It was not bad duty and both men became very full of themselves, believing they truly were the best of the best.

One day in November, Eddie came into the barracks where Jim was lying on his bunk. "Do you know where Dealey Plaza is?" he asked him.

"Sure," Jim said. "It's in downtown Dallas, why?"

"The president was shot there, just a few minutes ago."

"In Dealey Plaza, are you serious?" Jim was incredulous. It was almost unthinkable that the President of the United States could be assassinated—especially in Dallas. It just didn't make any sense.

The country was thrown into mourning, as the new president, Lyndon Johnson, took over and tried to calm the fear. Jim had never been politically inclined. He liked Kennedy, leaned a little toward Johnson because Johnson was from Texas, but nevertheless, he admired the man and was stunned by his death. They were placed on alert for about a month until it was certain there was no foreign conspiracy involved in the assassination. Then things slowly got back to business as usual.

In late May, there came great news for the two new warrant officers. They, along with several others, were to be sent to Fort Meade in Maryland. They received the cushy assignment due to several factors. Jim and Eddie had the best scores across the board of anyone else in their class, and they were the most, squared away Warrant officers in the unit. In other words, they were just more presentable than most of the other guys.

They would be chauffeuring generals around, their base commander told them. The best possible duty they could have drawn. They would also participate in some further testing of the UH-1D helicopter at Aberdeen Proving Grounds. The aircraft had just been put in service in Vietnam the previous year and the army wanted some of their best flyers to check it out further.

Eddie was elated. They would be close enough to Philadelphia for him to go home on weekends. Jim too was excited. He had never really been out of Texas except for boot camp and flight school. It was a new adventure for him and he intended to make the most of it.

They arrived at Fort Meade in July of 1964. Accommodations were better than they were used to and the food was good. The weather was mild and Jim found the countryside of Maryland to be very pleasant, lots of trees and hills. Eddie took the bus home and brought back his car, a 1958 Chevy. "Not much to look at," he said. "But it will get us around town." Jim had no complaints about how the car looked. It represented freedom to the two soldiers. He wanted to go to Washington. His mother had made him promise to send some post cards from the Capital and he wanted to see everything in this new place that was to be his home for the near future.

Eddie noticed the picture of Laura hanging inside the door of Jim's locker. "Who's that?" He asked. "She's a looker."

"Just a girl I used to know," Jim said.

"Now that sounds like a sad country song, Jim boy. Want to tell me about it?"

"Not much to tell. It just didn't work out. She couldn't see herself living on a farm." He told him about how he'd met Laura and how it had all ended. He was okay with it now, he said. It was just one of those things you have to deal with in life.

"Well, I know it may not be much comfort on a cold lonely night, my friend," Eddie said, "But it was definitely her loss. She won't find another one like you. Look at the bright side of it, Jim. She'll probably marry a wino and get as fat as a Volkswagen."

"I sure hope so," Jim said, and they both laughed.

Neither man was drawn to the boisterous night life that was common to the strip that ran past the main gate of Fort Meade. Eddie, being a married man, did not care to frequent the night clubs and pick up spots along Highway 32. On weekends when he did not have duty, he went home to be with his family in Philadelphia. Jim went along a couple of times too just for something to do. Off time without a vehicle was pretty boring and Jim came to look forward to Saturday duty because Eddie stayed in town and they could go out.

A friend told them about a place in Annapolis where there was good music and college girls. Eddie agreed to accompany Jim there just to watch out for him. "I promised your grandfather, remember.

The Driftwood was a popular night spot with a band and a juke box and hamburgers and French fries. The music was light rock and roll and the atmosphere was congenial. The friend had been correct in his assessment of the establishment. The place was busy with college girls. It was also busy with Navy men, Annapolis Midshipmen. There were dozens of them there.

The two army men looked out of place as they strutted into the nightclub with that air of superiority that was common to their kind. They found an open spot at the bar and ordered two beers. They drew stares from some of the female patrons of the place and some looks of disdain from several Middies.

They ignored both and finished their beers then ordered two more.

Three middies in perfect dress whites approached them as they stood at the bar. One was about Jim's height and the other two about the same size as Eddie. "We don't see too many army boys around here," the larger one said—you guys lost?"

"No," Eddie said. "We're not lost, are you guys lost?"

"It's just that Annapolis is a navy town, and I think you guys might be better off with your own kind."

"And what kind is that?" Eddie asked.

"Well, look around," he said. "You're pretty seriously outnumbered here."

"So, you're saying that as soon as I knock you on your ass, all these well-dressed girls are going to come to you rescue?"

Jim chuckled, loudly enough for the navy man to hear him and his attention was diverted toward him.

"Something funny, man?" he said.

"Not really," Jim said. "I was just wondering, what do you guys use to get blood out of those pretty white coats?"

The navy man's face blanched, and he realized that he was in over his head. His two friends started to drift away from the action, and he was alone. He turned quickly and went back to his seat.

"Okay, Jim," Eddie said. "You're gonna have to knock that shit off. You almost got me in a fight."

"Me, what did I do? You were the one threatening to knock the guy on his ass."

"'What do you use to get blood out of those pretty white coats?' That was a classic. Let's have another beer."

They resumed their former position at the bar. "See anything you like, pal?" Eddie said, looking around the room and smiling.

"I've been watching that table over there," Jim said, pointing toward the corner. "There are four girls sitting there. Three of them have gotten up and danced a couple of times but one of them, the little blonde, has been asked five or six times by navy guys, and she turned them all down."

"I think she's waiting for you to ask her," Eddie said.

"Why do you say that?"

"Because she's been stealing looks at you ever since we walked in here."

"And you think I should go ask her to dance?"

"Why not? What's the worst thing that can happen? You'll have to walk back over here in humiliation with four silly girls giggling their heads off at you."

"You're a lot of help. I'm not about to be the next one she turns down. There may be something wrong with her. She could be married, for all I know."

"She's not married, and she won't turn you down."

"How can you be so sure?" Jim was hesitant.

"Kemper, ol' buddy, there is only one thing I understand better than helicopters, and that's women. I saw the look in her eye when she glanced at you just a second ago. She's yours for the taking. If she turns you down, I'll go smack her for you, and then we can haul ass out of here at the double quick."

Jim gathered his wits and his courage and started walking over to the table where the four girls were sitting. Eddie was right, he figured. The worst thing they could do is laugh at him. The band had stopped playing and the juke box had not started up yet so the place suddenly seemed deathly silent to Jim.

A few of the men in the place watched him to see what would happen. There was an empty chair at the end of the table and he pulled it out and sat down without being asked. He was immediately staring into what he believed to be the most beautiful blue eyes he had ever seen, up until that moment in time. Natural blonde hair, not straight but not curly either, complimented her face in a most perfect way and caressed her neck lovingly.

She stared back at him, not sure what was coming next while the other three girls sat mute, waiting to see what this soldier was about to do or say.

At the bar, Eddie just shook his head, both amused and impressed at his friend's brashness.

"I was wondering if you might answer a question for me," Jim said.

"Are you doing a study on something?" she asked him. A slight smile appeared on her lips. He didn't seem at all nervous, she noticed.

"Sort of," he said. "I'm just curious. I noticed that several guys asked you to dance and you didn't dance with any of them. I was thinking, if another guy wanted to dance with you, and mind you, I'm not necessarily saying that I am that guy, but if some guy—any guy—wanted to ask you for a dance, what would he have to do differently from what those other guys did? You have to understand that if this guy risked humiliation and rejection to come over and ask you to dance, what would cause you to dance with him after you turned down all the others?"

"And what do you intend to do with this information should I choose to share it with you?"

"I suppose I would use it to my advantage," he said.

She leaned over, put her elbow on the table, and rested her chin in her hand with her index finger extended to her temple in mock pensiveness. "Well," she said. "I suppose the first thing he would have to do is not be a midshipman. He could be some other military person, I suppose, like perhaps a Marine—or maybe even a soldier. But not a panty-waist momma's boy, like most of the Academy guys are."

"Well, I guess nobody ever accuses you of being vague, do they? My name is James Kemper, I'm from Texas, and I am an army aviator. I go by Jim.

"My name is Matilda Ann McKenna." She extended her hand and he shook hands with her. "I go by Mattie," she said. "And I would love to dance with you, James."

"I go by Jim."

"Then I shall call you James," she said.

He took her hand and they walked over to the juke box. She put a quarter in and punched the buttons. The sweet, mournful voice of Skeeter Davis sang for them as they wrapped their arms around each other and moved as one, oblivious to everything else in the world.

He held her tighter and she melted in his arms and laid her head on his shoulder.

There was not much in this world, Jim was thinking, that could even come close to the feel of a woman in his arms, the soft warmth of her breasts pressed against his chest, the smell of her hair and the tenderness with which she gently stroked his neck. If he had listened to this song any other time, it would have reminded him of Laura and caused him pain. But tonight, was different. He wasn't sure what to think about this lovely girl who had graced him with a dance—him and no one else. He was almost afraid of her. He didn't know what to do next.

The sweet voice continued. He was hoping it would never end.

Mattie looked up and him and smiled, then put her head back on his shoulder. They stood wrapped in each other's arms for a couple of minutes after the song had ended.

The place erupted in applause as they returned to the table. The navy men seemed content to take second place to this intruder from outside their realm.

Mattie introduced Jim to her friends. Cindy Newsome, her best friend, asked Jim about his friend at the bar. "Call him over," she said.

Jim waved to Eddie to come on over. Eddie brushed him off but Jim insisted and he finally complied. Two of the girls placed a chair between them and motioned for Eddie to sit down.

"You're cute," one of them said. "Do you fly a chopper too?"

"No," he said. "I fly a helicopter. The aircraft we fly are never called choppers. They are called helicopters."

The two girls each took one of Eddie's arms and asked him to dance with them as Jim and Mattie finished another dance. "It never fails, Jim," he said. "Every time I meet a woman I really like, I turn out to be married."

They squealed in disappointment and Eddie comforted them. "Now ladies," he said, "I am perfectly content to sit here and engage in riveting conversation with two of the prettiest girls in the state of Maryland. But, alas, my heart belongs to another who is far away in a strange land."

"And what strange land is that?" Cindy asked him.

"Philadelphia," he said, and they both squealed again.

Jim enjoyed watching his friend interact with people, especially females. Eddie was charming and witty and would have made a perfect cad were it not for his high moral content. He was devoted to his wife and two kids and everything else in life was just supplemental.

That night when they got back to the barracks, Jim stood at his locker door looking at the picture of Laura and thinking about the evening and the girl he had met. He felt the same fluttering in the pit of his stomach he had felt when Laura sat down at his table that time in study hall. He took her picture off his locker door and put it in a drawer under his towels.

"I saw that," Eddie said, from the other side of his bunk. "I knew you were in for it when she danced with you. Life will never be the same for you, my friend."

"It sure feels that way," he said.

Jim applied for and was granted a week's leave to go home to Texas. He told his mother that he had met the girl he was going to marry. Her name was Mattie and, although she was not yet aware of it, she was going be the mother of his children.

"You're going to marry a girl you danced with one time?"

"We danced four or five times," Jim explained.

"Oh," Allie said. "That's different. You danced with her several times. What brought this on?"

"She's beautiful," Jim said. "The most beautiful woman I've ever seen."

"You mean the most beautiful woman you've seen this week?" she responded. "What do you know about her? What about her family?"

"Not much," he said. "She lives in Annapolis, Maryland. She's going to the University of Maryland, a psychology major, I think. Her father is a state senator."

Allie's demeanor changed. "A state senator? Well, that is impressive. I guess I should have known that my son would be attracted to quality. I just hope you don't get hurt again, Jimmy."

"Thanks, Mother. That won't happen. I want to take my car back with me. My friend Eddie goes home on weekends, and I don't like asking other guys for rides."

His grandparents were thrilled to see him. Mary started crying when she saw him in his uniform. "You look just like your father," she told him.

Alton took the news about the girl in Maryland with less strife than he would have before he met Eddie Csaba. The man from Philadelphia had convinced him that all Yankees were not from outer space. If his grandson had settled on this Yankee girl, then she must really be something special.

Jim started seeing Mattie on a regular basis. They usually met at the Mandris Restaurant on the square in Annapolis. They had sandwiches and cokes and conversation, intense conversation about nothing in particular. She wanted to know everything about his life in Texas. She wanted to know about his family and the farm to which he intended to return after his time in the Army was finished. Why he had not gone to Officer Candidate School, with his three years of college and his obvious qualifications, qualifications obvious, at least, to Mattie.

"My best friend was killed in a car wreck," he told her. "I guess it just took the wind out of me. I had to get away."

"Was there a girl involved in all this?" she asked him.

"There was, but she's not involved in it now." He smiled at her when he said that.

They walked around the little town that was the seat of Maryland State Government. She showed him the Statehouse where her father worked. She took his hand as they walked along the dock and around the Annapolis square. A quaint, beautiful little town, Jim thought. What a strange occurrence to find this girl here.

The town and the whole state were almost as beautiful as she was. He still could not believe that she had found him worthy of her attention. This was no camp follower, this girl. No, she was quality, as Grandpa had said. She was in her senior year at The University of Maryland, a psychology major. She wanted to write, not teach. Just what he needed, he told her, someone who would analyze his every word or act.

He remembered what his grandfather had told him about dealing with other people, especially women.

"Don't talk about yourself too much," he always said. "Let them talk about them. That's what most people want to do anyway. If you humor them and really listen to what they have to say, they will feel good about themselves and be drawn to you."

He'd always tried to heed his grandfather's advice, but Mattie was making it difficult for him. All she wanted to talk about was him. She must have gotten the same advice from someone older and wiser in her family because she was certainly making Jim feel comfortable and good about himself.

"Have you always lived in Annapolis?" he asked her.

"We moved here when my father was elected. I grew up in Baltimore and went to Junior High school there. I went to High School here."

"I told my mother about you."

"Oh, and what did she say?"

"Well, actually she was more impressed with your father being a state senator, but she hasn't met you yet."

"Living in the shadow of my famous father," she said, with dramatic flair. "Tell me about your family, James."

He did tell her, he told her his life story, how his mother and father met, about his Grandpa and the dairy farm. He was not going to mention Laura, but Mattie asked about her.

"Tell me about the girl," she said.

"There's not much to tell. It just didn't work out. She was accustomed to high living and just didn't want to live on a farm."

"So, you were planning to marry her?"

"I don't think I ever believed it would come to that," he lied, "she was only attracted to me because I'm so good looking and she just wanted to show me off to her friends."

"Superficial bitch, in other words," she said.

"Right, and I just hate being a sex object."

"I could tell that right away when you came over and asked

me to dance the other night. You seemed so shy and unassuming. I guess I felt sorry for you."

"Whatever works," he said.

She squealed with delight then grabbed his face and kissed him passionately. He returned her kisses with added interest.

"Now, about that sex object thing, I'm not totally averse to being—"

She squealed again. "I knew it was all bullshit, James Kemper, but I love your bullshit."

"There's more where that came from, missy," he said.

"It's Mattie, and don't forget that."

"I won't, Mattie," he said. "I won't ever forget you."

"Did you love that girl, James?" she asked him.

He pondered her question for a moment. "Yes, Mattie, I did."

"Do you think you'll ever fall in love again?"

"I'm sure of it, Mattie," he said, smiling at her and looking deep into her eyes.

The third time they met, she asked him to come to dinner at her house. The thought of meeting her family, especially her father the senator, was a little intimidating to Jim but he agreed. It was, after all, a necessary hurdle he had to jump in order to win this girl, he was convinced. "Wear your uniform," she told him. "I want them to see my soldier."

He found the McKenna house on Tolson Street, not far from downtown, using the directions Mattie had written down for him. And it was no small task given the corkscrew layout of the streets of Annapolis. The house was nice, very quaint, but not overly pretentious. He had expected to drive up to a mansion but this was not the case and he felt a little more comfortable about the coming encounter.

A fourteen-year-old scale model of Mattie answered the door. "Mattie!" she yelled, without saying anything to Jim. "He's here! Come on in," she said, motioning to him. She stared at the tall handsome soldier who had come in his best Class A uniform to visit her sister. Now she knew why Mattie wouldn't stop talking about him, she thought. "So, you're James."

"I am," he said. "And who are you?"

"I'm Andrea McKenna. I'm Mattie's sister."

"That would have been my guess," Jim said. "You look just like her."

Mattie came and ushered him into the living room where her parents, Charles and Aimee McKenna were waiting. He was impressive, they each thought to themselves. Tall, almost six feet tall, and he carried himself with confidence and poise. He seemed not at all uncomfortable to be there. Charles McKenna told him to sit down and then pulled his chair a little closer to his daughter's new suitor. This was a signal for the women to leave the room.

Mattie's mother summoned her and Andrea into the kitchen. "My god, Mattie," she whispered. "That's the most beautiful man I've ever seen."

"Isn't he, Mom?" Mattie said. "I think so too. He's wonderful. I love him."

Their courtship was a proper one. They did not sleep together before they were married, although Jim wanted to very much. Mattie was adamant about it, so he acquiesced to her wishes. He was going to "buy a car without test driving it first," as Robert Cunningham used to so crudely put it.

They were married December 16, 1964, and lived with Mattie's parents until she finished her degree at the university. Then, at her insistence, they moved into base housing at Fort Meade.

It was a big change for them, of course, because the McKennas had a maid and the house was always spotless. It took some getting used to, and Jim missed having Edie Csaba around all the time, but he and Mattie were happy. They were made for each other, Jim was convinced. She had no faults that he could discern. Their lovemaking taught him very quickly that the past was indeed the past and would remain ever so. It was a wonderful time for them both.

Early in March of 1965, Mattie told Jim that she was going to have a baby. "So, we're on our way to having grandkids," he said, beaming like a soon to be father should.

"Grandkids?" she shrieked. "We haven't had our first child yet and you're talking about grandkids. How do you know you will want to stay with me that long?"

"I'll never leave you—so don't get your hopes up. You couldn't get rid of me with roach spray," he joked. "Just don't ever leave me, Mattie."

"I won't, James. I promise," she said.

He stared at her for a few moments. "We're having a baby," he said. "It will be a boy."

"Yes," she said. "A boy, I guarantee it."

And she kept her promise. Alton Kemper II was born in September, the first of their four children. He was a beautiful boy who looked like his father. The McKennas accepted the boy's name, after Jim's grandfather, because Jim had assured them the next boy would be named Charles after Mattie's dad. Everything was well in the family.

In December, Jim's world was shattered when word came from Texas that his grandmother, Mary Kemper, had died after suffering a heart attack. He took his wife and three-month old son home to attend the funeral. Trenton and Allie were there and met Mattie, and little Alton for the first time.

It was a bittersweet time for them all. The joy that would have been Alton Kemper's, at meeting his great-grandson, was tempered by the loss of his dear wife. Still, he was very attentive to his new namesake and to his grandson's wife, "the purest quality he'd ever seen in a woman, except maybe for Allie," Alton said. He winked at Allie. Allie shushed him and said that Mattie was far better than she had ever been. Alton just shook his head at her.

Allie decided that her son had met his perfect match. She was now a grandmother and she loved it. The boy was perfect too, as she always knew her grandkids would be. Mary Kemper was laid to rest in Oakwood Cemetery, in Comanche, and the Kemper and Hargrove families gathered strength from their mutual love. Mattie confided to Allie, James already knew, that she might be pregnant again.

Jim spent as much time as he could with his grandfather, but time was pressing and he had to get back.

"You've done good, Jimmy," Alton told him. "Your family is beautiful...everything you deserve."

"They're more than I deserve, Grandpa. I'm very lucky."

"Well, it looks like you might not have to go off to that damned war. I was sure hoping you'd miss that mess.

"I won't," he said. "I'll have to go, they've already told me. It's just a matter of time. I haven't told Mattie. She's still living in a dream world about it—sort of blocking it out, you know?"

"Damn, Jimmy. You have to take care of yourself. I can't lose you, son—I just can't."

Tears welled up in Alton Kemper's eyes and he started sobbing. Jim hugged him, with his arms over his grandfather's for the first time, comforting the older man. Alton always hugged Jim with his arms over the younger man's arms, taking the dominant role of the comforter. Now they were switched. They had come full circle. Jim teared up at the thought of his grandfather, always so strong, so forceful, now showing weakness. But he continued to hold him while the older man wept in his arms.

In May, Jim and Eddie were given orders to Fort Rucker, Alabama, for further intensive training in helicopter tactics and low-level flying. He knew what that meant, and Mattie knew too. She was quietly terror stricken over the possibility of losing her husband in a senseless war.

"I'll be okay, Mattie," he told her over and over.

"Don't lie to me, James," she said. "Men are getting killed in Vietnam every day. Don't tell me it can't happen to you. Don't tell me you won't get killed and then go and do it. I'll never forgive you if you do that to me."

"Listen to me, Mattie." He took her face in his hands and looked right into her eyes. "I will not get killed in Vietnam. I promise. Do you understand that?"

She nodded. "Uh huh," she said. "You better not be lying to me. I'll never forgive you if you lie to me."

Mattie was six months pregnant now. He rubbed her belly and said, "you take care of you and Alton and this one. I'll take care of me. Don't worry about me. I will be okay."

Charles McKenna Kemper (Charlie) entered the world on August 28, 1966 at Anne Arundel General Hospital in Annapolis. He was not quite as handsome a child as their first grandson but the McKennas fell in love with him just the same.

Chapter 9

Vietnam

1966-1967:

Jim held the stick steady and increased power. The helicopter, trimmed and cocked, nosed down and headed out over the Delta. He watched its shadow racing along the ground, dancing with the bushes and the saw grass below, and leapfrogging over trees and other objects. It reminded him of when he was a kid riding in his grandfather's car as they sped down the road to town. The car's shadow would bounce off the fence posts by the side of the road. Crossing a bridge or passing a building would bring the shadow right up close to the car only to have it disappear a moment later into the bar ditch. He would sit very still and wait until the car again passed an object that would bring the elusive shadow back into his view.

His attention returned to the matters at hand and he abandoned the helicopter's shadow to the Delta below. He was on his first real mission. Since his arrival in Vietnam, he had flown only ash and trash missions, delivery boy missions, taking someone here or there or packing ammo and provisions to a firebase somewhere. Now, he thought, it was time to earn his pay.

In the back, a team of Special Forces troops sat quietly, their faces stoic and sinister. The black and green camouflage paint they wore gave them a fearsome look. It was no game to these guys. They were a serious bunch, for they approached their jobs with a definite sense of purpose. Their commander, a Captain Jacobs, peered out the doors of the ship, moving from side to side constantly, looking for anything suspicious.

The worst flooding in the Delta in twenty years had prompted the operation. All the low ground in the Plain of Reeds was underwater, leaving only scattered areas of high ground for the enemy to hide in. Headquarters wanted some prisoners and figured there would be easy pickings. Jacobs explained that all the *dinks* in the Delta had gone over to the Viet Cong so all were fair game. "There's only so much high ground so we know where the bastards will be."

Jacobs had to pay a visit to some of his old friends the Hoa Hao (wa haaz) he called them. The Hoa Hao were mercenaries who worked, from time to time, for the US Army. As brutal and as blood thirsty a people as one could ever encounter. Even the Special Forces guys hated them but used them anyway because they performed a valuable service. They killed Viet Cong in great numbers, for a price, of course, taking ears as proof of a kill, for which the army willingly paid.

A Green Beret sergeant named Rawlings told them that a common and favorite practice of the Hoa Hao was to steal a woman from a local village and use her, as long as it pleased them then, when they no longer wanted the woman, or if she became pregnant, they would send her out to the wire and shoot her, from a distance, then claim she was VC trying to penetrate their camp, and collect bounty for her.

It was a despicable practice, nobody denied that, but, as Jacobs justified it, "These people are all the same. Even the best of them is no damned good. It don't really matter who kills who in this fuckin' country. Any method of killing VC is acceptable."

Out of the corner of his eye Jim noticed Captain Jacobs pointing to something off on the horizon. He and Jim's crew chief, Specialist 5, Eugene Dolan, were pointing and speculating on what it was. Dolan grabbed his binoculars for a closer look.

"Two boats," he yelled.

Two small boats were scooting across the water, headed somewhere fast. Jacobs looked and confirmed that there were two figures in one of the boats and a single person in the other. "I wonder where those dinks are going."

"I don't know," Dolan yelled. "But they're sure in one hell of a hurry."

"Bring it around, Commander," Jacobs said, getting right up next to Jim's helmet in order to be heard over the noise of the props. "I want to check these people out."

He made a circling motion with his hand and pointed in the direction of the people in the little boats.

Jim responded and banked the aircraft to the left and headed toward the suspected enemy. They now realized that they had been spotted and were trying to take whatever cover they could find. "They're VC," the captain was saying, and the others loudly agreed. "Look at 'em haulin' ass. They're VC, all right, that's a definite." He made hand signals, indicating that he wanted Jim to pull up a short distance from them.

Jim bought the ship to a hover, as directed. The man in the rear sampan jumped into the water and tried to hide under and behind his boat. The other two, one of them a woman, continued trying to get away.

On Jacob's instructions, Jim brought the ship over to the boat. Just then the prop wash blew back a mat that had been lying on the bottom of the boat between the two people, revealing a rifle at the woman's feet. She lunged for the weapon and Dolan opened up on them with his M-60, knocking both occupants into the water. Their bodies jerked for a moment and then just floated lifelessly in the bloody water.

The other man was trying to hide under his boat, trying to keep himself between it and the Americans.

"So, you want to play games?" the captain shouted. "Okay, asshole, we'll play kill the dink." And he fired into the boat with his M-14, tearing away chunks of it and throwing pieces of its contents into the water.

Aware of his desperate situation, the Vietnamese swam away and took cover in some bushes about fifty feet away from the boat. "Where are you going to hide, ass hole?" The captain continued taunting the man. "Come over here." He motioned for him to swim over toward them but the man would not respond, still clinging to the clump of bushes that had become his poor refuge.

Jacobs dropped a rope to the boat and sent one of his men down to search it. Rummaging through it, the Green Beret whooped and held up some maps and a Viet Cong flag for the men in the helicopter to see. A further search revealed paperwork identifying the occupant as a sergeant in a Viet Cong company. Jacobs was beside himself.

"We've got a keeper, boys," he said. "We need to take this guy prisoner, he'll sing like a canary when we get him back to base."

They dropped off the captured Vietnamese at the Green Beret base at Muc Hoa and then resumed their flight across the delta.

At a small village, Jim noticed a couple of women working at the edge of the village.

"Are those women stolen like you were telling me about earlier?" Jim asked him.

"Probably," Rawlings said. "It's hard to say. Sometimes they might take a liking to one and hang on to her, depends on how hard she works and how good looking she is."

"They're some kind of Buddhist sect, I think," Colby said. He had taken off his helmet and peering through his little round eyeglasses gave him the scholarly look that had earned him the nickname Professor. "They think it doesn't matter what you do in the flesh. Kill, rape, burn down farmhouses, it's all the same to them. They think that shooting a pregnant woman gets you the same points in the hereafter as helping an old lady across the street."

Rawlings agreed, nodding his head. "I hope when this war is over we can come back here and blow the shit out of the dirty bastards, but right now Captain Jacobs says we need them. They're our ace in the hole, he says."

A strange war, Jim thought. How could America be involved with such people? Was winning that important? He didn't think so but then he'd always been naïve, or at least that's what Eddie, had told him. He was too damned innocent for Vietnam, Eddie said, but a few more days like today and he wouldn't be naive or innocent very long.

Rawlings had not stopped talking all the time Jim had been thinking. "Do you guys know a pilot named Grantham?" he was asking, "Captain Grantham, out of Soc Trang."

Jim nodded. "My platoon leader," he said.

"One hell of a guy, the best I ever saw," Rawlings said. "He's flown several operations with us. He's fearless, absolutely fearless. He ain't scared of the devil himself. When we came to pick up Sergeant Martin, and Martin said don't land, Captain Grantham told Captain Jacobs that if he wanted to go in and get his man out then all he had to do was say the word and they'd go in and get him. It might not have been the smart thing to do but it sure as hell made an impression on us."

He was right about Grantham. They had met when Jim arrived at the 336th Assault Helicopter Company at Soc Trang. He and Csaba got off the Caribou that had brought them from Saigon and standing there on the tarmac was Captain Jack Grantham. Six feet tall and about one hundred and seventy-five pounds, Jim estimated, with not an ounce of fat on him.

Ruggedly handsome, he had the look and demeanor of a man who would evoke confidence and respect from superiors and subordinates alike. He would prove to be the Quintessential Warrior, the kind of man with, and for, whom other men would go into combat and die, if it were necessary. They became friends immediately. No reason why that Jim could figure, it was just that, beneath the soldier facade and the cocky attitude, Grantham was almost a carbon copy of Jim Kemper. They shared many of the same values and attitudes about life and families and duty.

The road to Vietnam had been a lot easier for Grantham than it had been for Jim. Jack had gone to West Point and had married well, the daughter of a newspaper publisher in San Francisco. Jim had married well too, he knew. Mattie was far above his station in life, but he was thankful that she didn't place much value on such things and had never reminded him of it. His mother, of course, would have argued about whose station was above whose. Allie Kemper believed that her son had no faults and if anyone should be grateful for a marriage it was the McKennas of Annapolis. God, he missed Mattie. He'd only been here three months, but it seemed much, much longer. He missed his son too and now, with another baby on the way, he was starting to question his decision to go to flight school, knowing, as he did at the time, that it meant a certain tour in Vietnam.

Captain Jacobs was coming back now, circling his finger over his head for Jim to crank it up. Staff Sergeant Martin and the other soldiers followed. They climbed aboard the helicopter and Jim got airborne and headed back to Muc Hoa, where they would refuel before making the hop back to Base

They would learn from Jacobs, after landing at Muc Hoa, what had happened with Sergeant Martin at the Hoa Hao camp. The mercenaries had had an election of sorts, a change in command, more accurately. Two factions had argued over who should be in charge. Argument led to bloodshed and both sides, not wanting to risk an American's life and thereby place financial hardship on them all, had locked up Sergeant Martin and his radio. He sat, confined to quarters, not knowing what was going on but not wanting to risk his buddies coming in trying to pick him up. He issued the warnings on the radio. When they came to let him out, one group of men, the obvious losers, had simply disappeared.

Soc Trang

Jim Kemper and Eddie Csaba arrived at Soc Trang, Vietnam in June of 1966. About an hour's flying time from Tan Son Nhut, Soc Trang lay off the Mekong River along Highway one. Highway One was misnomer for it was a highway in name only. The Viet Cong kept it closed most of the time, leaving the base accessible only by air and boat, via canals that connected it to the river.

The first permanent helicopter base outside of Saigon, Soc Trang was generally regarded as a pretty good duty spot. It served the entire Army Fourth Corp area which included all of Vietnam south of Saigon, and housed Two Army Assault Helicopter Companies, one of which, the 336th, Jim and Eddie Csaba were assigned to. A Colonel, Eugene Davis, whom both

Kemper and Csaba found to be a congenial man although very professional in his approach to his job, commanded the base. The real backbone of the 336th, however, was Captain Jack Grantham, their platoon leader, almost a legend to the men who flew with him. Grantham had earned their respect by being the one pilot they could always count on to come to their aid in times of trouble. He was the best helicopter pilot in the Army, many agreed, and as the Green Beret, Rawlings, would say, absolutely fearless and seemingly not the least bit concerned about his own personal safety. It was almost as if the airmen believed they could never die as long as Captain Grantham was in charge. There would come a time, a few short months from now when Jim Kemper would share that honor and respect among the men and the two of them would earn the nicknames, Butch Cassidy and the Sundance kid, Grantham being Butch and Kemper, Sundance. The noms de guerre were assigned to them by Alex Colby, Jim's door gunner, and came as a result of an operation in which both men would commit acts of derring do as Colby would describe it.

They visited a tiny village on the Ba Sac River, to which the Viet Cong had paid a visit the previous night and had killed all the inhabitants. No reason, except, possibly, that the village people had not been sufficiently unfriendly to the Americans, they had just murdered them all, men, women, and children, as a warning to other villagers. Jim was shocked at the barbarity of the act. He could not conceive of such a thing, his mind would not accept it. These people killed each other with a ruthlessness that was almost evil. It was evil, to Jim, and to his down-home sensibilities, and he was convinced that day of the justness of the American cause in Vietnam.

After lift off from the village, Captain Grantham turned his ship south and headed down river toward home with Kemper right behind. Grantham spotted a line of sampans in the river below, five or six of them with several black clad figures in each.

"There's the sons of bitches," he yelled into the mike. He banked hard immediately. "Turn on 'em, Kemper. Bring them under fire."

Both ships dropped down right on the water and Colby and Dolan, as well as the two gunners from Grantham's ship opened up.

"Dumb sumbitches," Dolan yelled, "stupid sumbitches, right out in the open like that. Go professor, go," he yelled to Colby, who was stern faced, methodically, raking the little boats with a withering fire.

Some of the Viet Cong had made it to the riverbank and were attempting to scatter and Kemper brought his ship up and jumped over to where they were and Dolan killed them with several short blasts from his weapon. Grantham chased some more down river and his crew dispensed with them in short order. Both aircraft bounced around the area, like flies on a puddle of water," looking for any of the enemy that might have survived. There were none left alive.

"Paybacks are hell," Dolan said, as he released his M-60, letting it rest in the sling. He pushed back on his helmet. His cheeks puffed up as he breathed out the air his lungs had held captive for the past few minutes. "Yes, sir, paybacks are hell."

"Good shootin' Guys." Grantham's voice came over the radio. "We got 'em all."

Jim glanced at his watch. It had only lasted a few minutes. In the river, the remains of the sampans the American gunners had shot to pieces were torn and splintered, floating half in and half out of the water. Jim counted the bodies of at least fifteen Viet Cong bobbing up and down like corks on a fishing line. Along the bank five more black clad bodies lay twisted and tortured, in various positions of impact posture, the result of Dolan's handiwork.

Dolan complimented Jim on the intercom. "Great flying, Mister Kemper," he said. "Some of the best flying I ever saw."

Jim would have taken no pleasure in what they had just done had he not seen the atrocities that morning at the village. This was not murder, as was the work of the Viet Cong, this was war. This was justice. The Americans had brought justice to a wild and untamed land. Jim felt like Wyatt Earp in Dodge City. The exhilaration was overpowering, and the rest of the crew felt it too, he could tell. Even Colby, who was usually

very serious and somber, was smiling broadly as they sur-
veyed the scene after it was over.

"Sic Semper Tyrannous!" Colby said, the words of John
Wilkes Booth after he'd shot President Lincoln.

Jim remembered them from history class. Colby was, indeed, a scholar.

"What's that mean? Dolan asked, looking perplexed.

"Thus, be to tyrants," Colby answered, the smile disappear-
ing from his face. Dolan just shook his head and started working on his M-60. "Intellectuals," he muttered.

Grantham and Kemper, as well as the four gunners, would
receive letters of commendations for the day's work. And both
pilots, subsequently, would be awarded the Distinguished Flying Cross for this and other actions.

Later, when Colby spotted the two pilots together, he
jerked his head in their direction and said, "There goes Butch
Cassidy and the Sundance Kid," and the name stuck.

The 336th Assault Helicopter Company at Soc Trang was
part of the Army's 13th Aviation Battalion, which was head-
quartered at Can Tho, just up the Mekong River. An Assault
Company, in Vietnam, generally consisted of two lift platoons,
the troop carriers, and a gun platoon, which flew in support of
the lift operations. The 336th was equipped with the UH-1,
Huey, B and D models. The D's, which Jim Kemper flew,
were troop movers, able to carry about nine or ten fully
equipped dry ARVN (Army of the Republic of Vietnam) soldiers, or about six or eight similarly loaded Americans. The
Americans were larger and able to carry more weight. Five
each of the D-models made up a lift platoon. Their armament
consisted of two M-60s one operated by the crew chief and the
other by the door gunner. For most of his time in Vietnam,
Jim's crew carried ARVN's but on occasion would be called
on to transport Special Forces troops as they had on the trip to
the mercenaries' camp.

A gun platoon usually had five ships divided into two sections, a heavy section and a light section. The heavy section
was anchored by a D-model Huey known as the Hog, usually
flown by the platoon leader, in the 336th this was Captain

Grantham that was equipped with a 40-mm gun that protruded from the front of the ship. A "wonderful weapon," everyone agreed, "when it worked right," which it rarely did. The 40-mac mac was fond of jamming and, as a result, was hardly ever used. The Hog also had a large rocket pod on either side of the ship and, in addition to the M-60 door guns, carried a flex kit. This was an assembly of two M-60s, mounted one over the other that could be rotated a few degrees from side to side and up and down, giving added straight on firepower. Two B-models made up the rest of the heavy section of the gun platoon and two more B's made up the light section. The B-model helicopters were similarly equipped except that they did not carry the 40-mm gun and their rocket pods were usual-ly smaller than the ones on the Hog. In combat, a gun ship pla-toon could bring an awesome amount of firepower to bear on the enemy.

Jim and Eddie were assigned to a lift platoon and, after an easy period of ash and trash missions they were soon lifting payloads of ARVN's into combat operations.

Typically, the Huey crew was seventy five percent static. The aircraft commander, the crew chief, and the door gunner usually stayed with the ship and the fourth man, the co-pilot, was rotated from one assignment to another. There was not, in actuality, a co-pilot on a Huey crew. The pilot was the aircraft commander and the man in the right seat was called the pilot. The AC was the boss on a flight and could sit in either seat but usually chose the left seat because of the greater visibility af-forded by that position due to the arrangement of the instru-ment panel. There was then, no copilot time in a Huey. All time logged by either flyer was pilot time, a fact that would help many in their pursuit of civilian jobs after their tours were over.

Behind the passenger compartment, in the gun well, on the left side of the ship rode the crew chief. The most important man on the crew, without a doubt, because he not only operat-ed one of the M-60s but was also responsible for the mainte-nance of the aircraft. Jim's crew chief was Eugene Dolan, a black man from Chicago, who had joined the army looking for a better life than he could find in the hot Chicago streets. When he made Specialist 5 and was assigned to his own aircraft as crew chief, he approached the job with a religious fervor that impressed the entire company. Dolan was good at his job. He learned to detect problems with the aircraft, high and low frequency vibrations in the rotors, and the like, just by listening to the engine running. He could often feel a developing problem before the pilot did. Dolan allowed no one to perform maintenance on his ship but himself and if any major work had to be done he stayed with the mechanics every minute until the job was complete.

Jim decided there was no better aircraft maintenance program in the world than the one employed by the army helicopter crews. The concept of the maintenance being done by men who flew on the plane themselves was one that ensured that a thorough job would be done.

Dolan had found his niche in the army. In the pre-civil-rights days, in which he had decided to become a soldier, the military was the one segment of American society where it really did not matter what color a man's skin was. A man was judged by the job he did and nothing else. Of course, there was the occasional redneck to deal with, that was inevitable. But, for the most part, the army was pretty much color blind. These facts were even truer in Vietnam. In war, what mattered most was getting out alive with your anatomy still reasonably intact. If a buddy could help you in that endeavor, it didn't make a damn if he were black, white, brown, or even polka dot, for that matter. Jim was more than happy to have the big, easy going, black man on his crew. He felt it gave him an edge and he wanted every edge he could have to get through the madness in which he had landed. Dolan had four months left on his second tour and the experience that he brought to Jim's crew was invaluable. Dolan could smell trouble from a mile or more away and Jim had learned a lot just by watching and listening to him.

"It was quiet in 'sixty-four," Dolan said, "not like now, more fighting now. In 'sixty-four, the gooks had bows and arrows and bolt-action rifles. Soon as we showed up, they'd haul ass like scared rabbits. It's a different war now. Now they got AK-forty-seven and fifty calibers and they ain't scared of us no more."

Behind Dolan, the other gun well was manned by a slight, bespectacled man with a shock of blond hair which fell across his forehead when he took off his helmet. At five-eight and a hundred and thirty pounds he looked more like a company clerk than he did a door gunner on a Huey. Intense, book wormish, Alex Colby was a walking incongruity. Abandoning what everyone had called a promising future, he had dropped out of Indiana University in his third year to join the army. He handled an M-60 like he was born to it, and he killed with an easy style that belied his soft exterior. There was a dark under-current of torment deep down in Colby, the severity of which Jim could not completely grasp. Like a time bomb waiting to go off, he was sullen and detached at times and, at other times, likable and even jovial.

"There is something wrong with Colby," Dolan had con-fided to Jim. "But I'm glad he's on our side."

દ્લઝ

After the encounter with the sampans, Captain Grantham went to see Jim in his hooch. "You okay, Jim?" Grantham said. "It was a little intense out there today, and I was a little concerned about you."

"I'm fine. I guess I wasn't expecting it to be like that. It happened so fast."

"You must learn to separate yourself from all of this," Grantham told him. "This is not reality. Vietnam is an aberra-tion. Here you will see and do things that you would never have thought possible. We all do. For the rest of your life, after you leave Vietnam, you will see people shocked and outraged at acts of violence that here are accepted as commonplace. You must remain detached and not be affected by it all."

"I don't have a problem with killing the enemy in combat. It's the callousness with which it's done that amazes me."

"But you see, it's the callousness that makes the killing

possible. If we really thought about it, if we weighed the right and wrong, the morality of each act we commit, we would not be able to do the job which fate and circumstance, and the US Government, has dictated that we must do. Then we would die instead of the enemy, and that is not acceptable."

"I know what you are saying is true, Jack, and I'm grateful to you for everything."

"No need to be," Grantham said. "I want to see you go home in one piece, alive and sane. So just fly your ship and do the job I know you can do. Stick close to me, and we'll get through this together, and then you can go home to that farm in Texas you told me about."

After Jack had left, Jim lay back on his bunk and thought for a while about what the captain had said. If he got out of this place alive, he believed it would depend a great deal on this man who had suddenly become a good friend. Jim would take those words to heart, and he would live by them. More importantly, he would survive by those words. That day, Jim took on his war face, his persona de guerre, he would call it. He started looking at every situation in a detached way, as an observer would look at others in crisis or confrontation, and decide the best plan of action to take. Then he found that he was able to act or react very quickly to some opposing force just as he would have advised another to do in the same instance. He was like an impartial onlooker at his own actions, almost like having an out of body experience. Jim ceased to be the star of his own life story and, instead, became the director. Vietnam would be the defining influence on his life. From this day on, there would be no hesitation in Jim Kemper. There would no longer be any indecision, and he would cease to harbor any doubts about his own abilities. In times of crisis or confrontation, the warrior took over, and Jim would coolly and methodically take command of the situation. He gave himself the name Warrior One-Seven, after the numerical designation of the helicopter he flew, and this would be a buzz word for him the rest of his life. And, although he would never tell his secret to any one, not even Jack Grantham or Mattie, it would, when needed, push the buttons, the necessary buttons he would need to survive in and reach the very top of his world.

༺༺༻༻

After liftoff, Jim climbed to a thousand feet and was cruising at eighty knots. Eddie followed close behind, a little off to the left side. They would rendezvous that morning with other crews of the 336th and some elements of the 121st Helicopter Assault Company, at an airfield south of Soc Trang. They were to transport ARVN troops on a sweep and block operation. Intelligence had reported some enemy movement in the area and Battalion wanted it checked out.

Dolan leaned back in his compartment, his eyes half closed, appearing to be sleeping but, in fact, was keeping a curious eye on his crewmember at the other door. Colby had been getting stranger every day. Mister Kemper had noticed too, Dolan was sure of that, but hadn't said anything about it yet. The professor was poised at his gun, half out of the door, with a distant look on his face. He was somewhere else, Dolan believed, and he seemed to be talking to himself, nothing really noticeable unless you really studied him closely, as Dolan had begun to do recently. Colby was wound up pretty tight, Dolan observed. Men had different ways of dealing with Vietnam. Some moved through this phase of their lives seemingly unaffected by it all while others developed scars, deep scars, that they carried with them the rest of their lives. Colby was coping in his own way, Dolan guessed, but he certainly bore watching, and he was starting to get really weird.

The airfield lay ahead, and the two ships slowed and descended and set down at the edge of the ramp where the South Vietnamese soldiers were loaded and waiting. Colby watched them suspiciously. He did not like the South Vietnamese any more than he did the Viet Cong.

"Don't trust them," he said. "They're all draftees. They run at the first sign of trouble. Not like the VC. The VC fight 'cause they want to, and they'll fight you too. The ARVNs aren't soldiers, not real soldiers. One operation we went on, up near Cambodia, maybe in Cambodia, Dolan and I had to knock two of them off the ship. They were trying to climb back on board. I wanted to shoot them, but Dolan wouldn't let me."

Jim studied the slightly built soldiers. Colby was right, they didn't look like soldiers. He'd heard that some were good soldiers and fought well. Some, whose families had been murdered by the Viet Cong, had scores to settle. He guessed that would be motivation enough. Still, there were a lot of desertions and a good many more were killed, Jim believed, because their hearts were simply not in it. They wouldn't last long if it weren't for the Americans.

They linked up with two other crews from the 336th and three from the 224th and formed up to set down on the LZ that the flight leader had marked with smoke. It was near a small village that was the object of the day's operation. All the ships landed without any trouble, no incoming fire was received. And the South Vietnamese troops jumped out and ran for what cover they could find in the bushes and saw grass, not knowing when or if they would be under fire. The only sanctuary they had had, the helicopters, was gone in an instant as the Ships lifted off as quickly as they had landed.

The crew of Warrior One-Seven watched the little men slowly advance toward the village and then Jim banked to the right and left them behind. They would return later in the day to extract them.

A few miles from the village, Jim thought he saw something on the ground. He alerted his crew then broke off from the formation to investigate but, after descending for a closer look, found nothing. "I saw someone moving down there," he said, "maybe two or three people, but I don't see anything now."

"They're down there," Dolan said. "I've seen this before. They hide in the brush and weeds and, with those Cooley hats they wear, you can't see them from the air. Bring it down, Mister Kemper, low and slow across that field."

Dolan and Colby both leaned out of the aircraft and aimed their M-60s straight down at the ground. Both men watched intently as Jim flew across the field as his crew chief had requested. Slowly, menacingly, they inspected the landscape below them.

It was a quirk of human nature, whether Eastern or Western that, after apparent danger had passed, a man cannot keep from turning to look to verify that fact. It was this quirk, with which Dolan and Colby were familiar, that spelled death for five Viet Cong soldiers.

As the helicopter passed over them, one of the men on the ground looked back over his shoulder and, when he did, Colby spotted the man's face, now exposed, and opened up on them with his M-60. "I got 'em, I got 'em," he yelled. "Pull up, skipper, swing around."

Dolan, on the other side, couldn't see anyone on the ground but opened up with his weapon anyway, throwing up little geysers of mud and grass, just in case there were some Viet Cong hiding in his line of fire.

Colby killed four VC in a matter of seconds but the fifth got up and ran straight in line with the helicopter hoping to get to the trees about a hundred yards away. "There's one under us," Colby said, calmly, in his mike. "Back off so I can find him."

The man ran a short distant toward the tree line and then, as if he could somehow feel Colby drawing a bead on him, he turned to face his executioners. He just stood there staring at the American sitting in the door of the terrible, destructive machine, who would soon orchestrate his doom. Their eyes met. Colby held the man's gaze until the color and the life had drained completely, out of his face.

Colby spoke in a slow monotonous tone that unnerved the other three men on the aircraft. "'I was with the captives by the river Chebar, and the heavens were opened, and I saw visions of God. And I looked and, behold, a whirlwind came out of the north.'"

"Don't play with him, Colby!" Jim yelled into the mike. "I won't allow that. Kill him or let him go."

The short, staccato bursts from Colby's gun told him which course of action Colby had chosen.

"Weird shit, Colby, weird shit," Dolan said into the ship's intercom, you are one strange sonofabitch."

Colby turned and looked at Dolan and then glanced at Jim and the other man. "I kill, therefore I am," he said, not smiling.

Dolan repeated the phrase. "Three years at Indiana University and that's all you remember from philosophy one-oh-one. You must'a dozed off a lot in class," he said and laughed.

Colby laughed too and they all relaxed a little, but Jim was certain that Dolan had been right. There was something wrong with Alex Colby.

They returned later to pick up the ARVN troops who had, much to their great relief, encountered no Viet Cong. They had, however, encountered the village and had, apparently pretty well ransacked it, their packs being loaded down with the booty they had stolen. "Thievin' little shits," Dolan said, in disgust. "We chauffeur their asses around so they can steal from some poor villagers. You wonder why they hate us, Mister Kemper?"

They dropped the troops off at the airfield and headed for home. It had been a good day in Jim Kemper's war. They had engaged the enemy and had inflicted casualties and had not lost a man, with the possible exception of Colby. Jim was concerned about Colby. There was a thin line between efficiently doing one's job, as it was required of him, and enjoying the brutal art of killing. Colby might not have crossed that line yet, but seemed to be walking dangerously close to it.

After they had returned to base, Dolan motioned to Jim that he wanted to talk. "That was stuff from the bible that Colby was saying out there, wasn't it, Mister Kemper?"

"Yes," Jim said, "Ezekiel, I think, if I remember correctly from my bible classes when I was a kid."

"That's some weird shit, Mister Kemper, weird shit," Dolan kept saying and shaking his head.

Jim picked up his mail and headed for his hooch to read the two letters that had arrived, one from his mother and the other from Mattie. He weighed the decision over which to read first and decided on his wife's. She related all the latest things that little Alton had done. What her mother had said about this or that and how her father was doing in the state senate or one or another of his business ventures. There were more and more protests and demonstrations against the war in Vietnam on television every day now. Mattie was starting to question the prudence of "our involvement in the war," as she put it. She wanted to know how Jim felt about it. She told him to be careful and to bring himself safely home to her. She loved him, of course, and missed him and would write again in a few days.

Jim opened the letter from his mother slowly. A feeling that something might be wrong invaded his mind as he started to read.

Dear Jimmy, Allie wrote. *I made a visit to the farm this past week. I still try to go there at least once a month. Your grandfather is not doing too well, although he is in good spirits, you know how tough he is. Even at seventy-five, he is still as ornery as ever, but it's his heart, I think, that is causing him trouble. He had a full physical about a month ago, and the doctor told me that Alton had some scar tissue from a previous heart attack. It must have been a minor one, the doctor said, but it was still serious enough to be concerned about. He's got him on a strict regimen now, you know, taking it easy and watching his diet. I asked Grandpa about it and he said he didn't recall ever having a heart attack before. That would be just like him to have one and not know it. He said the doctor didn't know what the hell he was talking about and we left it at that.*

Danny Carlisle, you know Danny, is still working at the farm running things for Alton. I don't know what we would have done without him. He has helped us more than you can know. He is a good man and your grandfather trusts him as much, maybe as much as he does you. I know you will do right by him when you come home to take over the dairy.

Danny made a deal on some land that joins the farm on the north side, across the creek, and Alton bought it. They are looking at some more over beyond that. They have great plans for the old place. Grandpa says he has everything in the world now that he needs except for Mary, and forty more years and,

most of all, his grandson, Jimmy. I will close for now, son.
Take care of yourself and please be careful. I love you more
than anything.
   Mother

Jim sat on the side of his bunk struggling to hold back the tears. This was why he was in Vietnam, for the people back home. He didn't know about politics or policy or things like that. He was here to fight for the folks at home, and he had to keep it in that context if he were to continue to do it. God knows, these people weren't worth fighting and dying for. There would be plenty of time in the coming years to argue the right and wrong of the Vietnam War but right now all that mattered was getting the hell out of here in one piece.

He leaned back, lay his head down on the pillow, and closed his eyes. A minute later, he was asleep, his mother's words still weighing heavily on his mind.

Chapter 10

The Wrens Leave

Alton was sitting by his smokehouse enjoying the shade of the big twin oak tree and taking it easy as the doctor had told him to do. He heard the postman's car pull up to the mail box at the end of the drive and stop briefly, as the mail was deposited, and then speed off. A moment later, Danny Carlisle shuffled up with some letters in his hand.

"Letter from Jim, Mister Kemper," he said and handed the letter to Alton. "There's one from Allie, too. Couple more concerning the dairy. You want me to take them."

"Yes, Danny, thank you," Alton said, and Carlisle ambled off to the office trailer they had set up next to the farm house, to tend to business. Alton opened Jim's letter and began to read it.

Dear Grandpa,
Mother wrote me that you were not feeling so well. I am sorry for that. I wish I could be there to help you out when you really need it but I understand that Danny has been running things for you, and I am happy to hear that. Mother said that Danny has been invaluable to you these past few years. I want you to know that I still intend to come home and take over the farm when my hitch in the army is up. The confidence you have placed in me has been the driving force in my life. All I want to do with the rest of my life is take over for you there and keep the Kemper dairy going. I want you to know that I will certainly do what is right by Danny. I am grateful for all he has done for you.

*I wish I could be there with you now but I must first win
this war we are in. I still believe that I did the right thing by
coming here. I can understand, I guess, how Dad felt when he
went off to fight in World War II. Please forgive me for leaving. Take care of yourself and I'll be home before you know it.*

I love you, Grandpa,
Jimmy

Alton clutched the letter tightly, tears rising in his eyes, and
bowed his head, thinking back over the years of hard work he
had put into the place. He had come a long way from the horse
farmer he was forty years ago, when he inherited the little
farm from Mary's father. A hundred acres, that's all it was
then, and he raised peanuts and watermelons and such and
eked out a living for them. All the talk he had made about being a gentleman farmer, James had never believed in him. He
didn't think Mary had either, although she pretended to. Jimmy believed it. Jimmy always believed everything he told him
and shared the dream with him. Few people had dreams of
being farmers. Most were farmers because they were born into
it or got stuck in it. Not many thought of farming as a good
career move. Jimmy did though. He was never ashamed, like
James was. He was never ashamed of Alton Kemper. Jimmy
had the insight and the vision to understand everything that
Alton had tried to pass on to him ever since he was a boy.

He looked out across the creek at the cows grazing on the
new plot of land they had just bought. They were gentle, doc-
ile creatures, he mused, dumb as hell, but beautiful. They
made him a lot of money. He guessed he would love the cows,
even if they didn't provide him his living, but it was much easier to feel benevolent toward the curious, slow-witted, beasts
when they had done so much for him and his family.

Alton knew he would not see his grandson again. The pains
in his chest were coming more and more frequently, and he
knew that the instrument of his eventual demise was beating
precariously in his chest.

But he had succeeded after all. Now, in his waning moments, he was proud of his life and he was content, more con-

tent than he had been since his wife died. God, how he wished he could see Jimmy and Allie one more time. But they knew how he felt about them, they always knew. Now If Jimmy was killed in Vietnam, this old man wouldn't have to endure the loss of one so close to his heart. God had given him one final blessing, and it was the best of all. He would die before his grandson and his faithful daughter-in-law, the two people he loved most in the world. A man couldn't hope for much more than that.

 espan

Danny Carlisle finished his business in the office and went out to where Alton was sitting. He found the older man leaning back, motionless, against the smokehouse, his head still bowed, and Danny stopped a short way off, thinking that he was asleep. When Alton didn't move, Danny called to him but got no response.

"Alton," Danny called again. He went over, put his hand on Alton's shoulder, and realized that his friend of so many years was dead. "Oh no," he said. He took his old friend in his arms and just held on to him. "I'm sorry, Alton. I'm so sorry."

Seeing that something was wrong, two of the workers came over and, after realizing what had happened, removed their hats and stood off a few feet, giving Danny his time alone with Alton. One of them turned his head quickly to see two little birds flutter out of the eave of the house and fly away.

Danny sat with Alton for a while, talking to him as if he were still alive. "I know I have tried to tell you, Alton," he said. "I have tried to tell you how grateful I am for all you did for me. You believed in me when no one else did or would. I'd still be a drunk, of no use to anyone, if you hadn't took me in and helped me. It's been hard for me to say but you're my best friend, you're the best friend I ever had. You've been more than just a friend, you've been like a father or a brother to me. You're the best man I've ever known. I love you, old friend," he said as he broke down and wept, his chest and shoulders heaving. He hugged Alton tightly and sobbed uncontrollably.

They laid Alton to rest, next to his wife Mary, in Oakwood Cemetery on the seventeenth of February in 1967. John Beaty, a Comanche city official and a good friend of the Kempers for many years, said at the funeral that Alton's death marked the passing of an era in Comanche County, Alton being "the closest thing to a pioneer that was left in these parts."

Kinnie Sullivan, visibly shaken by his friend's death, went up to deliver the eulogy. The Sullivans were a unique and interesting chapter in the county's history. The first Republicans, and the first Catholics as well, in the area, they were a likable family of Irish Americans. Kinnie—known as Pat, for some unknown reason, to most who knew him—went by Kinnie because that's what his older sister had always called him when he was a boy. He was born in 1896 and christened Edward William McKinley Sullivan after the Republican President who took office shortly after his birth.

Kinnie went to work for the Post Office in 1924 and remained there for forty years, retiring in 1964 as the Assistant Postmaster. Kemper and the easy going, likable Sullivan had been friends since the twenties, ever since Alton moved into the county.

Alton had once told his grandson that Kinnie Sullivan was the best man he ever knew and the smartest too. "If you ever needed to know anything," Alton told him, "you could either look in a book or go ask Kinnie, 'cause you couldn't always rely on what a book said."

It was Sullivan who had brought them the awful news about James being killed, and he who had tried to comfort Alton, to no avail, and help him get through it.

Kinnie did not make a speech about his old friend. He simply told them that Alton's death was a great personal loss to him and that he would miss him greatly. "I don't know—what makes two people become friends," he said, "and remain that way over the years. I don't think anyone has the answer to that. All I know is that Alton Kemper was my friend and I was fortunate to be his. Now he has gone the way that all must go eventually and we who knew him are much less now than we once were because of it. Rest in peace, old friend."

Allie Hargrove laid her hand across the casket as it was lowered into the ground. "Poor Jimmy," she thought. "This will hit him hard." With him in Vietnam, now she had to start worrying about him again. She hoped he would be all right."

Trenton came down with the kids after Allie, and he now wanted to take them to the Matthew's house before they left to go back to Dallas.

"I want to stay a while," Allie told him. "Then I need to see to Alton's affairs. I may be a few days here before I come home."

He nodded. Allie hugged Sarah and Trent and then they left. She stood alone for a while, a short distance from the gravesite, watching the workmen removing the chairs and things and preparing to close it up. She felt a hand on her shoulder and was startled for a moment. She had not been aware that anyone was there behind her and turned to see George Matthews, her father.

"Oh, you scared me," she said. "I thought you had left with the others."

"I wanted to talk to you, Allie," George said. "It's time we talked, I think." He was nervous and having a hard time, she could tell. She had tensed up when she realized it was his hand on her shoulder and that didn't help his nervousness. "I know we've never been close, Allie. I don't know why. I know I wasn't a very good father to you and the boys, but you treat me like I'm a stranger. Ever since Alton Kemper came into your life you have treated your family like second best."

"Not my family. I've been good to Mom. John and Luke, well—my brothers are so resentful of Trenton, and the business, and my marrying him, I don't think we'll ever be close but I have treated them decently. I have seen to it that Sarah and Trenton were always close to you and Mom. I've brought them here regularly to see you. You've been a good grandfather to them and they love you and Mom very much."

"But I wanted for us to be closer, Allie. You're my daughter and you treated Alton more like a father than you ever did me."

"He was more of a father to me then you ever were," she

shot back quickly and knew that she had hurt him, but she didn't care. Years of resentment toward him, and now the loss of her first father-in-law, had put her in a hurtful mood. She wished he would just go away.

"That's a terrible thing to say, Allie. Why do you say things like that?"

"You *know* why, Daddy. You know why."

"Oh, Allie, I made a mistake. That was a long time ago. I know it was wrong, but it was a mistake. I never did anything like that again."

"I was fourteen years old, Daddy. Fourteen years old. A man doesn't try to do that to a fourteen-year-old girl, especially his own daughter. I was your daughter, for God's sake. How could you have done that?"

"Can you ever forgive me? I need to know that you can forgive me. I know this has been between us now for a long, long time, and I want to put it to rest."

"No, Daddy, I can't. I'm forty-four years old and every day I think about it. There isn't a day that goes by that I don't feel a little dirty, like there's something wrong with me, because of you. I never told anyone, and I never will, but not to protect you, to protect me. I never wanted anyone to know. I was too ashamed. Yes, Alton Kemper took your place. Because he wasn't just like a father to me, he was my father."

George Matthews turned and walked away, resigned to what his daughter had just told him. He would live several more years, but they would not speak again. No one in the Kemper, Hargrove, or Matthews families would ever know what had caused the destruction of the relationship between Allie and her father.

Allie stayed out at the farm for a few days until she was scheduled to meet with Alton's lawyer about the estate. Alton had asked Allie to see to his will, in the event he died before Jimmy came home from Vietnam, and she told him she would. The will gave her power of attorney to operate the business until Jim came home. All of Alton Kemper's worldly possessions, he left to his grandson just as he said he would do. If Jim were killed in Vietnam, then the property would go to Al-

lie and his cash and other assets were to be split fifty-fifty between Allie and Jim's family. His only request of his grandson
was that he deed to Danny Carlisle a ten-acre plot of ground
that he, Alton, had already laid out on the north side of the
farm along Duncan Creek and that Danny remain working at
the farm for as long as it was mutually advantageous to all parties concerned, those being Jim and Danny. Alton did not
write these items into his will but put them in a letter as requests only. Jim had the option to act on both requests as he
saw fit. Alton Kemper knew his grandson and knew he would
do the right thing.

Allie had been vaguely aware that Alton's financial well-
being had improved greatly in the past few years, but she was
surprised when the lawyer started going over the list of her
former father-in-law's assets. He had bought all the plots of
land adjoining his property except the one to the south. He
would have bought that too, the lawyer said, had it been for
sale at a reasonable price, which Alton decided that it was not.
With his life insurance, he'd kept the policy for over twenty
years, his cash worth was over sixty thousand dollars.

"I had no idea there was that much, Mister Bynum," Allie
said to the lawyer.

"Alton Kemper was a very frugal man, Allie," Bynum said.
"He was driven, absolutely driven, like a man who knew his
time was running out. He wanted to leave something for his
family. He knew you would be taken care of so he left it all to
Jimmy. He bought up the land around him when it came available, and he got some really good deals. He didn't go shopping
for it but when the other owners got in trouble, they went to
Alton first and he offered them a fair price, which they gladly
accepted.

"He's been accumulating cash for quite some time now.
You know, Allie, the dairy really is a profitable business.
Danny Carlisle helped Alton an awful lot but the truth is that
Alton knew the dairy business as much as anyone around here,
and he taught Danny most of what he knows now. Jimmy
should be able to do quite well with the farm when he comes
home."

Allie thanked him and left to go to the farm. She wanted to meet with Danny and work out a plan for keeping things going until the time that Jimmy got out of the army. She was faced with a situation that she was not certain she knew how to handle. Danny had worked for Alton for ten years and was certainly partially, if not primarily, responsible for the success that the dairy had enjoyed in that time. Now Alton was gone and all that he had left to Danny was the promise of a job and a plot of land, and both were now in the hands of his boss's grandson who had been gone for several years and would not be back for another four months yet. This had to be hard for the man to live with. Jimmy wasn't much more than a kid the last time Danny saw him, and Danny was ten years older than her son. It was indeed a delicate situation, and Allie pondered how she could approach it appropriately.

Danny was waiting at the farm when she arrived. He opened the door for her and they shook hands.

A strange thing, Allie thought.

Men were just beginning, in that day and time, to shake hands with women the way they did with men. Typically, they chose to just tip their hats or offer a verbal greeting. It made her feel really good, and she told him so. Men had treated Allie like an object of desire for most of her life, most either being afraid to touch her or trying to force themselves on her. Here was a man who was willing to treat her like a person. The only other man who had ever done that, except for Trenton, was Alton Kemper, and she found it refreshing.

"Danny, I want to talk to you about Alton's affairs and about running the dairy," Allie said.

"Mister Kemper went over everything with me, Mrs. Hargrove. I'll stay as long as you want me to and, when Jimmy comes home from Vietnam, he can work things out about what happens after that."

"Call me Allie, Danny," she said. "Did you know about the land, the ten acres, across the creek?"

"Oh, sure, Mrs—Allie, I mean. Alton set that up years ago. He didn't put it in his will because he wanted to give Jimmy the right to do it. Alton knew that a request from him was as good as an order to Jimmy. Jim is a good man. He'll do right by me, and I'll do right by him. I'll run the place for you, and you can come and check on me, if you like. Or I'll have the accountant send you a balance sheet every month, any way you want to handle it. Alton thought more of you than anyone, except maybe Jimmy, and he asked me to help you out in case something like this happened."

"I'd like to spend some time here, bring my kids and spend some time, but not to check up on you, there's no need for that."

"Sure," Danny said, "That would be helpful. I'm sure you could offer suggestions from time to time."

"What about your salary, Danny? Are you okay with that?"

"I'm fine with that. Don't worry about it. Ten years ago, Alton started a deal with me, a profit sharing deal I guess you could call it. He started matching funds that I set aside to build my house with. I have a little over fifteen thousand dollars now. When Jimmy comes home and signs the land over to me then, I'll build the house, but in the meantime, we'll just keep things going. You'll be a lot of help, I know. Alton always said you were sharp as a tack."

"Thank you," she said. "It's nice of you to say that. You have my number in Dallas. I'm going to Maryland next week to see Jim's family and in-laws, let me give you the number." She took a small book out of her purse and scribbled down the number, then tore the page out and handed it to him. "If you need anything from me, don't hesitate to call."

"Thanks, Allie, I will, I mean I won't, I won't hesitate. And don't worry about anything."

They shook hands again and Allie left. She saw him in the rear-view mirror watching her as she pulled out of the drive-way and she wondered what he was thinking. He was a strange sort of man. *Nice, but just a little different from most other men*, she thought. Perhaps he really believed that she was as smart as Alton had told him she was or maybe he found her attractive. That could be it, although she was ten years older than him. That was probably it, she concluded.

When Allie arrived at the airport in Baltimore, Mattie was

there, with little Alton and six-month old Charlie, along with her parents, to meet her. The daughter-in law she had met only once, over a year ago, when Mary Kemper died, was just as beautiful as she remembered, and the two boys were wonderful. It was no wonder Jimmy had fallen so quickly for her. Mattie had an easy grace about her, a soft vulnerable grace. She made a man want to wrap his arms around her and protect her. At the same time, she was attractive, extremely so, and, as her son had intimated to her. Mattie had a raw sex appeal that could make that same protective man to desperately want to get her in the sack. Allie was pleased with her son's choice of a wife, and the two of them became very close. They put away the notion that mothers-in-law and daughters-in-law could not be friends, especially if both were beautiful women.

Allie walked down the airport corridor to where the McKenna's car was waiting, with the senator carrying her bags and escorting her, and the rest of the entourage following behind. She could almost feel Aimee McKenna's eyes burning into her back as Charles had seemed to suddenly forget that anyone else was there. Allie's high heels made a clicking sound on the hard tile floor and her A-line skirt flipped back and forth with each step she took. Even at forty-four, men were still turning around to watch her as she walked past.

The McKennas did everything they could to make Allie feel at home. Even Mattie's mother eventually got over the hard feelings her husband had caused by his being overly attentive to Allie at the airport. Aimee McKenna warmed up to her. They were a gracious family, well-bred and cultured, Allie found. Not anything like she was used to. Texans, even well bred, educated Texans, usually came with a crude, arrogant sort of manner about them, like they owned everything and knew everything. The women too were often like that, apparently trying to compete with their men. Allie was glad that she had taught her son, from very early in his life, the proper way to speak and conduct himself. The hours and hours spent with him had paid off. Jimmy had class, and he had manners. He was full of confidence in his own abilities and he was not intimidated by a living soul. Allie had seen to that.

She had taught him how to act and know who he was. A loud-mouthed Texan, with all the accompanying bull, would never have gotten his foot in the door of the McKenna home, but her son was almost revered there. They seemed as proud of him as she was, and they were enamored with their grandson, Alton, especially Aimee.

Aimee McKenna was an attractive woman, and her daughters took after her. The senator, as he liked to be called, was full of himself but he was not a natural born blowhard, so he merely exuded quiet confidence rather than the bluster that was common to many politicians.

"I must tell you, Allie," Charles McKenna was saying, as his wife poured some more coffee for them at the dining room table. "I didn't want Mattie seeing James at first. When she said, she had met a soldier…well, you know what I mean." Allie nodded. "But James is such a fine boy. You did a good job of raising him. We feel about him just like he was our own son."

"Thank you," Allie said, "I had a lot of help from his step-father, Trenton. Trenton always treated Jimmy like he was his own. He never showed any favoritism toward the other two children. We have been a pretty close family but Jimmy was influenced mostly by his grandfather, my first husband's father, who just died this week.

"Yes, yes, I was aware of that. Jim talked a lot about his grandfather. He must have been a good man."

"He was," Allie said. "He was a wonderful man, A little rough around the edges, if you know what I mean, but he was crazy about Jimmy. And Jimmy loved him too. You know, he left his dairy farm to Jimmy and Mattie?"

"Yes, James—perhaps I should call him Jim as you do but Mattie calls him James, just to be different I think. Jim said his grandfather was going to leave him the farm.

"That's okay," Allie said, "we all know who we are talking about."

"I suppose they'll be moving there when Jim gets out of the army. That's going to be a little hard to take around here but I want what is best for all of them."

They smiled about that. Allie told him about the farm and the money that Alton had left and what potential there was for Jimmy to really make something for his family back in Texas and Charles seemed to be content with that. Being the practical man he was, McKenna could easily see that. If what Allie said was true, then his daughter and grandsons would certainly be well taken care of. He could rest easy with that knowledge.

Chapter 11

Fire Fight

February 10, 1967:

Warrior One-Seven was on another operation with the detachment of ARVN troops they had lifted on the last mission. Intelligence had again reported enemy activity near the village they had previously assaulted. On approach to the LZ, the lead ship reported that it was taking fire.

"This ain't goin' to be no walk in the park," Dolan said. "The gooks showed up today, guys. I can smell 'em. Our little buddies here are goin' to catch hell today."

Jim could see the flashes from the AK-47s, in the tree line as they zeroed in on the American helicopters and their South Vietnamese passengers. No fire had hit his ship yet, as he descended to the LZ to unload the ARVNs, who by now were starting to get skittish. Jack's voice invaded his headset, calm and cool and task oriented.

"This is Captain Grantham," he said. "LZ is hot. Repeat, LZ is hot. Lead ship has come under fire. It appears that Charlie intends to contest our landing. Stay in formation and unload troops as quickly as possible. Maintain covering fire after lift-off. My gun ships will cover and support the landing."

About fifty feet off the ground, Jim heard and at the same time felt rounds hitting the side of his ship. Dolan yelled but it was not an injury yell, more a yell of surprise. Jim could tell by the inflection in his voice.

"What was that?" he said.

"I told you this wasn't goin' to be an easy one. They're pepperin' us pretty good."

The aircraft sat down hard, and the ARVN soldiers jumped to the ground quickly, drawing fire from the Viet Cong in the trees. They dove for any cover they could find, wanting to put as much distance as possible between themselves and the helicopters, which were now all taking fire and darting off as fast as they could unload. A single round from an AK-47 buzzed by Jim's head, sounding to him like a bee or a housefly buzzing around his ear, and struck the overhead panel just above him.

"Damn," he yelled. "That was close." The man in the right seat, another warrant officer named Coogan, on his first combat mission, was visibly shaken and unable to offer much assistance.

"No big deal," Jim said to him. "A miss is as good as a mile, they say." This produced a wide smile on Both Dolan's and Colby's faces.

"Right on, Skipper," Colby said.

The enemy held his ground and continued pouring fire into the ARVN troops as the American helicopters gave it right back to them, with American firepower eventually winning the day. When it was certain that the Viet Cong had withdrawn, the lift platoons went back in to pick up the survivors and the dead and wounded. Kemper's ship was assigned to transport the ARVN dead.

"Damn! Why do we have to carry the stiffs?"

"Come on, Dolan," Colby said, "it'll be fun. They won't hurt you."

"Kiss my ass, Colby," Dolan yelled, waving him off with his hand.

"Knock it off, guys," Jim said, "Lend a hand. They're bringing some now."

Some of the South Vietnamese troops, their weapons gone, and looking like they had just escaped from hell, began placing two of their dead buddies on the floor of the helicopter. Colby reached for one of them and, grabbing the man's shirt at the shoulders, hoisted him aboard.

"You don't look so good," he said, talking right into the dead man's face. "Hasn't it just been an exasperating day?"

"Shut up, Colby!" Dolan yelled at him again. "You're giving me the creeps."

When they were loaded, Jim lifted off and joined the formation as it headed for the airfield to deliver the remains of the detachment of ARVN troops. Glancing over his shoulder, Jim could see the bodies of six, maybe seven, dead soldiers. They looked like boys to Jim, no larger than some twelve or fourteen-year-old American boys. They could be Boy scouts, playing war, had it not been for the blood and the mangled and missing body parts. Somewhere in Vietnam, a few days from now, some Vietnamese mothers, if they were still alive, would be getting the word that their sons had been killed in combat. Jim wondered if Vietnamese families went through the same tortured grief that American families did when they got the same kind of news. *They must*, he thought. *Everyone does.*

That was human nature. The constant presence of fear and death couldn't possibly lessen the agony of losing a son in the war. The only good thing about this, and he wasn't so sure the Vietnamese mothers would agree with him, was that they no longer had to worry about their boys any more. That, at least, had been taken away from them. The Americans had dropped their sons off in hell and were now bringing what was left of them home, piled up like cordwood in the backs of their awful machines.

About a half hour into the flight, Dolan coughed twice in the intercom, a signal he and Jim had made up to get Jim's attention, without anyone else on the aircraft knowing. When Jim turned to look, Dolan gestured with his thumb to the back of the aircraft. When he turned to look, Jim recoiled at what he saw. Alex Colby, apparently now completely over the edge, had taken two of the dead ARVN soldiers and set them in a reclining position next to him in his gun well. He was sitting there, his arms around both corpses, talking to them like they were just some grunts out on a night of drinking. One of the men's head was bowed, resting on his chest, but the other one's was slung back against the rear wall of the helicopter, the eyelids open, with the blank lifeless eyes staring off into nothing.

Colby was having a conversation with one of them and would turn, from time to time, to the other, punch the body with his elbow, and laugh like they had told a joke. Both men had taken multiple rounds in the chest area. They had gaping, bloody, wounds that Colby slapped at with his arms as he conversed with them. His forearms and his uniform shirt were covered with the men's blood but Colby didn't seem to notice.

Upon arrival at the airfield, Colby exited the ship quickly and motioned to the two men to follow. "Get out of there," he screamed at them. "Get out of my helicopter."

He reached for both bodies and, grabbing them by their shirts, right where their wounds were, yanked them from the ship out onto airfield tarmac.

The next day Jim went to see Captain Grantham to request that Colby be sent home. It was time, he knew, long past time. Colby had seen enough of war. *God help the folks back in Terre Haute*, Jim was thinking, *when Alex comes home.*

There was a big operation planned for the fifteenth of February and the platoon was short-handed, so Grantham informed Jim that Colby would go along for one more ride.

"I don't think that's a good Idea, Jack," Jim said. "Colby is over the edge." He told him how the man had been acting lately, about the ARVN corpses, and how Colby had been getting steadily worse in the past few weeks.

"I don't have any choice, Jim," Grantham said. "I'll have replacements next week but right now he's all we've got."

∽∾∽

On February 15, 1967, an ominous, foreboding feeling seemed to grip and permeate the lives of the army aviators of the 336th Assault Helicopter Company as morning spread across the flight line at Soc Trang. Intelligence had reported that elements of the Ninth Viet Cong Regiment were operating to the south of the base near the town of Vi Than. A reaction force had been ordered to search for and, if possible, engage and destroy the enemy.

The Ninth Regiment was both hated and feared by the army airmen. They were a tough and tenacious foe, true enough. But the real reason for the trepidation, with which the helicopter forces approached these Viet Cong troops, was an awful rumor. A rumor, though never fully confirmed, nor disproved, had been going around about a staff sergeant named Green who had gone over, defected, to the other side and was now aiding the Viet Cong in their war against the American helicopters. The staff sergeant, said to be familiar with helicopter design and tactics, was thought to be living among the Viet Cong and teaching them the best way to defeat and shoot down the American airships. No one knew if the rumor was true or not, or if a staff sergeant named Brown, or Green, or Black or whatever, had really defected. Perhaps army intelligence knew, and they were not saying, but it certainly made for some interesting speculation on the part of the army aviators who had to go out and fight the Ninth VC.

Up and down the flight line the crew chiefs and mechanics were doing their pre-flight inspections, checking fluid levels and pressure gauges and all the necessary tasks that are required to make the craft ready for a combat flight.

When Dolan arrived to start prepping One-Seven, he found his aircraft commander already there. He was taking apart the overhead panel.

"What's up, Mister Kemper?" Dolan asked.

"You remember that round that passed by my head and hit the overhead? I want that bullet. That bullet was aimed at my head and I want to keep it. You know, as a souvenir."

"Yeah, I know what you mean. Good idea, put it in one of those plastic cubes, you know what I'm talking about?"

Jim nodded. "Yes, a memento of the war to show off when I get old," he said, smiling at Dolan, amused at his crew chief's sudden interest in the matter. "Something to prove I was here."

"Yeah, yeah," Dolan said, "Tell them, 'Look at this bullet some bastard shot at Grandpa.'"

They laughed at that and Dolan helped Jim take the overhead panel apart but the elusive missile could not be found.

"Disintegrated, I guess, Mister Kemper. Who knows? Bullets do some crazy things."

Jim continued to look a while longer but found nothing so he closed up the panel and began preparing for the day's work. Coogan arrived. He would be the Co-pilot today. He climbed into the right seat and began going over his checklist. Jim patted him on the shoulder, a friendly welcome, and took his position in the left seat as Colby showed up and began helping Dolan with his work.

Colby and Dolan were arguing about the ammo load for the day. Standard compliment was usually five hundred rounds for each M-60 but Colby wanted seven-fifty, having heard that today they could definitely expect to get into some shit. A compromise had to be made if a larger ammo load was carried. The additional weight meant it would he harder to lift off and might mean less of a payload that the ship could carry. It was a rare case when the extra two hundred-fifty rounds were ever needed.

Few helicopters were shot down when they were alone and had to fight on their own, without support, and most firefights were brief enough that the standard load was sufficient. It was more or less a macho thing to load up with additional ammunition, so Jim sided with Dolan and nixed Colby's request for more ammo.

Jim and Coogan were briefed in the ready room with the other pilots. They went over the navigation maps together and strapped on their flak jackets and sidearm. It was like cowboys and Indians, it seemed to Jim, except that it was real, too real to be taken as lightly as the airmen tried to do. Captain Grantham called Jim aside, gave him a few more details about the operation, then told him not to worry.

"It's all in a day's work," he said. "Those little bastards are more afraid of us than we are of them."

"Then they must be crapping on themselves about now," someone said and drew laughter from the other crewmembers.

"I hope you're right," Jim said, smiling, and he threw a snappy salute which Grantham returned as he turned to go to his ship.

A short while later Grantham's voice boomed over the headsets. "Pull pitch in five minutes."

Jim and Coogan adjusted their seats and did a final check of the instrument panel. Jim checked the engine mixture as Coogan tuned the radios to all the frequencies on which they would be operating. All of them were blaring at the same time but the pilots had learned, in time, to listen to all of them at once, somehow making sense out of the confusion.

Grantham gave the final signal and Kemper and the other flyers pulled back on the pitch levers as the rotors got a bite of the hot, squalid, Delta air and the Hueys lifted off the Tarmac for their trip to the ARVN base, to pick up their human cargo, and for their rendezvous with the vaunted Ninth Viet Cong Regiment.

This day's operation was a joint affair, with some Special Forces coming along to aid the Vietnamese troops in the completion of the stated objective. They were along to assist the ARVN troops and to gather intelligence when the objective was taken. Colby said they were coming along to shoot the ARVN's when they started to run.

The ships were flying in a, Vee of five, formation with Eddie's ship at the head of the Vee carrying an overweight, obnoxious Major named Pennington. Pennington had already done a tour in Vietnam back in '64, when Dolan was there, and he believed that fact gave him an edge that the other pilots didn't have. It was, in fact, a diminishing factor to the major, for the Viet Cong's tactics and, more importantly, their weaponry, had improved greatly since his previous tour. This essentially meant that Pennington was not quite up to speed with the other airmen, this not being inherently dangerous except that Pennington was in charge of the operation, and that scenario was fraught with danger.

The marshy patchwork of the Vietnam landscape rushed below. From above it looked peaceful enough but the beauty of the country belied its torment and masked the terrible agony of its people. Jim saw some farmers tending their paddies on the ground, coaxing water buffaloes along. They barely even looked up as the formation of helicopters roared past. They were used to such disturbances by now.

Pennington's nasal voice came over the radio. "Three miles to the LZ."

The LZ was visible now and Jim made a last check of his sector map for comparison. The tree line loomed wickedly on the horizon. Jim knew they were there. The enemy was there waiting, he could feel it, waiting to kill him, kill them all.

"Look alive, guys," he said over the ship's intercom to his crew.

Dolan and Colby hunched over their M-60s, putting on their war faces, and Coogan sat up a little straighter and grasped the controls. When going into an LZ where there is a likelihood of contact with the enemy it was procedural for both pilots to take the controls. The reason being, obviously, that if one was hit the other would have immediate control of the ship.

They could see the landing area clearly now. There was a shallow canal, more like a drainage ditch, protected by a low dike, about seventy-five to a hundred yards from the tree line. Not enough room to land there and disembark troops safely. Too close to the enemy. Jim was certain that Pennington would direct them to set down on the other side of the dike, there by affording them some protection. It was about two hundred yards from the tree line.

Just right, he thought. *That would give the troops some cover and time to get formed up before pushing off.*

Pennington issued his orders. "All ships, your LZ is that open field between the tree line and that little dike running parallel to it."

It was almost as if a hush fell over the entire formation as each man wondered if they had heard the major correctly.

"Shit!" Dolan yelled. "We can't go in there between that dike and the trees. They'll cut us to pieces."

Captain Grantham's voice broke in. "Confirm your orders, Major. You don't intend to land that close to the tree line?"

"That's affirmative," Pennington repeated. "Next to that dike."

"Negative, sir, that's too close. The troops need more room to get set before moving out. The enemy will zero in on us and, from that distance, they'll cut us up."

There was silence on the line for a moment and Jim could visualize Eddie trying to talk some sense into the Major. "My orders were clear," was Pennington's response, and Grantham shot back immediately.

"I can't set my people down at that location, Major. It's too close to the enemy."

"You are very close to insubordination, Captain." Pennington said, trying to sound military, but coming across, in that high-pitched voice of his, as ridiculous.

"Then let me check it out first, let me take my gunships parallel to the tree line and check out the situation."

The major agreed and ordered the other pilots to hold their positions as Grantham banked his ship and flew past the suspected enemy stronghold.

"There's a line of bunkers, six or seven I think. Enemy is there in force. I repeat, in force and appear to be heavily armed. I can see Viet Cong in large numbers manning the trench line between the bunkers."

"Are you receiving any fire?" the major asked.

"No, they aren't firing. They're waiting for the troop ships. They are holding their positions waiting for us to set down. They have got to be hoping we attempt to land inside that dike. They set it up this way on purpose. We must land farther out."

"Why are they not firing at you? They aren't that well-disciplined to hold fire when they have a target like you just gave them."

"They are waiting for the troop ships, Major." Grantham was almost yelling now. "You're about to set us down in a hornet's nest."

"My orders have not changed, Captain. You will provide cover while we go in. All ships follow in formation. After first platoon discharges its troops, I will lead second platoon in."

The first five helicopters turned to the right and, on command, dove sharply toward the waiting LZ below. Pulling up, in a hover, no more than ten feet off the ground, they eased down on the marshy grass below them. The troops quickly disembarked, without receiving any fire, as yet, and started setting up a perimeter to wait for the rest of the force to land before they made the assault on the enemy position.

Warrior One-Seven, in the middle of the left side of the second vee, followed Eddie's ship as it duplicated the action of the first group of helicopters which were now lifting off and getting the hell out of there. It appeared, for the time being that Pennington might be right. *He must be feeling pretty proud of himself right about now*, Jim thought.

As the lead ship, with Eddie and Major Pennington aboard, started to land, the formation began to receive fire from the tree line. Eddie's helicopter suddenly flipped back over itself and came down on its right side. The rotors struck the ground violently and pieces of them flew off in all directions, smashing into the ship, ripping and tearing everything in their path.

Jim pulled up and flew over the stricken helicopter, to avoid being struck by the churning rotors, and quickly set down. Men started trying to exit the ship as Viet Cong gunners opened up on them at almost point blank range. Some were killed in the doorway, their fallen bodies blocking the other's attempts to disembark. Tumbling out onto the ground, the remaining ARVNs managed to get to their feet and run for the trees.

A murderous fire tore into them and they fell immediately in a heap. Warrior One Seven's entire load of South Vietnamese soldiers were killed in a matter of seconds. Jim moved at once to lift off but the enemy had brought them under fire and a blistering broadside of automatic weapons struck his side of the ship, killing Dolan instantly and wounding Colby and Coogan. The rounds had torn into the helicopter's control cables, severing them, and disabling the aircraft. Jim unstrapped his seat belt and climbed out of the seat, surprised that he had not been hit. He checked on Dolan, and saw that he was dead, then helped the other two out and onto the ground beside the ship. Colby was hit through the shoulder, seriously, but he was still conscious. Coogan's legs were shot up and he was unable to walk. Enemy fire was still coming in their direction.

Jim picked up Colby in a fireman's carry and headed for the little dike they had seen from the air and. Upon reaching it, he lay the man down behind it to shield him from the Viet Cong gunners. As he headed back to get Coogan, he saw that the other helicopter, the one directly behind him in the formation, had also been shot down. The other two had somehow managed to unload and lift off without being disabled. He grabbed Coogan and hoisted him up and again ran for the dike, as AK-47 rounds tore at the ground around him. Jim felt a round rip through his pants leg but it missed his leg. He tried to run faster, thinking any minute that the next one would hit him. He could feel the impact as several well-placed shells struck Coogan in the back. Jim knew the man was dead but he carried him to the dike anyway and laid him down beside Colby.

The gunships sprang forward and were laying down rocket and M-60 fire at the invisible little men in the tree line, and the enemy fire let up momentarily. Grantham's ship started taking 50 Caliber fire directly in the engine. Oil and smoke began pouring out and the engine ground to a halt. He quickly depressed the collective to flatten the pitch of the rotor blades in order to allow the ship to auto-rotate down, but he did not have enough altitude. Grantham managed to swing the helicopter over across the dike as it belly flopped into the ditch and buried up to its skids in the mud. The crew was shaken up but otherwise unhurt. He ordered them out of the ship and assisted in getting them to cover behind the dike and then ran in a low crouch along the back side to where Jim was seeing to Colby's shoulder wound.

"We're in deep shit," he said, almost out of breath. "How is he doing?"

"He'll be okay, but we need a dust-off quick. Dolan is dead. So is Coogan. I can't tell about Hardesty's crew. I haven't seen any movement in there yet.

Bullets were churning up the dirt around the top of the dike and both men flattened themselves out on the ground to avoid being hit. They chanced a look and saw someone climbing out of Lieutenant Hardesty's ship. It was Hardesty's door gunner, George Burton. Jim remembered Burton, a stocky muscular man from Somerset Kentucky, who always introduced himself that way, "George Burton, from Somerset, Kentucky." Burton had the presence of mind to remove the M-60 and the ammunition can from his stricken ship and was headed toward the dike lugging both items. It was no easy task, but Burton was doing it.

"We've got to move, Jim," Grantham said. "The enemy will attack if they think we can't stop them. I'm going to try to get to your ship and use the M-60. You check on the other crews and see if there are any more wounded that need help. You with me, buddy?" He grabbed Jim's shirt and looked him right in the eyes. "We may not get out of this, Jim," he said.

"Yeah, yeah," Jim yelled. "I'm with you."

His chest was heaving, as was Grantham's. They took several short, quick breaths, and Jack jumped up suddenly and was over the dike and headed across the field toward the downed helicopters.

"Aw, shit!" Jim yelled to himself.

He jumped up just as quickly and fell in behind Jack.

Being shot at was a strange sensation, Jim thought, as he ran as fast as he'd ever run before. Bullets passing close by made a kind of fluttering, vibrating sound. He resisted the urge to wave his hand and try to brush them away from his head. A thousand things went through his mind. He thought about zig zagging, like he used to see them do in the movies but that didn't seem as prudent now as it did to John Wayne. He wasn't about to slow down long enough to zig zag. There were men over there in those trees trying to kill him. They were doing all they could to send him home to his wife and mother in a body bag. It made him angry, mad as hell, and he swore to himself that, if he got the chance, he'd kill them all.

Jack made it to Jim's ship and was checking the ammo feed on the M-60 and bringing it into position just as Jim got to the other helicopter. Climbing aboard, he found the lieutenant, his co-pilot, and the crew chief dead. The five Green Berets, including their commander, a lieutenant colonel whom Hardesty had been carrying, were lying nearby in the grass. Two were dead and the other three, including the colonel, were seriously wounded.

"Lay still, Colonel," Jim said. "Keep low. I'll get you out of here."

"See to my men," the colonel said. "I'll be okay. Watch them, son, I think they may be going to attack us. Hand me my weapon and see to my men."

Jim checked one of the other men as he quickly found an M-14 and handed it to the colonel. The other Green Beret was shot in the legs, badly hurt. Their helicopter had taken direct fire right in the door as soon as they had landed. The crew had been killed almost immediately, except for Burton, who was shielded from the fire by the other men in the door of the helicopter. Jim picked the man up and headed back to the relative safety of the dike.

Three groups of enemy soldiers, about six men each, had formed up and appeared to be getting ready to come out and finish off whoever might be left alive on the field. Grantham saw them as they came out of the tree line and opened up with the M-60. The rounds smashed into the first group of six and they never knew what hit them. Pieces of bone and flesh, and bloody pink intestines, spewed out in all directions, painting the marshy grass all around as the six men collapsed in a stack of unrecognizable remains. Grantham continued firing into the bloody mess for a few more seconds, just to make sure, then turned toward a second group who suddenly became aware of the danger and turned around to go back to the security of their bunker.

"No, you don't, you sons of bitches," he yelled, as he opened fire on the running men and struck them in their backs, pitching them forward into the mud on their faces. A couple of them tried to hide in the brush but saw grass would not stop bullets and the M-60 killed them where they lay.

Burton was set up behind the dike on the right side of the ill-fated helicopters and had started pouring rounds into the tree line. The enemy fire let up as he raked along their entire front with his M-60, allowing Jim to go out and retrieve the other Green Berets without any bullets buzzing around his head.

As Jim bent over to help the Green Beret colonel, the man said, very calmly "Watch out, son, there's some gooks right over there." He pointed, and Jim turned to see two Viet Cong not more than fifty feet away. Behind them were at least a dozen more. Terror gripped his entire body. He reached for his sidearm but it was gone. The lead man drew back to throw a grenade.

"I'm dead," Jim thought.

But a fusillade of fire, from Grantham on the left and Burton on the right, tore into the enemy soldiers. The lead man dropped the grenade. It fell among the other Viet Cong and exploded, killing several of them.

Jim helped the colonel off the field and then looked at Eddie ship. A horrible sight awaited him. He could see one of the pilots, still strapped in his harness, hanging upside down and clearly visible in the chin bubble.

"God, oh God." Jim hoped it was Major Pennington and not Eddie. He couldn't tell from where he was standing. There appeared to be no movement in the aircraft. For an instant, a thought came into his mind that reviled him and made him shudder that he could even think it. He almost hoped they were all dead so he would not have to cross that field again. He wrote it off as human nature but, years later, it would still bother him that he could think such a thing.

Someone was now trying to climb out of Eddie's ship. Jim still could not make out who it was but as the overweight form of Major Pennington became visible, he realized that it was Eddie, his old friend since flight school, who was hanging there, dead, in the cockpit of his helicopter.

In the command ship, overhead the Vietnamese officer, a full colonel, who was in overall charge of the operation had called in air support. Shortly, a pair of A-1s, manned by the colonel's South Vietnamese pilots, out of their base at Can Tho, screamed in just above tree top level, strafing the Viet Cong positions below, and dropping their loads of 500-pound bombs. The roar was deafening and the Americans on the ground grabbed their ears and dove for cover as the bombs exploded over the bunker complex and hot mud and dirt and chunks of grass plummeted down on them.

Grantham, out of ammunition, abandoned his position at the M-60 and was making his way back to the ditch when he saw Jim at Eddie's helicopter. Jim had gotten Pennington out of the ship and the major was standing beside it now, dazed and cut on one leg.

Jim picked up a piece of a pilot's body armor, an insert called a chicken plate that somehow had been tossed out of the aircraft, and was using it to bust out the Plexiglas windshield in order to get Eddie's body out. He succeeded but was unable to release the buckle on the harness because of Eddie's weight against it.

When the 500-pound bombs struck, Grantham, Jim, and the major were knocked to the ground. They got to their feet and shook themselves off.

Jim tried again to release the seat belt but, being unable to, he gave up.

"Let the dead bury the dead," he said, philosophically.

Bible teaching from time spent on his grandmother's lap when he was a boy. It was strange how things came into your mind in times like this, he was thinking. The three of them made the ditch at the same time the enemy fire resumed. Burton's gun had fallen silent, and Jim saw him banging on it. Jammed.

Safe for the moment, behind the downed helicopters, Grantham grabbed Major Pennington by his shirt and threw him to the ground. "You, stupid son of a bitch," he screamed. "Why aren't you dead? Look at my platoon, look at my men out there, dead. I told you we were too close to the tree line." Jack drew back as if he was going to hit him but Jim grabbed his arm.

"Don't, Jack," Jim said.

Pennington was terrified, the bullets were still flying, and now he had to contend with this. "You can't talk to me like that," he said. "I'm your superior officer."

Grantham went for him again but Jim held him off as the matters of the moment regained their priority. "We'll settle this later," he said.

"I'm bringing charges against you, mister," Pennington whined. "You're a witness, Kemper. You saw him strike me."

"I didn't see anything, Major," Jim said, as the fire from the tree line increased in intensity.

Burton could not get his gun unjammed and the ammunition in Grantham's ship had been all but used up in the initial assault. They were, once again, in serious danger of attack by the enemy in the trees. The A-1s had apparently had little effect on the bunkers.

Then a sound overhead, like wind being torn apart, caused them to look up in time to see two F-105s turning for a run on the position the A-1s had unsuccessfully tried to silence. The air force was here, beautiful F-105s from Saigon, carrying napalm, lots of napalm. The orange balls of flame engulfed the enemy bunkers, rolling, churning, and boiling up above the tree line, destroying everything they touched and scorching the faces of the Americans crouching there behind the little dike. The firing from the tree line stopped and, when the napalm fire burned out, it did not resume. Jim could hear faint screams coming from somewhere underground in the enemy camp.

A medevac helicopter landed in the field across the ditch and Grantham and Jim helped the wounded, including Colby aboard. The relief force was arriving now, and they would soon be lifted out, but first they would rig the ships for recovery and oversee the retrieval of their dead comrades.

Sitting across from each other on the flight back to Soc Trang, their hands reached out to each other's, and one grasped the other in the soldier's handshake. They said nothing, there was no need to. They had been in hell together. There was no need for words.

Aboard the medevac ship, the heat from the napalm was still intense and the crew turned their faces away from it but

Colby kept staring at the enemy line, a faraway look in his eye. "In all this world," he said, "there is nothing more beautiful than a gook on fire." He looked thoughtful for a moment and then added, "Except maybe Ann Margaret."

After they had dusted off, the Green Beret colonel asked about Grantham and Jim. "I meant to get the names of those two men," he said. "Those were two of the bravest soldiers I ever saw. I wish I had gotten their names. Do you know them?" he asked, nodding toward Colby.

"Well, yes, sir, Colonel, I do," Colby said. "That's Butch Cassidy and the Sundance Kid."

Chapter 12

The Survivors

Within two hours after they had been taken off the LZ, Jim and Grantham were back in Soc Trang, exhausted and emotionally drained, but unhurt physically. Jim was covered from head to feet with mud, from the 500-pound bomb blasts, and oil and grease from the downed helicopters and, worst of all, the blood of the other Americans he had carried out of harm's way.

He sat on the floor, leaning against his bunk, his bloody clothes lying in a pile beside him. He was about to go to the shower when he heard his name being called. It was Jarvis, the company clerk, with an envelope in his hand.

"I had this telegram for you this morning, Mister Kemper, but I couldn't find you before you lifted off. It's from the Red Cross."

A stab of fear ran through Jim. *The Red Cross*, he thought, *must be bad news*. He opened the telegram slowly, afraid of what it would tell him. It read:

Alton L. Kemper died Feb. 14, 1967 Comanche, Texas.

Just as he had feared, short and to the point, now he knew why people hated to get telegrams. Well, at least his grandmother wasn't around to face this. Jim would have to deal with it later. He was too tired and too much had happened today for him to worry about things a half a world away. Now he needed sleep.

It had all been more or less fun and games up until now. He

had done his job and he was good at it. They had killed the enemy and they had been invincible, but today he learned what Vietnam was all about. He learned that they were not invincible, merely human. The, little people, had turned on them, like a dog backed into a corner, and they had fought back, viciously and deadly. Were it not for American technology and firepower, they would have all been killed.

Today he saw Americans killed in combat, not body bags filled with anonymous remains, but genuine red—blooded baseball playing, hamburger and French fry eating Americans, with broken and bloodied bodies laid out in dead repose on the marshy, muddy saw grass of a foreign land. Back home, their mothers don't even know yet. Back home their families were still planning for that wonderful day when their boys come home from the war. There should be a term for that period of time that passes between when a man is killed in war and when his family gets the word. It had to be the most deceptively cruel time in a mother's life, her boy dead thousands of miles away and she didn't even know yet.

The next day they were debriefed in the company ready room. They learned that they had indeed gone up against elements of the Ninth Viet Cong Regiment. They had performed their duty magnificently they were told, in the face of great odds. Reports were needed from all concerned, including Grantham and Jim. The Green Beret colonel, as well as the Vietnamese officer in charge of the operation, would file their reports and then a determination would he made as to what had happened and what recommendations might be forth coming.

An investigation of the bunker complex had revealed some interesting facts about the battle. The complex was typical. The Viet Cong had dug a trench along the tree line. At intervals of seventy-five to a hundred feet they had dug bunkers, six in all, which were covered with four feet of coconut palms, other debris, and dirt. To the rear of the fighting trench ran a second trench that was, in turn, connected to each bunker by a series of additional trenches. This communication trench permitted the enemy to move about the bunker complex freely, even during a fight, without hindering the soldiers in the primary fighting trench. In case of an air strike, the men would take shelter in a bunker and then come back out to fight when it was over. Only a direct hit from a 500-pound bomb could do much damage to the bunkers. The trees overhead absorbed most of the impact from the bombs. Even the napalm strike might not have been effective except for one fatal mistake on the part of the Viet Cong. It was this:

Normally, the series of access trenches which connected the bunkers to the communication trench were, of necessity, dug with a "zigzag" in them. This was to prevent napalm, dropped on the communication trench, from entering the bunkers through the connecting accesses. In the battle near Vi Thanh, the enemy had neglected to install the zigzag in the access trenches. Whether due to time constraints, or arrogance or just plain stupidity, which seemed unlikely, no one knew for sure. But that simple fact, just one small mistake in a war of huge mistakes, had saved Jim Kemper's life and the lives of the other Americans who had been there with him. When the F-105s came in and dropped their napalm, it hit directly on the communication trench and spread, unhindered, right into the bunkers where the enemy troops were hiding. All of them were suffocated and burned to death instantly. The battle of the tree line was over. A rough body count was made and estimates were that seventy-five to eighty Viet Cong had been incinerated in the bunker complex. Grantham's and Burton's guns had killed at least twenty more, they said, but no one could he sure because of the extensive damage done by the napalm.

The butcher's bill was in, and it was excessive. In addition to Eddie, Dolan, and Coogan, there were seven other dead Americans: Lieutenant Hardesty, his crew chief, and his co-pilot—Burton being the only survivor from that aircraft. Eddie's crew, except for Major Pennington, of course, and the two Green Beret soldiers, were killed. Of the sixty or so ARVNs who had gone into the battle, thirty-seven had been killed or wounded. The rest had retreated, and all but ten were eventually picked up.

It had not been much of a battle. It would be overshadowed by an operation called Cedar Falls, the war's first combined, and America's first Corps-sized operation, that was directed against the Iron Triangle, a Viet Cong stronghold twenty miles northwest of Saigon. There would not be any write-ups, no bands playing and that sort of thing, and hardly anyone, other than the men who were there, would ever even know it had happened.

The four helicopters that were shot down would never fly again. They were too damaged to repair, and two more, of the four that had managed to avoid being shot down, though they were hit extensively, had to make forced landings on the way back to Soc Trang.

A few days later, Jim went to visit Colby in the hospital and found him subdued, but in good spirits. "How's the shoulder?" he asked him.

"Couldn't be better, Mister Kemper," Colby said, showing no emotion. "It's all screwed up. They say I'll lose fifty percent usage of my left arm. Wonderful, isn't it? I'm going home. You know, the old 'million dollar wound.'"

"I hope you're okay with that," Jim said.

"Aw, well, you know there's a saying about having the courage, or something like that, to accept what you can't change. You know what I mean."

Yes, yes, I do. That's a good way to look at it, I guess."

"It's the way I have to look at it, Mister Kemper. But I'm going home now. That's all that matters to me. I'm sorry about Dolan, I know you liked him. Ol' Eugene was a good man. I'll go see his family in Chicago when I get home. I'm not that far away in Terre Haute."

"I hope you will," Jim said. "I know they will appreciate that. Dolan was a good man, a good crew chief. I'll miss him."

"I wanted to thank you for saving my life. It was rough as hell out there, I know and I wasn't much help. I think you should get a medal for what you did."

"I was so scared I didn't know what I was doing most of the time. Anyway, you would have done the same thing if you hadn't been wounded."

"Maybe," Colby said, "but you did it. I'm grateful to you just the same. Hold on a second. He reached for a pad of paper on the table beside his bed. "I wrote a poem for you."

"I didn't know you were a poet, Colby," Jim said, taking the paper from him.

"I didn't either, until I got in here and had some time on my hands. Don't read it now, wait until you're alone, and don't tell anyone. They'll think I'm weird or something." He put his index finger up to his ear and spun it in a circle, indicating a crazy person. "You can hang it up in your new helicopter when you get one."

Jim thanked him, wished him luck, and was turning to leave when Colby spoke again. "I should have let him go, shouldn't I?"

"What's that?" Jim said.

"That gook, the one that ran under the helicopter and turned around to face me down, you said to either kill him or let him go. I should have let him go, shouldn't I? I should have honored his bravery?"

Jim thought for a moment. "No, Colby," he said, "you did the right thing. He might have killed us next time."

"Thanks, Mister Kemper. I needed that. Good luck to you."

Jim reached for Colby's hand and shook it. "Take care of yourself, Alex," he said.

His whole crew was gone now, and his friend Eddie Csaba. Strange, how war did not play favorites. Death was totally impartial and indiscriminate. Officer or enlisted, it didn't matter, one was just as likely to get killed in combat as the other. Poor Dolan, he joined the army to get away from discrimination and to seek equality, and he found it. In the end, war had afforded him the highest measure of equality. Death draws no distinctions between race, religion, or creed. You get in front of a bullet, you die. Jim guessed he would not see Colby again. He wasn't sure if he would ever want to. Colby was the most disturbed man he'd ever met, alternating between brilliance and lunacy without any prior warning when a change was coming, and now he was going home to live amongst an unsuspecting public. Jim got hack to his hooch and unfolded the piece of paper that Colby had given him. He was amazed as he read the strange lines of poetry.

> *Firefight*
> *He rode upon a Cherub, and did fly:*
> *Yea! He did fly upon the wings of the wind*
> *Hueys rush with wail and whine*
> *Like locusts formed in battle line*
> *"Whump whump, whump whump"*
> *Reverberates*
> *Infolding fire and whirling wind.*
> *Descending angels touch the earth,*
> *Where tree line shelters "little men"*
> *Above on hovering wings of steel,*
> *Visions of "Ezekiel's wheel"*
> *Living creatures, mounted, ride*
> *Back to back and side by side*
> *Gunship's answering songs of death*
> *He sends his scattering arrows out*
> *And his lightnings trouble all beneath*
> *Lion, Eagle, Ox, and Man,*
> *With burning coals that curse the land*
> *Strike and kill. Regroup, extract*
> *Dust-off dead and soon to die*
> *Across the Delta, probe, react*
> *"He rode upon a cherub and did fly:*
> *Yea! He did fly upon the wings of the wind"*
>
> *For WO James E. Kemper*
> *336th Assault Helicopter Company*
> *Soc Trang, Vietnam*
> *Alexander Colby, 1967*

Jim eventually framed the poem and hung it on the rear wall of his next ship. Some correspondents he was ferrying around noticed it and ran a story about it that appeared, along with the poem, in an issue of *Stars and Stripes*, just before Jim left Vietnam. Colby would have been proud of himself, Jim thought. He didn't know if they got *Stars and Stripes* in Terre Haute, Indiana, but he hoped so.

In May, word came down from battalion headquarters at Can Tho that Grantham and Kemper were to be decorated for their actions at VI Thanh. Jim didn't think too much of it. He didn't think he had done anything out of the ordinary, not anything any other soldier would not have done. Jack, well it took a lot of courage to do what Jack did. Jim wasn't so sure he could have shot all those people or not, he hoped that if called on he would have been able to do exactly as Jack did but, the truth was, he just didn't know. He would consider himself lucky if he got out of Vietnam without having to personally kill anyone.

He and Jack both had caught some flak, a mild dressing down was more like it, because their reports of the battle had not contained any references to Major Pennington. Being the ranking officer on the ground, Pennington was determined to share in whatever glory that might be available. They could not accuse the major of incompetence. That might force Pennington to bring charges against Grantham for assaulting a superior officer and, even though Jim was prepared to deny that Jack had attacked the major neither Grantham nor Jim wanted that to happen. In the end, Pennington was awarded a purple heart, for the scratch on his leg, and a Bronze Star for directing the defense of the perimeter.

"It was a joke," Jim said. "George Burton was the one who should be getting the Bronze Star."

Burton had as much to do with defending the perimeter as anyone, Jack included, but that wasn't the way the army worked. The glory would go to the officers.

All that notwithstanding, it was announced that Captain Grantham would be awarded the Congressional Medal of Honor and would be promoted to major. As a side show, a side show to the big show, as these things were sometimes called, Grantham would be invited to the White House to be decorated by President Lyndon Johnson. Jack took it all in stride, accusing the president of merely trying to improve his own image by hanging out with Medal of Honor winners.

Jim would receive the Distinguished Service Cross, the nation's second highest award, and would be promoted to warrant officer 2. His receiving the Medal of Honor was nixed from higher up, simply because he had only participated in rescuing people and had not actually engaged in combat. He would have had to kill someone to get the higher award. That didn't matter, he thought. But it would have been great to get to go to the White House. The White House was only thirty miles or so from Mattie. Jim guessed that he had been wrong about the battle not receiving much attention. The army was indeed making a big deal out of it. He learned that he would be decorated by the Army Chief of Staff, General Harold K. Johnson, who was visiting Soc Trang as part of his inspection of army activities in the Mekong Delta.

When the base commander called out, "Warrant Officer, James E. Kemper, front and center," Jim stepped out from the ranks and marched to where General Johnson was waiting. He stopped, snapped to attention, and saluted. The general returned his salute and waited, while the commendation was read then pinned the medal on Jim's left pocket, and that was it. The activities were over.

"You did good, buddy," Grantham said, when Jim was finished with the awards ceremony. "Congratulations. It should have been the Medal of Honor."

"Thanks, Jack, but that's okay. The only thing I regret is not going to the White House with you. It's not far from where my family is."

"I'll look in on them for you while I'm there. I'd like to meet them. Jim, a lot of guys become friends in Vietnam and plan to keep in touch when they rotate out but never do. I don't want that to happen to us. I want for us to stay friends after the war. I'd like your permission to bring your wife and boys to San Francisco when you get back in September. You can stay with Holly and me at her parent's house. Would you like that?"

"Of course, I would, Jack, that would be great, but it's a lot of trouble for you to go to."

It's no trouble at all. It's the best way I know to start the rest of our lives. You'll like my wife, Holly, and she and Mattie will get along fine. Now, don't go and try to be a hero again. Just keep your head down and be careful. I won't be here to watch after you. Bring your ass back in one piece, that's an order."

"Yes, sir," Jim said, and saluted his friend. "And thanks Jack, thanks for everything."

"My caribou is here," Jack said.

Jim walked out to the ramp with him to where the C-7 was waiting to take off for Tan Son Nhut. They shook hands and Jack climbed aboard and the airplane taxied out to the end of the runway and carried him away from Soc Trang forever. Jack Grantham had a date with destiny.

Now they're all gone, Jim thought. He'd never felt so alone in all his life.

ℰⅉℰⅉ

Washington was a pleasant change from Vietnam, for Jack, not as hot and certainly not as humid. He was glad to be out of the madness, away from the heat and the insects and the constant need for vigilance, and the killing. It was good to be home, although Washington was not his home, any part of the United States was home. He had earned his walk in the sun, but he was philosophical about what had brought him here today for the honor his nation was about to bestow upon him. A man could get too full of himself and take all this too seriously if he were not careful. Jack had made up his mind that he would not be adversely affected by it.

Holly Grantham sat next to her husband in their assigned seats in the guest section of the ceremonial dais that had been set up on the south lawn of the White House. Noise, from the city of Washington, horns blowing, and traffic rushing by not more than a hundred yards away, invaded the quiet, pleasant oasis that was the home of the nation's president. She could see the Washington Monument not far away on the Capitol Mall, and several kites fluttered aimlessly in the breeze.

A voice rang out. "Ladies and Gentlemen, the President of the United States."

Everyone stood up as the large, commanding form and gruff exterior of President Johnson emerged from a side door and ambled up to the podium. He was a serious looking man, full of troubles, Holly Grantham decided, but there could never be any doubt who was in charge when Johnson was around. He radiated power and control.

Holly grabbed Jack's arm and squeezed it, almost giggling like a schoolgirl and she struggled to control her excitement. She could not believe she was actually here at the White House not fifty feet from the President of the United States.

The ceremony began with little fanfare. A couple of men gave short speeches and then several army and navy men received awards from the president. There were some Bronze Stars, and Silver Stars, awarded to a few lower ranking officers. What they were for, Jack could only imagine, and two Distinguished Service Crosses which went to two navy men, an admiral and a captain.

Jack was rankled. They could invite admirals and captains, who sat on their asses most of the time, to the White House to get the DSC, but not a warrant officer who risked his life to save his buddies. It made him mad as hell, but what could he do? That's how it was.

An army lieutenant colonel approached the podium. He began reading from a pad on the stand in front of him. His voice was stern and military

"For gallantry in action. For service above and beyond the call of duty. For his relentless fighting spirit in the face of a formidable foe and exceptional daring that is an inspiration to his comrades and reflects the highest credit upon the United States Armed Forces. The Nation awards its highest honor. The Congressional Medal of Honor."

He stopped reading and for a moment there was absolute quiet on the south lawn. It seemed that even the traffic out on Pennsylvania Avenue had come to attention. A flag fluttered in a sudden breeze and broke the silence. A slow drum roll began and the Colonel looked up from the podium. His voice rang in Holly Grantham's ears.

"Captain John Fulton Grantham, front and center."

Jack snapped to attention, his quickness took Holly by surprise and she released his arm. He executed a left face, and marched five paces to the aisle, then made a right face and proceeded toward the podium. Fifteen steps, a sharp right oblique, and five more paces brought him face to face with Lyndon Baines Johnson. Grantham gave his best salute which was quickly returned by the Colonel.

An account of the battle near Vi Thanh was read, relating how Jack had manned the M-60 machine gun until it ran out of ammunition. His actions had saved many lives, the account said. Captain Grantham was deserving of the nation's highest award. The president stepped forward. Jack studied the man intensely, looking at his weathered face as if to memorize it. He did not expect to have an opportunity to meet the President of the United States ever again and he wanted to record it in his mind. Johnson placed the blue, star graced ribbon around Jack's neck.

"Congratulations, son," he said. "Your country is grateful for all you've done. Good luck to you."

"Thank you, sir," Jack said and saluted again then turned and retraced his steps back to his seat. Holly watched him walking back and noted that he was every bit as handsome, in his Class A green uniform as the honor guards they had seen at the tomb of the unknown soldier, at Arlington. She was flushed with pride in her husband. The last few days had been like a dream, a dream that Holly wished would not end.

"It's not over yet," Jack told her, after they had left the ceremony. They had been invited back that evening for dinner.

"Are you serious?" she squealed. "I don't believe it. The president invited us. What do I say to him? How should I act? What if he asks me about the war? Should I give him my honest opinion or try and be diplomatic. Daddy always said I should speak my mind no matter what. But, Jack, he's the president?"

"Hold on," Jack said, "it's not going to be just the three of us there. I mean we're not going to sit around chewing the fat with Lyndon. There will be hundreds of other people there. We may not even get a chance to talk to him. But," he said, pointing his finger at her, "but if you do talk to him, or his wife, don't, I repeat, don't tell him your opinion on anything, especially the war. Just be gracious and beautiful. That's what you do best.

That evening, after dinner, Holly stood in the East room of the White House, sipping champagne and making light conversation with some of the other guests, who appeared to Holly to be just as nervous as she was. Across the room, she could see Jack talking with the president. Johnson was pointing to the gold oak leaf insignia of the rank of major that had replaced Jack's two silver captain's bars. Holly expected, at any moment to awaken from her dream. She couldn't wait to get back home and tell her mom and dad about it. They would want all the details, what she said to the president, or Mrs. Johnson. What the president thought of her opinions about the war, or the economy, and anything else that might have come up in conversation."

The truth was, it was Jack they were interested in. America needed heroes, real heroes who had been in it, and could serve as the embodiment of the American fighting spirit. Jack Grantham was their man, she thought. He was the best we had.

They were ushered into the Oval Office for a picture taking session.

As the generals and admirals jockeyed for a position near the president, Johnson took Jack and Holly by their arms and placed them beside him as the cameras started flashing and whirring in a mad minute light show. Jack was a bit overwhelmed by it all but managed to avoid embarrassing himself. He was talking face to face with the President of the United States, and no one could argue that it was not a little intimidating, even to a Medal of Honor winner. The president was taller than Jack, and he sort of leaned over a bit when he spoke to him.

"Now I want some straight answers, son." Johnson said.

"You've been out there. You've fought in this war. All bullshit aside, how is it going out there?"

Jack was surprised by Johnson's bluntness and that he would ask Jack's opinion about the war. He wasn't sure just what to say. "It's tough, Mister President," Jack said. "A lot of the men feel that there is no clear-cut plan to win the war, that all we are trying to do is run up the body count without really trying to win the war."

"But what do you, think, Major? Can we win this war?"

Jack thought for quite some time and then bit his lip and spoke, in what he hoped would he a clear, concise appraisal of the situation. "No, sir," he said. "I don't think we can win the war with our current policies."

The president was less shocked than Jack had expected he would be. "Can you tell me why you feel that way? All my generals and admirals tell me they see the light at the end of the tunnel. Why do you feel differently about it?"

"Well, sir, we kill the enemy by the thousands. We clear out an area and totally exterminate every Viet Cong we can find and, in a few days, they're back just as strong as ever. It doesn't matter how many we kill or how much technology and firepower we bring against them, they keep on fighting. And the people we are fighting for are no better than the ones we are fighting against, maybe worse in some cases. I don't believe our cause is a noble one. No, sir, I don't believe we can win this war.

"Thank you, Major Grantham," Johnson said. "I appreciate your honesty."

"I might have screwed up," he later told Holly. "I told you not to express any personal opinions about the war, and I did that very thing. I'm not sure how the President took my criticism of his policies."

"If you gave your honest opinion then there is nothing to worry about," Holly told him. "Nobody can blame you for being honest."

But Holly Grantham was naive to the ways of the military. The qualities that made a good soldier in a firefight could quickly ensure his demise in the sordid game of military poli-

tics. The president did not fault Jack for his comments, he rather appreciated the forthrightness. But others had overheard
and the president's subsequent questioning of his commanders, based on what he had heard from the young outspoken
major, caused no small furor among the army's upper echelon.
Jack's stock began to go down. A promotional tour and several
public relations films which were to have featured the Medal
of Honor winner boosting support for the war, were canceled.
And Grantham was told he would no longer be given his
choice of duty stations as had been promised him. He could
see the writing on the wall. Jack decided he would leave the
army when his hitch was up in December. He applied for the
two months leave he had coming, requesting September and
October and June to coincide with Jim's return date, and was
surprised when the army granted it. That would leave him only
two months in the service when his leave was over. "Well," he
told Holly, "fame is fleeting, they say, one day a hero and the
next day a dog."

"It's okay, Jack," she said. "You can come home to California. Maybe this is for the best. You know Daddy wants you
to help him with the newspaper. It's not as if the army is your
only option."

"It's for the best, Holly. I know that. There are a lot of
things I want to do, a lot of things I have to do now."

They drove out to Annapolis to see Mattie and Jim's boys.
The McKennas made a big fuss over Jack, a "war hero in our
home." Charles McKenna was elated. Mattie's mother pulled
her aside, out of earshot of the rest and said, "He's almost as
handsome as James."

"Almost, Mother, almost," Mattie said.

Jack noted that Mattie and Holly were getting along great.
Good, he thought. *That's essential.* If his and Jim's friendship
was to flourish over the coming years, it was critical that the
women got along. He watched them closely, glancing away
from time to time from his conversation with the senator, looking for any sign of female discord that he might detect. He saw
none.

The McKennas presented their two grandsons for Jack and Holly's approval. They were proud of the two baby boys. "Alton, named after James's grandfather," Aimee McKenna explained, "and little Charlie, after Mattie's dad."

"Don't call him Charlie," Jack said. "I don't know how Jim will take that."

They didn't understand at first but, when Jack reminded them that Charlie was what the Viet Cong were called, they apologized profusely.

"It's okay," he said, laughing. "I was kidding. By the time this boy is old enough to know anything about it, the war will be ancient history."

Jack made arrangements to get Mattie and the boys to California in September when Jim came home. Charles wanted to pay for the plane tickets but Jack said no.

"It'll be my present to them," he said. "It'll be something to help them start their new lives."

"There's a man with quality," Charles said, after Jack and Holly had left to go back to Washington. "Just like I knew James was when he first came here. I know quality when I see it in a person and I see something special in that young man. Yes, sir, Jack Grantham will make his mark on this world one day."

Chapter 13

Coming Home

Jim closed his eyes as the DC-8 taxied out to the end of the runway. Another minute or two and they would lift off from Tan Son Nhut, and it would all be over. The madness and the misery would be over. He would not look back. Others were peering out the windows for one last look at Vietnam, but Jim wanted no such memory of this place. From the air, it would look lush, green, and benign. It might evoke pleasant thoughts that would come back to him in later years. He wanted to remember Vietnam as it really was, terrible and dangerous, the land that sent young American boys home to their families in body bags. He wanted to remember the people as they were. Desperate and dirty, ugly little people that murdered each other's children without compassion or mercy. The only things of value he would take with him from Vietnam would be his friendship with Jack Grantham and the memory of his friend Eddie Csaba. That was some consolation. It was enough, he guessed, to compensate for the sacrifice, although friends came and went in life. He would have to save that determination for another time.

The plane was speeding down the runway now, and Jim felt each bump along the way. Trees and buildings and fuel trucks and other support vehicles and personnel were rushing past at ever increasing speed outside, but Jim didn't see them. His eyes remained closed until the wheels cleared the ground and the aircraft smoothed out and began climbing for the sky. A great cheer went up as Vietnam disappeared behind them, disappeared into the recesses of the mind of each man who had fought there and was now fortunate enough to be going home in one piece.

The sound of excited voices awoke Jim from his sleep. There was some commotion in the cabin as men from the right-side seats were trying to look out the left side windows.

"San Francisco," someone was saying.

Jim could see the city off in the distance as the plane banked for approach to San Francisco International Airport. Before he went to Vietnam, he had heard other men talk about this moment in their lives, the moment they first spotted a piece of America after leaving the war. He had never been able to understand the feelings they had tried to convey. It was like most traumatic experiences, he guessed. One could not fully appreciate the sensation until it had happened to him. Now it had happened to Jim. The image of San Francisco, fading in and out through the disseminating clouds over the bay area, caused his heart to beat rapidly and a tightening feeling in his chest and throat. *A piece of America, just a small piece of my country*, he thought, *but enough for now*.

It was strange, a boy from Texas getting misty-eyed at the sight of San Francisco. What would his grandfather say? Grandpa, who hated anything that wasn't in or from Texas, except Mattie, of course, and Eddie Csaba, would have been intrigued by it all.

Another cheer went up when the wheels touched down and there was almost uncontrolled exhilaration among the men on the plane, some headed for their new lives and others to resume their old ones. This was a wonderful time in a man's life, or at least it was for most, a life moment that each would remember forever, some with fondness and others with remorse.

For those who came home to wives and families who were no longer there for them, it was a bittersweet time. For Jim Kemper, though, it was the one event in his life he would always look back on as pivotal. Nothing would ever be as it was before Vietnam. He had indeed lost that innocence Eddie Csaba assured him would not survive the war. From this moment on, he would take things as they came and he would not allow anything to control him. The Warrior had returned. Warrior

One-Seven. Although Jim's nom de guerre, his namesake, was lying in a rusting heap somewhere back in Vietnam, Warrior One-Seven, the man, was back home to take on the world.

Some of the soldiers and Marines from the plane were kneeling down kissing the tarmac as they stepped off the stairs onto American soil, but Jim was too busy looking for Mattie. He spotted her, waving to him from inside the terminal. She was pushing her way through the crowd of people trying to get into the terminal and she shot through the gate with the baby in one arm and the older boy holding onto her hand being pulled along. She stopped and picked Alton up and carried him the rest of the way into her husband's waiting arms. He held the three of them and wouldn't let go. Mattie was crying. She released her grip on the toddler, took Jim's face in her free hand, and kissed him, deeply, almost desperately and would not stop. It was too much for him to take in all at once. His wife, one son he barely knew, and the other son he had never seen until now. He wanted to hold them forever.

"You're beautiful," he told Mattie, "more beautiful than I remember. It seems like it's been ten years since I saw you. The boys are beautiful too." He took both the boys from her and held them up close to him. "I can't believe you call this guy Charlie," he said.

Mattie laughed, that wonderful girlish laugh of hers. "Jack said you wouldn't like that, But Daddy was so happy to have a grandson named after him, and his friends call him Charlie, so I gave in. I hope it's okay."

"That's fine, Mattie, really," Jim said, "where is Jack?"

"I'm right here," a voice from behind him said.

He turned around and there was Major Grantham standing there with a lovely young woman, who was obviously his wife. Jack threw him a snappy salute and Jim instinctively came to attention and returned the salute.

"You didn't think I'd miss this, did you?"

"No, I didn't, Jack. Thank you, thanks for bringing them here, and thanks for being here too. God, this is like a dream. Coming home is just like a dream."

"We've got plans for you guys. It's time you had some fun for a change. We are going to show you San Francisco. Forget about the war. Forget about the army. Forget about everything except having a good time and getting on with your future."

They had dinner at Lefty O'Doul's Irish Pub, a place selected by Jack because of its baseball atmosphere. The first thing Jim noticed when they walked into the place was the display of pictures of Hall of Fame players posted all over the walls.

"I hope this suits your fancy," Jack said. "I picked it out myself.

"Are you kidding? It's great. How's the food?"

"You guys will love it," Jack said. "They have the best food in town."

They argued over who would pick up the check but Jack pulled rank, explaining, "I'm a big-time newspaper man now. This one is on me."

Jim laughed and acquiesced.

Later, they drove down to San Jose to Holly Grantham's parent's house, where Jack and Holly were staying while he was on leave. It was a mansion, Mattie said. Jack explained that Holly's dad was a newspaper publisher and that he did quite well. The paper, The San Jose Examiner, was a little farther to the left than Jack Grantham would have liked but he lived with that. His father-in-law was a good-hearted man, despite his political excesses, and Jack thought a lot of both of his wife's parents.

Holly's dad, Sam Dryden, had offered Jack a job on the paper, a job he simply could not turn down. He would move immediately into a management position and assist Sam in the day to day running of the business. In addition to that, he would write a political commentary column and would have complete say so over its content. This was important, Jack thought, knowing Sam Dryden's opposition to the war and his tendency to see things in an anti-government light. Dryden had no sons and the idea of his son-in-law coming into the business, and possibly taking over one day, appealed greatly to him.

"You're not staying in the army?" Jim asked.

"I don't think so." Jack told about his visit to the White House and about his conversation with President Johnson. "The army doesn't want soldiers who question their leader's policies."

"That's the army's loss," Jim said.

"Maybe, but one man doesn't matter much to the army. There is always someone who can do the same job and won't ask questions. I think it's for the best."

Later they had a few drinks and sat around talking about what lay ahead. Their lives and their futures lay ahead of them and what they all hoped would be the beginning of a long bond of friendship between their two families. Jim was pleased that the two women acted like old school chums.

"I know it's a long way from Texas to San Jose," Jack said, but it's only three or four hours on an airplane so we'll see you often."

Holly took Mattie upstairs and showed her the room where she and Jim would he sleeping, and, at about ten o'clock she took both boys to hers and Jack's room to put them to bed.

"The top floor is all yours," she said, "don't worry about the boys. I'll take care of them. You two need to get re-acquainted. "It's been over a year, you know."

"We know," they both said, as they got up and went up-stairs.

Mattie closed the door behind her and leaned against it. "What's the matter?" she asked. "You seem lost."

"I'm a little nervous, I guess. I think I'd convinced myself that this moment would never come. In the past year, I thought about you so much, thought about this time, how it would be and how I would act when it did come. I guess I'm just not real sure what to do."

Mattie reached for the zipper on the side of her dress and undid it then slipped off the shoulder straps and the dress fell to the floor. She stepped out of it and stood there in her half-slip and strapless bra and waited for him to come to her. Jim felt a pang in his stomach, in his solar plexus, not a hunger pang but like a hunger pang, a kind of burning sensation. The same sensation he had felt the first-time Mattie took off her dress for him. He would never get used to it. He didn't want to get used to it. It would always be just like the first time between him and Mattie. He went over to her and kissed her, lightly at first then with more passion. She responded, her desire for him slowly growing in intensity, with the desperation of kisses long overdue.

"You come here often, soldier?" she managed to whisper, between his kisses.

"Not in a long time," he said. "Not in a very long time." He ran his fingers into her hair and clinched it tightly, forcing her head back then kissed her neck passionately. She almost cried out, would have cried out, but his lips covered hers again and she couldn't.

He suddenly stopped and looked her in the eyes intensely. "Nothing's changed, Mattie," he said. "Nothing will ever change."

"I know," she said.

He woke up with her in his arms. She slowly came awake, reached around him, and hugged him tightly. "I guess you're a man of your word, James Kemper," she said.

"How's that?" he said.

"You promised me you wouldn't get killed in Vietnam, and you didn't. I appreciate that."

"Shucks, ma'am, it weren't nuthin,' just a walk in the park."

"Well, I don't want to know about it," she said. "I don't ever want to know about it. I am sorry about your friend Eddie. I know that hurt you very badly."

"Yes, it did. But let's not talk about it."

They spent the next several days touring San Francisco. It was a wonderful time to be alive for Jim and Mattie. San Francisco seemed like a magic city and they both fell in love with it. They agreed that it was fortunate they now had friends living here so they would have an excuse to come back often.

Jack and Holly showed them around for a while and then Jack let them take his car and go it alone. They visited Fisherman's Wharf and rode the trolley cars to Colt Tower. It was the most exciting city they had ever been in. At Golden Gate Park, several scruffy looking men and women were sitting on the grass as Jim and Mattie walked by. They said something that Jim did not hear. Mattie had heard but tried to ignore them. The men, three of them, and two women, looked like hippies to Mattie but they appeared to be more menacing than most of the hippies she had seen. They were yelling again and this time Jim heard and responded.

"What?" he said. "What did you say?"

"How many babies did you kill last week?" one of them said.

"What are you talking about?" Jim said, dumbfounded.

"Come on, Jim," Mattie said, tugging at his arm.

"No, I want to know what that asshole said."

He walked toward the group and one of them got up to face him. An angry sneer came across the man's face as the others prodded him on.

"Show the baby killer, Andy," they yelled. "Kick his war-monger ass."

"What did you say, asshole?" Jim said, his anger rising.

"I said, how many babies did you kill last week?" the man repeated with venom in his voice.

"I never killed anybody that didn't need killing," Jim said, and he hit the man in the face. The man went down and Jim turned to face the other two but they would not move. "You two want any?" he asked.

They remained motionless. Only the women continued yelling obscenities. They must have figured the warmonger would not attack them and they were right.

Jim looked at the unconscious man still lying on the ground and a sudden thought came to him, remembering Alex Colby's erratic behavior. Jim felt a little crazy himself. He went over and took the front of the man's shirt in his hands and pulled his dirty, bearded face right up next to his own. "You don't look so good, Andy," he said very calmly. "Been a rough day, hasn't it?"

Jim was chuckling when he got back to where Mattie and the boys were, and she stared at him warily.

"Sometimes you worry me, Kemper," she said, shaking her head at him.

Back in San Jose, the Granthams had dinner waiting for them. Jim and Mattie were leaving the next day and there was much to discuss. After dinner, they had drinks and Jack motioned for Jim to come into the other room.

"I want to run something by you," he said. "When I was in the White House, I was struck, I mean impressed, by the power, the awesome power that the president has at his command. One man, only one man, can send hundreds of thousands of men to war at the drop of a hat, on a whim, almost, if he chooses to. I felt drawn to the place, you know, like I belonged there."

Jim nodded, and Jack went on. "It hit me just how much good an honest man, a truly honest man could do in that office. I'm not saying President Johnson is a bad president but he has this war to contend with. He's done a lot of good things but I'm afraid the only thing he will be remembered for is the Vietnam War. We should never have gotten involved in this war."

"I agree, Jack, but what would you do about it now? We can't pull out. Wouldn't that be admitting defeat?"

"I don't know, maybe, but that is what I would do. I wouldn't lose any more Americans over there. I don't think it's worth it. I'm going to use the newspaper column to try and stop the war. I think it's that important. I just wanted to know how you felt about it, if you might be against that."

"I'm not very politically opinionated," Jim said. "I think the war is a mistake too but I don't know what the best course of action would be. I guess we just have to trust our leaders. I certainly wouldn't fault you for anything you chose to do about it. That's your business. Our friendship cannot be predicated on total agreement in every matter that we might encounter."

"Good, good," Jack said. "I was hoping you would feel that way. I think I'm going to run for president."

Jim looked stunned. He started to laugh but saw that Jack wasn't joking. "You're only twenty-six years old," he said.

Jack laughed. "I didn't mean in the next election. I mean one day. It will take years of planning and hard work and building a support base. I can use the newspaper to gain a following and support. It can be done, Jim. If a man makes up his mind to do it and he wants it bad enough, he can do it."

"You're serious," Jim said, half amused and half impressed. "You're really serious."

"I'm dead serious, as serious as I've ever been about anything."

"Well, I wish you luck. I don't know of a better man for the job than you. If you ever need any help from a poor humble dairy farmer, just give me a call."

"I'll remember that, old buddy."

"But take some advice, if you will," Jim added. "Don't play the anti-war card too hard. I mean don't turn into one of those idiots who go around flying the flag upside down and making assholes out of themselves. Don't get too radical. Most Americans will support the president in any war because their sons are out there on the line. If you do run for president someday, your biggest asset will be your record in Vietnam. That medal you won will open more doors for you than all the honesty and ability in the world. Don't turn your back on that."

"I won't. I am proud of that."

"Remember," Jim continued. "Courage and duty are still honorable, even in an ignoble cause. What you did in Vietnam was an honorable thing. You saved a lot of lives, including mine."

"Horseshit," Jack said. "You did as much as I did, even more. I had a gun. You were out there without a weapon, trying to save people. You were the one that should have gone to the White House."

"I'm not sure I could have charged over that dike if you had not gone first," Jim said.

"That doesn't matter. What matters is, you did it. That's all that ever matters in life, not what you should have done or could have done, just what you did."

"Well, maybe so," Jim said, "but twenty years from now I wonder if anyone will really care what you and I did in Vietnam."

The next morning, Jack and Holly took them to the airport to catch their plane to Dallas. The Kempers planned to spend some time with Allie and her family. They would then fly to Maryland to load up all of Mattie's and the boy's belongings in a U-Haul truck for the trip home to the farm. Allie would be happy to have her son back and the McKennas would be sad but happy that their son-in-law had come home from the war in one piece, although they would be losing their daughter and the two grandsons they practically worshipped.

Chapter 14

The Farm

1967-1977:

Comanche County, in central Texas was named after the Comanche Indians, whose territory once included the area. It covered 944 square miles of rolling hills, ranging in elevation from 650 feet to 1700 feet. Annual rainfall was around eighteen inches, making it an excellent locale for farming, which produces a variety of agricultural products including peanuts, pecans, grains, and hay. Beef, dairy cattle, hogs, sheep, and goats were raised in abundance.

The area was first settled in 1854 when a colony was established by a man named Jesse Mercer on land granted to Stephen F. Austin by Mexico. Cattle ranching became the most important economic activity up until the time of the Civil war. When the army pulled out to join the hostilities Back East, the settlers were left virtually without defense against Indian raids. Most of the white population fled and by 1866 there were only about sixty people in the region.

Once the soldiers returned after the war, the settlers did likewise and by 1870, the county was again booming. There were over a hundred farms, covering 17,000 acres. The area continued to boom until the 1930s when Great Depression and the Dust Bowl brought much hardship to local residents. Most had to watch helplessly as their land simply blew away. The droughts of the 1950s demanded a long-term solution to the county's water problems. Federal funding became available in 1960 and work was begun on construction of a reservoir on the

Leon River. By 1967, Proctor Lake was completed and began providing water for the farming communities of Comanche, De Leon, and other towns in the County.

The city of Comanche was established in 1858 when a man named John Duncan donated 240 acres as a site for the County Seat. A post office was built in 1860 and the local newspaper, The Comanche Chief, began business in 1873.

It was along Duncan Creek, named after the man who had donated the land for the town, that Alton Kemper began to work the 100-acre dairy farm, with a dozen cows that he and his wife Mary had inherited from Alton's father-in-law, James McCarthy in 1922. They, and their newborn son, James, lived in the small wood frame house that came with the property, along with a barn, a smoke house, and a windmill. He was thirty years old and had aspirations of turning the farm into a successful business that would support his family in a manner he thought appropriate. The work was hard and unrewarding, but he managed to scratch out a living. He did, at least, until the depression years of the 1930s when he was forced to take what work he could find in town, or on other farms in the county, just to make ends meet.

The war years, however, were good for the Kempers and, despite the loss of his son and his subsequent breakdown over the loss, Alton managed to prosper. By the late fifties, the little farm was becoming more productive, and Alton was starting to make improvements in the facilities and to purchase additional land to increase his herd size. His grandson Jim came and helped him on the farm every summer between school years and the extra labor was much needed, although migrant workers were readily available, and Alton used them on occasion.

It was at this time that Alton hired a man named Danny Carlisle, a local farm worker and handy man, to assist him on a regular basis. Carlisle had fallen into some disfavor with Alton's neighbors because he drank a little too much. Danny's wife had died in '56, and he just couldn't seem to get over it. Alton certainly understood how a loss like that could affect a man.

The farm house had an extra room, off the main house across a breezeway, and Alton offered to let Danny live in the room. He saw something in the man that no one else did, and Danny responded. He turned out to be a good worker and a smart man as well. In time, he became Alton's right hand man and good friend.

Danny was instrumental in securing a contract for the Kemper farm to provide milk exclusively for all the school systems in Comanche and Mills Counties. They still would have to have a company package the product for them because they had no means to perform that function. But it was nevertheless a boon for the dairy. It turned out to be a very lucrative deal for them, but a mystery to Alton Kemper as to how Danny had managed to pull it off.

"My wife's sister knows some folks on the school boards," was all he would say. Alton let it go at that and accepted his good fortune without any further questioning.

An opportunity came along to more than double the size of the farm and further increase the size of Alton's herd. A man named Jess Sprouse had a farm just on the other side of Duncan Creek and was ready to sell. He offered the property to Alton first, and Danny suggested they buy the land. Alton went to the bank, got a loan, and made the purchase. Danny would live in the house on the Sprouse farm and they started making plans to purchase more cows.

When Jim returned from Vietnam in June of 1967, four months after his grandfather's death, he found the farm very different from the place he remembered. It was bustling with activity like he had never seen before. Danny's hired men were hard at work, herding in groups of cows to be milked. Some were transporting the product to refrigerated holding tanks, while others filled the feeding troughs, and cleaned up the abundance of waste material created by the bovine creatures. It was a never ending, seven days a week, operation that required constant replenishing of materials and feed and attention to the cows.

"Cows don't take off on Sunday," Danny said. "They have to be milked every day."

The very first thing Jim did was sign over the ten acres that his grandfather had promised to Danny. Danny had cleared Alton's things out of the farmhouse and had made it ready for the new Kemper family. It was comfortable, but small and, with two little boys running around, it was going to be a challenge for Mattie. Jim knew he would have to build a new house for them to live in.

"I'm at a loss, Danny," he said. "There is so much going on here, I'm lost. I just realized how little I actually know about this farm and about the dairy business. You'll have a lot to teach me, if you are willing, that is."

"It's not hard," Danny said. "Your grandfather taught me just about everything I know. It will take time, but you'll learn."

"Let's sit down and talk about this. I need to find out what your long-term plans are, and I'm sure you want to know what I have in mind. I know this may be awkward for both of us. I just want to make sure there are no misunderstandings between us.

Some time back, Alton and Danny had bought a small trailer house, and set it up next to the house, to be used for an office. Two desks, some file cabinets, and a few chairs were the only furniture in the office. "Alton finally got a telephone in the house and I had one put in here so I didn't have to drive to town every time I needed to ask somebody something.

"I'm surprised," Jim said, laughing. "Grandpa always said he had no use for telephones."

"He adapted. He had to," Danny said. "It just got too big for us to run it like the old days. We've got five hundred cows now, Jim, that's a lot of work and a lot of responsibility."

"I had no idea." Jim studied the older man as Danny continued speaking. At thirty-five, Danny was not a handsome man but neither was he unpleasant in appearance. He was taller than Jim, maybe three or four inches, and his curly blond hair was usually matted from dust and sweat. His nose was slightly too large and pointed, and it dominated his face. Danny was not shy and had never given Jim the impression that he was intimidated by anyone or anything. His friendship with

Alton Kemper, despite their age difference, had become almost legendary in the county and that told him all he needed to know about the man. Alton treated Danny almost like he was another grandson. He trusted him that much.

"We profit about seventy-five cents per cow per day. That comes to $375.00 a day, seven days a week, or more accurately, $2,624.00 a week. Some of the profit goes to improvement of the facilities, how much just kind of depends on what our needs are. I guess, from here on out, that will be your decision. Alton has a profit sharing plan set up for all the permanent workers, myself included, and it seems to have been working out well. Our guys all seem pretty content."

"My gosh, I had no idea this farm could generate that much money."

"It can be a lot better," Danny said. "I'd like to talk to you about putting in a pipeline. That's a conduit system that takes the milk from the milking machines directly to the holding tanks, saves a lot of labor."

"I've thought about this ever since I got out of the army, while I was moving the family here from Maryland. What I'd like to do, Danny, is offer you part ownership in the dairy. It's obvious that you know this business, and you helped my grandfather build it to what it is today. I want to turn this into the biggest dairy in Texas. I can't do that without you. What are your thoughts on that?"

"Well, I'd like that very much—it's not necessary—"

"No, I think it is," Jim interjected. "I think that is what I have to do to make this thing work the way I want it to work. I don't want you working for me, I want us both working for us."

"We have the means here to do that," Danny responded. "Can I make a suggestion, though?"

"Sure, what is it?"

"Alton always wanted you to finish your education at the university. My suggestion is that you go back and finish your last year and get that business degree. I think it will help us in the future, I mean with the bankers and high rollers. They place a lot of importance on a business degree. It'll open some doors for you, believe me."

"You really think so?"

"I know so, Jim," Danny said. "Alton helped me take some classes at Tarleton and it made a big difference for me. I learned a lot—about feed mixtures, additives, and all kinds of things. You're only a year away from a degree. It'd be a waste not to see it through."

"Well, let me talk to Mattie about it and see what she says. I agree with you that it might be helpful to us. Anyway, about that partnership, I'm thinking of twenty-five percent owner-ship in the business as it is now, all assets, tools, equipment and land…except for five acres around Grandpa's house. I want to build us a new house, one big enough for my family. We'll incorporate and the twenty-five percent shares of stock will be yours to do with as you will. My only stipulation would be that, if you decide to sell out in the future, you will sell it to me at the fair market value."

"I won't ever sell it, Jim," Danny said.

"I hope not, but people sometimes change their minds."

"I won't."

"Then we are agreed."

"That is more than generous of you, Jim. You just told me I'm going to be rich someday. Yes—we are agreed."

"Okay, then I will have the lawyer draw up the paperwork and we will get on with this thing. I'd like to call it Kemper Farms, if that's okay with you. I plan to expand."

"Absolutely, Kemper Farms, it is. Thank you, Jim."

"No, Danny, thank you."

They shook hands and the Kemper-Carlisle partnership was an entity. "Oh, one more thing, I see that my grandfather was paying you four dollars an hour but you never charged more than forty hours a week, and I am told you work a lot more than forty hours. I'd like to put you on salary at, say, two hun-dred fifty dollars a week, if that is okay. It's easier to budget with salaries, and I don't want you working long hours for no pay."

"That's more than fine, Jim. Thanks again."

Jim decided to take Danny's advice and return to the University of Texas to finish his last year of business administration. It would mean living in Austin and staying away from home at least four days a week, for a school year. He could rent an apartment and bring Mattie and the boys with him some of the time and come home on the weekends.

His most pressing need at the moment was a house for the family to live in. The old house was just not big enough and was too hard to heat and cool. When he was growing up, it had never occurred to him that the house was small. But, now, he wanted a proper house for Mattie and the boys, a house with plenty of room to grow. A call to his stepfather, Trenton Hargrove, produced a contractor from Dallas who was willing to come and stay at the farm for the next two months, get the slab work done, and complete the framing.

By the end of August, the structure was up and dried-in. Jim contracted with a local plumber to do the plumbing work, and Trenton brought an electrician, a man named Tom Wilcox, down from Dallas to do the wiring. Jim paid everything out of pocket, preferring not to finance the construction with a lender. He still recalled adding up in his head the cost of the house in Arlington, that Trenton had financed on the GI Bill, and vowing that he would never do that. His future business ventures would soon change his mind on the need to finance projects. But for his own home, he wanted it paid for when they moved in.

The dairy owned a pickup truck, but it was used for business and Jim had only one vehicle, the Tempest, which was still in pretty good shape, but he had to leave for school the first of September so he needed a car for Mattie. He decided on a Ford Bronco, rather than a car, so it could be used to haul stuff around on the farm.

"Go see Bill Clemens at Clemens Ford in town. Alton bought the truck from Bill and he did him right," Danny told him.

So Jim did as Danny had suggested. He paid $2,600.00 cash for the Bronco and let Mattie drive it home.

"When I get finished with school, I'll buy you a new car,"

he told her. "And I'll drive the Bronco. But for now, it will be more use to you than it will to me."

With help from Danny, Mattie would oversee the interior finish out of the house, selecting the paint colors, the cabinets and floor finishes, doors, etc. The house would be Mattie's house, and she threw herself into the job, helping the workers when she could, and often annoying them, but they got the job done.

Austin had not changed much in four years, at least not in appearance, but Jim had certainly changed. His mind was drawn momentarily to Laura and the time they spent together there. He resisted the temptation to drive by her apartment, and he did not go to Threadgill's. He did not wish to dwell on the past. He went to see Mrs. Gutterman, the owner of the rooming house where he had stayed before and was told by one of the tenants that she had passed away just this past year and that her grandson now owned the place.

Lot of that going around, Jim thought. He was blowing through his grandfather's money pretty quickly. What with building the new house and buying a truck, not to mention going to school full time and using his share of the dairy profits as his only means of income, he was feeling a little guilty. But they had a plan, he and his grandfather had a plan, and now he and Danny Carlisle had a plan. Jim was driven to make that plan work. The class work was easy but the time away from home was excruciating. It seemed to drag on forever. He looked forward to the weekend trips back to the farm when he could spend time with his boys, help Mattie with the new house, and continue learning the dairy business from Danny.

Contractors were busy installing milk pipelines in the two barns currently owned by Kemper Farms, and Danny was having a third barn built next to the one on the Sprouse Farm that Alton had bought several years back. With these new facilities and tools, they would be able to double their production as soon as they could acquire more cows. The normal birthrate of the *company cows* was not nearly sufficient to supply their need so Danny and Jim went to local auctions to make purchases when Jim was at home on the weekends. His schedule was grueling and Jim longed for the day he would be through with school and would have his degree.

By November the house was almost complete. Mattie was putting the final touchups on the paint, cleaning and waxing the hardwood floors, and buying new furniture. It would be ready in time for a Christmas party, and Jim planned to invite everyone down from Dallas and friends from around the area for a housewarming and Christmas get together.

The finished product was a marvel to behold, a classic two-story country estate with a walk-around porch that almost completely circumvented the entire house. It was a 3,000 square foot structure with stately columns supporting the porch roof and a steeple window that provided the foyer with natural light.

The entry was dominated by the stairway that led to the second floor bedrooms and directed those entering the house into a giant great room which, in turn, faced the kitchen and dining rooms. The Master Bedroom was on the first floor. Upstairs there were three bedrooms that shared a bath. The children would live upstairs.

When a final accounting was done, Jim learned that they had spent almost $20,000.00 on the home, quite a bit more than he'd expected, but he figured Grandpa Alton would approve and it was, after all, going to be their home forever, so he was okay with it.

Christmas was a happy time at the Kemper Farm. The Hargroves drove down from Dallas and Mattie's folks flew in from Maryland. Jim met them at Love Field and drove them to the farm. Charles McKenna was fascinated with Texas and with the farm he had heard so much about from his daughter. Jim took him on a guided tour of the property.

"We have five-hundred cows now," Jim told his father-in-law. "And we are planning to buy more. They walked out to one of the barns and Jim pointed to the stainless-steel conduit system that ran down both sides and through the middle of the building. We've just installed pipeline to carry the milk from the milking machines to the holding tanks. That cuts our labor dramatically."

Charles looked at the equipment admiringly. "I am taken completely by surprise, Jim," he said. "I guess I had a picture in my mind of a small farm with a few cows and a plow. You have a booming industry here."

"It will be one day," Jim said. "We're planning to expand, buy some more property, and install more facilities. Eventually, I want to package our own products and have our own brand name. This dairy will be more than even my grandfather ever imagined. I've got a lot of ideas on branching out into some other areas too, when I finish this year at school. Danny Carlisle, my partner, has an idea to build a feed and farm supplies store in town, and I want to sell equipment there too—you know, tractors, combines, and stuff like that."

"I want to tell you something, Jim." Charles McKenna stopped for a minute.

It almost appeared to Jim that the older man was going to choke up.

"I want to tell you how proud I am to have you for my son-in-law. I have to confess I was skeptical at first when Mattie said she had met a soldier. Then when I met you, I changed my mind, of course. But we were all so afraid you wouldn't make it home from Vietnam. Well, I'm just glad you did, and I am proud that you married Mattie."

"Thank you, Charles, I appreciate that. If it had not been for Mattie, though, I wouldn't have had much to come home to. This farm would have been useless to me without her and the boys—without all of you, for that matter. Mattie is my inspiration. Everything I do and plan to do is for her."

"You're both very lucky. We are all very fortunate for life's blessings. Keep in mind, I am not without influence in Annapolis and to some lesser degree in Washington. If I can ever be of help to you then, as they say, do not hesitate to ask."

"I won't hesitate a bit, thanks for the offer," Jim replied.

The Hargroves showed up on Saturday before Christmas. Trent was with them but Jim's sister Sarah was not.

"Where is Sarah?" Jim asked. "Surely you didn't leave her in Dallas, did you?"

"No," Allie explained. "Sarah is coming down with her

boyfriend, Tom Wilcox, the young man who wired your house for you."

"Boyfriend, "Jim said, frowning "Isn't Sarah a little young to have a boyfriend?"

"She's seventeen," Allie said.

"Doesn't seem right," he said.

Allie laughed. "You act more like her father than her brother."

"I guess I just lost track of how old she is," he added. "How old is this Tom Wilcox?"

"Tom is twenty years old," Allie said. "And he is a very nice boy. He reminds me of you—very ambitious. He wants to start his own business one day. Tom is very respectful. Trenton approves of him going with Sarah."

"Well, okay, Mother, if Trenton approves of him, I guess it's okay with me. When are they coming?"

"They'll be here tomorrow. Tom had to work today."

Jim's brother, Trent, was sixteen years old and almost as tall as he was. Trent quickly retrieved his ball and glove from the car and asked his older brother to play some catch.

"But I don't have a glove," Jim said. "I must have left it in Vietnam."

"Yes, you do," Trent yelled, "I brought your old glove with us just in case."

He still had the old heat on the ball. Trent's glove popped as he fielded each throw from his brother and slung it right back to him. They played for over an hour, and Jim told his stepfather to take a few, but Trenton begged off. "I'm getting too old to be taking hits from a major leaguer."

"I'm not a major leaguer," Jim said, "more of a sand lotter."

"You are in my book, Jim," Trenton said. "You'll always be a major leaguer in my book."

The women all pitched in to prepare Christmas dinner while the men hung around outside discussing politics and business. Jim took Charles McKenna aside, and they talked about his long-term plans to branch out into other industries.

"Look into prefab housing, Jim," his father-in-law advised him. "It's a coming thing—decent housing, easy to install, and affordable to poorer folks."

"Prefab, how does that work?" Jim asked.

"It's a simple two or three-bedroom house built in two sections. They are shipped together and put together on site. The slab is prepared beforehand, of course. The electrical system is in place and the walls are already paneled or sheet-rocked. You have to have an electrician to connect the wiring to the electrical service, and a plumber too, of course.

"That's sounds interesting, Charles," Jim said. "I might just look into that when I get the feed store business operating. Thanks, I appreciate that."

The feed store and farm supply store was a high priority on Jim's list. The county had a real need for such a facility, and Jim was convinced that it was a good investment. He'd have to stop by the city office to find out if there were any zoning issues or other regulations that would prevent his building on the property that he wanted to acquire for that purpose.

The women were announcing that dinner was ready so everyone started heading for the house. It was a lavish feast of baked ham and turkey, sweet potatoes, mashed potatoes, green peas, okra, cornbread dressing and hot rolls with giblet gravy. Mattie had insisted that they make the dining room exceptionally large for just such occasions. The table was hand crafted by a local carpenter, recommended by Danny Carlisle, and designed so that rather than being rounded on the ends it was angled at the corners to offer four additional seating positions. The massive table would seat sixteen people.

Jim had already planned the seating arrangements and made the announcement. "I want the two dads, the patriarchs of the clan, Charles and Trenton, at the heads of the table," he began. "I will sit to the left of Trenton and Mattie will sit to the left of her dad. My mother will please sit to the right of her husband and Mrs. McKenna will please be so kind to take the same position next to hers. I'd like for Danny to sit in the middle on either side, to referee."

There was some chuckling at the seriousness with which Jim seemed to be conducting the task he had assigned himself. There was not a small degree of shuffling around as each person assumed their designated spaces. Alton and little Charlie were served at a small table that was placed in the corner of the dining room just for them.

"Now," Jim continued. "Hargroves, and guests," he said, looking at Sarah's boyfriend, Tom Wilcox. "Sit wherever you can find a seat, you're on your own."

They all laughed at that and soon the food was being passed around the table and the digging in had begun. The first Christmas at the Kemper Farm, in the new house and with the new generation, began a tradition that Jim and Mattie would treasure for the rest of their lives.

After dinner, Jim asked Tom Wilcox to step outside. Jim's intention was to size the boy up and see what he was like. "You did a good job on the house wiring, Tom," Jim said. "Do you work for yourself or for a contractor?

"I work for a small company in Dallas," Tom answered. "I can't work for myself until I get my master license. Right now, I'm just a journeyman electrician. A journeyman has to work under a master for four years before he can take the master's test."

"I see," Jim said. "Have you ever wired any prefab houses?"

"No, sir, I haven't, but I've heard they're pretty simple. The connections, between the pieces of the house, are made in the attic and usually a hundred-amp service is all you need on one of them."

"That is my understanding too," Jim said. "I'm thinking about building prefab houses.

Would you be able to wire them for me, you know in a factory situation?"

"Oh, sure, I could do that. Wiring a house is simple, but I'd need a few helpers, depending on how fast you put them out."

"I understand," Jim said. "We'll get all the help you need, I'd let you hire your own people. Think about it if you will. It may be a year or so but perhaps by then you'll have your master license and may want to start your own company."

"I will think about it. Thanks, Mister Kemper."

Tom was not an overly handsome boy, Jim decided, but he was pleasantly congenial and honest. He seemed to be likable. If his sister Sarah liked him, that was a good sign.

Tom stood about five-eight and weighed around 160 pounds, Jim estimated. His frame would almost guarantee that Tom would be fat when he got older, if he didn't work hard to prevent it.

သာသာ

The Comanche city office was located on the south side of the square across from the courthouse. The office was administered by an old friend of Alton Kemper's, a man named John Beaty. Beaty was a tall man, extremely tall, and a good-looking man, whose size and intimidating appearance belied his good-natured congeniality.

Jim found Beaty sitting at his desk. When he saw Jim, Beaty stood up and extended his arm and the two men shook hands. "Jim Kemper," he said. "I'm surprised I recognized you, I haven't seen you since you were a kid. You look a lot like your grandfather, though. How have you been?"

"I've been fine, John, thanks. I've been meaning to come and see you. But I spent the past year at school, and it's really getting busy at the farm."

"I bet it is," he said. "There is never a lack of work on a dairy farm. So you finished your degree at Texas?"

"I did. Now I'm ready to embark on some things and I thought I'd come and talk to you. Grandpa always told me that if I ever needed to know anything to talk to either you or Kinnie Sullivan. What I need now involves you, so here I am."

"I appreciate that. Alton was a good friend. I wish I could have seen him more often before he died but it always seems that we all get caught up in our own lives and never really get around to what's most important. I'll help you any way I can, Jim. What do you need?"

"First, I want to build a building out on the Fort Worth Highway. It's going to be a pretty big building, about forty-thousand square feet. I need to know what the city needs as far as plans and inspection fees."

"Comanche has no building inspections," Beaty said. "No plan review either. You can pretty much do as you please. You will have to pay property taxes, of course. I expect your insurance company will make an inspection to ensure that the building is safe. But as far as we're concerned, there are no regulations. What are you going to use the building for?"

"I'm going to start a feed business. I'm also thinking about getting into farm equipment sales and rental. I may have to start slow, depending on financing. But that is where I eventually intend to be with it."

"I think that's a fine idea," Beaty said. "Now everyone has to go to Brownwood or Stephenville to rent farm equipment. I think that's a real good idea. But don't wait too long, or else someone may do it first. Business is booming in the county."

"I won't," Jim answered. "Grandpa always said you have to do everything today because tomorrow never comes."

Beaty laughed. "That reminds me of a story I told Alton once when he said that very thing. When I was a kid, my mother always cut my hair. Well, this one time, I didn't want to get my hair cut so I asked her if I could get it cut tomorrow instead. She didn't go for it, at first, but I kept on and finally she said okay. Well, the next day she told me to get ready for my haircut and I reminded her that she had agreed to do it tomorrow. I told her that tomorrow never comes."

Jim laughed. "My mother would not have bought that for a minute," he said.

"Neither did mine," Beaty said, and they both laughed.

Jim got up to leave, satisfied with the information he'd received. Beaty walked him to the door. "Good luck on your new adventure, Jim," he said.

"Thanks, John," Jim said. "John, I need to ask you—just how tall are you? I swear. I could get a crick in my neck from standing next to you."

"I'm six foot six and a half," Beaty said. "I just never stopped growing."

"Did you ever play basketball?"

"I did, in high school, and I had a scholarship to play in college—should have gone, but my dad had a peanut farm at the time and he needed help so I passed on the scholarship. It's one of my regrets but I did what I thought I should at the time.

"Too bad, but you did the right thing for your family," Jim said. "Well thanks for everything. My grandfather always liked you. I'll stop in from time to time just to talk."

"I'll look forward to that," Beaty said.

Jim contracted with a company out of Fort Worth to build the metal building that would house the feed store. It would be just a basic steel frame with metal siding. A wood frame office was put up in the back of the store and several cash registers at the front near the double wide roll up door. Rows of shelving, about thirty in all, would present the product to potential customers and an enormous covered lot out back would house the farm equipment and provide additional storage for any overflow from the store. A new sign at the street welcomed the buying public to "Kemper Feed and Supply."

Jim had originally figured on financing everything out of pocket, but he quickly discovered, after getting all his quotes in, that his pocket was not deep enough, not nearly deep enough. He found he would need two-hundred thousand dollars to open the doors. The dairy was not producing enough money at that time to float his dream very far. So, he violated a principle he'd had vowed he would never violate. He would have to get financing.

The only businessman he knew was his maternal grandfather, George Matthews, and Matthews had a thriving leather goods business with branches all over Texas. Jim had never been close to the Matthews, and he was reluctant to seek advice from his mother's father. Instead, he went to Trenton who managed one of George Matthews's stores in Dallas.

Trenton took Jim to see Abel Hansen who owned Hansen Trust and Investments in Dallas. Hansen Trust financed all of George Matthews's business ventures and had helped him grow the little factory in Comanche into a booming concern.

To his dismay, Jim would have to put the Farm and house as collateral. It was the last thing he wanted to do, and his naiveté had sheltered him from reality. Nevertheless, he had a plan and so he entrusted Abel Hansen with his affairs, and the funds were made available in an escrow account to begin the construction.

There were more time-consuming matters involved in the construction of a building than he had foreseen. Sub-contractors were usually smaller companies that were almost always on a tight budget. Jim started getting requests for pay-ment as soon as some of the installers were through with their work. He had to submit invoices to the bank and then wait for the inspector to approve the work that had been billed for. Then payment would be made. This process sometimes took forty-five days, and Jim was forced, by himself alone, to front some of them operating capital until bank payments were made.

Tom Wilcox took a leave of absence from his regular job and did the electrical work on a labor-only basis. He made ma-terial lists and Jim bought the material out of pocket. Tom stayed at the farm during the project and that gave Jim a chance to get to know him a little better.

Jim found Tom to be an honest boy. Using his inherited abilities of discernment, passed on from his mother and grand-father, Jim knew that his most likely future brother-in-law was an individual with whom he would do business one day. The wheels were already turning in Jim's head as he watched Tom work. The steadiness and professionalism with which he ap-proached everything he did, impressed Jim and, before the feed supply store was even open for business, he was planning his next adventure.

"How long will it be until you can get your master license, Tom?" Jim asked him.

"Well, I've been a journeyman for two years so I'll have to wait another two years, then I have to pass the test. I plan to take some classes to help me with that. Why, are you wanting to do the pre-fab housing right away?"

"No, not necessarily," Jim replied. "I'm just doing some thinking. I expect it will be at least a year before I want to move on anything. I was just curious about the process."

"I have to have four years of documented experience from the company I work for," Tom said. "I'm not ready, though. There is still a lot I have to learn yet. I would appreciate you keeping me in mind, Mister Kemper."

"You can call me Jim," he said."

"I'm not sure I can do that, Mister Kemper," Tom said, "but I'll try.

The feed supply store opened for business officially in August of 1968. Product was still being delivered, and Jim had traveled to all the major farm equipment manufacturers to price and pick options on tractors, plows, and combines He ended up buying only one combine, due to the price, for rental purposes.

The Ford Company representative came to visit and made the case for Ford tractors. "The Ford Three Thousand is an all-purpose agricultural tractor, which the company began producing in 1965, and is the best tractor in the business," he said. "Some were made in Belgium," he continued, "and some were made in England."

There was an American produced model, the model C. and Jim ordered four of them, along with four John Deere, two model 4230s and two 4320s. He also bought two International Harvesters for a total of ten tractors, at a total price of just under twenty thousand dollars.

Seven of the tractors would be for the rental operation and the other three, one of each brand would be for display only. The three companies, from which he had bought the tractors, in exchange for the advance purchases, offered Jim a good markdown multiplier for future purchases and promised quick delivery, dropped ship to a designated location.

Jim also bought a small forklift to move product to the shelves, and for deposit into a customer's vehicle. Stocking the place with all the various brands of feed and seed and other miscellaneous items of use to farmers and homeowners came to right at fifty thousand dollars.

He planned to increase the in-house maximum quantities when the initial stock was sold out. Hopefully, it would not be very long.

Jim had planned ahead for the employment situation. They would use school kids during the summer and after school during the school year, strong boys, typically, because lifting feed sacks all day long was hard work. Comanche High School would provide a good portion of his labor force. He would pay them a dollar an hour, a little more than they would willingly work for but Jim wanted dependable and responsible kids who would show up for work on time and would be honest and hard working. He didn't want screw-ups or screw-offs.

Cashiers were pretty easy to come by. Jim hired three away from local stores with a quarter an hour increase in pay, and a better opportunity for advancement. Advancement to what, he wasn't sure just yet, but he did have long-term plans for all his employees' future well-being. A greater problem, however, was finding a manager for the store. It would be impossible to entice someone to move from Dallas to Comanche, Texas, for a job that paid less than a hundred dollars a week, so he ran an ad in the Tarleton University newspaper, over in Stephenville, for a business manager.

One interview after another left him cold. He desperately needed a good manager, to free him up to help Danny at the dairy, but as one liberal arts major after another failed to impress him with their over-inflated opinion of their own value, he was on the verge of giving up and just doing the job himself. That's when he got a call from one Emma Sue Brown, requesting to interview for the job. Jim had not considered that a woman might apply for the job. He was just old fashioned enough to find it a bit strange, but nevertheless he told her to come on in.

Emma Sue Brown, and she went by Emma Sue, proved to be a bit of an enigma. At five feet nine inches and about a hundred and twenty pounds, Emma Sue cut a nice figure. She dressed well. Jim noted that she wore a dress to the interview and, apparently, had taken good care of herself. Her short brown hair gave her a boyish look, and she didn't smile broadly, as did most females he'd encountered in his life. Emma was not noticeably pretty, but neither was she homely. Sort of common looking, she was, Jim thought, but that would not interfere with her work. In fact, it might be a help to her in running the store. He didn't imagine any of the guys making a big play for her.

Jim introduced himself and they shook hands as he directed her to follow him into the office. "Have a seat Ms. Brown," he said, motioning to the chair on the other side of his desk, and she sat down across. "So, what do I call you, Emma?" he asked her.

"My folks always called me Emma Sue, sir, and it sort of stuck. I know it sounds countrified, but I haven't been able to shake it off."

"Nothing wrong with that," he said, chuckling. "It's a nice name and if it was good enough for your folks, then it should be good enough for the rest of the world. So, tell me your qualifications for a management position. You see what we have here. It's pretty simple actually. You would be in charge of maybe five workers, mostly kids, at any given time, and three or four cashiers, in rotating shifts depending on the need."

"I worked in my dad's drug store while I was growing up," Emma told him. "We had a similar number of employees. I worked full time during the summer, and weekends during school. I took care of the inventory, ordering whatever was needed, and scheduling the help. I have been going to Tarleton for the last two years. I just got my associate degree in business management."

"How about working with people? Did your age, and being a girl, ever cause any problems for you?"

"A couple of times, yes," she said, shifting slightly in her seat. He could tell the question made her uncomfortable.

"I'm not trying to put you on the spot," Jim said, "but it is a possibility that some guy could get all butt-hurt over having to take orders from a woman. It's just something we'll need to be prepared for."

"I know. I got through it okay. My dad taught me some things about dealing with people so I could prevent that from happening, rather than so much how to handle it after it had happened. He told me to not give orders, or at least not to shout orders at people, I would always ask a person to do this or that and not tell them to do it."

"Right," Jim said, nodding his head. "My grandfather had a similar manner. He would go up to a worker, put his hand on the man's shoulder, and call his name. Then he'd say, 'Can you get me this or that, or we need to get this or that done.' They never seemed to mind doing what he asked them to do."

"Exactly," Emma said, "you put them at ease and avoid making them feel like it's a superior and subordinate situation."

"Did you ever have to fire anyone?"

"I never did," she said. "I'm not sure how I would handle it. It can't be a fun thing. I suppose I'd try to be as professional as possible. If it comes to that, I might have to ask you to help me with it."

Jim laughed. "I'll tell you a secret, but don't tell anyone, I've never had to do it either. I guess we'll learn together.

Emma Sue laughed at that. "I think if you catch an employee stealing or doing some other serious offense, it would not be as difficult as if someone just was not able to do the job."

Jim agreed. "I think the trick is," he told her. "If it has to be done, I mean if there is absolutely no way around it, then don't wait so long that it becomes fun to do. That's just not fair to either the employee or the business."

Jim knew he was going to hire Emma Sue Brown right then but he wanted to display some professionalism, if only to himself. "Well, Emma Sue, everything looks good," he said, "give me a couple of days, and I'll be in touch. I want to talk this over with my business partner and work out a few details, so I'll get back you by the end of the week."

She thanked him, and they shook hands. She left. Jim wondered if his first impression was right again. It always had been in the past but hiring a woman to manage a business that was essentially a man's business was a big chance to take. Granted, Emma was by far the most qualified of all the applicants he'd interviewed, and that was really all that mattered. But he wanted to run it by Mattie and Danny just for their input.

The milk delivery system was just about complete, and the contractors were checking and testing the motors and valves and all the miscellaneous moving parts and electrical connections. Soon they would double their output of milk and have to expand the bottling plant. Fortunately, Grandpa and Danny had established a really good line of credit with the bank and financing improvements on the dairy was not a problem. But he'd used the farm as collateral for the feed supply business, so it would be essential that he pay down that loan as quickly as possible.

He addressed that issue with Danny in their weekly meeting and assured him that the loan would not hinder dairy operations. Danny seemed unconcerned about it but did ask Jim about hiring one of his nephews, his sister's son, as a salesman for the dairy products. The boy had just graduated from Texas Tech with a degree in marketing. Danny believed he could be of help in getting the product into more markets in Texas and other states as well.

Jim agreed. "Let me know how he does," he said. "If your nephew is anything like you, I'm sure he can help us a lot."

"He's very smart and very ambitious. I'd like to give him a try."

"Then let's do it," Jim replied. "Don't look back. When can he start?"

"I'll let you know," Danny said. "Right away I hope. Oh, there is one more thing. Marcus is half Mexican. My sister is married to a Mexican, I mean he's an American, of Mexican descent, but a good man, so is Marcus." Danny looked at Jim, not sure what his response might be to hiring a Mexican for such an important position.

"Well, hell, Danny," Jim said, "I married a Yankee. I don't care who or what a man is, as long as he is responsible and honest. I know you would not recommend someone who is not. Hiring your nephew is your decision. If we can't help out our families, and help ourselves in the process, what good are we?"

"Thanks Jim," Danny said, relieved that his proposal was well accepted. "I'll get him down here."

Jim told Mattie about Emma Sue Brown, and the look on her face told him that he had made the right decision. "You're an amazing man, James," she said. "Most men would be afraid to hire a woman in such a position.

"She's the best man for the job," he said, laughing.

Jim made the call to his soon-to-be-manager. "Emma Sue?" he asked, when he heard her voice on the phone."

"Yes," she responded. "This is Emma Sue.

"This is Jim Kemper, when can you start to work?

❦

In July of 1968, Mattie announced that she was going to have another baby. She was wrong, as it turned out, because the doctor later confirmed that she was pregnant with twins.

"Two for the price of one," her husband said.

"You're always looking to cut corners, aren't you, James?"

And on March twelfth of 1969, Mattie Kemper presented her family with two brand new baby girls at Blackwood Hospital in Comanche. Both mother and father decided that there were only two possible names for the two newest Kempers. They would name them Allison, after Jim's mother, and Aimee, after Mattie's mother. They would have no middle names because neither of their namesakes had middle names. Jim's life would never be the same again.

It took three years to pay off the loan for the feed supply store. It had been a struggle but clearing the debt left him in a better position for future ventures. He had already sat down with Abel Hansen and presented him with a rough draft of his business plan. Jim Kemper's plan for the future was to start new businesses by backing responsible people he trusted. He would be senior partner or majority stockholder and would finance and oversee the operation of these enterprises and build them to the point at which his participation in them was not needed in order for them to continue flourishing.

His next outreach would be to set up his new brother-in-law, Tom Wilcox, in his own electrical business just as soon as Tom had acquired the necessary licensing required to start an electrical contracting business. Jim had taken the whole family to Dallas for his sister's and Tom's wedding. It was a special ceremony. Jim had a hard time accepting that his baby sister was getting married. He still thought she was too young, but accept he did. He could tell by the manner in which Tom Wilcox catered to Sarah, and how he treated all the older people, that he was a good man. Sarah would be in good hands, he decided. He tried again to stop Tom from addressing him as Mister Kemper but it was to no avail it seemed so he let the issue drop.

The feed supply was pretty much self-sufficient now, thanks to Emma Sue Brown. Every day she proved that Jim had been wise to hire her to manage the business. Emma Sue had accepted his offer of a hundred dollars a week salary and a two percent profit sharing plan. She had paid holidays off and paid vacation and, since she had developed one of the high school kids into an assistant manager, she was able to have some personal time off during the work week, if needed. She never abused the privileged and Emma Sue seemed to be married to that feed store.

Emma worked hard, put in the long hours without complaining. And she had earned the respect of every employee at the store. Her salary had increased twice from one hundred a week to one twenty-five and then to one-fifty, and Jim raised her profit sharing rate to three percent. Only one thing could go wrong now, Jim thought.

It happened in May of 1970. Emma told Jim that she was getting married, but she quickly advised him that she would not be leaving her job and that her marriage would have no negative effect on her commitment to the store. His name was Raymond Trumble. He lived in Comanche and worked as an auto mechanic at a local car repair place in town.

"He's not good enough for you, E-Sue," Jim said. He had become fond of calling her E-Sue.

"You don't even know him, boss," she said, laughing. "He's a nice guy and he's really good looking."

"Well, I guess you know better than anyone what is best for you."

Still Jim was a bit concerned. He'd never seen Emma with a man, not that it meant anything, and she didn't have many friends. At twenty-seven she was getting married for the first time. He just hoped it worked out well for her and her new husband. He'd take a look at this fellow and see what he thought about him. He didn't ask Emma if she loved this Raymond Trumble. Something about her demeanor told him that Emma might just be ready to get married, like she thought her time was running out. He hoped that was not the case.

The Kempers attended the wedding at the First Baptist Church. Mattie, the two boys, and the twins all paid their respects to Emma while Jim spoke to her new husband and sized him up. Raymond Trumble was a nice-looking fellow, Jim noted, just as Emma had said, but Jim wasn't completely comfortable that the man was good enough for her. The man was about Jim's age but looked older, according to Mattie. Jim believed he had shifty eyes, a certain quality that was just slightly unpleasant. He brushed it off as simply a case of his being pre-conditioned not to like the guy because he was worried about Emma Sue. Nevertheless, he would reserve the right unto himself to form a more lasting opinion at a later date.

The couple would live in the house Emma had built, with Jim's help, in Comanche. That didn't set well in Jim's mind but he let it go. It gave the appearance, he thought, that Trumble's reason for marrying Emma might have been to make things more comfortable for himself. She had a nice house and a job that paid her more than he made. Jim expected that, at some point, the man would either stop working or start missing work frequently. He didn't mention any of this to Emma because he seriously hoped he was wrong.

It wasn't until Jim visited the Hargroves in Dallas and told his mother about Emma's marriage that he learned a little about Raymond Trumble. "You don't remember that name?" she asked him.

"No, should I?" He said.

"Raymond Trumble is the grandson of Leland Trumble, who was the town drunk in Comanche when you were a little boy."

"Really?" he said, still puzzled. "I don't recall that name."

"Leland Trumble was the man your grandfather Alton, knocked down on the square that time when he took you to town with him. I never did find out what caused the fight, but I always suspected it was over something Leland said about me. Alton never would tell me any details about what happened."

"I remember that," Jim said, "but it wasn't much of a fight, two hits, as the saying goes, Grandpa hit Leland and Leland hit the street. I don't know what caused it either. So, I better keep a close eye on this Raymond fellow. I won't take kindly to someone mistreating my E-Sue."

"I don't know anything about the boy," his mother said, "but his dad, Leland's son, was a good man they say. He always tried to live down his father's reputation."

In August, Tom Wilcox called Jim and informed him that he'd passed the Dallas Master Electrician's exam, but he wanted to wait a while before going into business because the company, for which he was working, was training him to do estimating. Tom believed, and Jim agreed, that any additional experience he could get, on somebody else's dime, would help him out immensely in the future. They agreed to wait for the time being before considering a new venture. But circumstances changed their plans late in 1970 when the owner of the company passed away suddenly from a heart attack, leaving only his wife to run the business, a task for which she had no appetite. She asked Tom Wilcox, now being the only master electrician with the firm who could legally take over, if he would be interested in taking over and buying the company. She would be willing to let him pay out the note, which she would finance for him.

"How much does she want for the business?" Jim asked him.

"A hundred and twenty-five grand," Tom said.

"And what would we be buying for a hundred and twenty-five thousand dollars?"

"I'll have to get a more complete list together, Mister Kemper, but they have five service vans, a pretty good inventory of tools and equipment. The building is an old house but it's on an acre of land. The customer list is pretty extensive, a lot of long-time customers, prompt paying customers, and twelve field employees, five journeymen, and seven helpers. Mister Simpson's wife handles all the bookkeeping and check writing. I can get a complete list together for you to look at."

"Good Tom, do that, and I will be in Dallas this week sometime, I'll call you and let you know when. We'll take a look at the place and then sit down with the lady. What's her name, by the way?"

"Mrs. Simpson," Tom said, "Leda Simpson. The owner's name was Adam Simpson."

Simpson Electric Company was located on the southeast corner of Northwest Highway and Plano Road, in Dallas. The deceased owner, Adam Simpson, had been mildly successful for a small contracting firm. Jim had the property appraised and decided that the asking price of a hundred and twenty-five thousand dollars, for the entire company was a fair price. The building was small but adequate for a new startup business. There was a reception and bookkeeping area and desk, three additional office spaces—one for an estimator, two for managers, and a small conference room. A covered area behind the building afforded space for the vehicles and some equipment. A small storage building held miscellaneous material, extension cords and the like.

Jim and Tom sat down with Leda Simpson to discuss terms of the deal. Jim asked her to keep working for the company for at least a year in order to facilitate a smooth transition. He would get the money from Abel Hansen and pay Mrs. Simpson the hundred and twenty-five grand in full. She was agreeable to stay on the job, but she had never charged the company for her time so they agreed on an hourly rate. All parties shook hands and the deal was done. He had a lawyer draw up the papers and he arranged the loan through Hansen Trust.

A week later, Jim presented Leda Simpson with a check. "Don't spend it all in one place," he said, smiling at her.

"It's going in the bank, Mister Kemper," she replied.

"Now hold on a minute. Let's drop this Mister Kemper business, call me Jim," he told her. "I've been trying to get

Tom here to do that for several years now. Maybe you can convince him to be tad less formal."

"I'll try, Jim, but Adam never could stop him from calling him Mister Simpson, so it's an uphill battle."

So, on October third, 1970, Kemper Wilcox Electric Company officially became an entity. Business went on as usual but under a different name. Jim would eventually initiate some great changes in the company. They would seek bigger and more profitable projects, and eventually build a larger office building, hire more estimators and electricians. The name would one day change to Kemper Wilcox Engineering, when they started doing HVAC mechanical contracting. Jim imagined the company becoming the best, if not the biggest, in Dallas. Anything with the Kemper name on it had to be the best.

Chapter 15

The Senator

The incongruity of Jack Grantham's being subtly forced out of the army due to his honest comments to none other than the President of the United States demonstrated, at least to Holly Grantham, the depth of corruption to which the military service had fallen. She had urged her husband to write a letter to Lyndon Johnson and inform him of the wrong which had been done to him.

Even after Jack's explaining the futility of such an action, Holly was still incensed. While she was pleased that he would return to what she considered a normal life, her sense of fair play was seriously damaged. The president had asked Jack if he thought we could win the war, and Jack had given him his straightforward opinion that he did not believe we could win under the present circumstances. For that, he was ostracized and even told by one general that he had most likely gone as far as he would in the army. Some high-ranking officers had been replaced and some others reprimanded because Johnson deduced that he had not been given correct information.

"You people are blowing smoke up my ass," he was reported to have said to some of his top commanders.

So Jack Grantham was out. His winning the Congressional Medal of Honor notwithstanding, he would not be allowed to advance any further. He was more angry than hurt, remembering Major Pennington. Pennington was the incompetent officer who had forced them down so close to the tree line in in the battle near Vi Thann. Jack realized that much of the upper echelon of officers in the army were more concerned with sav-

ing their own asses than they were with winning the war.
Johnson's generals had lied to him, played down the gravity of
the situation and how badly the war was actually going. Jack
hoped one day to sit behind that big desk in the Oval Office
and make a difference. But first Jack Grantham had to learn
the newspaper business.

Hell, he thought, he'd never even had a paper route when
he was a kid. His immediate fear was that his father-in-law,
Sam Dryden, might just use him for curb appeal because of his
service record but Sam assured him that he really needed Jack
to take over the business for him. So Jack was shown his new
office, a rather plush office, he observed. The sign on the door
said: *Jack Grantham, Editor-in-Chief.*

Sitting behind his desk with Sam Dryden smiling at him
from the other side, Jack tried to get a grasp on the whole
thing.

"How does it feel, Jack?" Sam asked him.

"I think it's going to be harder than flying a helicopter,
Sam," Jack said.

"Maybe so, Jack, but there won't be anybody shooting at
you here," Sam said, chuckling.

"I hope not," Jack replied. "I appreciate it, Sam, I really do.
I'll give you my best."

"That's all I ask for, Jack."

Jack had been up front with Sam about his political ambitions. Sam Dryden, being the avid supporter of all things associated with the Democratic Party, had no problem with his
son-in-law's plan for the future. In fact, Sam was enthusiasti-
cally supportive and expressed a desire to play a role in helping him meet all the right people, employ fundraisers and other
personnel who could help move him along the road winning
elections.

Sam explained that the man who had been in the job Jack
would now be doing had retired and the position was legiti-
mately open. "I didn't fire anyone to make room for you. Joe
Creel, the managing editor, is a hands-on type of guy, and he
honestly did not want to be editor-in-chief. So don't be concerned that there will be any hard feelings at any perceived

nepotism. Jim Phillips, the man who retired, had wanted to leave a year ago but I asked him to stay on until you got back from Vietnam. I guess I made some assumptions that you'd throw in with me. It seems to have worked out."

"I am grateful, Sam, I really am. The opportunity you have given me is exciting. It will be different, but my army training prepared me for different and evolving contingencies, and how to deal with them. I can do this, Sam."

His first day on the job, Holly came in with a box of miscellaneous items with which she intended to decorate his new office. She had taken his Medal of Honor and had it mounted in a glass enclosed frame and wanted to hang it on the wall. He forbade her to do it, very sternly.

"We just don't do that, Holly," he said, "it's pretentious and vain. Every time somebody came into my office their attention would be drawn to it. I'd look like the biggest asshole in town."

But he did let her hang the picture he'd sent her from Vietnam, of him standing by his helicopter. He loved the picture because it reminded him where he'd been and what he had survived. It also made him aware of how precious it was to have lived through it and that he had the rest of his life to live. Holly hung the picture on the wall behind his desk.

"There," she said," my handsome warrior, now everyone will know what you did for us."

"That's the past, honey," he told her, I'm glad it's behind us. Now we just have to get on with things. I have a newspaper to run—let me correct that. I have a newspaper to learn how to run. Your father has been great to me. He knows I don't know anything about all this and yet he's willing to take a chance on me."

"He loves you, Jack. You're the son he always wanted. I think he was disappointed that I was not a boy."

"Not as disappointed as I would have been if you had been a boy." He took her arm, turned her around, and wrapped his arms around her, fondling her breasts. "No, you are definitely not a boy."

She giggled and they kissed, for a long time.

"When can we have some kids?" he said.

"Whenever you want me to, my darling," she purred. "Just say when."

"I'd like to start tonight."

"It's a date, soldier. Shine your boots," she said, giggling again.

Sam gave Jack a list of the newspaper staff, each position they held, and their associate assistants. It was an extensive list that would take some time learning. "Your job as editor-in-chief, Jack will primarily consist of delegating these positions. They are fairly well staffed at this time so I don't expect you to have to make any changes right away, but there will come a time when you have to either reassign someone or let them go. After the military, I don't think you'll have any problem delegating."

Jack shook his head. "I'm a pretty good people person, Sam," he said. "I've had to relieve men and or demote them. Sometimes a man has just advanced a grade or two above his capacity. He will most often think it's unfair, but I had to look at the bigger picture."

"Exactly," Sam said. "Now take a while to get familiar with the folks on the list. You won't be able to memorize all the names overnight but, in time, as you work together with them, you'll know them all. I'm going to have you sit in on the content meetings. That's where we decide which stories to run and which ones to bury. There is only so much space so we have to be very selective sometimes. Murder and mayhem get top billing. The war protests, not so much anymore. Missing children, or a cop getting shot, have to be covered. Every department head will be trying to get their stuff on the front page. You and Joe Creel will have the final say. Joe being the Managing Editor, and he has thirty years in this business, will carry some weight, so unless it's something you really have a good feeling about I would defer to him. He knows what he's doing. I mainly want you to observe and see how things are done. You will be making assessment of how each person is doing his or her job. Mostly you will delegate, but you need to know enough about the job each employee does in order to be able to make that assessment."

Jack studied the list intently, trying to tie the name to the job. Both name and position labels were attached to the office doors and the assistant's offices were cubby holes next to the office of each department head, and their names were on those doors. It wouldn't be that hard. He'd just read the name before he went into each office and eventually each name would match the face.

At the first meeting, Sam Dryden introduced Jack to the staff. He had each department head stand up and introduce him/herself and tell a little bit about their jobs. When he was finished, he said to Jack, "Now, Jack, repeat the names of everyone at the table."

Everyone laughed as Jack said four or five names and then threw up his hands and said. "I'll need a little more time but I'll get to know you all."

After a year of living with Holly's parents, Jack decided it was time for them to buy a home where they could start a family. He and Holly began a search for the right house for them. It was none too soon because Holly discovered that she was pregnant.

"Finally," Jack said, "I was afraid that I might be shooting blanks."

"Apparently not," she told him, "I went to the doctor and it's confirmed. I'm three months along."

"Thank you, baby," Jack said, "You've made me very happy."

"That's my job," Holly said.

The search for a house continued for several months. "I'm not too picky, am I, Jack?" she asked.

"Don't ask me, dear, talk to the three hundred real estate agents we've worn out over the past several months."

"But I want it to be right for us," she said, "We'll live in it the rest of our lives."

"Unless we move to Washington," he said, winking at her.

"Unless we move to Washington, of course," she responded, nodding her head up and down. "That's what I meant."

They found a house that Holly finally put her blessing on. It was in Cupertino, near the mountains. It was perfect, Holly told Jack—five bedrooms, three baths, a den and family room and a huge backyard. The house was located on San Leandro Avenue. They barely had time to get moved in before the baby arrived. That happened on January 6, 1968. A boy arrived and the Granthams named him James, after Jack's best friend from Vietnam, James Kemper. They painted his room blue but they kept him in their room the first few months after they brought him home from the hospital.

Jack made a call to the Kempers at the farm in Comanche.

Danny Carlisle picked up. "Kemper Farms," he said, how can I help you?"

"This is Jack Grantham, Jim's friend from California, is Jim around?"

"Hello, Jack," Danny responded. "I've heard a lot about you. No, Jim is not here right now. I can have him call you when he gets back."

"Just give him a message for me, if you will."

"I'd be happy to," Danny said.

"Tell him that James Fulton Grantham was born yesterday, January sixth."

"Jim will be happy to hear that, I'm putting it on my board right now. Thank you."

"Thank you, Danny," Jack said, "I look forward to meeting you someday."

"I look forward to that too, Jack, thanks and congratulations on the new boy."

When Jim came back to the office, he saw a note on Danny's chalkboard, *James Fulton Grantham born January sixth, mother and child doing well.*

Jim went into the house and called out to Mattie, "Jack and Holly had a baby boy, they named him James."

"That's quite an honor," she said. "I wish we could go visit them."

"I've got a lot going on right now, maybe we can in a month or so. I'll give him a call later."

By the time the next son came along, Jack and Holly were

settled into their house and baby James was eighteen months old. They named the next boy Samuel, after Holly's dad. Holly was hoping that the third time would be the charm and that she would get the girl she wanted, but it was not to be. They named the third boy Jack but he was not a junior. Jack wanted to make Edward the boy's middle name, after Jack's dad.

The Grantham house was filling up quickly.

Sam Dryden and Jack disagreed on the growth issue for San Jose and the Santa Clara Valley. There was much discussion in the newsroom but it was typically good natured. Dryden was a slow-growth advocate, preferring to halt the building and development at the current city's edge. Jack, on the other hand, believed that more people meant more building, more jobs, and greater newspaper circulation.

"I want to protect the environment, Sam," Jack said. "But not at the expense of people and their families. We can be environmentally responsible and still expand. We just have to reach a happy medium."

"I don't think that's possible," Sam often contended. "I don't want to see the mountains and the valley covered with condos from one end to the other. The city council has a good grasp of what's right, and I think we should support them."

"I'll defer to you on that, Sam," Jack responded. "You've lived here a lot longer than I have, and you know the valley much better. Right now, I just want to help make the paper successful."

"We have the lion's share of circulation in the bay area," Sam said. "We're growing as fast as the city is."

Jack began writing a weekly editorial opinion column. It was time consuming, but he had discovered that his job as editor-in-chief took very little of his time. Joe Creel actually did the daily managing of the newspaper. Jack sat in with Joe on interviews for new hires, and reviews for existing employees. Occasionally, he accompanied the reporters on assignments just to get the feel for their jobs and how they approached their work.

Initially, Jack wrote about the ongoing controversy over accelerated growth in the valley, slow growth as advocated by

Sam Dryden and many others, and a level of compromise between the two. He discovered some things. The unfettered
growth people tended to be builders and contractors, develop-
ers and speculators, people on the way up who, to be very
honest, were mainly interested in making money in great
quantities. They were typically Republicans. But their numbers also contained many thousands of working people, the
common man, so to speak. These were people who only wanted jobs and the opportunity to earn a living and prosper.

The folks on the other side were almost exclusively Democrats and tended to be men like his father-in-law who were
either well off or made their living in businesses or pursuits
not dependent on a building boom. They were environmentalists primarily, and not unreasonably so. Jack too often be-
moaned the overdevelopment of land that destroyed animal
habitats and the pristine beauty of the wilderness.

He walked a fine line between the two. It was a learning
process in the honing of political skills, the art of compromise,
and the ability to not offend anyone on either side. Jack was
beginning to understand why no one could ever get a straight
answer out of a politician.

His column became so popular that people from both sides
of different issues began trying to recruit him for their public
face.

"I report the news, I don't make it," he often commented to
someone wanting his participation in one issue or another.

He began to learn political speak—the art of discussing an
issue of interest without actually taking a definitive stand. Po-
lice and firemen were easy to defend. They were heroes to
most people. One could, if sufficiently careful, praise them
and extol their necessity and virtues while, at the same time,
defending the need for fiscal responsibility and keeping control of runaway cost without having someone in the back row
yelling, "Bullshit, which is it, more cops or let's save money?"

Jack and Sam had often talked about Jack's desire to run
for president. "There has never been a Democratic president
from California," Jack said, "I want to change that."

"I do too," Sam replied. "You could run for state senator in seventy-two. That would be a platform from which you could run for the United States Senate, maybe in nineteen seventy-six. These are long-term goals, but public service is a long-term pursuit."

"So, what do you suggest we adopt as a long-term strategy?" Jack asked.

"We need to start building a campaign organization right away, Jack," Sam told him. "I have some ideas for a campaign manager and we can begin setting up offices in every district in the state. Volunteers will flock to you, I guarantee it. You're a family man, a war hero, and most importantly, a Democrat."

"So, what's our first move?"

"I'd say run for the state senate in seventy-two. That gives us four years to get organized. We'll start a profile series in the paper. I'll get Paula Simpson, she's the assistant to Martha Rutledge in layout and design, to interview you and write the profile. She's done some similar stuff for us in the past, she's very good."

"Can I still work here while I'm campaigning? I still need to make a living."

"I'll put you on the board of directors on a retainer," Sam said. "You can take a leave of absence to campaign. You won't take a cut in pay. I don't want you to worry about anything but winning. Once you win, state senator is a full-time job in California, and your salary will be close to what you make now. I can put Holly on the payroll to make up the difference. That way we'll avoid any perception of conflict of interest. Have you talked to Holly about this yet?"

"Only in the realm of maybes and possibilities, I haven't told her that we are going to start right away, but I will soon."

"Good idea, she'll be okay with it but it's best to level with her. Now I need to be certain that you are one hundred percent up for this."

"I am, Sam, but I must admit that, after seven years at the paper, I was starting to get pretty good at the job, and I was really enjoying it."

"You'll always have a role here in this organization, Jack"

Sam told him. "You're doing a fine job, but we need to focus on the bigger picture."

"I know, that's what I want too."

Paula Simpson was a frumpy looking girl, if it be proper to call her a girl. She was twenty-eight years-old and wore long skirts and baggy shirts that almost hid her abundant breasts. Jack observed that, when she removed her glasses, she was quite pretty, not stunning but capable of drawing a second look from a man. But she was all business and, as Sam had told him, she was good at what she did.

Paula spent a week with Jack in his office, gleaning every bit of information she could from him that she could think to ask. "I grew up here in San Jose, met Holly at San Jose High, played football, although I never did shine. I was second string quarterback, even played in the Big Bone game in 1958 against Abe Lincoln High when the star broke his ankle. We won the game twelve to zero, but that was my last year of football. I wanted to concentrate on my military career and getting into West Point."

"Tell me about Vietnam, Jack," she said.

He told her about Vietnam and how he had met his best friend, Jim Kemper, there, about the firefight in which he had won the Medal of Honor for his actions. He played it down, giving the credit to Kemper. "Jim should have won that medal, instead of me. He's the bravest man I ever knew."

"We can't over play the war hero angle. It defines who you are and where you came from."

"You sound like Jim," Jack said. "He said those exact words to me when we first came back home."

"Where does Jim come from and what did he do in Vi-etnam?" she asked.

"He's from Texas, owns a dairy farm somewhere near Co-manche, Texas. He was a warrant officer, flew a helicopter in my company. We saw the elephant, together but were fortu-nate enough to come home in one piece."

"Saw the elephant?" she said, looking confused."

"It's too hard to explain, Paula. It means we had a life changing experience together, after which we would never be the same again. I'm sorry. I just don't like talking about myself."

"It's a human-interest story, Jack, once you thrust yourself into the public arena, they'll want to know whether you wear boxers or briefs and what you eat for breakfast. Politics is, by its very nature, a vanity game. Men must continually praise themselves and tout their own accomplishments or risk being outdone by their opponents."

Jack just shook his head. "It's just so new to me," he said.

"When you start to hear the lies and bullshit they say about you, you'll learn to fight back."

"I suppose you're right," he said.

"So, which is it, Jack?" she asked him.

"Which is what?" he responded, not sure what she meant.

"Is it boxers or briefs? Every woman in the office wants to know."

"Oh," he said and started fidgeting around in his seat. Her question made him uncomfortable but at the same time intrigued him. He was sure she was coming on to him but he didn't want to even entertain the thought. "Boxers, but don't let that go any further."

"Your secret is safe with me," she said. "Okay then, that's it for today. I'll see you tomorrow."

He was tormented by the exchange that had just occurred between them. She had caught him one time staring at her breasts, and he knew that she knew what he was thinking. *Damn*, he thought, *how can a man let something like this happen?* It was just an innocent flirtation but here he was still thinking about it. Next thing he knew he'd be fantasizing about getting her into bed. No, he was not going to do that, this was not what he wanted.

A couple of days later, Sam called Jack into his office. "There's someone I want you to meet," he said. "Jack, this is Nick Devoss, he's been managing political campaigns in California for twenty years. Nick, this is Jack Grantham, my son-in-law. He's headed for Pennsylvania Avenue."

"Are you sure you want to do this, Jack?" Devoss asked him.

"I'm sure, Nick," Jack said. "I've been planning this for over five years now."

"Well, you better be damned sure because, once you commit, your life will not be your own again, ever. Your family will be scrutinized top to bottom, side to side every minute of the day. You wife leaves the house with a hair out of place, it'll be on the six o'clock news. You fart in an open stadium, and you'll see it on the Sunday morning news shows. I see you're smiling, but I'm only half joking. You gotta be a hundred percent committed to this coming fight, a hundred and ten percent because it's brutal. It can ruin your marriage, make your kids hate you, and drive you insane. It takes a strong man with a strong family to survive a run for the presidency."

"Then why does anyone ever do it, Nick?" Jack asked.

"Because it's the top of the world, you'll be the most powerful man in the world. Winning the presidency is the culmination of a successful life in public service. You have to start winning now and build a resume that exudes success and evokes confidence. Are you registered to vote?"

"Am I registered to vote? Yes," Jack said.

"Are you a registered Democrat?"

"I've never registered with either party."

'You need to get that done right away. If you don't, your opponent can, and will, make an issue of it. You have to be thirty-years-old in California to run for the senate. How old are you, Jack?"

"I'm twenty-nine."

"That's okay, you'll be thirty-one in 'seventy-two. We don't know yet who you'll be running against, but you can bet your ass they'll make an issue of your youth. Say you're up against a woman. How do we counter that?"

"I'd ask her how much time she spent in Vietnam," Jack replied.

Nick laughed out loud. "You have a sense of humor, but that's a good way to piss off women. You catch half the female population of California during their periods, and you come off like you're talking down to a woman and the shit will definitely hit the fan.

"I wasn't joking, Nick," Jack said. "Why can I not say, 'I was old enough to fly a helicopter in Vietnam, I was old enough to lead men into mortal combat, and I was old enough to kill people. Why am I not old enough to serve the people of my state in the senate?'"

"Okay, your point is made and taken. Next, do you have any skeletons in your closet?"

"He's squeaky clean, Nick," Sam Dryden interjected. "Hell, he married my daughter right out of high school, went to West Point for god's sake. Jack has never even so much as had an impure thought."

Jack and Nick looked at each other and burst out laughing. "I'm not going to put that in your bio, Jack." Nick said.

"Please don't," Jack said. "Somebody might put me on a lie detector."

Sam started laughing too. "Maybe I got just a bit carried away," he said.

"But just for the record, so you can't say I never warned you. Whatever you do, don't ever, I mean never, lay your hands on a woman who is not your wife. I don't care if the Forty-Niners cheerleaders walk into the room naked—don't even sneak a peek. You're a good-looking guy, Jack, and you're a war hero. Don't be surprised when women start throwing themselves at you."

"To be honest, Nick, I really had never even thought about that. It's kind of scary. My plan is to have Holly by my side everywhere I go. I've never even considered having anything to do with another woman."

"Just keep your pecker in your pants, Jack, don't ever take your pecker out of your pants on the campaign trail."

"You're telling me to piss in my pants, Nick"

"If that's what it takes, son," Nick said, "if that's what it takes. We can't have female trouble is all I'm saying, it will kill your career and ruin your life."

"Yes, sir, I know what you mean, and I appreciate it. I'll be careful."

Paula finished the profile and the paper started running it in weekly segments for six weeks. It generated a lot of interest and people began calling the paper to find out where to either volunteer or donate money to the campaign.

Nick Devoss was a rumpled man, about five foot eight inches tall and overweight. Even in a suit, he looked as if he'd just rolled out of bed. He drank too much, Jack discovered, but it didn't seem to interfere with his work. He had shepherded many candidates into office and was very much sought after for his ability to build a viable political campaign, organize volunteers, and scare up large donors. Sam Dryden was paying his salary until the campaign could raise enough money to pick up that expense. Nick only took on Jack's campaign because Sam convinced him that Jack's ultimate goal was to go to Washington.

Paula Simpson's bio on Jack did so well that Sam asked her to set up and manage the main campaign headquarters in San Jose. She was quite capable and, in no time, had the place staffed with volunteers, answering phones, taking pledges, mailing out copies of the bio, and asking for money.

Jack would have preferred that Paula not have such a prominent role in the campaign, but he could hardly tell Sam he didn't want her. What possible reason did he have other than the fact that he was afraid of her, or more specifically of his feelings toward her? He was not falling for her, he knew that. And she had given him no indication that she was interested in an affair with him. It was just that she was perfectly proper in the office, around others. She hardly even looked at him when they passed in the newsroom, she remained totally focused on the business at hand. But when they were alone, she looked at him in a way that told him there was more going on than she let on. He eventually decided to pretend that it was innocent flirtation and meant nothing. It was most likely his own guilt that made him uncomfortable.

Nick told Sam and Jack that the race for the state senate would be a shoo-in for Jack. He was a perfect candidate and the power of the newspaper behind him made it a cakewalk as Nick described it. Sam had sought and gotten endorsements for Jack's candidacy from other newspapers in San Jose and San Francisco and many others across the state as well.

Jack won his first election by a fifty-three percent margin. Polls showed that he lost the bulk of the environmentalists because he appeared to be taking more of a pro-growth stance than they were comfortable with.

"We'll have to appease the whackos a bit, next time," Nick told him. "They're a pain in the ass but they do have some influence. Don't worry, Jack, I'll make it play to them next time."

Next time, would be for all the marbles, a run for the US Senate and that would not be as easy as winning a seat in the state legislature. Nick began quietly getting people on board state-wide, so he would be able to quickly set up campaign offices all over the state when the time came.

Jack immersed himself in his job. The work was not hard but it was demanding and time consuming. In the beginning, he drove back and forth between home and Sacramento, but the two-hour drive one way slowly began to wear on him and his nerves.

Holly suggested that he rent a small apartment or a hotel room and stay over when he'd had a long day. It would mean driving in on Mondays and then back home on Friday afternoon—at the most, three days away from home during the week. It was a good idea, Jack decided, and he found an appropriate place. It was an extended-stay hotel not far from the capitol that offered a cooked-to order breakfast every morning.

Although he missed being at home and seeing his wife and boys every night, it was a lot easier on him. He could only imagine that, if he became a US Senator how that commute would be. He'd have to move his family to Washington, that was all there was to it.

In January of 1975, Jack's oldest son, James, turned seven years old and a party was planned. The Kempers were coming with their bunch.

With the exception of Jim's visit in mid seventy-four to visit Fleetwood homes, this was the first time the families had seen each other since their coming home. Sam Dryden was looking forward to meeting Jim Kemper, having heard so much about him from his daughter and son-in-law.

Sam queried Jim about his political affiliation. "Are you a Democrat, Jim?" Sam asked him.

"I'm not sure what I am, Sam," Jim replied. "My grandfather was a Democrat and my father-in-law still is. Charles McKenna, that's my father-in-law, he's a state senator in Maryland. Jack and Holly met him. When Jack went to Washington to receive his medal, they went out to Annapolis to look in on Mattie and my boys. They ask about Jack every time we see them. I told Charles that Jack was now a state senator in California. He was very impressed."

"Senator McKenna is a fine man, Sam," Jack interjected. "He's crazy about his grandsons, just like you are."

"Yeah, the boys spent their first year or so with the McKennas while I was in Vietnam," Jim told Sam.

"It certainly doesn't hurt for kids to spend time with the grandparents. They need somebody to keep their mom and dad in line."

"You're right, Sam," Jim said. "I grew up with my grandfather, and I wouldn't have had it any other way. He was a great man."

Sam nodded and smiled. "Jack is going to be running for the US Senate in two years," Sam said.

"So, you really are going to do it? You told me that when we stayed with you guys when I came home. I only half thought you meant it. I mean, it's a nice ambition but I figured when you got into politics you might discover that it's more trouble than it's worth."

"Oh, it is more trouble than it's worth," Jack said, "but I want to do it."

"Good, then I'll expect an invite to sleep in the Lincoln bedroom when you are president."

"You got it, Jim. So how is your business going?"

"Going well, the dairy is growing by leaps and bounds, and I've got three of the feed and supply stores, found a very capable young woman to manage them for me. I recently bought an electrical contracting company. My sister's husband is a master electrician. I made him my junior partner. He's a good man."

"Wow," Jack said, "Now I'm impressed."

"I'll be back out here in a couple of months for a second visit to Fleetwood in Riverside. I'll stop in to see you again."

"That's quite a trek but you're always welcome here," Jack said.

"I won't ever come to California without looking in on the Granthams," Jim said.

Sam Dryden left and the two friends sat back and watched the activity around the pool. Kids were jumping in, doing, cannonballs, as close as they could to other kids, and mothers were admonishing them to be careful."

"I can see why we became friends, Jim," Jack said, "our wives look enough alike to be sisters."

"You mean the blonde hair and blue eyes and built like two brick shithouses?"

"Yes, that's what I meant."

They held up their beer bottles in a toast.

ಬಿಬಿಬಿ

Jack was in his Sacramento residence when he received a phone call from Sam. "Jack, I'm going to have Paula Simpson do a promo-piece, for the paper on your current activities in the senate. Can you prepare a couple of pages on what's on your table at this time? I'd like to do this every few months just to keep you in the news."

"Of course, Sam," Jack responded, "I'd be happy too. I appreciate your doing that. I can drop it off at the office on Friday."

"That won't be necessary. She's coming to Sacramento to deliver some paperwork for the paper. She can pick them up from you Thursday evening at your place."

"Oh, well, I don't mind bringing them in, I hate to put her to any trouble."

"No, it's okay, Jack, she has a sister or cousin or something who lives there. She's going to stay the weekend with her."

The knock on his door told him that Paula had arrived. He noticed immediately that she was not wearing her hair up on her head as she normally did. "You've let your hair down," he said and motioned for her to come in.

"I got tired of everyone telling me I look like a school marm."

"I never thought you looked like a school marm," he said.

She looked at him coyly. "What did you think I looked like?

"I think you look like a writer, and you are a pretty good writer. You should write a book or something," he said as he pointed toward the couch for her to sit down, and he sat down on a single chair in front of her. She kicked off her shoes and crossed her legs.

"Thank you, I'd love to write a book," she said. "I've thought about it."

"Good, you should, I hope I didn't put you to any trouble. I told Sam I could bring this by the office but he said you were visiting your sister here in Sacramento."

"It was a cousin, but I'm not staying with her. I just told Sam that so he wouldn't feel bad about asking me to work late."

"I see," Jack said. "Well, look this over and see if you can do anything with it."

She began perusing the pages he had given her, nodding her head and pursing her lips a couple of times and then she laid them down on the couch beside her.

"So, what do you think?"

She looked at him seductively, and he immediately grew nervous. Then she stood up and started fumbling behind her back with the button and zipper of her skirt. She unhooked it and let it fall to the floor. She stood there in just her panties, still wearing her baggy sweat shirt, and walked over to where he was sitting. She straddled him on the chair he was in, took hold of the hair on the back of his head, and pulled it back then placed her lips on his. She began kissing him, passionately, emitting low moans and whimpers as she continued. He felt the tip of her tongue touch his. It was not obtrusive but touching his with little flicks back and forth.

She stopped for a moment, just long enough to remove her

shirt and thrust her breasts into his face, then went back to kissing him. His arms had thus far been down beside him. He put his hands on her waist with the intent of making her stop, but it was useless. He felt himself getting an erection. She stopped to catch her breath and to check his reaction. He was looking at her body and she was smiling down at him.

"Dear God, Paula," he said, struggling to catch his breath, "this is what you've been hiding under all those baggy clothes—why?"

"I enjoy the look on men's faces when they see me naked for the first time, that's why."

"I can't do this," he told her, "I just can't do this."

She kissed him again. "I'm going to go get in your bed and wait five minutes. If you don't want me, then don't come in to me, and I'll leave and never tell anyone this happened. But if you want me, I'm yours for the taking and I swear that, unless you tell someone, no one will ever know about this."

The light was off in his room when he went in. He took off his clothes and slid into bed beside her. They wrapped themselves around each other in a lover's embrace and began kissing again. He grew dizzy from her kisses. Jack thought for a moment that he must be dreaming or that he was losing his mind.

He didn't know where he was or who he was. Her fingernails dug into his back but she was careful not to leave a scratch mark. He was lost in this magnificent creature with whom he was committing the most grievous of sins. The greater sin was that he didn't care.

When it was over, they lay next to each other and she slid into him and laid her head on his chest. He pulled her close with his right arm and kissed the top of her head. "You do realize, don't you, Paula," he said, "that I have placed my political career, my marriage, everything I am and everything I ever hope to be, in your hands? I would have been better off getting hooked on heroin than doing what I just did."

"But you like me, don't you?" she asked him. "Was I good for you?"

"In all my life, I never imagined that a woman could make

me feel the way you just did. I had no idea women like you even existed. God help me. I mean that."

"Then don't worry, Jack," she said.

But he did worry. Jack spent the next week in a deep, all-consuming depression. The experience was something he could not have imagined would ever happen to him, but the cost might be more than he could bear. He was not immediately fearful that Paula might tell someone. He believed her when she said she would not. But his greater fear was that he would want her again and such behavior, especially for a man in the public eye, always had a way of getting out. He regretted what he'd done to Holly and his family. Hidden secrets ate your insides. Like he told Paula, she had the means to destroy him. He knew now that he had a ticking time bomb around his neck that might go off at any time.

えべる

The surprise winner of the 1976 Democratic presidential nomination was Jimmy Carter, a former state senator and governor of Georgia. When the primaries began, Carter was relatively unknown at the national level, and many political pundits regarded a number of better-known candidates, such as Senator Henry M. Jackson of Washington, Congressman Morris Udall of Arizona, Governor George Wallace of Alabama, and California Governor Jerry Brown, as the favorites for the nomination. However, in the wake of the Watergate Scandal, Carter realized that his status as a Washington outsider, political Centrist, and moderate reformer could give him an advantage over his better-known establishment rivals. Carter also took advantage of the record number of state primaries and caucuses in 1976 to eliminate his better-known rivals one-by-one.

The contest for the Republican Party's presidential nomination in 1976 was between two serious candidates: Gerald Ford, the leader of the GOP's moderate wing and the incumbent President, from Michigan, and Ronald Reagan, the leader of the GOP's conservative wing and the former two-term governor of California. The presidential primary campaign between the two men was hard-fought and relatively even. By the start of the Republican Convention in August 1976 the race for the nomination was still too close to call. Ford defeated Reagan by a narrow margin on the first ballot at the 1976 Republican National Convention in Kansas City, and chose Senator Robert Dole of Kansas as his running mate in place of incumbent Vice President Nelson Rockefeller. The 1976 Republican Convention was the last political convention to open with the presidential nomination still being undecided until the actual balloting at the convention.

Jack Grantham was faced with two battles in his coming election. He had to beat the incumbent Democratic senator, a weak and ineffective man named Johnson Thomas.

"A man whose policies are as backward as his name," said Nick Devoss on a national news show, creating an instant bumper sticker which he exploited and had thousands of them printed to be sold to Grantham supporters.

Thomas had some crooked dealings in his past, and Nick had people who could find such weaknesses. Evidence of influence peddling and misappropriation of campaign funds came to light and were carried in the *San Jose Examiner* and eventually in other news media across the state. Thomas denied all charges, but it didn't sell well with the media.

The Thomas campaign accused the *Examiner* of foul play, claiming that Senator Grantham was on the paper's payroll. Sam Dryden denied the charge and offered to open up his payroll to state election officials. He also revealed that his daughter, Grantham's wife, was actually on the payroll, instead of the senator. There were some shaking heads and rolling eyes but polls determined that the dust-up did not cost Jack any serious loss of support.

Thomas was accused of using campaign money for personal expenditures. Jack never asked Nick if the charges against Thomas were true or not, or where he got the negative information.

Jack won the Democratic primary and would face the Republican candidate, Steve Mogens, on November second.

"We have another damned Dutchman." Nick said, being of Dutch extraction himself, he relished the coming conflict.

Sam Dryden pondered the possibility of finding some dirt on Mogens, but Nick assured him that it would not be necessary because Mogens was vulnerable, due to the perception that he was in bed with big business.

Mogens had been CFO of a Silicon Valley computer company and had resigned his position to run for the US Senate. "He's an unfettered growth advocate," Nick said, in one of their strategy meetings. Jack started to say something but Nick put his hand up. "I know, Jack, you are too, but like I told you before, we're going to play that down and throw some chum to the environmentalist sharks. You have to walk the line. Say you favor controlled growth as long as it lends deference to the land and the rivers and the mountains. It's all bullshit anyway. If everyone running in a political race said what they truly believe, no one would get elected."

"So, you think I have good shot at beating this guy?" Jack said.

"I wouldn't be here, Jack, if I didn't," Nick responded. "I know you can beat him. I'm going to have that girl, who did the profile piece on you when you ran for state senator, work that up again with some added stuff from your first term. What was her name?"

"Paula Simpson," Sam told him. "I can get her in here." He picked up the phone, dialed Paula's extension, and asked her to come to his office. In a few minutes, she walked into the room.

Sam went over with her exactly what he wanted. He showed her how to slant some of Jack's accomplishments as senator in the most positive light. She said she understood what he wanted, turned, and went out the door. Nick watched her walk out but said nothing.

"Come on, Jack, let's go down to the SJ on second street," Nick said. "I want to talk to you."

"Sure, Nick," Jack said. "Let me get my coat."

They ordered drinks and Nick started going over some strategies for the campaign. He rambled a bit about some of his past campaigns and how this one was going to be his easiest one yet because of the diversity of the candidates. "One is a whore for big business and the other is a war hero and a champion for the working man."

"Just keep reminding me which is which, Nick," Jack said.

Nick chuckled. "That not why I asked you to join me here, Jack, I have to ask you something."

"Okay, shoot." Jack said.

"What's going on between you and that woman in the office?"

"Nothing, Nick," Jack responded emphatically, "nothing at all. Why do you ask me that?"

"You're a good-looking man, Jack. When we walk around the newsroom, every woman in there can't take their eyes off you. I Envy you, I really do. But Paula goes to great lengths to pretend that you are not even in the room. I know she dresses like a bag-lady, but she can't hide those tits. There is more going on there than meets the eye. So, if you're stiffing her, it can get us into trouble."

"There was some mild flirtation once, Nick, nothing more than that. She's attractive, any man can see that, and why she tries to hide her looks, I have no idea. But there is nothing going on between us, I promise you that."

"Okay, that's the right answer, even if you're lying to me, that's the right answer."

Jack made a call to Paula and told her about his exchange with Nick Devoss and what had made Nick suspicious in the first place. "I'm sorry, Jack," she said. "I was trying to be discreet. I'll act differently in the future."

"No, don't change anything," he told her, "Nick is a crafty old geezer. If you change anything, you do, he'll know I talked to you."

"Okay," she said. "By the way, Jack, I'm going to leave California."

"Really, that's a surprise, where are you going?

"I'm going back to my folks in Ohio. I can work for the local paper and have more time to pursue my writing career."

"Well, I wish you the best. I do think you have talent. You've helped my campaign a lot, and I appreciate it. And, Paula, I'm sorry there couldn't be more between us. I just didn't meet you in time."

"I'm sorry too," she said. "I'll watch your career and hope the best for you."

"Thank you, and you take care of yourself." He hung up and felt both relief and regret. He truly hoped he'd never see her again but knew that he would think of her from time to time.

Jack was elected to the US Senate and Jimmy Carter won the presidency. In January, Jack went to Washington to begin his tour as a freshman senator. His first challenge was to find a place to live. Jack had named Nick Devoss to be his chief of staff and left the hiring of additional staff members to him. Sam Dryden flew to Washington to assist in a solution to the living situation. He suggested they buy a condo somewhere near the capitol, in easy walking distance to the office. Sam loaned Jack the money. Rather, he financed the purchase of a two-story row house in the one-hundred block of Fifth Street Southeast. Nick would share the quarters, and Holly and the boys would have a place to stay when they came to visit Jack.

The near disastrous tenure of Jimmy Carter, specifically his mishandling of, and bad luck with, the Iranian hostage crises threatened his chances for a second term. The 1980 US Senate elections coincided with Ronald Reagan's election to the presidency. Reagan's large margin of victory over incumbent Jimmy Carter pulled in many Democratic voters and gave a huge boost to Republican senate candidates. The Republicans gained a net of twelve seats from the Democrats, the largest swing since 1958, and gained control of the Senate, 53-46. Majority and minority leaders Robert Byrd and Howard Baker exchanged places. This marked the first time since 1954 that the Republican Party controlled the senate.

"We dodged a bullet," Nick told Jack, "If we'd been up for reelection this time, it would have been a hard fight. A lot of Republicans rode Reagan's coattails into office. Eighty-two will be different, midterm elections favor the party out of power. We should be a shoo-in for reelection in eighty-two."

On August 3, 1981 13,000 of the 17,500 members of the Air Controllers Union (PATCO) walked off the job in what was, in effect, an illegal strike. Their aim was to get higher wages and expanded benefits.

President Reagan issued an ultimatum that the strikers were to return to work within forty-eight hours or face termination. In 1955, Congress, had made strikes by the air traffic controllers a crime punishable by either a fine or of one year of incarceration. The law was upheld by the Supreme Court in 1971.

The striking controllers were demanding a $10,000 per-year across-the-board increase in wages and a reduction of a five-day, forty-hour work week to a four-day, thirty-two-hour week. They also were demanding full retirement after twenty years of service. The whole package would cost the American taxpayer 770 million dollars a year.

Jack was careful not to be publicly outspoken on the standoff between the strikers and the White House. He personally agreed with the president but any outspoken support, on his part, for Reagan's action, if he actually fired the strikers, might be perceived as being anti-union, and no Democrat could ever risk that.

In the end, President Reagan did fire the striking workers but the impact of his action was minimal because 2,000 or so supervisors, and the employees who had not joined the strike, pitched in and filled the vacancies. Eventually, many of the striking workers were hired back.

The whole affair was a learning experience for Jack Grantham. Nick explained how one wrong move could often ruin a career or put you in a hole you couldn't climb out of. "Had you made the typical Democrat response and supported the Union publicly, we would now have egg on our faces. And had you vocalized your support for Reagan, you could rest assured that some asshole would use it against you in the next election."

"So, in every single issue that comes up, we have to sit down and formulate our response, weighing both sides and

deciding which position has the best positive political outcome?"

"Sort of, Jack," Nick said. "More accurately we have to examine the issue and list all the possible responses then we have
to decide which position has the least, negative, political impact."

"It's kind of crazy, isn't it Nick?" Jack said.

"No, Jack, it's fucking nuts. It's upside down. It's contrary
to everything you've ever been taught to believe and do. You
have to change the entirety of your personality and how you
interact with people and how you approach life itself. For instance, on Thanksgiving, you visit a homeless shelter to help
serve turkey and dressing to indigent souls. Now you really
and truly have compassion for these people, you're even spon-
soring a bill to help them get back into society and become
productive members of same, but someone on the other side,
an opponent, or a newsperson, or whoever, blasts you for
merely taking a photo opportunity. It doesn't matter if you
worked there ten hours that day, they will belittle you for it
and diminish your actual motive."

"Can't a man just do what his heart tells him? I mean can't
I just do what is right and honest and let people say what they
will? Won't people acknowledge that?"

"Your friends will, sure, they'll love you for it but the other
guys will try and turn it into political advantage for them.
There is no room for heart in politics. Even if you have it, you
must count it as a weakness because ultimately it *is* a weakness."

"It all sounds so cynical, Nick."

"It 'is' cynical," Nick responded, "politics *is* cynical. Politics is man at his very worst. But it's the price you have to pay
if you want to sit behind that big desk one day. To get to the
White House, you're going to have to play the game. It's like,
oh what's that guy's name—Harvey Mackay? You have to
learn how to swim with the sharks without being eaten alive.
I'll get you a copy of that book. You need to read it. Another
thing, you will often see a politician refer to another member
of congress or the senate, as his esteemed colleague and very

dear friend. That's all bullshit, and it's pure hypocrisy. They hate each other because they are all lying snakes. I know you are a good man, Jack, I know you are rightly motivated, and I don't want all this to corrupt you. Stay focused on your goal to do good things for the people of California and eventually for all Americans, and don't get sidetracked by the bullshit."

The election of 1982 was a surprise to just about everyone but Nick Devoss. As he had told Jack, the midterm elections tend to favor the party out of power. After the gains of 1980, twelve additional Republican seats in the senate and the presidency, they only picked up one seat in the '82 election. Jack won his race by a landslide. He was becoming a favorite son and a very popular senator in California.

The time away from home was wearing on Jack's nerves. He missed his family and he hated being alone. Nick Devoss offered a suggestion that he move them to Washington. The condo was not nearly as big as their house in Cupertino, but it was large enough for the five of them. Nick would move out and find other arrangements.

"I can afford it," he said. "I have no debts and my salary is sufficient for me to rent a place to live. I'd rather have you happy, Jack, rather than save some money. I know you fly home every weekend but that is hard on a family. You lose continuity and your kids grow up without you around. You can put your boys in a private school here in Washington, there are some good schools to choose from."

"What about public schools?" Jack asked. "Don't you think it would send a good message if I put my kids in public schools?"

"It would send the message that you're an idiot. Public schools in DC are a lot like pre-prison training centers. If you lived in Virginia, or Maryland it would be a different story, but you have a house here. I'd put them in private schools, they're safer and better."

Holly was elated at the notion of living in Washington and the fact they'd be a family again. The move was made in December of 1983. It was a happy time for the Granthams.

"I miss sleeping with you," he told Holly, "and I don't mean the loving, well, that too, but I just miss having you beside me in bed at night."

"I know what you mean, and that's the hardest part, you not being there."

"I won't ever let it happen again," he said, "I promise."

They made love every night the first week after the move. "You're going to spoil me," Holly said when they had finished their latest encounter.

"That's what I'm trying to do, baby," he said, "but it sure doesn't take long to get caught up, at least not for a man to get caught up."

"I'll let you know when I'm caught up," she said.

"Well, I hope it's sometime before I have a heart attack," he said, struggling to catch his breath."

"Please don't tell me you're getting too old for this," she said. "My dad uses that line all the time, 'I'm getting too old for this shit or that shit,' he says. So I don't want to hear it from you. You're only forty-two years old."

"Not at all, Holly baby, I'm in my prime."

The national election of 1984 was a rout of biblical proportions. President Reagan carried forty-nine out of the fifty states, beat Walter Mondale by 58.8% to Mondale's 40.6, and captured 525 electoral votes, the highest total ever received in a presidential election. But despite the Reagan landslide, the Republican Party had a net loss of one seat although it retained control of the senate. They picked up sixteen seats in the congress but did not win control.

Jim Kemper came to town to do some business with the Republican National Committee. Jack expected he was making a big donation. Jim told him later that he'd had a meeting with Phil Gramm, who had just been elected to the US Senate in the recent election. "Gramm is one of my senators and I just wanted to pledge my support in person and go over some things I'd like him to consider getting on board with us on the production of milk in impoverished countries."

"So you're a crusader, are you?" Jack asked him.

"If there's money in it, I am," Jim replied and Jack laughed.

"I want to take you guys out to dinner, Jack. I have to leave tomorrow, can we go out tonight?"

"We'd love to, Jim," Holly said.

"Yes, of course," Jack answered.

They went to Washington Harbor to the Leonardo de Vinci Ristorante. An easily recognizable United States Senator caused no small stir in the restaurant. The class of people who frequented the place was not given to autograph seeking or public fawning over celebrities, so they were pretty much left alone except for some staring and smiling.

Jim ordered a bottle of their best wine and toasted Jack and Holly and their boys. "Here's to friendship and success," he said. Their glasses clinked as the three Grantham boys looked on. "Oh, I'm sorry," Jim said, looking at the boys. "Would you boys like a beer?" The twelve-year-old said yes but the other two just looked at him. "I'm joking guys, don't look so serious."

"Yeah, James," Jack said. "No beer for you, you have to drive."

The boys laughed at the two older men. They were having fun and they rarely saw their father so relaxed and laughing so much.

Jim looked at the oldest boy. "I understand you're named after me," he said.

"Yes, sir," the boy said, "and my dad. My middle name is Fulton."

"Nothing wrong with that," Jim said. "Your mom and dad paid me quite an honor by naming you after me. You give me a call if you ever need anything, you understand?"

'Yes, sir, thank you," the boy replied.

"And you are Sam, right, named after your grandfather," Jim said, pointing at the middle boy, "so you must be Jack." The younger boy nodded. "You've done well, Jack. Of course, Holly did all the work so I suppose she should get the credit."

"She's a great mother, Jim."

"We are fortunate, you and I. We are so far away from the past that it seems now like it was only a dream. I am still amazed and proud of how you set your sights on doing what you have done and then went out and did it."

"No different than you, Jim," Jack said. "You were talking about building a commercial empire when we were in Vietnam. Now you have done it."

"I've had a lot of help from some very good people. It wasn't all my doing."

"I'm not buying that," Jack said. You are the engine that drives that train."

Jim spent the night in the condo and then Jack took him to the airport the next morning to catch his plane to Dallas. "You're going places, Jack. I am starting to actually imagine you as president someday."

"I've got one more election to win, in eighty-eight, then I figure I'll make my run. It seems to be coming together."

They shook hands and Jack left. Jim went to the counter to confirm his flight. He watched as his old friend walked down the concourse. Almost everyone he passed reacted to him in some way. A few went over to shake his hand but others just spoke or waved to him. They had lived separate yet parallel lives. Both of them had risen to the top of their worlds and yet had remained the very same people they were when they started out. At least that was Jim Kemper's take on it.

Senator Grantham won reelection to the senate in 1988 by a fifty-one percent margin. "A landslide," he told Holly.

In 1994, despite the popularity of President Montgomery, the Republicans took the congress. But the loss of the congress did not affect Jack's hold on the seat from California. He won his race easily with a fifty-three percent margin.

He could smell the fragrance in the Rose Garden.

Chapter 16

Dallas

Tom Wilcox was a natural born leader, Jim discovered as he watched him go about his daily duties. Tom scheduled the work crews, talked to customers on the phone, and did the estimating for new jobs. Jim spent most of the first six months since the beginning of the business in Dallas. He watched, helped out where he could, and tried to learn as much as he could about the electrical contracting business. At Christmas, they closed the shop for a long weekend and went back to the farm for the annual get together.

Jim advised Tom to hire a full-time estimator who would lighten Tom's workload and give him more time for promoting the business. He and Tom worked out a progress review system that would track each employee's performance and advancement. Initially the review would take place every six months for the first few years. Once the employee reached the journeyman level, he would be considered for a foreman's position to run jobs. He'd be in charge of other workers and would be offered a salaried pay scale. The review would then typically be held once a year.

They had begun to land some commercial contracts and needed more electricians. Jim sat in on the interviews with Tom. Tom assessed the potential employee's trade skills and Jim studied him for any personality defects he might have. Jim might tell Tom, "that guy is a bit shifty," or another one "seemed honest and straight up." He rarely had an incorrect first impression, and he discovered that Tom was pretty good at judging people as well. Occasionally, a bad seed might get through the screening process and would have to be let go later. It was all part of business.

The personnel performance reviews were very popular with the employees and served the company well. An employee would be brought into Tom's office, with Jim sitting in, and given a complete assessment of job skills, leadership skills, personal appearance, and wage rate. Often a review meant a pay raise of at least a quarter, or fifty cents, but on occasion it might be an ultimatum for the employee to improve his position by being more dependable, or by working faster, or by dropping some other detrimental trait, like cursing or smoking in company vehicles. Before too long, many other companies in Dallas were initiating a similar program.

In 1974, Kemper Wilcox, Electric Company bought an HVAC Company—Mechanical Contracting—and became Kemper Wilcox Engineering. A new building was built to incorporate both trades. The new building was a two-story, to conserve space on the property and a much larger enclosed warehouse and truck maintenance shop was added onto the old building, to make use of that structure, rather than tear it down.

It had some sentimental value for Leda Simpson and that fact weighed heavily on Jim's decision to leave the building in place. He did have it remodeled and, with the addition of the warehouse and truck maintenance facility it would be of good use to them.

Danny's nephew Marcus had expanded the Dairy's customer base as far south as Austin and had as his goal to take them into every major market in Texas and Oklahoma. Soon they would be providing milk to schools all over the state and to the contiguous states. Jim intimated his fear to Danny that Marcus would outrun their ability to meet contractual agreements. "I hope we don't get too far in front of our supply line," he said.

"We'll need more refrigerated trucks," Danny told him. "I suggest we contract with a hauler to make deliveries. We can rent the tankers and have our name on them. That will save us several million dollars over buying new trucks."

"That sounds like a plan, Danny. By the way, how is Marcus doing? We sure don't want to lose him."

"He made fifty grand last year and will probably double that next year, I'd say he's not going anywhere. Oh, he's had some job offers but Marcus is very family oriented, very loyal. He appreciates the opportunity we have given him."

"I hope he makes a million dollars," Jim said."

"I do too," Danny replied.

"I'm flying to California next week to tour a factory that builds prefab houses, and see my old army buddy, Jack Grantham. I'm considering getting into manufactured housing before too long," Jim said. "Any thoughts on that?"

"I don't know much about that field," Danny said, "but if it means more affordable housing for poorer people, then I think it's a good idea. With the right managers and salesmen, you could market the things all over the country and even in Mexico, maybe."

"You have any more nephews, Danny," Jim said, chuckling.

"It might be something Marcus could help with. He worked in construction when he was younger, only as a laborer, mind you, but he does know a little about it."

"Would you be able to spare him from time to time?"

"I think so. I wouldn't mind getting back into the sales side of the business, for a while at least. If you need him, we can figure something out. He's fluent in Spanish, and that will help a lot in Texas, and especially Mexico."

"I'll keep that in mind," Jim said. "I've been thinking of taking some Spanish classes myself. I had several years of it in school but I've lost a lot over the years. We'll talk more about this again. Now I have to go into town to see Emma Sue. There's a problem with one of the guys she wants to talk about.

In the business world, it was a given that there would inevitably be employee problems. Much of the discontent arose from one simple fact. Most human beings only had a job because they had to work to live. Most would prefer not to have to work, to be independently wealthy. The benefits of being independent was not so much the ability to buy stuff but rather that your time was your own and did not belong to an employer. The dairy had not been as susceptible to disgruntled slackers as had the construction company. Jim lent that to the fact that most of the dairy employees were boys from small towns and farms in the area. They had worked all their lives and, family ties were strong. Reputations were at risk if one proved irresponsible and had to be let go. In Dallas, things were different, attitudes were different. There was more competition for good help, and an unhappy employee could easily find another job very quickly.

Until now, Jim had not heard of any conflicts between Emma Sue and the employees at the feed supply store. There was always a ready supply of high school kids, who would work hard and long hours for seventy-five cents an hour. Every school year there would always be a new supply of strong young boys looking for work. Most eventually went off to college or better paying jobs, and few stayed working at the store for more than a few years. But he'd gotten a letter from Clayton Settles, the man Emma had designated as her assistant manager. Clayton was upset with Emma Sue and thought he would be more qualified to run the store. Jim told Emma to fire Clayton, but she was reluctant and wanted to have a meeting with Jim in attendance. Clayton had been with them for five years and, as far as Jim knew, he had been a good employee.

Emma Sue sat behind her desk and Jim took a chair next to her. The body language was not lost on Clayton. He became noticeably nervous and began to shift around in his seat. "Tell me what's on your mind, Clayton," Jim said.

"Well, Mister Kemper," he said, "I've worked hard here for you, and I'm just not sure I see any way to move up in the company."

"You started as a stocker, didn't you?" Jim asked him.

"Yes, sir, five years ago, and I know you made me an assistant manager, but—"

"Emma Sue made you her assistant manager, Clayton, I didn't."

"I know that, and that's part of the problem. I just don't like workin' for no woman. It just ain't right, Mister Kemper."

Emma Sue could feel Jim looking at her. She shifted in her seat and lowered her eyes from his gaze.

Jim cut his eyes back toward Clayton with a look of disgust on his face and asked him, "What have you been doing here since Emma made you her assistant?"

"I've learned all the inventory, all about maximums and minimums, I learned about what they call first in last out and so forth, you know, sell the oldest product first before it goes bad."

"That's good stuff to know," Jim said. "Do you know about markups and why we price the feed and other products the way we do?"

"Yeah, I mean Yes, sir, I know about labor burden, profit and overhead. I've been handling all the time cards and helping with the bills—the payables. Emma is teaching me about collecting money that is owed to us."

"Receivables?"

"Yes, Receivables, that's the most important."

"How much are you making now, Clayton," Jim asked.

"Well, I started at seventy-five cents an hour, just like everybody else, and after a year I got a raise to a dollar an hour, then a year after that I got a buck-fifty. And when I made assistant manager, Emma Sue raised me to a dollar seventy-five."

"So, the money is not the problem," Jim said. "It's just your having to work for a woman?"

"Yes, sir, I'd just rather work for a man."

Jim felt himself getting angry but he didn't show it. "Who taught you everything you've learned at the store here, Clayton? Did you take classes or something?"

Clayton shook his head, knowing where the conversation was headed.

"Times are changing, Clayton," Jim told him, "and folks who are not willing to change could get left behind. Listen, when Emma first told me about the problem you had with working for a woman, I told her to fire you."

Clayton wrinkled up his mouth and nodded slightly.

"But the reason you are still here, and the reason we are having this meeting is that Emma sees some potential in you. Perhaps it's some hidden quality, and she didn't think you should be tossed aside so lightly. I expect she also might have welcomed the opportunity to let me see what she has to deal with on a daily basis." With that, he winked at Emma Sue, and she smiled back at him. "Now, I have to tell you that Emma's record as manager of this store is unquestionable. I could not have built this business without her, and if you can get past this silliness—and I don't mean to hurt your feelings, Clayton, but it is silliness—and if you can get past it, you can move up. We have plans for a branch store in Brownwood, and that store will need a manager. I anticipate that Emma Sue will become a division manager, and she will have to assign some-one to run this facility while we find someone to run the Brownwood store. I'll give you some advice—learn every-thing you can from Emma Sue. She knows this business better than I do and, unless she just up and quits on me, she's here to stay."

"I will, Mister Kemper," Clayton said. "I'd really appreci-ate the chance to be a manager full time."

"Okay," Jim said, "then I guess we're are all done here. If you'll go on back to work, I want to talk to Emma alone be-fore I leave."

"Yes, sir," Clayton said, "thank you, Mister Kemper." With that, the man shuffled out of the office to go back to his duties.

Emma Sue looked at Jim with a puzzled look on her face. "When did we decide to put a store in Brownwood?" she asked him.

"Oh, I've been thinking about it for a while," he said. "I made the final decision a couple of minutes ago."

She laughed at that and hit his chest with the back of her hand. "Thanks for coming, Jim. I'm sorry for the trouble, I know you're busy."

"I'm never too busy for you," he said. "Just don't take any shit from these guys. You don't have to. You're the boss and if they don't like it, they can go someplace else.

"Thanks, boss," she said:

❧❧❧

Fleetwood Homes began building prefab houses in 1950 and had become the premier name in that field. Jim sought to model his business plan after Fleetwood's approach. The concept was fairly simple. The houses were built in two or more parts with all plumbing and electrical wiring complete, and the walls sheet-rocked and painted. The houses were joined onsite, and set on a pre-poured concrete slab. The trusses and roof were then installed and an electrician and plumber would make the final connections and bring utility service to the property. The finished product was a comfortable three or four-bedroom home at a substantial savings over the standard built-in-place structure.

The manager of the facility in Riverside, California, had agreed over the telephone to take Jim on a tour of the factory. The building was huge and housed the entire process from framing to the touch-up paint. There were dozens of crews working on the various stages of construction. It seemed to Jim to be organized bedlam.

The manager of the facility, a former carpenter named Martin Forsyth, was more than eager to show off his work. He walked Jim through each step in the building process, all up and down the line, introducing him to the employees and the office staff. Jim was impressed by the professionalism and by Martin's knowledge of the job. The thought crossed his mind that maybe one day he might offer the man a job, but that would be just a bit unethical. He would not repay the company's graciousness by hiring away what was obviously a good and loyal employee. But he took Mister Forsyth to lunch and dinner the two days he was there touring the factory.

Martin gave him a complete list of all the different trades that were involved in the process of building the house from ground up to the shipping department. "If you do decide to get into manufactured housing, Jim," he told him, "give me a call anytime, and I'll help you anyway I can."

"That's very kind of you, Martin. I appreciate it, I appreciate it very much. And don't be surprised if you get a call from me soon."

Jim called Jack Grantham from his hotel room and got directions to Jack's home in San Jose. Although they had talked on the phone frequently, he had not seen his old friend nearly as often as they had planned. and the two families had not gotten together since the 1974 visit. They had vowed to get together either in Texas or San Francisco, on a regular basis, but life took over sometimes and changed people's plans. It was going to be different now, he promised himself that it would be different now.

He found the Grantham house with little trouble and Jack and Holly met him at the door. Jack grabbed him and hugged him then Holly did the same. "Wow, it's been a long time," Jim said. Is this the same wife you had last time? She gets prettier every time I see her."

"She's the same one," Jack said, "she just keeps getting better."

"You're too kind, Mister Kemper, "Holly said, laughing. "And you're still the second best looking man I've ever met."

"Thanks, Holly, my wife says the same thing about Jack."

"Well come on in Jim, we've got a lot of catching up to do," Jack said. "How are things going with your farm?"

"It's been like a miracle, Jack," Jim said. "We've been very successful. The dairy is in high production, and we are shipping milk all over Texas and Oklahoma and a few markets in Arkansas and Louisiana. I started a feed and farm equipment supply store in Comanche and we're going to build another one pretty soon. Holly will be pleased to learn that I hired a woman to manage those businesses."

Holly smiled and nodded her approval.

"So, you're rich now, are you?" Jack asked.

"I'm getting there, Jack. I've been more fortunate than I ever imagined I would be. But I've had some good help from folks I've come across." Jim told Jack about Danny Carlisle, and Emma Sue, and Tom Wilcox, his brother-in-law, and the engineering company, and how they'd been so instrumental in his success.

"You always had a knack for spotting good people, didn't you? I mean you liked me right off."

"I did, and I inherited that gift from my grandpa. He taught me how to analyze people very quickly, as soon as I meet them. I've yet to be wrong, as far as I know, but enough about me. You're a state senator now. I guess you were serious about that political business."

"It's working out pretty well for me. I've made my first step just like I planned.

"How are you doing personally, Jack, you and Holly?"

"I couldn't ask for a better life. Holly's father, Sam was ready to retire and put me in charge of the newspaper but he put that on hold when I won the state senate election. I was getting good at the job, although it is tedious sometimes and dealing with newspaper people can be a pain in the ass. I was making good money, and Holly was happy, and that's all that matters, but now I'm off to public service."

"Do you recall that you told me you were going to run for president one day?"

"I did, and I still am. I have a plan...well, sort of a plan. Sam suggested I run for the state senate first, before I move into national politics, and now I've done that."

"I sense some hesitation in your voice," Jim said. "Is there a problem? Are you sure that is what you want to do?"

"I have a passion for it, Jim," he said. "But the crap you have to go through and the people you have to deal with are a pain in the neck. I've never been politically active, and Holly's people are all Democrats so I guess I'll have to run as a Democrat. Sam said I won't stand a chance as a Republican in the bay area. I don't honestly know what I am."

"My grandfather was a Democrat and just assumed I would be too when I grew up, but grandpa hated FDR, mostly because my father was killed in the war. Grandpa thought we should have stayed out of the war. One of Grandpa's lifelong friends in Comanche was a man named Kinnie Sullivan. And well, Kinnie was a Republican, the only one in the county, apparently. Kinnie taught me the Republican philosophy on business and what they call Conservatism. I discovered that I was probably a Republican. I didn't know for sure but about six months ago I was asked to join the Texas Coalition of Republican Businessmen. I didn't think it could hurt anything so I joined. I found a lot of business people. They have women in the coalition of Republican businessmen. Imagine that. But I met a lot of people itching to invest in new companies, and I'm going to need investors with some of the plans I have in the works. I can't finance it all myself, and I can't use the dairy or the engineering company for collateral because I have partners and it wouldn't be fair to risk their livelihoods with my adventures."

"It sounds like you've got your shit together, Jim." It's very impressive, I have to tell you. I can't see myself running a newspaper thirty years from now, reporting on things other people do. I want to make news, not report it."

"I believe you will," Jim said. "I'll help anyway I can. I think you'd be a great president. Just remember what I told you when I came back from Vietnam about not using your war record in your campaign. You're a Medal of Honor winner, Jack. That is a hell of a deal. I mean it."

"I know it is, and I appreciate your reminding me."

"Make a plan, and be specific," Jim said. "Set a timeline and stick to it. Don't give up, if you really want it, don't ever give up."

∽∾∽∾

Since the beginning of business, Kemper Engineering took most of Jim's time. He spent the better part of 1974 in Dallas, except for the few days he took to go visit Fleetwood and the Granthams. He stayed alternately with his mother and stepdad, Trenton, and in hotels. Eventually he rented an apartment, but being alone was something he just didn't do well. He had Mattie hire a live-in housekeeper, and nanny for the children, so he could bring her with him on occasion. Mattie went with him one week out of every month. Being more accustomed to fine dining than Jim, Mattie insisted they find and discover new places to eat every night. Jim explained to her that, unless she developed a craving for barbeque or fried chicken, it would be very difficult to impress her with the cuisine of Big D.

"It's not Baltimore or Annapolis, Mattie," he told her."

Mattie loved her life on their farm. The nice house made the difference but she was not disappointed with the choices she had made. Marrying Jim Kemper and moving to Texas, as different as it was from Maryland, was her life's choice and she was not sorry. But the time in Dallas for that year made her long for some social interaction with other people. She liked Dallas, she discovered, and when Jim hinted that they might eventually need to move there so he could be closer to his business and his family, at the same time, she was pleased. She didn't let him know she was pleased for fear of hurting his feelings about the farm.

Later, when he asked her what she thought about making the move, she responded as she often did. "I go where you go, James Kemper," she said. "You should know that by now."

"I know it gets lonely there by yourself on the farm and I miss you every minute I'm away, the kids too. I just don't like being away from my family."

It took a year for Jim to put together a business plan for the manufactured housing factory, and to get the money. This was no feed and farm supply business. It would take a lot of property and a huge building, plus equipment and tools and skilled workers. It would also take ten million dollars, which he didn't have yet. So he got half the money from Abel Hansen and took in five investors, each with a million dollars, which all but one had to mortgage themselves to the hilt to get financed for their investment capital.

Jim retained controlling interest in the venture and asked them to agree to sell their shares back to him, at fair market value in about five years or so. He promised them they would be multi-millionaires by then.

Abel Hansen had put up a million dollars of his own money to invest in the company that would be called Kemper Enterprises. Abel made it a point, every so often, to remind himself that Jim Kemper was only in his early thirties—he was, in fact, only thirty-three years old when the deal was signed to start the business. But Jim Kemper was no ordinary thirty-three-year-old man. He was a natural born entrepreneur, with business sense far beyond his years and energy and drive to succeed that was unrivaled by anyone Abel Hansen had ever known. Hansen and the other four stockholders had invested their money, their hopes, their dreams, and their futures, not in a pre-fab housing business but in Jim Kemper himself. Abel Hansen knew a winner when he saw one, and Jim Kemper was a winner, if he'd ever seen one.

Construction on the factory began early in 1975 and by summer of '76, it was fitted and stocked and operations began. Marcus Hererra came to Dallas, on loan from his Uncle Danny, to learn the products, the different floor plans, and the installation process. Jim asked him to embark on a mission to set up sales offices all over Texas and into Mexico. By the end of the decade, they would have sales offices in most states across the south and a few as far West as New Mexico and Colorado. Marcus proved to be an amazing young man with a business acumen that was self-taught more than learned. Jim was going to find it hard to give him back to the dairy when the time came that Danny requested his return.

Carlisle seemed content to handle the sales and promotions for the dairy, for the time being and, whether for his own purposes or out of a desire to see his nephew become a larger figure in the bigger picture, he told Jim to keep Marcus for as long as he needed him. Jim was more than happy with the arrangement. Marcus bought a house in Dallas and moved his family there so he could be closer to his job.

Marcus's move to Dallas made Jim accept a hard reality that he would also have to relocate to where his business interests were. It would not be easy, although Mattie did not seem to have a problem with living in Dallas. Leaving the farm after only eight years there, a place he'd planned to live the rest of his life, would be an emotional blow to him and the kids as well. The two boys were in their seventh and sixth grades in school and the girls had completed the first grade. They had friends in Comanche, they had lives there.

Jim found a house he wanted to buy but would make no offer on it without bringing Mattie and the kids to see it. So, one Saturday morning, he loaded the whole gang in the car and drove to Dallas to show them the house. He had made arrangements to meet the realtor there to show them the inside.

"Get ready, guys," Jim said, as he turned off of Preston Road onto Beverly Drive. "We're going to be living in Highland Park. This is a very nice house, and I am hopeful that you will all be happy here. I won't buy it, though, if we don't all agree that we can live here."

Turning onto Lakeside Drive, he told them to cover their eyes, and they all did, including Mattie. He parked on the curb in front of the second house on the right, 4907 Lakeside Drive, and told them to remove their hands from their eyes.

"My heavens, Jim," Mattie said, "it's a mansion. I had no idea it would be like this."

The house that Jim wanted to buy for them was a mansion indeed. It was a stately mansion, all white with a front portico and elegant columns. "It looks like the White House," Alton said.

"I'm glad you noticed that, Alton," Jim said. "That was one of the reasons I liked it right off. My good friend Jack Grantham wants to be president one day and when he comes to visit us it will fire him up even more."

"But how can we afford this, Jim?" Mattie said. "How much does this thing cost? I mean, it's beautiful but can we do this?"

"It's already done just as soon as you agree," he said. "I've secured financing and all that's left is for us to sign the papers. Now don't make up your mind right away, we still have to see the inside."

"How much is it?" she asked him.

He mumbled something that she could not hear and she asked him again. She knew he didn't want to tell her the cost when he mumbled something again that was unintelligible.

She began to laugh. "You don't want to tell me the cost, do you?" she said.

"It's right around a million," he finally said, and she heard that.

"Holy shit," she exclaimed and then apologized to the kids for her outburst. "How can we do this? I mean, how can we afford this house?"

"We can't," he said, "but we will be able to before too much longer. We have a lot of collateral now with the new business, and the two feed stores. I can swing it. Don't worry."

Mattie knew they were doing well. She knew they were making money. Her husband was a good businessman and was fearless to start new adventures. She'd seen the bank accounts and the tax returns so she was aware that the family was comfortable. But for the first time since they had married, she realized just how special her husband, James Earl Kemper, really was. He would be a force in this town and in the country as well one day. The Kempers were rich. She wasn't sure just how rich yet, but she knew they were rich. Yes, they would live in this house on Turtle Creek but they would not become snobs. She would not let them become snobs. Their children would attend public schools, and she would see that they remained grounded in humility and inculcated with the values they'd learned at the Kemper farm.

⟡⟡⟡

It took a month for them to get completely relocated from the farm to Dallas. Mattie managed the move, coordinating with the movers, marking boxes, and making certain that nothing was left behind. It was hard, frustrating work. A family of six accumulated a lot of stuff in ten years and there was very little that could be thrown out without protest from this kid or that one.

Jim had offered his brother Trent a job at the dairy, and Trent accepted, albeit with less enthusiasm than Jim would have liked. Jim's motivation was two-fold. First, he wanted someone to stay in the house and maintain it. Second, Trent had, at his father's insistence, attended four years at UT Arlington but as yet had no degree and no apparent plan for his own future. Jim knew Danny Carlisle would watch over the boy and make him work and thereby motivate him to make something of himself. Jim had contemplated letting Emma Sue teach Trent to manage the feed store in Brownwood but decided against that because there would not be sufficient direct supervision, and Jim was not sure his younger brother could be trusted to work unsupervised. So, Trenton would be living and working on the farm.

The Kempers would visit the farm about once a month so Jim could confer with Danny on issues regarding the dairy. They often went back for holidays and four-day weekends and occasionally for vacation. Trent seemed glad to have them all there because it had to be very different for a young man to leave Dallas to live and work in the more austere surroundings of the Kemper farm. Danny said the boy was doing a good job and learning quickly. Trent was up early and was not in the habit of being late or missing work. Jim was pleased and he gave credit to Danny Carlisle for his brother's progress.

Jim's workload was becoming overwhelming, and he found that he seemed to be working or traveling all the time. He decided to make a move that he would have to justify to himself that it was not unethical. Kemper Industries, specifically the pre-fab housing division, was booming and quickly becoming unmanageable for one man. He knew he was going to need some help. He contacted Martin Forsyth, the plant manager for Fleetwood Homes, and offered him a job. Forsyth was open to the offer and agreed to fly to Dallas for a sit-down with Jim.

Jim met Martin at Love Field and drove him to the facility. Jim took him to a new office on the second floor that had just been finished out with new furniture and a huge desk that would make the Oval Office envious. "Go ahead, Martin," Jim said. "You sit in the desk and I'll pull up a chair."

The move was not lost on Mister Forsyth, and he chuckled. "It's a beautiful desk, Jim. You may not get me out from behind it once I sit down."

"That was my plan, Martin. I would like to entice you to come to Texas and run this place for me."

"It's a challenge I would relish, Jim. It will be hard leaving my home in California, and I'd have to convince my wife and kids but they might be open to it. What exactly do you have in mind for me to do? I've been running the plant for Fleetwood, but I wouldn't mind taking on some more responsibility."

"I'm going to offer you the top desk, Martin. That's the one you're sitting behind now," Jim said.

"Wow," Martin said. "I know the business pretty well, but, I'll be honest, I'm not sure that I can do that job. I only graduated high school, I have no college degree, and I've been doing my current job for almost twenty years. Are you sure you want to offer me this job. Don't get me wrong, Jim, I'd love to do it, but I don't want to make the move and put you to a lot of expense just to disappoint you later."

"I've thought about that, and I appreciate your honesty. I knew your credentials before I called you, and here is why I think it will work. We have bookkeepers, a CPA, and office staff to do billing and the normal functions of a large office such as ours. You will need to interview people for the various departments and basically just manage everything through them. We have some good department heads but I want you to evaluate them and make any changes you deem appropriate. Spend as much time in the plant as you think is necessary. We'll go over the books, with the accountants and the financial officer once a month and anything you don't understand, we'll learn together. When I started this operation, I didn't know anything about it except what I learned from you out in Riverside. I'm ready to take this thing to the next level so I need to get some professional help.

Martin swiveled his chair from side to side and then rolled it up to the desk. "Well, Jim," he said. "If you have that much confidence in me, then I'm on board. I won't let you down for lack of trying."

"Just promise me that if you get in over your head, or if you think you're in over your head, call me, and we'll work it out."

"I will," Martin said. "You can count on that. I'd rather admit I need help than to screw something up."

"That's all I ask," Jim said. "Now, I guess you'd like to know what financial benefit this move will be to you."

Martin smiled broadly. "I'm glad you brought it up, because I didn't want to."

"Okay, well, the entry level position is a hundred K plus insurance and benefits, of course, holidays and vacation, pretty much standard stuff. It's a salaried position so you'll keep your own schedule. Also, you'll need a place to live for you and your family, here is what I have in mind. I have an acre of land in North Dallas. We'll build one of our four-bedroom units, the biggest and the best, on it and get it set up. You commit to fifteen years with me and the house will be yours, free and clear. Let me assure you, Martin, we're talking seven figures a year at some point in the future. Don't let that scare you, let it inspire you."

"That's very generous, Jim," Martin said. "Thank you."

"It's not generosity, Martin, it's business. If I didn't know you can do this, you wouldn't be here."

"I'll give you the best I've got."

"And I'll give you mine. So, we have a deal?"

"Yes, sir, boss, we have a deal."

They shook hands on it and Jim suggested they go to lunch.

૯∕ЭC∕Э

George Matthews died in February of 1981, and Jim went to his funeral in Comanche. Allie and Trenton were going as well, mainly for Allie's mother, Mae Ellen. Allie had little desire to see her brothers. Jim took Mattie along because he needed some insulation from his two uncles. He never liked the boys because they were so jealous of Trenton and made no secret about it.

It was a pretty dry and ritual affair. Jim spoke to a few of the people he knew. Most of his grandpa's old friends were all dead now. He never really knew George Matthews. Grandpa didn't like him, his mother was resentful toward him. Jim never knew why there was so much tension between Allie and her family. There just was, and he never gave it much serious thought.

Mae Ellen talked to Trenton about running the business, but he had little interest other than continuing to manage the Dallas operation. Matthews's two sons had always wanted to run the business, and Trenton suggested that Mrs. Matthews let them have a go at it. He didn't have much hope that they would do anything but play at running a business, but, at this stage of the game, she didn't have much choice.

At the gravesite, Jim sought to comfort his mother. He hugged her after the service was over. "I'm sorry, Mother," he told her. "He was your father so I know it can't be easy."

"I'm okay," Allie said. "Alton Kemper was my father. He was the only father I ever had."

"I can't say that hurts my feelings, but you should try to comfort your mother. She needs you now, more than ever."

"I will," she said. "I love my mother. She deserved so much better than the life she's had."

"I have to go. We'll talk again in two weeks. We're going to Maryland next week, the whole family, to take Alton for his summer with his foreign, grandparents."

She laughed. "Alton showed me a picture of the reason his heart is in Maryland. She's breathtaking, you know. You're going to lose that boy not too long from now."

"I know, he is in love and, you know what? I think it's the real thing, for both of them. We're going to see her again next week. Shadow is of Japanese descent, adopted by her parents, the McCormicks. She's a beautiful girl, a wonderful girl. And she and Alton seem to be hopelessly in love."

Alton's and Shadow's wedding took place in the park not far from Mattie's parents' home. There were at least a hundred people in attendance. Most were from the University, friends of Alton's and Shadow's. Charlie was there, with his girlfriend Jenny, to stand as best man for his brother. They gathered around the tree where the two newlyweds had first kissed. Shadow came up a few notches in Mattie's view if that were possible. The uniqueness of that struck her as just a beautiful thing to do. It also confirmed her earlier suspicion that the McCormicks were ex-hippies. The earthiness, of it all confirmed that in her mind.

She hugged her daughter-in-law and told her, "Welcome to the Kemper family, darling. You will make a valuable addition. I can't imagine a more perfect girl, excuse me, a more perfect woman to take my son away from me."

"I knew he was quality the first day I met him, Mattie," Shadow said.

"And you were, what, twelve years old at the time?"

"I've always been ahead of my age, at least that what my daddy always told me."

"Well, I believe it is so," Mattie said. "You know, my father used to bring me to this park when I was a little girl."

"So, did mine," Shadow said. "We spent a lot of time here. It's one of my favorite places, especially now. This is where I realized that I was in love with Alton."

In March of 1989 Charles McKenna suffered a heart attack and died, having never met his soon to be born greatgrandchild. That was the saddest part for Mattie, losing her father before what would have been one of his greatest joys. Coincidentally, former Maryland Governor George P. Mahoney died on the eighteenth, just a few days after Charles.

Aimee McKenna was in poor health and Mattie worried that she might lose them both so close together. Her parents had always been very close, codependent, and inseparable as long as she and her sister Andrea had been alive. The funeral had been more of a state affair than a family event. Governor Schaefer even showed up to say a few words. It was nice, Mattie thought, but she would have preferred a more private service.

In July of 1990, Jim's and Mattie's attention turned to the growing trouble in the Middle East. Iraq accused Kuwait of stealing oil from Rumaylah, Iraq's oil field near the Kuwait border, and was threatening military action. Squabbles in the Mideast ordinarily would not have drawn any attention from the Kemper family but this could turn into a full-blown war that might disrupt the flow of oil that was vital to United

States' interest worldwide. On the twenty-second, Saddam Hussein started deploying his troops to the Iraq border with Kuwait. And on the second of August, 100,000 Iraqi troops invaded Kuwait.

President Bush made a declaration that "This will not stand" and a deadline was set for Iraq to withdraw from Kuwait by January 29, 1991 or face military action. The U.N. Security Council immediately passed Resolution 660, demanding that the Iraqis withdraw from Kuwait immediately and unconditionally. On August 6, Resolution 661 was passed, imposing a trade embargo on Iraq. Saddam Hussein responded by annexing Kuwait. On August seventh, the US launched Desert Shield, and the first American troops began arriving in Saudi Arabia.

On January ninth, talks between US Secretary of State James Baker and the Iraqi Foreign Minister Tariq Azis broke down and were ended. On the twelfth, the US Congress passed a joint resolution authorizing the use of military force to drive the Iraqis out of Kuwait.

That same day, Charlie received orders to report to his national guard unit for immediate deployment to Saudi Arabia.

"Now I know how my grandpa felt when I went off to Vietnam," Jim told Mattie. "This shit just never ends, does it?"

"He'll be okay," Mattie said, "we have to believe that and keep believing it."

Charlie's unit arrived in Saudi Arabia on October 15, 1990 and received their equipment. He and his crew, with the exception of the loader, had trained together every summer at Fort Hood since Charlie had received his commission. His driver was Corporal Henry (Hank) Wilson from Topeka, Kansas, with six years in the army. His gunner was Staff Sergeant Martin (Marty) Phillips from Lubbock, Texas. And the loader, Specialist 1, Arlen Green was from Chicago. They all shook hands with the new man.

"So, what do we call you, Arlen?" Hank asked the new guy. "Arlen don't sound like much of a badass name. What's your war name?"

"Shine," Arlen said, "I go by Shine."

"Damn, Arlen," Charlie said, "how the hell did you get that name? It doesn't bother you to be called by a racial slur?"

"No, sir, Lieutenant," he said. "I gave it to myself. The last crew I was on didn't like Black folks so I took that name as a sort of, in your face, thing. It shut them up. You don't have any problem with me being on your crew, do you, Lieutenant?"

"Hell no, Arlen," Charlie said, "and knock of that lieutenant shit, unless there are big shots around. If you don't have a problem riding with a Honky from Dallas, then we'll get along just fine. When the shit starts, I don't want some 'why are we here' shithead watching my back. I'd rather have a badass Black dude from Chicago that will help me kill the bad guys."

"All-fucking-right, LT," Arlen responded. "I won't let you down, Charlie, and thank you."

The others patted him on the back and scuffled around with each other. Charlie had his crew.

Saturday February twenty-third, at four a.m. Saudi Time, they were given the Go Ahead, along with eighteen hundred plus other Abrams crews to begin the ground war into Iraq.

"Charge" came the command over the intercom and Lieutenant Kemper told his driver, "Let's go, Hank, we've got places to be and people to kill."

The Abrams roared to life and headed out across the vast Iraqi desert. Charlie and his crew would be in intense mortal combat for one hundred hours—four days in which the US military would win its quickest and most lop-sided war, in terms of casualties and equipment lost.

Charlie Kemper had honored his father and gone to war, just as Jim Kemper had done twenty-four years before. It was relatively painless for Charlie and not nearly as long and as great a personal sacrifice as it had been for his dad, but he had done it.

ↂↄↂ

In 1994 Jim bought fifty acres of a plot of land on the east side of North Collins Street, just north of SE Green Oaks

Boulevard in Arlington, on which he planned, at some future date, to build an office complex that would house Kemper Enterprises, a holding company under which he planned to bring all his business entities. It would also offer extensive office space and services to many other companies and ventures. He planned to build two separate buildings of about forty stories each which he would name after his grandfather. Alton Kemper Towers would be the premier office complex in the area, and Jim hoped would rejuvenate the commercial and residential building market in Arlington.

The project would be a year in the planning and ground-breaking was tentatively scheduled for the spring of 1996. Charlie had taken over the management of the construction project and was fully involved in every decision. He'd set up a huge office trailer complex and was spending the bulk of his time on the jobsite. It was a burdensome job keeping track of every single trade on the project. The electrical and HVAC installation were being done "in house" so to speak, with Kemper Engineering doing the work on a cost-plus basis. Mike Andrews, for whom Charlie had worked when he first started with the company, was the electrical project manager on the project. He had an office next to Charlie in the construction trailer. It had been awkward at first. Mike was forty years old and Charlie still only twenty-nine, but they got past any potential problems. Charlie, like his dad, did not try to throw his weight around. He asked people to do things rather than ordering them. It worked wonders to alleviate any bitter feelings that might arise because of his youth. Charlie Kemper had that special aura about him, the same mysterious element possessed by the older Kemper that made people not even realize that he was as young as he was. They followed him instinctively, without hesitation. At this point in the game, most of the men and women who worked for him were years older than he.

It was the confidence he exuded that inspired trust and loyalty. Admittedly, some of the respect he received was due to the great confidence that people had in Jim Kemper. The years had proven that Jim's plan to bring his son into the business and to prepare him to take over one day had worked and was bearing fruit. Employees of Kemper Enterprises were beginning to accept that the younger Kemper was his father's equal and that the company was in good hands.

Chapter 17

Alton Kemper II

Jim's and Mattie's firstborn son, who was named, with Mattie's permission of course, after Jim's grandfather, spent the first two and a half years of his life in the presence of his maternal grandparents. The McKennas were a more genteel bunch than the rougher cut Kempers of Texas and the youngest Kemper would take on their ways and their attitudes as he grew up. He would be less Texan than his younger brother, a fact that Jim eventually had to accept. It was not necessarily bad, he reasoned, for a boy to attain a certain amount of culture.

His mother, Mattie, certainly was cultured enough and it hadn't hurt her. She had been down to earth enough to fall in love with Jim Kemper, hadn't she? And that not being at the time, given his circumstances and prospects for the future, the prudent course of action a sensible father would have desired for his daughter.

Alton II, was so named, by compromise, after Jim's grandfather, with the understanding that the next male Kemper would be named Charles, after the Honorable Charles McKenna, the state senator from Maryland, Jim's father-in-law, a good-hearted man, Jim came to realize. Alton was drawn to his grandmother, Aimee McKenna. He was drawn to her much the same way that Jim had been drawn to his grandfather Alton Kemper when he was growing up, believing that his grandparent had no faults and was incapable of wrongdoing. The boy's relationship with his grandmother would be an impenetrable one, one to which even his father Jim, whom he would come to respect more than anyone else in the world, would have to accept second place. It was a small price to pay for having the boy for a son, Jim thought.

Alton and his grandmother Aimee exchanged letters on a weekly basis. At first it was just some scribbling and pictures Alton drew but later, as he got older, he kept up the routine and his grandmother was faithful to send a return letter every time. She taped each and every picture he sent her to the refrigerator or on the wall, until their house was practically covered with Alton's works of art.

Jim's firstborn child was a remarkable boy, very smart and studious. He was not the loud and boisterous boy that his younger brother, Charlie, was. Self-assured and confident, quietly confident, Jim learned early on just how smart Alton was. Jim played checkers with him regularly when Alton was just six years old, and the boy would quickly get bored with the game, so Jim bought him a chess-set and began to teach him the game.

Trenton had taught Jim how to play chess when he was a kid but he never had passion for the game. Still, he could easily beat a six-year-old and he would let Alton win sometimes so he would not get discouraged. Eventually the boy got better, and Jim found it a little harder to win each time, and then a lot harder. Soon he had to fight to win a game. Alton's grandmother sent him a book on chess and he studied it religiously, plotting strategies, tactics, and different defenses, His father wanted to give up but he didn't dare. Jim was amused and proud that his son could make him look like a rookie on a chess table.

Once the family moved to Dallas, the McKennas made more frequent trips to visit and the Kempers were able to repay the visits to Maryland with more ease. It was just easier to fly out of Dallas into BWI than getting to and from Comanche. Jim and Mattie walked through the little park that ran the length of Lakeside Drive and along Turtle Creek with her mother and father. The McKennas marveled at the beauty of the place. "This is one of the most beautiful places I've even seen, Mattie," Aimee McKenna told her daughter.

"It's just perfect, Mother. I couldn't be happier. Can you believe that soldier, who walked into our home in Annapolis that time, has done all this?"

Aimee nodded. "I could tell you I'm not surprised, but it wouldn't be the whole truth. My heavens, Mattie, I would have been satisfied just knowing he came home from that awful war in one piece. If he'd turned out to be a mechanic or a plumber, we'd still feel the same way about him. He's still the most beautiful man I ever saw."

Mattie laughed at that. "I remember you said that the first time I had him come over. And yes, I still think so too. He's wonderful with the kids, spoils the girls rotten, though. I can't make Aimee do anything lest she tell her Daddy on me."

"Mattie, your father and I would like for the boys to come and stay with us next summer if it's okay with you and Jim. I know the girls are too young yet to go away from home for that long but the boys would be such a blessing for us. Do you think Jim will be okay with that?"

"Let me talk to him, Mother," Mattie said. "Charlie plays baseball so that might be a problem but Alton only seems to be interested in academics, mostly history. It might do him good to see some of the Civil War battlefields around Maryland and Pennsylvania. I'm sure he'd enjoy it."

Alton Kemper, like his namesake, was a quiet boy but he had an inner strength that Jim recognized right away. He'd often step into the fray that frequently broke out between his two sisters and calmly talk them into apologizing to each other. He'd make them hug each other and remember that they were sisters and that sisters never stayed mad very long.

Once when the boys were in junior high school, Jim got a call from Mattie at his office. "Guess what, Jim," she said. "Your son got suspended for fighting after school."

"Dammit," he said, "what's Charlie done now?"

"It wasn't Charlie this time, it was Alton." There was silence on the other end of the phone. Jim could not believe what he'd just heard.

Alton had apparently gotten crossways with another boy. Jim and Mattie got the story from Charlie, who told the tale in

great detail. "See, Pop, this kid named Edmond has been messin' with Alton all year. Alton didn't do anything to Edmond
but Edmond just took a dislike to Alton for some reason. And
every time Edmond would say something bad to Alton, Alton
would come back with something like 'You must have low
self-esteem if that's the only way you feel you can communicate.' You know how Alton is, he never gets mad, but ol' Edmond kept getting pissed, oh, sorry Mom, anyway, Edmond
kept getting madder and madder, so he invites Alton out after
school. So after school," he continued, "we all meet on the
baseball field. Edmond said he was going to kick Alton's
ass—ah, I'm sorry, Mom, can you go in the other room?"

"Not on your life," Mattie said. "Go on with your story and
I'll absolve you of any inappropriate speech. I want to hear
this."

"Okay, well, Alton said something about how fighting never solved anything. I know he got that from Grandma Aimee,
so I told Edmond that if there was going to be any ass kicking
it was going to be 'me' kicking 'his' ass. Well, he didn't want
that to happen, and I could tell that by looking at his eyes. He
was about to piss his pants. But just as I was about to get on
him, Alton said, 'that's okay Charlie, I'll fight him.'

"Well that was not what Edmond was expecting but he'd
come too far to back down so he walked up to Alton, and Alton knocked him on his ass. Then Edmond gets up and runs at
Alton and they go down rolling around on the ground until
Alton gets on top of him and starts hitting him in the face.
About that time the principal grabs Alton by his shirt and pulls
him off. We all had to go to the office. I told the principal that
Edmond started it and just got what he had coming. He suspended Edmond too. And that's how it happened."

"Okay, Charlie," Jim said, "thank you, and thanks for sticking up for your brother."

"I don't think he needs me sticking up for him anymore,"
Charlie said. "Alton is tougher than he lets on."

It was decided that Alton would spend the summer of '76
in Annapolis with his maternal grandparents. His brother
Charlie would go along but would only stay two weeks, being

the star of his little league baseball team required him to be at home because the team needed him.

The McKennas were ecstatic to have the two boys with them. Mattie's sister had not yet married so Mattie's four children were the only grandchildren they had. It was not easy for them living so far away from the kids when they wanted so desperately to have an active part in their lives. It was the price they paid for their daughter's chosen life. But Aimee McKenna was not bitter about how things had turned out. She spent many nights crying silently in her room for all of her daughter's children, fearful that something might happen to one of them.

She was afraid that she might die before she had formed a strong enough bond with them that they would always remember her fondly after she was gone. Alton was her favorite, everyone knew that, although she never said it out loud. She had received hundreds of drawings and letters from him over the years and had finally, at her husband's insistence, she took them down from the walls and refrigerator and stored them in a box in the attic. Only the latest four or five remained posted in her bedroom and kitchen.

The advent and availability of personal email, in the early '70s was changing the way people communicated, and changing it drastically. Her husband Charles was able to get letters from Alton, at his office, and would dutifully bring them home to his wife. They had decided that it was time for a home computer, so when the two boys came to visit this summer, they would all go and buy one so Aimee could more easily stay in touch with her beloved grandson.

She bought an Apple I which, the salesman explained, came with a video interface, 8k of RAM, and a keyboard. Keyboard was about all she understood of the pitch and her husband complained of the $700.00 cost, but nevertheless reluctantly shelled out the money. If it made his wife happy, then he was okay with it. If it kept them in closer contact with their daughter and grandkids, then it was a small price to pay.

"I'll show you how to use it, Grandma," Alton told her. "Daddy bought us one for the house and it's easy to use.

"I'm sure you can, my darling boy," she said. "You're a lot smarter than I am."

They spent the summer going places. Charles McKenna took his grandson to the Maryland State House to show him what he did for a living. Alton asked a lot of questions, Charles assumed that the boy had spent a lot of time listening to his father doing business on the phone. "Are you a Democrat, Grandpa?" the boy asked him.

"I am, Alton, most of the folks in Maryland are Democrats. Now, don't get me wrong, your father is a Republican, but he is a good man, a very smart man. We just disagree on some things. That doesn't mean we don't like each other though."

"I guess I am a Republican too because my dad is, but I don't really know."

"You have a lot of time before you're old enough to figure that all out, Alton," he said. The boy didn't respond but appeared to be very thoughtful about what his grandfather had said.

All in all, it was pretty boring, Alton later confided to his grandmother.

"Please don't tell your grandfather, Alton," she said. "It would hurt his feelings."

"I won't, Grandma. Daddy has always told me to be careful of hurting people's feelings. Daddy says that not saying something that is the truth is not always lying."

"Your daddy is a smart man," Aimee said.

"He's the smartest man in the world," Alton quickly responded.

"Well, he may very well be, Grandson. I suspect he may very well be."

At least one day a week they had lunch at Middleton Tavern, on the square, commonly referred to as just Middleton's. It was Aimee's favorite place to eat. Then they would walk down Compromise Street to the marina to look at the boats. The McKennas had a small sailboat, a sloop it was, to be exact, a Catalina. The three of them went sailing on the Chesapeake Bay at least once a month. By the end of the summer, Alton fancied himself quite a sailor.

Alton was content to sit for hours in the sunroom with his grandmother. Once she noticed him staring at her, deep in thought. "What's on your mind, Alton?" she asked him.

"I like it here, Grandma," he said. "Can I come back every summer?"

"Well, honey," she said. "We'll have to check with your mom and dad, but, if it's okay with them, then I would love to have you here every summer. I know your grandfather would love that too. But are you sure you'd not rather stay at home with your brother and sisters and all your friends?"

"No, I'd rather be here," he said, "I don't have that many friends. I'd rather stay here every summer."

"Well, of course I'd rather have you here too. We'll ask your folks when they come to pick you up, okay."

He nodded his head up and down. "I love you, Grandma," he said.

Aimee started to cry and motioned for him to come to her. "I love you too, honey," she said. "Come give me a hug." He ran to her and she squeezed him in a loving embrace and he hugged her back. "You give good hugs, Alton."

"You give good hugs too, Grandma."

The summer came and went, like they always do, too quickly it was over for Aimee McKenna, but the last week of summer blessed them with the rest of the Kemper clan. Jim had some business in Washington. He wanted to get to know the players at the RNC and meet his congressman and senators from Texas. Mainly, he wanted them to get to know him. It was always business with Jim Kemper. He came back to the McKennas very elated that he had met John Tower, the first Republican senator from Texas since Reconstruction. His father-in-law was not as impressed, as was Jim. Republican was not a dirty word in the McKenna house but neither was it considered sacred.

"It's just business, Charles," Jim said. "I really don't care much for politicians, no matter which side they are on."

"Well, Jim, I guess I wouldn't either, if I were not one of them. It's a job like anything else, only as good as the man who does it."

"We've got an election coming up," Jim said. "I assume you'll be toeing the party line and casting your vote for Carter?"

"I suppose," Charles said. "I don't much care for that peanut farmer, but I have a duty to do."

"I understand, sir. I was a little put off with Ford after he pardoned Nixon, I thought that was wrong. But I'll vote Republican and hope my grandpa never gets wind of it." They both laughed at that.

Charles said, "So your grandfather was a Democrat?"

"Yes, dyed-in-the-wool, whatever that means. All my family, and all their friends, were lifelong Democrats, except for one good friend of my grandpa, a man named Kinnie Sullivan who was a very conservative fellow. He turned me into a Republican. Thankfully, my grandpa never knew."

The McKennas waited until the night before they left to go home, at dinner, to bring up the possibility of Alton spending the summers with them. It was a surprise, to say the least, to Jim and Mattie. It had been hard enough to let one of their children leave for the entire summer, once, but to consider it for every summer…well, Jim wasn't sure he could handle that.

Aimee made her case. "Charles and I would, of course, love to have them all come every summer but I know you cannot do that, it would be too disruptive, I know. But if maybe Charlie could come with Alton for a week or so and then Alton could stay the summer, like he did this summer, it would mean so much to us."

Alton came to his grandmother's assistance. "Dad, you're going to be busy with your work, and with Charlie playing baseball. You won't have a lot of time in the summer so, if I come to stay with Grandma Aimee and Grandpa Charles, I won't be any trouble for you at home."

Jim stared lovingly at his oldest boy for a moment. "Son," he said, "you've never been any trouble to me and your mom, never. Alton, you're the best—" He stopped for a moment and glanced over at Charlie, who had stopped eating and was listening intently for what his father was about to say. "Alton," Jim continued, "I could not ask for a better son than you have been. I was blessed, your mom feels the same way too, since the day you were born, you're a blessing to us every day." Charlie shrugged his shoulders and started eating again. "I just want you to be happy, son, and if you want to spend summers here with your grandma and grandpa, then it's okay with me. I expect your mom will agree.

"I do understand the relationship between a grandparent and a grandkid. Remember, my grandfather was the only father figure and male role model I had, until my stepfather, Trenton, came along. He was a good man and treated me like one of his own. But it was my grandpa who shaped my life. The influence such a relationship can have on grandparent and grandkid alike, is immeasurable. You just can't replace it."

His seven-year-old daughter, Aimee, spoke up. "What about me, Daddy?"

"What about you, Aimee?" Jim asked her.

"Am I a blessing too?"

"Yes, my dear, you are a blessing too, you are all blessings to me," he said.

Eventually, Jim and Mattie started letting the girls go for the two-week visit along with Charlie. Mattie would fly with them to Baltimore and, on several occasions, she stayed with them as well. Then she flew back with the three kids while Alton stayed the summer.

The McKennas bought a bicycle for Alton the next time he came for the summer. The bike opened up his world, since his grandparents lived close to downtown Annapolis, and he rode it in and around the quiet, pleasant neighborhood and even around the square and to the marina.

Alton asked a stranger how to find the Driftwood in Annapolis. And the man, although a bit surprised why a boy would want to know how to find a bar, nevertheless gave him directions to the place. Alton found the bar, locked his bike to a parking meter, and walked into the place like he belonged there. He didn't get far.

"Whatta you want, bub?" an older, bearded man asked him. "Kids can't come in here."

"My mom and dad met in this place and I just wanted to take a look," Alton said.

"How long ago was that?"

"I don't know for sure, maybe fourteen or fifteen years ago."

"I've only been working here about five years," the man said. "Aw, hell, come on in, I guess it won't hurt to give you a tour."

There wasn't much to see. It was just one big room with a bar on one side and bathrooms on the other. Alton noticed two tables with chairs on either side. One table had a board and checkers on it and the other one had chess pieces.

"People play chess in here?" Alton asked him.

"Some of the navy guys do, most of the other folks who come in are too stupid to play chess. That's what the checkers are for—the dumbasses.

The boy started laughing at the man's use of profanity. It was different for him to be around such talk. His mother protected him from it and his dad, although he slipped up once in a while, usually watched his language around the house. The only person in the family who cursed was his brother Charlie.

"Was your dad in the navy?" the man asked.

"No, he was in the army. He flew a helicopter in Vietnam."

"No shit?" the man said.

"No shit," Alton replied, enjoying himself in the candid talk.

"Now look here, bub, I don't want your momma coming in here getting on me for teaching you bad words."

"Don't worry, my parents live in Texas."

"Texas? Then what are you doing here?" the man asked.

"I spend summers with my grandparents," Alton said as he started playing with the chess pieces on the other small table.

"You play chess?"

"Some," Alton said. "You want to play me?"

Alton moved two pawns to the next line and then brought his bishop to the second line. When the man moved his bishop's pawn onto the next line, Alton captured his rook with his previously situated bishop.

"Bullshit," the man yelled. "You're a ringer."

"What's that mean?" Alton asked him.

"It means this is not your first rodeo, it means you're a pro."

"I told you I could play some."

"Some? Some is right. You snookered me, boy," he said, smiling at Alton, obviously enjoying the time he was having.

His beard was full and white but fairly well kept and his face, though wrinkled, was not harsh but rather had a soft benevolence to it. To Alton, he looked more like how a grandfather should look than did his own Grandfather McKenna.

The man yelled across to a man behind the bar. "Hey, Tommy, this kid just waxed my ass on the chess board."

Tommy yelled back. "Grady, you know you don't know nuthin' about machinery."

Alton had no clue what that meant, but the old man laughed so he figured it must have been funny, so he started laughing too.

"So, your ol' man was chopper driver in Vietnam?"

"He was a helicopter pilot, they don't call them choppers," Alton said.

"Well, son, I rode enough of them damned things to be able to call 'em what I want to call 'em."

"Yes, sir," Alton responded.

"Where was, your dad based in Nam?"

Alton thought for a minute and then said," I don't know, sir. He talked about it but I don't remember what he said."

"You don't have to call me sir, you can call me Grady. Hey, what is your name by the way?"

"Alton, sir, I mean Grady. My name is Alton the second. I'm named after my dad's grandpa."

"That's nice," Grady said. "You seem to be a smart boy. Maybe you can come back and teach me how to play that damned game sometime."

"I usually ride my bike to town on Wednesday, I go to the Marina or just ride around the square. I'd like to come back."

"I look forward to it, Alton," Grady said. "The afternoons are usually slow so it'll be okay if we set down for a nice game of chess. I'll have some cold drinks for you next time."

Alton raced back to the McKennas' house. He wanted to tell his grandmother about his afternoon but he quickly thought better about it. She might not understand that he had been in a bar all afternoon. He decided to keep that conversation for another time.

The very next day, which was Thursday, was warm and sunny. Alton went to town with his grandmother. They had lunch again at Middleton's, as usual, and Aimee McKenna took him shopping for "anything he wanted" as she put it.

"I don't really need anything, Grandma," he told her. "You got me the bike, that's the best thing you could get me. I've been able to go all over town and see everything and meet people. It's been a fun summer, I wish it wouldn't end."

"I do too, honey," she said. "I wish it would never end."

Just down Tolson Street from the McKenna house was the home of John and Lydia McCormick, a couple in their forties, who owned an importing business that they ran from their home. They had been childless until they were thirty or so years old. Mrs. McCormick's being unable to bear children had left a tremendous hole in their lives. For that reason, they decided to adopt. Their association with a Japanese export/import business led them to consider a Japanese child who had lost her natural parents in a typhoon. They named her Shadow, Shadow McCormick, actually Lydia named her Shadow, but her husband agreed it was a musical name for a lovely, musical baby girl.

The child grew more beautiful every day, it seemed to her parents. Lydia McCormick home-schooled Shadow and the girl proved to be very intelligent. She was smarter than they were, her parents often bragged to friends. The McCormicks showered their daughter with love and attention. They spared no expense or labor to keep her happy and well taken care of. But the girl was not spoiled, as one would think. She was confident in her own abilities and treated friends and strangers alike with respect and consideration. Her manners were impeccable and her perfect English caused a good deal of amusement and surprise, given her appearance, when she opened her mouth to speak. Such perfect speech coming out of a girl, who was obviously of Japanese extraction, always made a big impression on anyone with whom she came in contact.

Shadow's life might very well have continued, uneventful and mundane, had not the Maryland State Senator, Mr. Charles McKenna, who lived down the street, asked his thirteen-year-old grandson to carry some paperwork over to John McCormick one bright summer day in 1978.

Alton Kemper rang the doorbell at the McCormick home and waited, as he heard footsteps approaching from inside the house toward the door. The boy was moonstruck when the door opened, and he was staring into the dark, alluring eyes, of the prettiest girl he'd ever seen. He stood there, unable to speak for a few moments. A smile came alive on the girl's face as the boy remained mute and did not appear to be able to reverse his condition. "Can I help you?" she asked him.

"Uh, I have a package for Mister McCormick," he finally managed to say as he handed her the folder in his hand.

"He's my father, I can take it," she said. "Would you like to come in?"

"Oh, I don't know, I guess not. I was just supposed to bring the folder for your father."

"You can come in if you want to," she said, giggling. "We don't bite, well at least some of us don't. Would you like some iced tea?"

"I guess so, sure," he said.

She led him through the house and out onto the backyard patio. "You can sit down if you want to," she said, and he dutifully complied. "I'll get us something to drink, what would you like?"

"Just some water," Alton said.

And she went off to the kitchen while he waited nervously trying to think of something to say. Words would not come to him, and yet she seemed so at ease and self-assured. She returned after a short while and handed him a glass of ice water then sat down across the coffee table from him. She set her glass down on the table in front of her and then grasped the hem of her skirt to make sure it didn't ride up as she slid back in her chair.

All the time she was looking right at Alton to see if he was looking at her. Alton was looking at her face and was being very careful not to glance down at her legs. She smiled at him, innocently, although she knew she was toying with him. She wasn't sure if he knew it, though.

"Who are you and why are you here?" she asked him.

"You invited me in," he said.

"No, silly, I mean why did you come to Annapolis? I've never seen you here before."

"Oh, I'm visiting my grandparents, the McKennas, just down the street. My name is Alton Kemper the second, I'm from Texas. Well, that's not quite true, I was born in Maryland, but I live in Texas."

"Alton Kemper the second," she said. "You mean there are two of you?" The girl was having fun with Alton and he wasn't sure how to respond.

"No, I was named after my dad's grandfather, Alton Kemper the first. He and my dad were very close. My brother Charlie is named after our grandfather Charles McKenna who lives down the street from here."

"I know Mrs. McKenna," she said. "She's a nice lady. Sometimes she has me come into her house for tea. Why haven't I seen you before?"

"I don't know," he said. "Just my bad luck, I guess. I was here the past two summers but I didn't see you," he told her.

"Oh," she said, "you do have a sense of humor. I was about to think you were afraid of me. I was at summer camp last year, and the year before that I was taking some advanced courses. My parents want me to graduate early so I can get a head start on college."

"I'm not afraid of you," he said. "I just get a little nervous around pretty girls." Alton had heard his brother say that to a girl once and he never imagined that he would ever come upon the occasion to use it himself, but here it was and he did it.

Shadow smiled broadly and batted her eyes at him. "You

think I'm pretty? You're not just saying that because I said your grandmother is nice, are you?"

"No, I wouldn't do that. But I'm going to ask my grandma why she never told me about you." Alton could feel himself loosening up a bit and he was getting more confident, a little at a time. "You'd be pretty even if you said my grandma was a mean old woman."

"Thank you, Alton," she said. Maybe we can write to each other when you go back home."

"I'd like that, I really would like that. I'll write you. And I'll be back next summer. If you're still around, we can talk and maybe go downtown and walk around and get some lunch or something."

"Where else would I be?" she said. "This is my home."

At that time, John and Lydia McCormick came out onto the patio deck and introduced themselves to Alton. "So, you're Charles McKenna's grandson, are you?

"Yes, sir," Alton said.

John said, "I've known Senator McKenna for quite a few years. We go way back. Charles is a fine man." He noticed Alton staring at him and his wife, with a confused look on his face. "She's adopted, Alton. We got Shadow when she was a baby. That's why she doesn't look like us."

"Oh, I didn't mean to—stare. I didn't know. Is it okay with you if I write to Shadow when I go back home? I just come here in the summertime, every summer, all summer."

"Of course, it's okay," John said. "I think that would be fine."

Alton spent his last Wednesday of the summer at the Driftwood playing chess with Grady Booker. The two had become good friends over the past two summers. Alton enjoyed talking to the older man and found him to possess a soft and gentle nature that belied his outward appearance and rough manner.

"I've made myself stop cursing in front of you, Alton," Grady told the boy. "I don't know if that's a good influence you've had on me or a bad one, but that's what happened."

"Well, I'm glad I could be of some assistance to you, Mister Booker," Alton said. "And you finally beat me in a chess game, so good things have come out of all this."

"Indeed, it has, and you better not have let me win. I won't have you feeling sorry for me."

"It was fair and square, Grady," Alton responded. "You are getting better and better. After next summer, you'll be able to compete in the world championship tournament."

"Yeah, right, I'll put that on my calendar."

The day before he was to fly back home, Alton met Shadow in the little park that was a couple of blocks over from the McKenna home. She reached out to take his hand, and he quickly drew it back and wiped it off on his shirt. She giggled and said. "Do I make you nervous, Alton?"

"A little," he said, "just a little."

"I don't know why, it's just me. You don't have to worry about saying or doing something wrong when you're with me. We're friends, aren't we?"

"I hope so, Shadow." He loved saying her name. A million things were going through his mind at one time. This girl made him feel like he'd never felt before in his life. He wanted to tell her how he felt but he didn't know how. Every time he started talking to her he lost confidence in himself and was afraid he'd say something really, really stupid. That was why he let her do most of the talking. She didn't seem to be burdened with the same inadequacies he believed he possessed.

She stopped and leaned back against a tree and pulled him closer to her. He'd never been that close to her face before, and he felt his heart fluttering, or at least something was fluttering in his chest or stomach or somewhere. "You are going to kiss me bye, aren't you?" she said.

He couldn't speak so he didn't even try. He placed his lips on hers and they kissed. The boy was afraid he was going to pass out, but he didn't. *So, this is what it was like to kiss a girl*, he was thinking. *This is why everyone makes such a fuss about it*. He pulled back, looked into her eyes for a moment, then embraced her, and kissed her again, this time with more confidence, and she kissed him back with the same enthusiasm.

This was one of those life experiences Alton would never forget. He knew he was in love, hopelessly in love. But it would be several summers before he would tell her. His task now would be to get through the next school year until he would see her again.

"I'll write you, Shadow, I promise, and I'll be back next summer to see you, if you want to see me."

"You better write me, Alton Kemper," she said, "and of course I want to see you. Why would you think I wouldn't want to see you?"

"I don't know," he said, "it's just a long time until next summer."

"It'll be here before you know it, and so will I."

Alton struggled to keep his mind on school. When his first report card came, his grades had slipped from all A's to a couple of B's. It was not a serious fall from grace for a normal student. But Alton had never been a normal student. He had always approached everything he did, with the requisite seriousness and had strived to be the best at everything he did. His mother Mattie was worried until a telephone call from her mother in Maryland informed her that Alton had met a girl. And the girl was not just a girl. She was, according to Aimee McKenna, the girl of Alton's dreams.

Mattie tried to discuss the situation with Alton and found herself being slightly amused at his inability to talk about his new love. "I'll be all right, Mom," he told her. "I'll get the grades up. I just dropped the ball a bit."

She let it go at that and, sure enough, Alton's grades did come up. But the boy was definitely changed. She asked Jim to talk to his son, to have that talk with his son about love and life and the pitfalls of losing one's focus. So Jim went into Alton's room one night after dinner and took a seat next to the desk where he did his homework. "Can we have a talk, son?" he asked.

"Sure, Dad," he said. "What's up?"

"Your mom tells me you met a girl in Annapolis. You want to tell me about her?"

"Well," Alton said, and started fidgeting around. "She lives down the street from Grandma and Grandpa McKenna. She's a year younger than I am but she's very smart. She may graduate early because she so smart."

"So, do you like this girl?"

"Yeah, I do, a lot. I think I love her."

Jim almost smiled but he forced himself not to, knowing the fragility of the young male ego, but certain that his son, at thirteen, could not possibly know what it meant to be in love. "What's her name, son?"

"Shadow, Shadow McCormick," Alton said. "She lives down the street from Grandma and Grandpa McKenna."

"Yes, I seem to recall you said that. Shadow McCormick, you said? I could almost fall in love with that name. My guess is she's as beautiful as her name is. Now is this a mutual thing? I mean does she feel the same way about you?"

"I think so," he said. "She made me kiss her."

"She made you kiss her?" Jim said and chuckled. "She got you in a headlock, did she?"

Alton laughed. "No, it wasn't like that. We were walking and she was holding my hand, and she pulled me close, and it just sort of happened, and then it happened again."

"Sometimes that's all it takes, son. Women are strange and wonderful creatures. They can make you happy and sad, all at the same time. I assume you will be writing to her or talking on the phone a lot until next summer?"

"Yes, we're going to stay in touch. I don't have a picture of her yet but when I get one I'll show it to you."

"I look forward to that," Jim said. "Just don't let this interfere with your schoolwork, Alton. Remember your first priority is to get your education."

"I won't, Dad, I promise."

Jim had a suspicion that this girl, his son had found, would quite likely, become a very important part of their lives at some future date. His and Mattie's first-born son was not a flighty boy, as was his brother Charlie who often talked about a different girl-friend every week and fell in love faster than a dog could scratch a flea bite. Alton was just not like that. Jim could easily envision his son meeting the love of his life at a very early age and never veering from that course. He could also see the possibility that Alton might get hurt by this girl and never get over it. He was just that kind of serious boy. Jim hoped that this girl with the musical name was as serious as his son was.

The picture of the girl was not what Jim and Mattie were expecting. "She's Japanese?" his mother asked. "How in the world did a Japanese girl get a name like Shadow McCormick?"

Alton told them the whole story. "You don't have a problem with her, do you?

"Of course, not, son," Jim said. "We were just curious. She's a beautiful girl, just like you said. I can certainly understand your attraction to her."

The summer romance that Jim and Mattie assumed had filled their son with infatuation for the girl from a different place, turned out to be anything but infatuation. He continued his yearly sabbatical to his grandparents' home in Maryland with no less enthusiasm and no dimming of the twinkle in his eye. Aimee McKenna confided to her daughter that she didn't think the boy was coming to see her any longer so much as he was the bright and beautiful girl down the street. She and her husband Charles had been taking Shadow with them to the airport, to meet Alton when he arrived, for the last few summers. The two kids did have the good manners to hug each other in front of the elderly couple, rather than "locking lips" as Charles put it.

By the summer of '81, Alton was almost sixteen years old. Before long he would be getting out of high school and making plans for what he planned to do with the rest of his life. Jim and Mattie decided they needed to sit down with him and discuss his future.

The meeting took place in their dining room, the night before he was to leave for the summer. "Son," Jim said, "your mother and I have been thinking a lot about your future and we thought it might be best to get your input. Have you thought about your plans for college?"

"I want to be a writer, maybe a journalist or something like that. Grandpa says he'll get me a job at the state capital so I can make some money during the summers there, and I want to marry Shadow," he told them.

"Have you mentioned this to Shadow?" his mother asked him.

"Not yet, I'm going to do that this summer."

"Okay, that's a good idea," Jim said. "You should always get a girl's permission before you marry her."

Mattie and Alton both laughed.

"I know she feels the same way I do. I just know that."

Mattie asked him "Have you two, uh, you know, been close yet?

"You mean are we doing it? No Mom, we're not. But I love her."

Mattie let out the breath she'd been holding in and breathed a sigh of relief.

Jim too was relieved. "Son, I certainly can understand the hold that a Maryland girl can have on a man. I went through very much of the same feelings you are going through now. And the love of my life lived on the very same street where Shadow lives. It looks like that street has captured the hearts of two Texas boys."

"I know," Alton said. "I went to the Driftwood, met a man named Grady and played chess with him."

His parents looked like they had been struck dumb. "You did what?" they both said at the same time.

Alton told them the story, and that he had been going there most Wednesdays every summer since his very first trip. After the story was finished, it didn't seem quite as shocking as they had first imagined.

"Well, you don't seem any worse for it, so I guess it's okay," Jim said. "Anyway, let's talk about your college. Your mother and I have been thinking about some options you might want to consider. We haven't discussed this with your grandparents yet but we are thinking that, given the situation with your love for Grandma and Grandpa McKenna, and of course your love for Shadow, you might want to think about attending the University of Maryland. They have an excellent journalism school, and you could stay with your grandparents. We'll pay them for the extra expense, and we'll pay for your schooling. What do you think about that?"

"You'd be okay with that?" Alton asked.

They both nodded their heads.

"I was thinking about asking you if I could do that but I didn't think you'd agree with it."

"I'm not looking forward to you being so far away and out of our lives sooner than we were expecting. I mean, your mother and I both had hoped you'd go to school in Texas where you could come home regularly, but it is your future, Alton. You should have some say in it, don't you think?"

"Well, yeah, I think so too. Thanks, Dad. Can I tell Grandma Aimee?"

"Why don't you let your mother discuss it with her first? Is that okay?"

"Sure," Alton said.

"We are all going with you this summer to Maryland. Call it a short vacation and we want to meet this girl you seem to be so taken with."

Alton smiled at that. "You'll like her, I know you will.

On the fourth of July, they had fireworks, shot from barges, over the water off the Annapolis Marina. Alton and Shadow sat on the dock with their legs dangling over the edge. Shadow lit up and giggled with every starburst or Roman Candles that went up and off into the air.

Alton was staring at her and hardly noticed the fireworks display. She looked over at him several times and realized that he was looking at her. There was a lull in the show while the people doing the fireworks reloaded, so she turned and looked him right in the face. "You're not watching the show," she said, "you're watching me."

"I enjoy watching you more than any old fireworks show."

"What are you thinking, Alton Kemper?" she said. "You're very serious tonight."

"I'm thinking about you," he said, "you're about all I ever think about."

She stared back at him, looking him right in his eyes. "Do you love me, Alton?" she asked him.

Alton swallowed hard. "I do, Shadow," he said, "I really do. I think I loved you the first time I saw you."

"I suspected as much. I didn't think you were coming back here every summer for the crab legs."

He laughed out loud. "Well, I do like the crab-legs, but I love you more."

"So, what do you propose to do about it? I mean what is your plan for our future?"

"I'm going to move here and go to the University of Maryland. I'll live with my grandparents or maybe rent an apartment in College Park near the campus."

"Do you want to marry me someday? I mean if you love me, should I assume you want to marry me?"

"I was getting to that," he said, smiling. "Yes, Shadow, I want to marry you. I love you, will you marry me someday?"

"Yes, Alton, I will marry you, whenever you are ready."

"Thank you," he said, "so should I assume that you love me too?"

She leaned her head over and kissed him. But the kiss was not like all the other times they had kissed. This was more serious, more determined, delicious—to him, almost ravenous.

After a short while he pulled away. "We better calm down," he said. "People are looking."

"Yes," she said. "I love you too."

When the Kemper family arrived, the Mckennas planned a party and invited the McCormicks from down the street, along with some other friends. When Shadow walked in, Mattie smiled broadly, went over to her, and hugged her tightly. "This is going to sound like a cliché, but I feel like I already know you. You, my dear, are everything Alton said you were, and more."

"And you are too, Mrs. Kemper," she said. "I feel like I know all of you already."

Jim and the girls gathered around to get their hugs too. The girls were giggly and laughing as they each hugged her and told her they had many secrets to tell her about their brother.

Jim said, "Now I know why Alton walks around with his head in the clouds all the time."

Shadow smiled, appreciatively, and graciously. But Jim was certain that she was not unaccustomed to be told how pretty she was.

Charlie stood back, next to Alton. "Holy shit, brother," he whispered, "did you drug this girl or something? There is no way you had that coming."

"Don't you pop off to her, Charlie, I'm serious. I'll kick your ass if you say anything out of line."

"I don't doubt you for a minute," Charlie said. "Don't worry, I'll make you proud." Charlie walked over to Shadow. "God, she is good looking," he said to himself, almost out loud. He took her hand, as Alton watched nervously from behind him. "I want to thank you, Shadow," he told her," for turning my big brother from a shmuck into a pretty cool guy. It had to be you who did it because I've been trying all his life and I had no luck. Because of you he's even fun to be around now."

Alton breathed a sigh of relief, as did Mattie. They met John and Lydia and they all talked about the two kids. The McCormicks seemed totally happy with the ongoing relationship their daughter had with the boy from Texas. And the Kempers shared their joy over the love that was so obvious between their two children.

Mattie decided that the McCormicks were most likely former hippies, or at least Lydia was, or maybe a flower child. They were congenial enough, and obviously good parents. Lydia was a pretty woman, and John was smart, and a good business man, but not handsome by any stretch. His nose was too big, as were his ears, and his complexion was reddish and rough. She noticed Lydia looking at Jim with what Mattie could only describe as "hungry eyes." But she received no such response from John toward her, for which she was thankful.

Still, they were the parents of this beautiful and intelligent girl, with whom her son had fallen madly in love, and that was enough for her.

When Alton graduated from high school, in 1983, the McKennas flew in to attend the ceremony. They brought Shadow with them. After the graduation ceremony, Jim loaned Alton his Lexus to take Shadow out to dinner. They went to Patrizio, an exclusive Italian restaurant in Highland Park Village. The Kempers often dined at Patrizio. The food was good and the atmosphere was party like, due to the abundance of college kids from SMU who frequented the place.

When they returned to his house, there was no one home. Alton remembered that the girls were staying overnight with friends, the parents and grandparents had gone to visit the Hargroves. Charlie was off to nobody knows where. Alton took Shadow to his room to show her his desk, adorned with her pictures, and his books and computer. He sat down in his chair and she sat on the side of his bed as they talked about the house and the park along Turtle Creek and made small talk about various other insignificant things. She was staring at him intently.

"Are we alone?" she asked him.

"Looks like," he said, looking at her just as intently as she continued looking at him.

They sat there for a few moments, just staring at each other. Alton felt his heartbeat increase to what he thought must certainly be a medically dangerous level. They stood up at the same time and moved into each other's arms. Their lips met and they begin kissing, feverishly. "I love you, baby" he said in her ear.

"That's the first time you've called me anything but Shadow," she whispered back in his ear.

"I know," he said, "it just came out."

"Do you want to make love to me?"

"I do," he said," but I'm trying to decide if it's the right thing to do before we're married."

"Let me see if I can help you with your decision," she said.

With that, she got up from the bed and took off her clothes in front of him, walked over, and turned off the light switch then ran back to his bed and jumped on top of him. They were kissing and trying to get his clothes off at the same time. Finally accomplishing that task, they came together for their first time. He grasped her long black hair in his fingers and she whimpered from the pain.

"I'm sorry," he said.

"No, it's okay, don't stop."

Her fingers dug into his back, and he squeezed her so hard he was afraid he might break her. It was the first time for both of them and their awkwardness would have been humorous to an observer. The physical impact on the girl was more pronounced than Alton's emotional experience, but it worked for them in spite of the fumbling and embarrassment. When it was over, they collapsed together, and rolled over, each struggling to catch their breath, in a lover's embrace, both exhausted and amazed at the marvelous thing that had just happened between them.

He had always known that this would happen and he'd hoped, no, prayed that he would know what to do. He'd been told that it came naturally, and he learned that indeed it did. He didn't know how many times he told her he loved her or how many times she told him the same, but the fact was well established that night.

Afterward, she sat on his bed again looking down and appeared to be deep in thought.

"Is something wrong," he asked, "are you okay?"

She looked up and smiled at him. "Nothing is wrong, Alton," she told him. "Nothing will ever be wrong as long as I'm with you."

"You'll never be sorry about this, Shadow, I promise you that. I'll love you till I die. And maybe even after that if it's possible."

The big people, as Charlie liked to refer to them, came home about eleven o'clock. Alton and Shadow were sitting next to each other on the couch, watching television and drinking cokes.

"Where is Charlie," Mattie asked.

Alton shrugged his shoulders. "Probably down on McKinney Avenue," he said.

She didn't say anything about their being in the house

alone, but Alton knew she was thinking about it. He could read his mother's mind.

Charlie came in around midnight and found his brother sitting at his computer. "So, did you nail her?" he asked.

"Shut the hell up, Charlie," Alton yelled at him. "What makes you say things like that? It's not your business."

"Is this one of those 'saving yourselves for marriage' kind of weird contracts?"

"Why was that the first thing out of your mouth? Why is something inappropriate always the first thing out of your mouth?"

"Now hold on, brother. Come on down off your high horse. Your bed looks like somebody had a come-as-you-are party, in it. Do you think Mom would not have come to the same conclusion?"

Alton's demeanor changed. He lowered his head and wouldn't look at Charlie. "Aw, shit," he said. "Just don't say—"

"Forget it, bro, this is Charlie. I'm your brother. I'm proud of you. And besides, I understand the problems it would cause you, and her, if the big people found out, especially Shadow's parents. Listen, Alton, you've got something going for you I probably never will have. Shadow is not just beautiful, she's smart and a very decent person. I can tell. I just wish I'd met her first. Hell, I'd get straight As and stop cursing for that girl. Oh, sure, I've nailed half the girls in school…well, maybe not half but I have—"

"I know where you're going with this" Alton said, "and I have to admit, I've been envious of you from time to time, but I never could be that way, and I sure can't be that way now."

"I don't expect it from you, you've got a lot more going for you than bedding down a different girl every weekend. I mean you're going to marry a girl who probably farts rose petals."

"You almost make me believe that you believe that," Alton said. "And Shadow does not fart."

"Everybody farts, Alton, and you think my lifestyle makes me happy?"

"I don't know, Charlie, you tell me. Does your lifestyle make you happy?"

"Hell, yes, it makes me happy," Charlie said. "Now, either straighten up your bed or get in it and pretend you're asleep, in case Mom comes in."

"Thanks, Charlie," Alton said. "And Shadow does not fart."

"Whatever," Charlie said. "Jenny is pretty, not as pretty as Shadow but pretty enough, and she farts like a plow horse."

They both laughed at that.

Alton registered at Maryland for the '83-'84 season. Shadow, although she was a year younger than he, started the same year, as a pre-law major.

They were married in his second year. Alton's family all came up for the event. Shadow insisted that they get married in the little park near Tolson Street where the McKennas and the McCormicks lived. They tied the knot by the tree where they had first kissed. Charlie was Alton's best man. He whispered in his brother's ear, when the pastor called for the best man to come stand by the groom, "maybe not best man, but definitely the better man."

Alton laughed and everyone wondered what Charlie had said.

The newlyweds rented an apartment not far from the campus. Alton continued to work for his grandfather at the Maryland State House. Shadow and Alton graduated in 1987 together. Alton earned a journalism degree. Shadow would continue in law school for three more years. After graduation, Alton started looking for a job.

The McKennas offered to let them come and live with them in the big house on Tolson Street. They could stay there as long as they wanted to and Shadow could be close to her parents while she finished law school. Aimee confided to Alton that Charles intended to will the house to him and Shadow, in hopes of keeping their grandson in Maryland and close to them until both he and Aimee passed on. Alton and Shadow decided to accept the offer to live in the big comfortable house that was, in actuality, as much his home as the Kemper home on Turtle Creek.

At Alton's suggestion, Shadow did not take the Kemper name, but rather chose to keep her maiden name. Alton loved his wife's name. Shadow McCormick, It was musical, almost magical, and he thought it would enhance her career as a Washington lawyer.

Alton interviewed for several different news organizations, not the least of which was the *Washington Post*. But he had received no offers and was still not sure just what he wanted to do with his hard-earned journalism degree. As he often did when something was troubling him, he called his father.

Jim admonished him about seeking employment with Liberal outlets like the *Post*. "And for God's sake don't talk to the *New York Times*," he said. "You want to work for a company that will let you tell the truth."

Alton, not being politically wise, didn't know what his father meant but he trusted his judgment so he spent some time trying to figure out what he wanted to do. The next week Jim was in Washington on some business with the dairy industry and Alton asked him to come to the house for a talk.

"I'm just not finding anything I really want to do, Dad," he said. "I'd like to be a correspondent and travel some. I have an idea for a book but I need to go to Iraq for some research."

"Iraq?" Jim said, perplexed. "Why in the world would you need to go to Iraq? It's a dangerous place for Americans."

"I've been talking to people who are telling me that The United States bankrolled the Iraqi war effort against Iran, even gave him chemical weapons. I think that's wrong, don't you, Dad?"

"Of course, it's wrong, son, if it's true. You'll learn about the politics of Washington in due time, I suppose, but keep in mind that everything you hear is almost always slanted with a political advantage in mind. Don't believe everything you hear or see. Whether it's a Democrat or a Republican, be careful what you take as truth."

"That's why I want to go, to find out for myself."

"Do you need any money?"

"No, we're doing okay. I have some money saved from my job with Grandpa Charles. We don't have to pay rent, staying with the McKennas, and Shadow's parents help us out. But I don't want to ask you for money, that would be like I never left home."

"Okay, son, but a loan is a business deal, not a gift. You could take a loan from me, at a reasonable interest rate, and pay it back when your book sells."

"Let me see how it goes, and if I need help, I'll call you. Thanks, Dad," Alton said.

That night after they went to bed, Alton told Shadow about his plan to go to Iraq. She tried to be supportive, but it was clear she did not favor the idea. She tried to talk him out of it for fear that something might happen to him.

They were on their sides facing each other, talking, and, like every time they tried to discuss important issues in bed, she gave him *that* look, and they were in each other's arms. He looked at her after they had made love. "You are so beautiful," he said. "Every time with you is just like that first time in my room. Are you, like, magic or something?"

"I could ask you the same thing," she said. "You're beautiful too."

"Not like you, Shadow, there is no one like you. If you don't want me to go to Iraq, I won't go."

"I don't want you to go, Alton. I don't want you to leave me. I don't ever want you to ever leave me."

"Then I won't go," he told her. "I can do research at the library and talk to people involved in what I want to write about. My Dad will be relieved too. I'll tell him you talked me out of it."

Alton got an offer from a Baltimore newspaper to write a weekly column on local and state-wide issues. He suspected the Kemper name might have had something to do with the offer, but he didn't care. The job would give him some income and the time to work on a book. He could write the column from home and email it in every week. The problem would be finding significant things to write about. His grandfather, Charles, offered to help him out with relevant issues currently on the table in the Maryland legislature. As it turned out, it was not his family name that played a role in his getting the job. It was the fact that his grandfather was Charles McKenna, the state senator.

Alton's consternation over that was soon alleviated by his grandpa. "There is no dishonor in getting help in your career by people you know, or by people who know you," he told his grandson. "The newspaper recognized that you have access to a variety of important issues that affect the citizens of this state. That fact just opened the door for you. The rest is up to you. I can't write the column for you."

By the end of 1988, the Iraq-Iran war was over and Alton had completed his book. The book was not a chronicle of the war itself, but rather was a chronological expose of the arming of the Iraqi regime under Saddam Hussein, by the Reagan Administration.

He titled it, "Short of the Glory," a play on Romans 3:23, the bible scripture. "For all have sinned and fall short of the glory of God."

Alton was most disturbed that the United States would, as some were charging, provide Saddam with chemical weapons. Weapons, they claimed Saddam had used to kill thousands of Iranians and thousands of his own people, the Kurds, in March of 1988. Alton found no irrefutable evidence that the Reagan Administration actually committed the heinous act. Some evidence pointed to the Soviets as the perpetrators of same, so Alton wrote it into his book only as an accusation and not as fact.

The book was picked up by a major publisher and became an instant success. It made the *New York Times* best seller list in the first month after its release.

Alton took Shadow, her parents, and his grandparents to Washington Harbor, on the Potomac where they had dinner at Leonardo de Vinci's, an upscale Italian restaurant run by a chef named Vittorio Testa, who owned his own island off the Italian coast near Naples. The bill came to $300.00 without the tip. Both Charles McKenna and John McCormick offered to pick up the tab, but Alton insisted that it was his party, and he paid the bill.

Alton Kemper II, the writer, was on his way to fame and fortune.

About the time, Alton was starting to get comfortable with being a celebrity—he was busy doing book signings all over the country—he also discovered that he was going to be a father. Shadow was three months pregnant and was starting to show it. He had often observed that expectant women had a certain glow about them and even with their bulging bellies did not seem to lose their beauty. Shadow was no exception. She grew more beautiful to her husband as her shape changed and there were other changes to her body at which Alton marveled.

Shadow was not a large breasted woman but neither was she underendowed. Alton thought she was perfect but as her body started preparing itself for the coming blessing, her breasts grew fuller and rounder, and she became even more perfect. He had always had trouble keeping his hands off her but with the new changes he almost became a nuisance to her.

"I think you only love me for my boobs," she told him, laughing.

"I can't help it, Shadow," he said, "I guess I'm just depraved."

"I'm going to nurse the baby, is that okay with you?"

"Of course, it is," he said, "I love that. You'll be a wonderful mother, I know you will."

"And if it's a girl I'd like to name her after my mother, it would be Lydia Kemper, of course. If it's a boy you can name him whatever you want, okay?"

"You should know me by now, baby, I don't have a problem with anything you want to do. I think Lydia would be a perfect name for our daughter."

"If it's a boy what will you name him?"

Alton thought for a moment and then said, "Charlie, after my brother."

On July 19, 1989 Lydia Marie Kemper came into the world, wide-eyed and ready for life. She was followed a year later by the baby boy whom Alton, with his wife's permission, named after his brother Charles McKenna Kemper. Alton Kemper's life was about to get on the roller coaster of life.

Chapter 18

Charlie

February 26, 1991:

On a signal from HQ, the 2nd Armored Cavalry Regiment jumped off in line and headed out across the wide expanse of the Iraq desert in search of the Iraqi Republican Guard. They made contact at a coordinate in the desert that was named 73 Easting. This was no more than designated point appointed as such to measure progress of the overall offensive.

The first tank to engage an Iraqi tank was commanded by a first lieutenant named Charles Kemper. Kemper was a recent graduate of Texas University and a product of ROTC training. During the run, up to the ground war, he received his promotion to full lieutenant from second lieutenant and given direct command of five M1A1 Abrams Tanks, in Eagle Troop, which were accompanied by thirteen M3A2 Bradley fighting vehicles and several M113 based mortar carriers.

At around three-thirty in the afternoon, Eagle Troop ran into elements of the Tawakalna IRG (Iraqi Republican Guard) Division, the 18th Mechanized Brigade and the 9th Armored Brigade. Lieutenant Kemper acquired his first target through his Abram's thermal view finder and advised his gunner.

"Plink," he yelled, again and again, as the Iraqi tanks exploded and burned.

Tank plinking was a term that had become popular among the tank crews because the Abrams superior target acquisition and destroy attributes reminded some of them of shooting tin can with a BB gun when they were kids.

It was a shooting gallery as the American tanks went through the Iraqi T-72s like, shit through a goose, as Kemper told it later. Eagle Troop destroyed twenty-eight Iraqi tanks, sixteen personnel carriers, and thirty trucks in twenty-three minutes with no American losses.

On March 17, 1991, Jim and Mattie Kemper were waiting at DFW airport for the troops to come down the concourse. As the soldiers became visible to waiting parents, and wives, and in some cases, husbands, Mattie watched intently for her son, Charlie.

"There he is," she yelled and pointed at him for her husband.

Jim spotted him too and they both started waving and calling his name.

ഇന്ദ

Charles McKenna Kemper was born when his father was away at war, in Vietnam. He made up his mind early on that, should the opportunity present itself, he would go to war too. Somehow, he felt he owed to his father and to his father's friends who did not come back from that war. As the Kemper family became more and more financially successful and a greater and greater impact on the business and social communities, it grew more and more unlikely, in his parents' minds that Charlie would ever actually go into the military. But Charlie was not an ordinary boy. He was, from the time he started walking and talking, so different from the Kemper clan that Jim often asked Mattie, jokingly of course, "Are you sure that boy is mine?"

Charlie would have grown up in the shadow of his older brother, Alton, had he accepted his station in life. Alton was smarter and better looking, not that Charlie was an ugly boy, he was not. But the older Kemper boy had striking good looks, just like his father. But what Charlie lacked in looks and scholastic interest, he made up for in personality.

Charlie was cocky and possessed an arrogance that his parents, and most people who knew him, found unwarranted. He struggled in school but did make his grades with some tutoring from his brother, the honor roll student. Charlie was more interested in girls and baseball than he was in academics. And girls were interested in him. Charlie was a charmer. He always seemed to know the right thing to say to a girl. To his mother's chagrin, Charlie was sexually active in high school. He never admitted it to her, but he carried himself in such a way that there was no doubt about it.

Charlie had no aversion to fighting and was suspended several times for that offense. He was given to profanity, a vice that troubled his mother greatly. Jim had tried to discourage him from cursing, with minimal results. He finally decided that the boy was not doing it to be rebellious or disrespectful. It apparently was just something inherent in his nature. Jim recalled how his own mother had to talk him out of a suspension for telling a teacher that he talked like he had a mouthful of shit. So, Jim gave Charlie a pass most of the time.

Charlie seemed to find humor in seriousness, or more precisely, he thought that those people he considered to be overly serious people were funny. Preachers, teachers, and politicians always impressed Charlie as being too serious about things, about life in general.

The boy was adventurous and curious, about everything. When he was a baby, he climbed on kitchen counters and got into drawers. He would remove all the contents from any container which he was able to get open. Then he would spread them all over the room or in other rooms in the house. They locked up everything, kitchen cabinets, bedrooms, bathrooms and garage doors, but it was to no avail. Charlie managed to break into any device that was intended to be "Charlie proof." He took people's things and either broke or lost them. Jim often had to look for his shoes, and even his wallet, which he occasionally found with all the money missing. Charlie often got out of the house and was found in the barn or in some other part of the dairy.

Even after Jim built the new house, reinforced with new locks and even chains placed high up, hopefully out of reach of the innovative toddler, he was not always successfully contained. Mattie once caught him standing on the tray of his high chair, which he had pushed over to the front door, attempting to take off the chain lock which was just out of his reach. Another time, she stopped him from using the broom to undo the same chain in an effort to gain his freedom.

After the move to Dallas, as Charlie got older, his brother Alton sort of ran interference for him. He stopped Charlie from screwing up, when he was able to. And he covered for him when it was possible without telling his parents a bald-faced lie. Alton made it clear to Charlie that he would not lie to their parents under any circumstances.

"But will you repeat a lie that I tell you?" Charlie asked him. "So, you're saying I have to lie to you too?"

"If you don't want the folks to know the truth, you will."

"Damn, Alton, you're my brother, I look up to you. You're supposed to be my rock, my confidant. Who else do I have to talk to when I fuck up?

"Why don't you try not to screw up so much?"

"I don't try to screw up, Alton, it just happens. I don't suffer fools easily, and I don't put up with no shit."

"You don't put up with any shit," Alton said, correcting his grammar.

"That's what I said."

"You said you don't put up with no shit, that's a double negative. You need to work on your English grammar."

"See, that's what I'm talking about. I need you on my side. You've always helped me. Now, there may come a time when I need you to back up a bullshit story for me."

"I'm not going to lie to Mom and Dad to get your ass out of a jam, Charlie."

"Okay, okay, I understand. If I have to lie to them, I'll lie to you too.

"Thank you, that way I'll have plausible deniability"

"What the hell does that mean?"

"It's a bullshit political term that means I know you're lying but I can say I don't."

"Is it okay if I give you a wink when I'm telling a lie, so you'll know?"

"No, Charlie, I don't want to know. Just keep me out of your intrigue."

Both boys completed grade school at Armstrong Elementary School, in Highland Park then they attended Junior High at Highland Park Junior High. In 1981, being one year behind Alton, Charlie joined his brother at Highland Park High School. Charlie struggled with his grades a bit and Alton helped him, practically doing his homework for him almost every night.

Charlie was not stupid, merely lazy, Alton discovered. When he briefed Charlie on the homework he did for him, he found that Charlie already knew the lessons, he knew them quite well, as a matter of fact. Alton was constantly amazed at the information his brother actually retained.

When Alton went away to college in Maryland, Charlie was devastated. As different as the two boys were, they were, in actuality, very close. Their relationship was based on a good degree of envy. Charlie admired his brother's intelligence. It seemed to Charlie that Alton got it all. Alton never had to really work at getting through school, it just came easy for him. Charlie, on the other hand possessed a personality that Alton often wished he had himself. Alton admired the easy manner that Charlie had with people, young and old alike. His younger brother was never at a loss for words. He seemed to be the center of attention wherever he happened to be. Charlie could talk to the prettiest girl in the school as easily as he could to another member of his family.

One time, the rest of the family went to spend the weekend at the farm in Comanche, leaving Charlie at home because he had a Saturday baseball practice. And they left Alton there to watch Charlie. As Alton ascended the stairs to the room that he and Charlie shared, he could hear a girl's voice coming from inside the room. There was no mistaking what was going on. Alton didn't open the door but stood there in the hall, listening. He couldn't help himself. It was both funny and exciting, and he found himself, for a moment, living vicariously through his baby brother. The girl was very animated and was either in great distress or experiencing great pleasure. He listened until they were finished and then went downstairs. He sat in the den but did not turn on the television so they would not know he was in the house.

After a while, he decided he would go back to his room and pretend he had just come home. At the foot of the stairs he met a blonde-haired girl coming down. She had no clothes on, not a stitch.

"Aw, shit," he yelled, and the girl squealed loudly and ran back up the stairs.

She entered the room, yelling to Charlie, "There's a guy downstairs. I ran into him"

"That's probably my brother, Alton," he said. "Did you bring the Cokes?"

"No, I didn't bring the Cokes," she yelled back at him. "He saw me naked."

"He'll live through that. Go get the Cokes, I'm thirsty."

"I'm not going back down there naked," she said. "You go get the Cokes if you want one." She was busily putting her clothes on.

Charlie left the room, still naked, and went down the stairs, He was smiling when he saw his brother still standing where he had encountered Charlie's naked girlfriend. "What's the matter, Alton? You look like you've seen a ghost—a naked ghost."

"We don't see a lot of naked girls running around this house, at least not since the twins got older," Alton said. "I was a little bit surprised, believe me."

"Oh, I believe you, Alton, I almost swallowed my tongue the first time I saw Jenny naked. Come on up, I'll introduce you to her."

The girl, now fully clothed, was hiding her face in her hands, and was looking at Alton through her fingers.

"Come on, Jenny," Charlie said, "stop being silly and meet my big brother. Alton, this is Jenny Benson, the love of my life, Jenny, this is my brother, Alton Kemper. You two shake hands. Don't touch anything else, Alton."

It was awkward for a few minutes but eventually they loosened up. This was the first time Alton had seen a full-grown girl naked, except in magazines, and he was not unhappy about it. "You're not going to tell Mom and Dad about me having a girl over here, are you?" Charlie said

"What girl?" Alton said, "I don't see any girl."

They all laughed. "That's my bro," Charlie said.

Charlie left to take the girl home, and when he returned Alton was lying on his bed.

"So what did you think of those jugs?" Charlie asked him.

"Big is the first word that comes to mind," Alton responded, "big and quite pretty."

"I really like Jenny," Charlie said.

"I could tell, I listened at the door for a while when I first came in."

"I bet you watched her run back up the stairs too, didn't you?"

"Yes, I did," Alton said. "She looked almost as good going up as she did coming down. Can I ask you a question, Charlie?"

"Shoot, brother, what's on your mind?"

"How do you do it? I'm really curious, I mean I'm better looking than you are."

"Oh, yeah, says who?"

"Well, it's just common knowledge. I think everybody pretty much agrees with that."

"Yeah, maybe, but it's not always about who's the best looking. You got to know what to say. Take Jenny, for instance. She's beautiful but she has low self-esteem. She doesn't know she's beautiful. Half the guys in school want to nail her and she doesn't know she's beautiful. Can you believe that?"

"No, I can't," Alton said, "there is no way that girl doesn't know how pretty she is."

"I didn't believe it either, so I never told her she's beautiful, like every other dipshit who was after her. Until she officially became my girlfriend, I acted like she was just any other girl, nothing special. Once I told her she needed to do something with her hair, it was too long. She cut it down to shoulder length like you saw her tonight, and I never stared at her boobs. She knows she has big boobs, she doesn't need to be told. Oh, I sneaked looks from time to time but I was discreet, you know, reflection in a window, sunglasses, when her dad says grace at the dinner table. But after you're going with a girl, an item, so to speak, you can pay her compliments and fawn over her. But you got to get your hand up her skirt first."

"Are you going to marry her, Charlie?" Alton asked?

"Oh, I don't know about that, I don't look that far down the road. Jenny is fun to be with, and she's great in the sack, but marriage? I'm not sure she's the one I want to spend the rest of my life with."

"Well, I know who I want to spend the rest of my life with."

"I know too, and I don't blame you," Charlie said. "Shadow is more than beautiful, she is the one you bring home to meet mother. You're a lucky guy, Alton. I envy you."

"Apparently, she, is because Mom has met her and she loves her too."

"Just don't fuck it up."

"How would I do that?"

"Just go easy. No matter how much you love her, don't show weakness. Don't let her know that you can't live without her, but don't take her for granted. Act like you have to win her every day that you're together."

"That sounds like just the opposite of what you said first."

"It's a tightrope you have to walk. Don't show off and don't fall of," Charlie said.

"I'm just thankful for her, and for you too, brother. You've helped me out a lot. I probably never would have seen a naked girl until I got married, if it were not for you."

"You know what I'm thankful for, Alton?" Charlie said.

"No, what's that?"

"I'm thankful the big people don't have security cameras in the house."

When his brother Alton went away to college, Charlie felt as if he'd been abandoned. Alton was a bit of a nerd, he knew that, but he was Charlie's brother, and despite their differences, they were as close as two brothers could be. Ever since the time in junior high when Alton fought that kid, rather than letting Charlie do his fighting for him, Charlie had held his brother in much greater regard than he held himself.

Now he was gone, at least that was how it seemed, and now he was the prodigal son. Charlie had long enjoyed being the proverbial black sheep of the family, but now more attention would be focused on him. Alton's accomplishments would no longer shield Charlie from taking responsibility for his role in the Kemper experience. So Charlie decided to get real. He decided to step up to the plate and be the son he was expected to be. He asked his dad for a job.

"What do you want to do, Charlie?" Jim asked him.

"I want to work for you, Pop," Charlie replied. "I want to go into the family business, but I have a military obligation to fulfill first. I'll do whatever you want me to do. I'll shovel shit if that's what it takes. Tell me what I should do."

"Well, there's plenty of shit to shovel on the farm," Jim said, and Charlie looked at him hoping he wasn't serious, "but I've got my brother Trent doing that and I wouldn't want to burden Danny Carlisle with another one of my projects."

Charlie let out the breath he'd been holding in.

"Why do you feel like you have a military obligation?" Jim asked. "You don't have to go into the military."

"Because you did, Pop, I want to be like you."

"Your mother and I were hoping you'd go to college. If you want to move up in the family business, you'll need a degree."

"I've thought about that," he said, "I'd like to go to Texas, like you did, and then go to officer school. I want to join the army."

"Will you get a business degree?

"If that's what you think is best, Pop, I will. Can I work summers when I'm out of school?"

"Let me think on it, son, I'm sure we can find a place for you somewhere. I'll get back to you."

"Yes, sir," Charlie said, "Thanks, Dad."

Jim was troubled by what he perceived as quixotic behavior on the part of his youngest son. First the boy wanted to go into the family business and the next thing out of his mouth was a desire to join the army. The boy had always been impulsive but, generally, had been more responsible than his behavior revealed. Still, Jim was glad that Charlie seemed set on doing something worthwhile with his life rather than just screwing off and partying on his old man's money. He was willing to work for a living, and that was a good thing. Jim thought on it and discussed it with Mattie and then decided what he wanted to offer his son and what he was going to suggest the boy do.

Charlie had made the Dallas all-city baseball team and, like his father, was being touted as a good prospect for the Texas team. But like his dad, Charlie did not really want to play baseball in college, despite the fact that his dad played for Texas and had done well. Charlie thought about trying to make the team. The Longhorns were the national champions in 1983, and it would be fun, he thought, to help them repeat that in 1984, but he needed to make his grades, and baseball would be a huge distraction for him. He was thinking on this when his dad walked into his room.

"Can we talk, Charlie?" Jim said.

"Sure, Pop, what's up?"

"Charlie, I've been thinking about what we were talking about the other day. I would like nothing better than for you to work for the company, and it's never too soon to start. You'll be graduating from high school soon, and you'll have most of the summer free before you start college next season. You'll have four summers to find a niche in the company. I propose to let you work in a different branch or division for each of the four summers. Are you following me?"

"I'm not really going to have to shovel shit on the farm, am I?" Charlie asked.

"No shoveling shit, Charlie. I'll have you live at the farm and work with Emma Sue Brown managing the feed and supply stores, probably next summer. We have five stores now, and it's a pretty big operation. Emma Sue can teach you more about it in a summer than I can in a year. But this summer, I think I'd like to start you with Tom Wilcox in the electrical business. You'll work as a helper on a service truck with a journeyman electrician. I want you to start at the very bottom so you can get a handle on just what all we do and how we do it. Are you okay with that?"

"I told you I'd do whatever you want me to do, Pop, I meant it."

"You did say that, I just hope you understand what it really means. Some of the work is going to be hard and dirty. You'll have to forget who you are, I mean the people out in the field won't care that you're the boss's son. And I don't ever want to hear you make that case. Do you understand that? You can never try to pull rank on anyone. You'll lose their respect and that could hurt you in the future. Many of the people, more accurately, most of the people you'll be working for could very well be working for you one day"

"That's a great concept, Pop. I can do this, I know I can. I've never been one to flaunt you and the family to other kids. I'm a real person."

"I believe you, son, I just wanted you to understand. Some of the folks you work with will resent you and others may try and suck up to you to curry favor. Just ignore all the bullshit and be yourself. This will be good for both of us."

"I appreciate you taking a chance on me, Pop. I know you wanted Alton to go into the business with you, but I won't let you down. I may not be as smart as Alton, but I'll work hard."

"I only wanted Alton to come into the business, if he really wanted to, Charlie," Jim said. "It's the same with you. I only want you to do this if you're sure it's what you really want."

"I do want it, it's what I want to do with my life. Oh, and about the army. I was talking to buddy of mine, nobody you know, and he is going to join the national guard. I'm going to do that too, I think, when I start to school this next year. They go one weekend a month and two weeks a year on a deployment thing. And I can still go to officer school. I think they call it the ROTC or something. I don't know what that means."

"Reserve Officers Training Corp, Charlie," Jim said, "and I think that a fine idea. So okay, I'll talk to Tom Wilcox and get him to find you a place in the company."

After graduation, Charlie was up early for his first day of work. He had been to the shop with his dad on several occasions, and he also knew Tom Wilcox, so getting to the location and finding his way around was not a problem.

Tom told Charlie to come into his office and pointed to a chair. "Have a seat, Charlie," he said.

Charlie pulled the chair around to face Tom's desk and sat down.

"Charlie," Tom said, "I'm going to ask Mike Andrews to join us. Mike is the project manager on a school remodel we are doing this summer. I'm going to have you work there for the time being and if something else comes up where I need you, I might switch you over."

"Sure, Tom," Charlie said, "whatever you need me to do."

Mike returned in a few minutes with the man Tom had previously identified as Mike Andrews. Andrews was about Charlie's height, maybe an inch shorter, at around five feet, ten inches and appeared to Charlie to be about thirty years old or so. He wore starched Levis with a Dallas Cowboys belt buckle, and a long-sleeved white shirt. He seemed amiable enough.

"Mike," Tom began, "this is Charlie Kemper. Charlie is my wife's nephew but I don't want that fact to have any impact on how he is treated, or not treated, either in the office or the field. He's going to work as an apprentice this summer. I'd like to put him on the Garland school project. I'm sure we have a place for him."

"No problem, Tom," Mike said. "Hello, Charlie, Mike Andrews, glad to meet you." He extended his hand to Charlie and they shook hands. "We're short-handed a bit anyway so the extra help will be appreciated. I have some paperwork to finish up that will take me about a half hour, so if you want to go back to the warehouse and talk to some of the guys, I'll come get you and drive you out to the job."

"Okay," Charlie said. "Do I call you Mister Andrews or Mike?"

"Oh, hell no, call me Mike. Mister Andrews is my dad's name."

Charlie laughed at that familiar saying. He remembered his dad trying to stop Tom Wilcox from calling him Mister Kemper by telling him that Mister Kemper was his grandfather's name.

"All right, Mike, thanks," Charlie said. "I'll be looking around in the back."

Tom walked into the warehouse with him, as Mike went back to his office, and showed him a set of electrician's hand tools with a belt and pouch. "These are my old tools, Charlie, they have a lot of experience. Your dad wanted to get you a brand-new set, but I told him that, if you show up on a jobsite with new tools, the guys will make fun of you. If anyone asks you about it, just tell them you got the tools at a pawn shop or borrowed them."

"Thanks, Tom," Charlie said. "What are all these things? I mean in case someone asks me to loan him something, what do I say?"

"First off, don't loan out your tools, every man is supposed to have everything he needs, so don't loan your tools. That's a good way to lose them. But you have a point. You do need to know what each tool is called." Tom went through the tool pouch and named each tool for Charlie. "It won't take long for you to remember what they all are. You'll, be fine, Charlie. Your dad helped out a lot when we first started up, doing the same thing you will be doing."

"My dad worked in the field, with tools? I never knew that."

"Well, he did some, enough to gain the respect of the men, but mainly he ran the company. He knew a lot more about this than I did back then, not electrical work, of course, but about the business."

Mike drove a new Ford F-150 pickup. It was the standard for the company, which had five of them for the four project managers and Tom Wilcox. The trucks were white with the company logo and name on the sides and on the tailgate, Kemper Wilcox Engineering. Charlie found it strange to see his name on almost everything in sight. He'd never given it much thought growing up but now his concern was that he might not measure up, he might be an embarrassment to his dad and the family. He decided he was not going to let that happen.

"Your name, Charlie," Mike told him, "can be a help to you or it can be a hindrance, depending on how you handle it."

"You don't think I should go by Charlie?"

"No, that's not what I meant." Tom stopped and then laughed out loud. "Aw, shit, Charlie, with your sense of humor, you'll get along anywhere you go. I had a speech all made up that I thought might help you handle the pressure of being the boss's son, but I don't think it will be necessary."

At the jobsite, a crew of electricians was installing cables in an underground conduit that went from a large piece of switchgear on the side of the building to distribution panels inside. Mike told Charlie to watch the men working while he went and found the foreman. When he returned, Charlie was at the end of the cable bundle, forming up the individual conductors, and helping the men push them into the conduit. No one had told him to pitch in, he just did it. Mike patted him on the back, said, "Good job," and then introduced him to the foreman.

"Charlie, this is Bobby Gonzales, our job foreman. He'll be assigning your jobs and helping you to get acquainted with everyone and with the job."

"Glad to meet you, Charlie," Bobby said, and Charlie returned his greeting as they shook hands.

"Bobby will bring you back to the shop after work today but from here on out just report to the jobsite here at seven a.m. sharp. Okay?"

"No problem," Charlie said, "thanks, Mike."

The foreman, Bobby Gonzales took Charlie into the school to show him the scope of the work. "We are remodeling the school classrooms," he said, "adding outlets and replacing the old lights with fluorescents. These jobs are always very quick turnarounds because we have to be through before school starts in September. I'm going to put you on the wire pulling crew. They'll show you what to do. It's not hard, but you do have to pay attention and keep your mind on the job so we don't get anything crossed up. We don't want somebody to turn on a light switch and flush the toilet instead."

"I'll be careful not to do that," Charlie said, laughing.

"You see these pipes running through the ceiling," Bobby said, "those pipes are called EMT, which means electrical metallic tubing, commonly referred to as thinwall. We run the pipes from point to point—main service to branch panels and from there to the switches, plugs, and lights in the different rooms. Then the wire goes in, and you'll be helping with that. Don't worry about what goes in each pipe, your crew chief will tell you that."

"It looks easy enough," Charlie said, "but I guess it takes a long time to learn how to do everything."

"Some take longer than others but, yeah, generally it takes about four years to become a full journeyman. You'll pick it up quick enough. It's just like anything else. If you want to learn something you can, you just gotta try."

Charlie's first work day was over before he knew it, and he found himself looking forward to the next day. "It was pretty cool, Pop," he told Jim. "I picked it up really quick. It wasn't that hard."

"I'll be following up," Jim told him, "I don't want anybody taking it easy on you just because you're my son."

"I don't think anybody knows. I didn't tell anybody and nobody mentioned it."

"Good," Jim said. "That's the way I wanted it."

Charlie's first month went well for him, and he was picking up the routine. He'd not been late a day and had stayed to work overtime a couple of days when the foreman asked him to. Charlie had learned that the typical grouping of wires consisted of four wires, a black, red, and blue "hot" wires—or correctly, ungrounded conductors—and a white "neutral" for a standard 120/240 volt, three-phase system, or a brown, orange, and yellow with a gray neutral for a 277/480 volt system, plus a green for a ground wire. He didn't know exactly what they did, other than that they carried electricity form one point to another, but he learned that many of the workers on the job didn't know either. Most of them just learned how to install material, without having a good understanding of electrical theory. It was fun work for a young guy, but he imagined that it could tedious and ordinary the longer one stayed in the trade.

When a service truck crew stopped at the job to help out, the journeyman and his helper joined them for their lunch break. Charlie bought a drink off the lunch wagon and sat down, leaning his back against the building, and opened up his lunchbox. The journeyman looked at Charlie as if he knew him. "Hey, I saw your picture in the paper a while back, didn't you play baseball for Highland Park?"

"Yeah, that was me," Charlie said.

"Are you any good?" the guy asked.

"Bet your ass I am," Charlie said.

The guy looked surprised, and just stared at Charlie.

"I'm just messin' with you man," Charlie told him. "I made All City last year. I love the game but I don't expect to play in the majors."

"That's cool, man, really cool. I played in junior high, but I never made the team in high school."

"It takes a lot of time and hard work, you really gotta want it bad."

The guy nodded his head in agreement. "I heard you were kin to one of the big shots in the company, is that true?"

"Tom Wilcox is married to my Aunt Sarah," Charlie said.

"Really?" the guy responded, "then why are you out here in the field, working your ass off?"

"Because I don't know shit," Charlie said. "I have to learn the trade just like anyone else."

"Okay," he said, "that's cool. I gotta admire that."

The summer came and went and the school opened on time. That contingency was of utmost importance in the building trade. When a job was completed on time, and hopefully at a profit, everyone concerned was happy and/or relieved. The general contractor held a catered barbeque dinner, outside in the school yard, for every worker on the job. The school officials were all there, along with management personnel from all the trades. Tom Wilcox showed up with Mike Andrews, and they all sat together at the same table.

Tom congratulated them and thanked them all for a "job well done." The general contractor's superintendent stood up and did the same thing. New job assignments were given out to the crew, and they all pitched in to clean up the mess and help carry the tables and chairs back into the school.

Charlie had no new job assignment. He would have a few days off before registration started in Austin. He picked up Jenny and drove to McKinney Avenue. They had dinner and then drove to White Rock Lake and walked around the west side shore. Charlie felt some responsibility to Jenny to discuss his future plans. She knew he would be starting to school right away and had been noticeably distant from him lately.

"What are you thinking?" she asked him.

"I'm thinking about what to do with you," he said.

"About what to do with me, you mean how to lay me without having to put up with me on a regular basis?"

"That's not what I meant, Jenny, I'm just trying to process everything and make some plans. That's why I wanted for us to talk."

"You don't owe me anything, Charlie. I'll leave quietly if you just tell me to."

"I don't want you to leave quietly, Jenny, or any other way. I care about you, a lot"

"That time at your house, you told your brother I was the love of your life. Was that true or just more of your bullshit?"

"It wasn't bullshit, Jenny. I do love you, but I have a lot on my plate right now. I have to do well in school, or I'll be in deep shit with my dad. I'm going to sign up for the ROTC, so I won't have much time to be with you."

"It sounds like you might be too busy for me, Charlie. Just tell me what you want me to do, and I'll tell you if I can do it or not."

"I want you to wait for me, and I'll wait for you. I'll come home on weekends when I can and see you. I don't want you going with any other guys and I won't either."

"You won't go with any other guys either?" she said and snickered.

"No, you know what the hell I meant. I won't see any other girls."

"Okay, what then?"

"I'm staying on campus my first year, in the dorm. Then when I start my second year, I'm going to rent an apartment. If you'll marry me, we can live there until I finish school and get my degree. I'm going to work for my dad."

Jenny was awestruck. "I didn't see that coming," she said. "I had no idea you wanted to marry me, I thought I was just a roll in the hay for you."

"Well, yeah, but you are one hell of a roll, Jenny. No girl ever made me feel the way you do. No girl ever came close to being you. You do want to marry me, don't you?"

"That's all I've ever wanted, Charlie," she said. "Yes, I'll wait for you."

"Then it's a deal. Now, in the summers I will be working for my dad in some part of his business, I don't know what I'll be doing next summer but I can see you at night and on the weekends."

Typically, an MBA consisted of core classes heavy in the first two years with electives being added gradually in the second year and more liberally after that. Charlie registered for a business strategy class, accounting, economics, finance, marketing, and operations management.

It was almost overwhelming to Charlie. He had slid through high school with very little effort, making his grades but not excelling in any one particular field except, as he put it, chasing girls. He knew right off that college was not high school. If he were going to complete the commitment he'd made to his father, he was going to have to buckle down and get serious.

He had not been ready for all the additional work required out of the class room. During his first semester, he only went back home twice, on the weekends and took work with him to finish over the weekend, and once for the Christmas break. Baseball tryouts began in December and the challenge of making the team presented him with an even heavier schedule. The season would start in February. Out of necessity, he took on a lighter class load in order to give him time to play.

He asked Jenny to come to Austin to see him because, when he was home, there was little opportunity to get her out of her clothes, as he phrased it to her. She willingly came to visit him. Being unable to take a girl into his dorm, he rented a motel room, and they spent the weekend together. As she was leaving to go back to Dallas, he leaned in the window of her car and kissed her. "I love you, Jenny," he told her.

"I almost believe you, Charlie," she said.

"I wish you would believe me, it's true. Why is it so hard for you to believe?"

"Because you screwed half the girls in our high school, I was just one of the harem girls."

"Listen, Jenny," he said, "we have to get past this. I haven't been with another girl since you and I started going together. You have to believe that. I've changed. I'm not that guy anymore. Next year we'll get married, and then you'll see who I really am. And it wasn't half the girls in the school—more like twenty-five percent."

She smiled at that, softened a bit, and looked at him with a pretend pitiful face. "I'm trusting you, Charlie Kemper, you better not lie to me. If you hurt me, I'll never forgive you."

"I won't hurt you, Jenny, I promise."

This relationship between him and Jenny had grown into something he'd never expected. He found himself telling her things, that he had never imagined he'd ever say to a girl, and actually mean it. He knew how to charm them, perhaps bullshit was a more appropriate term for his approach to the opposite sex. But maybe his inner longings for a more stable life were directing him toward committing his life to this girl.

He had good role models, no disputing that. His parents seemed to have the perfect marriage. Charlie never imagined that there had ever been any conflict between them. As far as he knew neither of them had ever even looked at another person in a lustful way. And then there was Alton, his older brother, who met the love of his life when he was thirteen years old and never deviated from that path. He and Shadow would be married soon, they had already made plans, and if any two people were ever made for each other it had to Alton and Shadow. Perhaps Charlie was trying to be like his dad and brother, and thereby gain some legitimacy in his life. He really had not "screwed half the girls in their school" as Jenny had exaggerated. There were a few he remembered more than others, but, in all honesty, none had ever made him want to change his life. No, Jenny was the one, he knew that. She was flighty and emotional, she would occasionally get mad at what he considered nothing and then get over it just as quickly as her temper had flared. It was going to be a rocky ride for them.

The summer of '84 presented both opportunity and emotional conflict for Charlie. His dad wanted him to work for Emma Sue Brown in Comanche learning as much as he could about the feed stores. He would stay at the farm and sleep in his old room. Charlie liked the idea but it would keep him away from Dallas, his friends, and most disturbing of all to him, away from Jenny. He made secret plans to have her come and stay with him for a few days, but he quickly nixed the idea because he knew his Uncle Trent would rat him out and Danny Carlisle would probably not allow it.

Kemper Feed and Supply now had four additional locations in Brownwood, Goldthwaite, Hamilton, and Dublin. Charlie would work out of the Comanche office, helping Emma Sue. He'd met Emma when he was a kid but had pretty much forgotten what she looked like. He found her pleasant enough but not pretty. At first, he thought she might be a dike but she was married so he guessed she was not. She was a couple of inches shorter than he was and her shoulder length brown hair was often kept tied up in a bun on her head. She was slender but not skinny, and he decided that she looked better from the back than she did when approaching him. Anyway, she was his boss for the summer so it really didn't matter to him how she looked.

She set him up a desk in her office and had an extra telephone put on it. Charlie wasn't sure why he would need a desk, he assumed he would be doing grunt work, loading and unloading trucks and cleaning up around the place.

"Your dad wants you to start learning the business, Charlie," Emma Sue told him. "We have kids to do the hands-on work. You need to learn how to keep inventory up and how to assess the needs of all five stores and how to get everything delivered to them in time. It's not as hard as it sounds but you have to stay focused. I'm going to show you the files, where all the hard records are kept. They are kept in the locked cabinet in the storage closet. I have a key and you'll have a key, no one else has a key."

"Okay, Emma," he said, "is it okay to call you Emma? I know my dad calls you Emma Sue all the time, or should I call you Mrs. Brown?"

"Well, I'm not Mrs. Brown, Charlie, my married name is Trumble but we are not that formal around here. You can call me Emma if you want to. This is going to be quite different for you than last summer. Your dad said you worked at the electric company last summer. Tom Wilcox called me and said you did an excellent job and helped them out a lot. Your dad has great expectations for you, you know, so he wants to get you started actually managing people and learning to run a business. We have an IBM AT computer that we keep all our files on. We keep everything for all the stores here in this store on the computer. In the other stores, they still do things the old fashion way, with pen and paper."

"We have a computer at home so I know a little bit about them," Charlie said.

"That's good," she responded. "I will probably take you with me on the weekly runs to introduce you to the other managers and let you get the lay of the land, so to speak. I'll be taking a week's vacation in August, and you'll be in charge while I am gone."

"Shit," Charlie exclaimed, "I hope I am ready for that."

"Jim may come down to help you. He usually fills in for me every year when I take vacation."

"Okay and, oh, my brother is getting married in July. I'll need a couple of days off if you can swing it.

"No problem," she said. "I knew that, your dad told me, so don't worry."

"Thanks, Emma, I'll do you a good job."

The job came fairly easy to Charlie. It mainly involved checking the stock on hand of each store, projecting sales figures and ordering new product to be dropped shipped to each individual location. He spent a lot of time on the phone with all the managers. After two weeks, he was doing his job like it was second nature. Occasionally, he would have to deliver some items to replenish product that had been sold out unexpectedly. He got to know the managers and most of the employees at each of the other stores.

The company truck had car phone which was a radio tower "trunking" system with a handset that looked like a regular phone. Calls were made just like a normal land line but the calls were routed through two-way towers. Users were asked to limit their calls to no more than two minutes. Charlie used the phone occasionally to let Emma, or the manager of a store know when he would arrive.

The manager of the Brownwood store was a man named Clayton. Emma Sue told him about Clayton, as they drove over there to introduce Clayton to Charlie. "I had some trouble with Clayton, a few years back," she explained. "He just didn't want to work for a woman. Your dad said I could fire him if I wanted to, but I took a chance and he has been a good manager. I think he still harbors some resentment because he has to work for me."

"What a shithead," Charlie said. "Oh, I'm sorry, sometimes I forget where I am. My dad is always getting on me about it."

"That's okay," she said, "Clayton is a shithead, or was at least. He may be fine now. You'll have to decide that for yourself."

"If he's still a shithead, I'll let you know," Charlie said. "If there's anything I know it's how to spot a shithead when I meet one."

Emma had Charlie spend two full days with the local accountant, Morgan Tolleson CPA, in Comanche, who handled all the bookkeeping for the stores, so he could learn how the profit and loss statements are calculated and generated.

"So, it's basically just adding up what you spend and subtracting what you bring in, Mister Tolleson?" Charlie said.

"Call me Morgan, Charlie, but, yes, that is it basically. But you have to know all your expenses, and expenses include everything it costs you to deliver a product to a customer. You see, we have the labor burden, overhead, and taxes to contend with. The labor burden is what an employee costs you. For instance, if you make eight dollars an hour, which I know you do, and you work forty hours a week that is three-hundred and twenty dollars a week it costs the store for you, but that is not all it costs."

"Really," Charlie said, looking surprised. "What else does it cost?"

"It's called the labor burden, Charlie. You see, the government has us hold out a certain amount of your money for Social Security, and the company is required to match those funds, and deposit them into your Social Security account. Then when an employee gets a paid vacation or a paid holiday, the pay he draws while not working is part of our overall labor burden. In some companies, it can run as high as thirty percent. Since the feed stores use a lot of part-time summer help, who don't get paid holidays and vacations, our labor burden is usually around fifteen percent, sometimes a little more. Now, overhead is the cost of doing business. Electricity and other utilities, office furniture, copy paper, telephones in the office and like the one in the truck are all part of the cost of doing business. It's very important for a business to know its actual cost of doing business. If you don't know your total cost you can't price your product properly. You could undercharge, and not make enough profit to stay in business, or you could overcharge and get beat out by the competition.

"It seems simple in concept," Charlie said, "but accounting for every single thing you buy must be very hard."

"It can be, yes, that's why we do inventory from time to time. If an employee steals ten dollars' worth of product, and you would have made five dollars from the sale of that product, then you have to sell two more of the same thing just to break even and get your money back for the initial cost of the product. That's a simple example but it gives you an idea of how important it is to know what you have in stock and how much it is worth. I've been doing the books for your dad since he started the store in 1968, and we have kept a pretty tight rein on the business, mainly because he and Emma have been very diligent about doing the hard work that is necessary to accomplish that. So, you have to have a good system and you have to actually use the system you have. A system can only help you if you employ it faithfully."

"Thanks, Mister Tolleson, I mean Morgan," Charlie said. "I'll file all that away for future use."

Clayton Settles was an enigmatic character. Rough and unkempt on the surface, he possessed an intellect that Charlie found both engaging and surprising. He was an amiable person, though not given to much talking. Charlie noticed, after several trips to the Brownwood store that Clayton always wore a baseball cap. It was usually a cap with a farm equipment logo on it. Only once did he see him take it off and expose a head of short blond hair.

He was stocking some shelves when Charlie introduced himself to Clayton. They shook hands and Clayton kept right on with his work, leaving Charlie standing there until he finished what he was doing. Then he apologized and introduced himself. "I'm Clayton," he said, "Clayton Settles. So, you're the boss's son?"

"That's the rumor," Charlie said, "but right now I'm working for Emma."

"Good luck with that," Clayton responded, a slight smirk show on his lips.

"I don't know what you mean. She seems okay to me. She's taught me quite a bit."

"You going to be running one of these stores?" Clayton asked.

"I don't know. I have to finish school first, then I'll have a hitch in the army. I plan to work for my dad someday, doing what, I don't know yet."

"Army, why the army?

"My dad was in the army. He flew a helicopter in Vietnam."

"I was in the Marines," Clayton said, lifting his left shirt sleeve to reveal an "Eagle Globe and Anchor" tattoo with USMC under it. "We used to get lifts to the combat zone by those chopper drivers. What are you going to do in the army?"

I'm in ROTC at Texas, I want to be an officer."

"Why?

"Because I do, I want to move up as fast as I can. I don't plan to make a career of the army, but I want to do my obligation."

"Well, I have no use for officers but I admire your determination to do your part."

"Thank you," Charlie said. "How long have you been working here."

"Right at ten years," Clayton told him. "I'd hoped to be running the whole shebang by now but they'd rather have a woman doing it."

"The profit and loss statements don't lie, Clayton, unless somebody wants them to," Charlie said. "Emma has done a good job, that's why my dad keeps her. I haven't heard any bad things about you, so I wouldn't get discouraged, if I were you. The business is always expanding. If you keep doing your job, you never know what might happen."

"Well, I appreciate that. Keep me in mind when you get to the top."

"*If* I get to the top, I certainly will, Clayton, just keep up the good work," Charlie said as he left. "He wants your job," he told Emma, when he got back to the office. "But I'm not yet convinced that he's a total shithead. He is a little strange, though."

"He has some good qualities, he does a good job, and that's why I kept him on. He's always wanted my job. But I'm not going anywhere."

"I hope not," Charlie said.

In July, the family flew to Maryland for Alton and Shadow's wedding. Charlie took Jenny with him. "You remember Jenny, don't you, brother?" Charlie said, smiling, when they arrived at the airport.

"I do," Alton said, looking at Jenny, "but I almost didn't recognize you with your clothes on."

She put her hands over her face and pretended to be embarrassed.

"Well now, look at you," Charlie said. "You're starting to come out of your shell."

Jenny was impressed with the wedding, being held in a park by the tree where Charlie's brother and his new wife had first kissed. It was romantic, the way she wished Charlie was romantic. He had his own manner of romance but it almost always involved his groping her or slapping her on her butt. She wanted to be a part of this family, and she wanted to marry Charlie, but she hoped he would eventually grow up. What she didn't know at the time was that Charlie was already starting to grow up. The confidence placed in him by his dad, and now by Emma Sue Brown, had sobered him a bit, and he was beginning to see the possibilities that lay before him.

Emma was going on vacation in August, and he would be in charge of the whole operation. Although it was intimidating, it was also exciting. He looked forward to doing the job and not letting it go to his head.

In the days before cell phones were readily available to the general public—at least before they were available in Texas—people could not hide their whereabouts. If a person had to be on the job, at a particular time, he actually had to be there to take a phone call. There was just no way to fake being there. Charlie called each store every morning around seven a.m. for two reasons. First, he wanted to make sure each store manager was on the job, and second, he wanted to let them know that he was as well.

Cell phones changed all that, both for good and for bad. A cell phone permitted a person to claim he was someplace he was not. It also permitted the boss to call an employee, who might be guilty of showing up late for work, and ask him where he was then show up a minute later at that location.

Cellular phones were coming into popularity and greater availability in 1984. After years of research and development at Motorola, Martin Cooper and Rudy Krolopp delivered a small working model in 1983. Towers and infrastructure, were still being perfected but the little personal communication devices began to change people's lives. It was 1985 before they were readily available in the DFW Metroplex from Metrocell Cellular. The first models were hard mounted in a car with the transceiver mounted in the dash. In December of 1985, Mattie Kemper bought her son a cell phone, "so you can stay in touch with me," she told him. "And so I can find you when I need to."

In his first year at Texas, Charlie applied for the ROTC program and was accepted. He had signed up for the basic course which would not require him to serve in the regular Army after graduation but rather would allow him to serve in the Reserve or National Guard in order to fulfill his military obligation. The classes were invaluable whether a student planned to make a career of the Army or not. He had an impressive array of classes from which to choose.

In addition to the classroom work, Charlie found the physical training to be more strenuous than he imagined it would. He was in good shape because of his baseball background, but the training was hard, and it took a while for him to reach the point where it was not so hard. The effect on his body was dramatic. His mother noticed it first and then his two sisters.

"Feel Charlie's muscles," Aimee said as she squeezed his left bicep while Allison held on to his other one. "Charlie is strong, Mother."

"Yes, he is," Mattie said, "and quite handsome, I might add."

Jim was happy with the changes he saw in his son. It was starting to look like the boy was actually going to make something of himself. "I'm proud of you, son," he told him. "Last year I got good reports from Tom Wilcox about your work, and now, after this past summer, Emma Sue tells me that you're a natural. You handled business very well while she was on vacation. That is quite remarkable for someone with no more experience than you have."

"You don't think they said that because I'm the boss's son, Pop?"

"I considered that but I've known both of them for many years now, and I asked them to be perfectly honest with me. So, no, I don't think they were sugar-coating your performance. You did a good job. Next summer we'll work you into the office here and let you get your feet wet in the big pond."

"I'm looking forward to that. The ROTC training is giving me a lot of confidence in myself, but I need some help with something else."

"Okay," Jim said, "shoot."

"It's my girlfriend Jenny. I told her I wanted to marry her in my second year in college, you know like Alton did. Well, now it's time, and I'm not sure how to go about it."

"Do you love her, Charlie?" Jim asked him.

"I think so, Pop, in fact, I know I do. She's not like any girl I've ever known."

"So, what's the problem?"

"I still look at other girls, all the time, and I still want to, well, you know, I still want other girls."

"Have you been with any other girls lately?"

"No," Charlie said. "I haven't laid a hand on another girl since I told Jenny I wanted to marry her. And I have had offers."

"I don't doubt that, Charlie," Jim said, "you do have an endearing manner about you. But I'm glad you have kept that commitment."

"So, you think I should marry her?"

"I don't know, son. You have to decide that for yourself. My advice would be for you to go talk to her father, make your intentions known, and ask him for permission."

"People still do that?" Charlie said. "I've never seen anyone do that."

"Alton went and talked to Shadow's dad before they got married. If some boy comes for one of my girls, he's going to have to go through me first, unless she just runs off. Then I won't be able to do anything about it, except shoot him later."

Charlie laughed at that. "I imagine that my sisters will tell the guy to go ask her dad first."

It was with some trepidation that Charlie approached the front door of the Benson home. He almost hoped her dad was not home, but it was Saturday, and he did not anticipate being able to postpone the deed he had to do. Jenny's mother answered his ring. "Well, hello, Charlie," she said. "Jenny isn't home right now."

"I know Mrs. Benson, I'd like to talk to Mister Benson."

"Of course," she said, and directed him to the study. "Tom, there's someone here to see you." She smiled at Charlie, as if she knew why he was there and said, "Can I get you something to drink, Charlie?"

"No, ma'am," he said. "I'm okay."

"Then I'll leave you two alone." And she left the room.

Tom Benson spun his chair around and motioned to Charlie to have a seat. Charlie sat down on the sofa across from him. "To what do I owe this surprise, Charlie?" he asked.

"Well, Mister Benson, as you know, Jenny and I have been going together for a couple of years and, I don't know if you know this or not, but I love her. I want to ask her to marry me if it's okay with you."

"Well, Charlie, that is quite a revelation. I did know you and jenny have been going together but I was not aware that you felt that way. I appreciate your coming to me first. That took some courage, I imagine, and it shows a lot of character on your part. Thank you. Now, if she turns you down, that doesn't mean you and I cannot still be friends."

"No, sir, not at all. Can you give me any advice on how to ask her?"

"Take her out to dinner and do the knee thing," he said.

"The knee thing?"

"Yes, get down on one knee and ask her, you have a ring?"

"My mom will let me use hers until I can save up the money to buy one."

"That sounds good, oh, and Charlie."

"Yes, sir?" Charlie said and turned back around.

"What would you have done if I'd said no?"

"I don't know, sir, I hadn't thought that far ahead. Would you not say anything to Jenny about this until after I ask her, I'd like for it to be a surprise?"

"I won't say a word," Tom said. "Good luck to you, son, and thanks again for coming by."

Charlie took Jenny to Patrizio for dinner. The place was always loud so proposing to her without yelling would have been out of the question. He'd thought of that, though, and he had a plan that he was hoping would impress her. When they had finished eating, Charlie stood up and struck his water glass with a knife. Jenny looked at him dumbfounded as to what he was doing. No one in the restaurant even noticed him, so he put down the knife and glass and waved his arms to the crowd.

"Can I have your attention please," he yelled loudly.

Slowly the place started growing quiet as more of the patrons became aware of the 'wild man' waving his arms and saying something. When the restaurant was totally silent, Charlie began to speak.

"Thank you," he said, "thank you all. I just need a minute of your time if you will be so kind as to indulge me." Pointing to Jenny, he continued. "This is my girlfriend, Jenny, I love her and I'm going to ask her to marry me, if you don't mind holding the noise down for just a minute."

Everyone started clapping and yelling and shouting "go for it." Jenny buried her head in her hands.

Charlie took her hand, dropped to one knee, made her look down at him, and said, loudly so everyone could hear. "Jenny I love you, will you marry me?"

"Yes," she screamed, stood up quickly, jumped into his arms, and wrapped her legs around his waist."

The restaurant exploded with cheers and clapping as people came over to shake his hand and to congratulate them.

Later, they drove back to his house to tell his folks and then to Jenny's house to tell hers. Tom Benson would have been skeptical about the impending marriage had not Charlie come to him before and asked his permission. That one honorable act put Jenny's dad solidly in the Charlie Kemper fan club forever.

Mattie was overcome with mixed emotions. She was happy that her youngest son would be settling down but she felt once again like she did when Alton went to Maryland. She was afraid that she had now lost both her sons. She blessed the marriage, of course. Jenny Benson seemed to be a good match for Charlie, both were free spirits. She knew they had been having sex for quite some time but she had put it out of her mind. She didn't approve but what could she do about it? At least now it would be legal, she decided.

Jenny wanted to have the wedding in Lakeside Park, just down the street from the Kemper home. Mattie, assuming that she had gotten the idea from Shadow, asked her about it. "Does the park hold some significance for you and Charlie? I mean was the park where you both decided you were meant for each other?"

"Oh, no, Mrs. Kemper," Jenny said. "That's where we used to go skinny dipping when we were in high school."

Mattie just shook her head. *I should have known*, she thought.

It was a lovely wedding, Mattie agreed. A more beautiful place to get married she could not imagine. Alton came to stand as best man for his brother. There were about two-hundred people at the wedding, most were friends of Charlie and Jenny, but some were friends and relatives of the in-laws. They all walked back to the Kemper home for the reception, which Jim had catered by a local, what else in Texas, barbeque restaurant. Mattie preferred the more genteel culinary fare of her native state but she, nevertheless, appreciated the effort her husband had made to make the affair successful.

Charlie asked his dad if he could use the funds that had been set aside for him to live in the dorm, to rent an apartment in Austin. "Jenny is going to get a job to make enough for us to live on," he said, "but we wouldn't be able to pay rent too."

"We budgeted an amount of money for your education and for your living expense while you are in school, and as long as you attend class and pass your courses," Jim told him, "I have no problem with your using the money to live in an apartment. If Jenny wants to get a job, I think that's a good idea. If you get in a bind and need money, I will help you out. That's the same deal I made with your brother and the same I will make with the girls, unless they get married before they get out of high school. That would save me a lot of money but it would not make me happy."

"I'm just starting to feel like a mooch," Charlie said. "I mean, I saved most of the money I made during the summer but it didn't last long."

"Don't, Charlie, don't feel like you are taking advantage of me. I am just thankful that I have the means to help my kids get an education. You don't owe me anything. Look at it like it's an investment for me. When you come into the business, you'll be on salary and that means you will get paid the same amount of money no matter how many hours you work, and they will be many, believe me. I'll get my money back from you, and then some. I'm just building my future CEO."

"Thanks, Pop," Charlie said. "I really appreciate it."

"You just be good to that girl, son, she loves you I can tell. I'd be very disappointed if you hurt her."

"I won't hurt her, Pop, I promise. I love you, Dad."

"I love you too, Charlie," Jim said. "I'm glad you're my son."

"I am too," Charlie responded.

He went over to his dad and they hugged. Charlie had never been one to show much affection toward his parents, unlike his brother Alton. No, Charlie never seemed to take relationships all that seriously. Jim believed his youngest son was capable of deep feelings but that he hid them inside so as not to appear weak.

The conversation about Charlie's renting an apartment in Austin brought some old memories out of the dust bin of time. He wondered if Laura's father still owned the apartment house in Tarrytown. He'd read that Laura had gotten married and had moved to Houston. He could have done some investigating just to see how she was doing but he would not. He didn't want to know. He would not allow himself to even take a step down that path. Everything he had now, including Mattie, especially Mattie, was a consolation prize for Laura. It was "spilled milk under the bridge," as Eddie Csaba used to say. Eddie loved to mix proverbs and metaphors.

In his third summer, back home from Austin, Charlie went to work at the main office for Kemper Enterprises. The company was expanding its pre-fab housing market, and Jim wanted Charlie to get some experience in setting up new offices in other states. He assigned him to work for Marcus Herrera and to help in the hiring of new sales people and office staff. Charlie traveled to Mobile, Alabama, with Marcus to set up a sales office and hire staff. The office manager would be someone from the company in Dallas, the rest would be hired locally. Jim and Marcus wanted a known entity managing any company facility remote from home.

The first order of business was to find an office and warehouse facility that would suit their needs. The would need at least two thousand square feet of office space at the front of the building and a 10,000-square foot warehouse where portions of the manufactured houses could be built as demonstration models.

They located a facility that would fit their needs on Bel Air Boulevard. The front office would have to be remodeled to provide several sales offices and a conference room, as well as a reception area. Marcus contacted a building contractor, and he and Charlie met the man at the address. The man drove a pickup truck and wore a baseball cap. He was eyeing Marcus suspiciously. "Who are you?" he asked Marcus.

"My name is Marcus Herrera, and I am Vice-President of Sales for Kemper Industries, and this young fellow here," he said, nodding toward Charlie, "is Charlie Kemper, son of the owner of the company. May I ask your name, sir?"

"I'm Joe gibbons," the man said, "and I don't mean to come off abrupt, but I don't see many Mexicans with a title like that. I was just surprised for a minute."

"Well, come back in about a month and you might see me painting the walls. Would that be more what you expected?"

"No offense, Mister Herrera. I was just surprised. Don't hold it against me, please."

"No offense taken, Joe. Let's just get this job done."

Marcus already had a typical drawing, drawn by the company architect in Dallas showing how he wanted the office laid out. It would be simple metal stud walls and sheetrock. The final painting and decorating would be done once the remodeling was complete and Marcus would most likely contract with a designer or decorator to make the place presentable.

"I wish you were on board full time now, Charlie," he said, "I could sure use you. I have four more of these places to set up all over the country. It's really simple, just time consuming."

"I do too, I've got one more year in school, and then I'll be back forever. I just hope I can learn enough to really help out."

"You'll do just fine. There is a lot to learn but you'll have a lot of help. Your old man is the best businessman I've ever known. He's taught me a lot, even at sales, and sales is my thing."

"I wish I'd known that my brother, Alton, was not going to go into the business with my dad, I would have started paying attention a lot sooner."

The contractor came with a quote for the work, and Marcus approved the price. The man Left and returned about two hours later with a contract. Marcus read the contract and noticed that the terms called for fifty percent payment up front before any work started. "We typically pay half the contract when all the material is delivered, then the rest when it is finished. I don't hold retainage so you won't get final payment until the job is ready for move in."

The man shuffled around a bit and seemed to be in deep thought. "Okay," he said, "I'll get it rewrote and I'll be back."

"What was that all about?" Charlie asked.

"My guess is he doesn't have the money to buy the material. We have to be careful. If I gave him half the money before he starts, he might not show up again. I have to treat the company's money like it's my own."

"What do you think he will do?"

"I expect he will make a deal with a supplier to front him the material and then pay it off when he gets our check. If not, then we might not see him again. If he comes back with a hard luck story, I'll probably go to the supplier with him and guarantee payment using a joint check procedure."

"Okay, so let me see if I am correct. You didn't offer to do that for him right away because you wanted to check his honesty, right?"

"That right, Charlie, very good," Marcus said. "How did you know that?"

"That's what I would have done."

"Excellent, but I hope it doesn't come to that. I'd rather he be able to handle his own affairs. We'll probably run into situations like this again in the future. These office remodels are not big jobs and the contractors who do this kind of work are usually small businesses, sometimes one-man operations, or one man and a helper."

Joe Gibbons came by to tell them that the material would be delivered in two days and that he would be there with his son to start work. He needed about two weeks to complete the job, he said. Marcus agreed, and they shook hands.

They were staying at the Adams Mark Hotel in downtown Mobile. Marcus had rented two separate rooms with a common door between so they could have plenty of working room. Charlie was given the task of setting up the electric account and the telephones. Marcus also had him find a janitorial service to set up an account.

The furniture would be shipped in from Dallas. Marcus made a list of everything they would need and called Kenny Stafford, the "quartermaster" so to speak, for Kemper Industries, Kemper Engineering, and the feed stores as well. He would put the order together, buy the equipment, and give them a ship date.

It amazed Charlie just how much they had gotten done in such a short time span, "without even breaking a sweat," he commented to Marcus.

"How many of these things have you done?" Charlie asked him, one night at dinner.

"Four, so far, three in Texas, San Antonio, Houston and Corpus," he replied, "and one in New Mexico in Santa Fe."

"It must be hard on your family with you being gone so much."

"It's actually kind of a nice break sometimes to get away for a short while. I don't mind it so much. I hate living out of a suitcase, but I meet lots of new people and see new places. For a kid who never got out of Brownwood, Texas, until I went to college, and never left Texas until I went to work for your dad and my Uncle Danny, it's been a lot of fun."

"My pop speaks very highly of you," Charlie said. "He has this knack for sizing up a person right off the bat. He can tell a good man from an asshole faster than anything. He told me that he knew you were quality the minute he met you. I'm not just blowing smoke up your ass, Marcus, he really said that."

"I know, he told me that much later. I've seen it many times since I have known him. Martin Forsyth and Tom Wilcox are just two, that I know of, that he recognized as real quality."

"And Emma Sue Brown too," Charlie added. "I worked for her last summer and she's very special to my dad."

"He sees the same thing in you Charlie, don't forget that. Your dad has big plans for you in the company. I'll probably be working for you one day."

"I doubt it will ever come to that."

"I don't, Charlie, I think it's a given. When that day comes, we'll both be ready. I'll bring you your first official cup of coffee as the new CEO of Kemper Enterprises. We're setting up a new entity, by the way, an umbrella company to incorporate all phases of the Kemper businesses."

"I knew that, he is going to build an office complex in Arlington and name it after his grandfather, Alton Kemper. He named my brother after the man, I thought that would be enough but, no, not for my Pop."

"I came on board in sixty-eight after Alton Kemper had passed away so I never met him. My Uncle Danny says he was a great man, though, and if my Uncle Danny says something, I believe it."

"Yeah, I do too. My dad says the same thing about your Uncle Danny. I was a kid when Danny came to work for Grandpa Alton. I guess I was two years old when you came to work for my dad. I don't remember Grandpa Alton either. My brother and I spent our first year or so in Maryland until Pop came back from Vietnam."

"I remember you two when I first came on board. You were the mean one, if I recall correctly, always into some mischief."

"That's what I've been told," Charlie said, laughing. "I guess it's true then, your Uncle Danny used to tell me the same thing. My brother was the good one, and now he's a writer."

"Your dad is mighty proud of both of you. That's about all he ever talked about when you were still at the farm, and of course his girls. He practically worships his girls."

"Yeah, they're spoiled little shits, but we all love them a lot. Hey, Marcus, I've been wondering how it is that you are kin to Danny Carlisle. He's an Anglo and you're Hispanic. Do you mind telling me how that happened?"

"Not at all, Charlie," Marcus said. "My mother is Danny's sister and she was a school teacher in Brownwood, still is, actually. Well, my father, Felipe Herrera, was working as a janitor at the school where my mother was teaching. As incongruous as it sounds, they met and fell in love, and got married. And here I am. Poppy died when I was thirty-four, ten years ago. My mother has never remarried. I don't think she ever will."

"I'm sorry to hear about you dad, that's gotta be tough to lose someone so close."

"It was and it is. I miss him still, every day. But Mom became superintendent of schools in Brownwood and it was she who helped my Uncle Danny and Mister Kemper land some huge milk contracts in the early years that got the dairy off and running."

In a month, the Mobile office would be open for business and they would be selling manufactured houses to folks all along the gulf Coast. Charlie would accompany Marcus to Denver to repeat the process to set up the western states operation. In the coming years, Kemper would have offices all over the country and building contractors would be developing whole tracts of the manufactured houses.

Before they went to Denver, however, Charlie had to report to his national guard unit for his two-week summer deployment. Just as he had done his previous three summers he would deploy to Fort Hood in Killeen, Texas. Charlie was fascinated with tanks, especially the Abrams tank. Charlie had expressed his desire to get into armor early in his ROTC training. The army had been accommodating and had sent him to Fort Hood to help him achieve his goal.

Training began with a week of classroom instructions. The duty this week had fallen to a Major Phillip Fremont, as spit and polish as any military man Charlie had ever seen, even in the movies.

"Gentlemen," the major began, "I'd like to welcome you to Fort Hood and to the Second Armored Cavalry Regiment. This class will provide you with the knowledge of, and prepare you for, combat in the M-One Abrams tank. Now before I begin the class, I'd like to say this. It's been twelve years since the end of the Vietnam War. The United States has had a major war approximately every twenty years since its inception. That means that, if we are lucky, and if God is kind to us, we will have another war within eight years or so from now. My job is to make sure that you men, as officers in the US Army, will be ready when that time comes."

Charlie wanted to laugh at the man's mannerisms and the seriousness with which he approached his job, but he forced himself to refrain from such action, knowing it would not have been appreciated.

The major began again. "The Abrams tank was developed as a replacement for the MBT-70 tank that was canceled due to several inherent flaws, not the least of which was that the damned thing was just too heavy, and too expensive. Congress then put its support behind the Abrams tank, which was named after General Creighton Abrams, who was the Commander of military operations in Vietnam from 1968 to 1972. The Abrams tank entered service in 1980. From 1979 until today, over three thousand Abrams tanks have been built, and more are being built as we are speaking. The primary armament of the M-One Abrams main battle tank consists of the M-Two-Five-Six, one-hundred-twenty millimeter, four-point-seven-inch smoothbore cannon. The machine also has been equipped with CBRN defense systems. These are protection measures that can be taken when any of four hazards may pose a threat. These hazards are, chemical, biological, radiological, and nuclear. It has day or night fire-on-the-move capability which is provided by a laser range finder, thermal imaging night sight, optical day sight, and a digital ballistic computer. Both the fuel and ammunition are compartmented to enhance survivability.

"The tank is thirty-two feet long, twelve feet wide, and eight feet high, and weighs in at just over sixty-seven tons. It is manned by a crew of four, one of whom will be an officer, the tank commander. That means one of you guys if you have what it takes to get there."

Charlie knew that he had what it would take to get there, as Major Fremont had so bombastically said. He took to the tank like the proverbial duck to water. By the time his training was finished that summer, he was as confidant as any young soldier could be. The potential tank commander had to learn all four positions of the tank crew in order to fully understand how to use the machine in actual combat.

The driver sat in the front section of the hull right under the main gun. The space was very confined and, in order to get into position, he had to lean back in the bucket seat and slide into place. The tank was steered using a motorcycle-style handle bar and accelerated by twisting a handle. He navigated using three periscopes, called vision blocks. For night operations, a night vision, sensor was substituted for one of the periscopes. There was a digital integrated display (DID) which provided navigational data and other information such as speed, fluid levels, and engine performance.

The rest of the crew worked in the turret basket—the turret's interior compartment. The commander sat in the center station with the gunner at his feet to the right. The loader rode on the left side of the turret, toward the back. The 1500 horsepower gas/turbine engine drove the Abrams at a top speed of just over forty miles per hour.

The tank commander oversaw the tank's operation, communicated with other tank commanders, and directed the rest of the crew. He had several periscopes and a joystick-controlled independent thermal night vision viewer to survey the battlefield. He could monitor the tank's various systems and its position on his integrated display.

The gunner targeted enemy vehicles and bunkers and fires the main gun. He pinpointed targets using a stabilized sight, with day vision and thermal night vision capabilities, and a laser range-finder that precisely measures the distance to the target. He also controlled the front machine gun and monitored the main gun's general condition.

The loader pulled rounds from the ammunition compartment and loaded them into the main gun. Generally, the gunner told the loader which sort of round to load. The loader and commander might also operate the two machine guns mounted on top of the turret.

Charlie completed the training course with commendations. He was going to be a tank commander, Major Fremont assured him. He would get his commission when he graduated this coming spring.

After finishing the office set-up with Marcus in Denver, Charlie and Jenny returned to Austin to the apartment and, despite wanting to get it all over with so he could start his day job, he put on his game face and knuckled down to passing his final year in school. Everything now relied on his finishing school with flying colors, so to speak.

His first day home from classes, Jenny met him at the door with no clothes on. He was only slightly shocked for he had come to expect the unexpected from his sexy tease of a wife.

"So, you're saying dinner is going to be late tonight?" he said as he picked her up and carried her into their bedroom.

The next hour or so reminded him of why he fell in love with Jenny Benson, to the exclusion of so many other girls who had followed him around in high school like he was a rock star. Jenny's mannerisms during lovemaking were both exciting and distracting. She constantly talked, speaking in his ear, sometimes with unintelligible moans and comments and at other times just saying his name with alternating degrees of volume, sometimes very low and then louder. He often found himself stopping his involvement in the mutual activity just to listen to what she was saying. She would always admonish him and order him not to stop. They finished with him gasping for air and trying to catch his breath. He rolled over with his chest heaving, completely spent and in awe of the beautiful creature now lying in his embrace.

"So, what's for dinner?" he asked her.

She hit him in the chest and said calmly, "You're an asshole."

"Well, I'm the asshole who wants to take you out to dinner tonight. Check your schedule and see if you can make it."

"I think I can work you in," she said."

They went to Threadgill's on Lamar Boulevard. Charlie ordered the chicken fried steak, the standard fare for Texas men, almost a rite of passage in some circles, and Jenny had a salad.

"My dad used to come here when he was in school. He got into a fight in the parking lot outside. And get this, he was defending one of his professors from some rednecks. Can you believe that?"

"I guess you're going to pick a fight with some rednecks when we leave?"

"No, why would you say that?" he asked her."

"Excuse me, Charlie but it's obvious to me that you are trying to be your father. You're getting a business degree at Texas. You joined the army, and now here you are at the place he hung out, wishing you could get into a fight with rednecks."

"Aw, bullshit, Jenny," he said, rolling his eyes at her. "I'm doing no such thing. I admire my dad and I appreciate everything he's done for me. You and me are going places, baby."

"You and I," she said, shaking her head and correcting him.

"You and I are going places, baby, and thank you for pointing that out. I'm trying to improve my speaking skills, I have to. I can't come off talking like a yay-hoo to customers or in business meetings. I really do appreciate your help."

"You asked me to correct you when you use improper grammar, but you need to get some tutoring on your own."

"I don't think so, you can teach me." He paused a moment and then said, "How's my grammar in bed?"

She smiled at him alluringly. "Perfect," she said, "no mistakes."

∼∽∽

Charlie graduated at the end of the 1988 school year. He received his commission in the national guard as a second lieutenant, and his business degree. It had been a long, hard, four years but now it was over. He and Jenny decided to stay at his parents' house on Lakeside Drive until they could save enough money to buy their own house.

Jenny laughed at the prospect of living in Charlie's old room which he had shared with his brother Alton, and where she and Charlie had sex on many occasions. The aforementioned room was a dormitory style space which was big enough for a pool table and two full sized beds. They decided to leave Charlie's bed and move Alton's out to give them more room. Charlie's sisters, Aimee and Allison, now eighteen years old, would still sleep just down the hall in their separate bedrooms that were joined together with a common bathroom.

Jenny was only four years older than the sisters so there was the opportunity for both camaraderie and for conflict. The girls were just out of high school and planning to attend SMU the coming school year.

Aimee was prissy and self-absorbed, a trait or character flaw that Jenny did not possess. That fact about her husband's sister annoyed her relentlessly.

Aimee would "borrow" things and not bring them back. She would leave her clothes piled up on the floor and have to rummage through her things to find a blouse or a skirt. The housekeeper, a woman named Emily tried to help keep her things in order but Mattie forbade her to do Aimee's laundry. "I won't have my children being dependent on Emily for their daily lives. Emily is not your personal handmaid, Aimee," she told her, "So pick up you own stuff and wash it or go to school wearing dirty clothes."

Allison, on the other hand, was a quiet and serious girl. Allison had a secret desire to go into her father's business just like her brother would be doing. She was constantly sucking up to Charlie, offering to get him things, or do things for him. Allison was learning Spanish and learning it with a passion. After meeting Marcus Herrera when she was a few years younger, and at his suggestion that she learn the language because they would eventually be taking the business into Mexico, she drove herself to become fluent in the language, taking Spanish her last three years of high school.

Charlie often commented that Allison's room looked like a military barracks while Aimee's looked like a landfill. "I hope she marries a doctor," he also said. "Or a lawyer who can afford to buy her enough clothes that she never has to wash them, just throw them away when they get dirty."

In August of 1988 Charlie's Grandma Allie passed away. He knew his dad would take it hard, they had been very close all of Jim's life. Charlie did what he could to comfort his dad but Jim seemed resigned to it.

"She was a good mother," he told Charlie. "I'm thankful to have had her in my life."

Allie was buried in Comanche next to Mary and Alton Kemper, in accordance with her last wishes.

"Why wouldn't Grandma want to be buried with her own parents, Pop?" Charlie asked Jim.

"I don't know for sure, Charlie," Jim said, "she had some issue with her father that she never would talk about. I expect that he was pretty mean to her and her brothers when they were growing up. My mother was always closer to the Kempers."

"Maybe he was 'diddlin' with her, you think?" Charlie said.

"If that was it, she never told me or anyone else as far as I know," Jim responded.

"Didn't you tell me once that Grandma's brothers were half-wits?

"Yes, they were."

ⅇↃⅇↃ

Charlie went to work full time for Kemper Industries in June of 1988. Jim assigned him to work for Marcus for the time being, but wanted him to learn every aspect of their business. The elder Kemper was working toward a plan he'd originally had for his son Alton but which had fallen on his younger son to fulfill. He wanted Charlie to be able to take over the total operation at some time in the future, become CEO of Kemper Enterprises so when Jim retired he knew the company would be in family hands. "I'm starting you at sixty-five grand a year."

Charlie's jaw dropped. "Holy shit, Pop, I had no idea I would make that much money, ever."

"That's not all," Jim said, "you'll have a car, full benefits, and an expense account. But keep in mind, this job will require some sixty-hour weeks, more often than not. It's tough and you will have a lot of responsibility. And the pay is just the beginning. I'm going to prepare you to take over this seat right here." He patted the edge of his desk chair.

"I hope that's a long way from where I am now," Charlie said. "I don't want to see you leaving any time soon."

"I'll never leave completely," Jim said, "but your mother wants to do some traveling, and I'd like to see the world too. I may semi-retire in a few years but it won't be until you are ready to take over for me."

"I appreciate your confidence in me, Pop, but it seems to me that so many of your people are more qualified than I am. I mean Marcus seems like the logical choice to be CEO, or Mister Morgan, the CFO. I want to do it but are you sure it won't cause some conflict if you jump me in over the other folks?"

"It might," Jim said, "but Marcus is a salesman, one of the best I've seen, and he is in the best possible position to help the company and himself. Frank Morgan is a numbers guy. He doesn't want to be top dog. He told me so quite a while ago. Listen, Charlie, you will probably have to face some resentment because of my pushing you to the top. There will be some talking behind your back about your being the boss's kid. Unless you fail big time, and we won't let that happen, all that will go away once you get a couple of years in the big chair, and the company continues to prosper. So don't worry, I know what I'm doing. If I didn't think you could do the job, I wouldn't offer it to you."

"Okay, Pop, I'm all pumped up, what's my first assignment?"

"As soon as your company car is ready, I want you to visit every business in the company. You can start with Emma Sue and the feed stores. E-Sue has been talking about retiring. Apparently her husband turned out to be a better guy than I anticipated, I might have misjudged him."

"First time for everything." Charlie said.

"Indeed, a little embarrassing but I'm glad I was wrong. Anyway, she's been with us twenty years and her husband has started his own mechanic shop in Brownwood, and I guess he's doing pretty well. I am pleased for them, but I don't want to lose Emma right now. I want you to go over her retirement plan with her. I think she has about fifty-thousand in it. Tell her if she really wants to hang it up we will pay her a two-thousand-dollar bonus for every year she has worked for us. If she stays ten more years we can offer her three-thousand a year for the last ten years. That's a total of seventy grand for staying another ten years. Tell her if she is dead set on leaving, that we'll have no hard feelings, and tell her you'll bring her to Dallas for a going away party."

∽∾∽

"I'm just tired, Charlie," Emma Sue said. "My mother has cancer, and I really need to take care of her. I wouldn't leave my job for anything, I love my job. Your dad has been wonderful to me but I'm just tired."

"Would a leave of absence help you out? I mean we can get someone to fill in for as long as you need, if you think that will work."

"My attention span is reduced and my work is starting to slip. I would rather leave before I become a detriment to the company. The offer for another ten years is generous and appreciated but I'm just afraid I'll reach a point where I won't be able to do the job the way it has to be done."

"I understand, Emma," Charlie said. "I'll hate to lose you but you are the only one who knows what is best for you. So here is what we'll do. You have your retirement plan and there is a substantial amount of money in it. I'll tell my dad I want to give you a retirement bonus of three grand a year for each year of service, that's sixty-thousand dollars. Pop will have no problem with that. Does that seem fair to you?"

"My God, Charlie," she said, "I had no idea I would get that much money. That is more than fair. Thank you and tell Jim thanks for me."

"I will tell him, also, we want to bring you and your husband to Dallas for a going away party. We'll put you up in a fancy hotel, wine and dine you, and give you a tour of the company you helped my dad start. But first, we need to find a replacement for you. That won't be easy. Do you have anyone in mind to take over?"

"I'd recommend Pete Richards at the Dublin store. He's my best guy, very smart and very dependable. He hasn't missed a day's work in the five years he's been with us. He can do the job."

"I'll go talk to him, Emma. Also, I want to ask you about this Clayton fella, Clayton Settles. You know he told me he was a Marine in Vietnam but I checked him out and found that he was rejected by the Marines for some sort of medical situation. Do you know anything about him?"

"Clayton has been troublesome ever since I first hired him. He's a good manager, has a lot of potential, but he's sneaky, and I've never really been able to trust him completely. That's why I didn't recommend him to replace me."

"Okay," Charlie said, "we'll have to decide what to do with him. If I fire him, do you have anyone else who can slide into that job?"

"I have some good assistant managers but they're young, I'm not sure they are qualified for an unsupervised management job."

"Well, then if Pete takes on the job, I'll make sure he knows that he may have to cut Clayton loose, especially after he discovers that he's being passed over for the top job."

"Thank you, Charlie. It's so good to see you starting to assert yourself. I knew when you came here that one summer that you'd be running things one day. You dad is lucky to have you."

"He's given me a pretty long leash, and I'm grateful for that. I haven't started tugging at it yet. I've watched him operate for years now, and I'm just trying to do what I think he would do. Now be sure and tell your husband that you and he are going to come to Dallas. We'll acknowledge your service at the Christmas party. You know, my dad will make a speech and recognize you and have you say a few words if you want to."

"I'll pass on that, thank you, I don't do well in front of a big audience, but the party will be nice."

"I'll send you a check for the sixty grand as soon as I get back to Dallas."

Pete Richards agreed to take on Emma Sue's job beginning on the first of the month. Charlie advised him of his increase in pay and benefits, and gave him his personal phone number, telling him to call anytime for any reason, if he had a need to. Pete assured him that he would not hesitate.

Charlie made the circuit visiting the other stores and met with the managers, two of whom, like Pete Richards, manager of the Dublin, he already knew. Bud Montgomery, in the Hamilton Store was the only new employee. Charlie introduced himself to Bud and informed him that Pete Richards would be taking over for Emma at the end of the month. Bud was an amiable man and told Charlie he'd help Pete any way he could. Clayton Settles was visibly upset when Charlie told him about Pete.

"I really thought that I was next in line for Emma Sue's job," Clayton said.

"We have some trust issues between us, Clayton," Charlie said.

"I don't know what that means, Charlie."

"Well, Clayton, it means that you told me some things that just aren't true. That, and the fact that you have been a real pain in the ass for Emma, is why you were passed over for division manager."

"What trust issues are you talking about?" Clayton asked.

"You claimed you served in the Marines in Vietnam and you didn't. You were washed out in boot camp."

Clayton shuffled his feet around and started to fidget a bit. "Umm, well, ah hell, Charlie I didn't mean no harm. I always wanted to be a Marine. I was willing to go, I would have gone if they'd let me."

"I believe you, but you didn't need to make up a story to get hired on here, and Emma brought you up to a store manager position. The lying makes it difficult to put you in an unsupervised job. You'll be working for Pete now, so make the best of it. You can quit if you want to, but I'm not going to fire you over this."

"I don't want to quit, Charlie," Clayton said. "I like the job and I need the job. I'm sorry and I appreciate you not firing me."

"That's fair enough, just hang in there and get the job done."

⌘⌘⌘

Charlie had a check cut and mailed to Emma Sue for the promised amount of severance pay. He called her to tell her that he would send the company plane to Comanche to pick her and her husband up for the coming Christmas party in two months and that they would be put up for a couple of days at the Ritz Carlton on McKinney Avenue with all expenses paid. Emma had been an integral part of the Kemper business dynasty for twenty years and Charlie wanted to reward her appropriately, but it was more than that. He wanted other employees to meet her and see how a loyal and dedicated employee was treated when they contributed so much to the success of the company.

It happened that Christmas season of 1994. Emma Sue Brown Trumble was a big hit with so many people who had only heard stories about her involvement. The department heads had met her at the semi-annual meetings but to most of the office staff of Kemper Enterprises, Emma was almost legendary.

Charlie and Jim drove Emma Sue and her husband, Raymond, to Love Field to take the plane back home.

Waiting on the tarmac for the aircraft to be serviced, Jim directed his attention to Raymond Trumble. "You know, Raymond, when E-Sue told me she was getting married, I was a bit jealous. I had my doubts about you, but I was wrong, and I'm glad I was. I am grateful for both you and Emma. I have to tell you, if I had not found you, Emma, I probably would have still been in Comanche running the feed stores and none of this would have ever happened."

"It was my pleasure, Jim. You have been more than a boss to me. You've been a good friend and mentor. And you, Charlie, I love you. I knew you were going to be great when I first met you when you were two years old."

They all laughed, Jim and Charlie hugged Emma and shook hands with Raymond.

"Thank you, sir," Raymond said, "for everything you've done for us. I really appreciate it. Emma does too."

"You're welcome, it was my pleasure. Good luck with your mechanic shop." Raymond nodded and shook Jim's hand again. "And you, E-sue, if you ever need anything, you call me."

"I will, boss," she said.

And with that, a milestone had been crossed in the Kemper legacy. Jim was happy and sad at the same time.

ல௸ல

Charlie spent two days at the Electric Company. Mike Andrews was now the senior project manager, and Bobby Gonzales, for whom Charlie had worked his one summer in the field, had been promoted to project manager and was running the service department.

Mike took him on a tour of all the ongoing jobs and introduced him to every employee on every job. "I hope you're not going to give me a test later," Charlie said. "I can't remember all those names."

Mike laughed. "It took me a while too. I remember most of them because I do the hiring, but I still forget a lot of their names. The job foremen are better at it because they work with them every day."

"I'd like to know more about the hiring process. What are some of the tricks you use to weed out people you really don't want to hire?" Charlie asked him.

"The first thing is just his general appearance. If a guy comes in with a tattered shirt or blue jeans with the knees out then, no matter what his qualifications might be, we are limited as to where we can use him. We obviously can't put him on a service truck and send him to people's houses or to a business. Sometimes I tell them that we have a dress code and that he will not be able to work in clothes like he is wearing.

But more often than not, I just don't hire him. If he's dumb enough to show up for a job interview looking like a hippie, then most likely he won't be a good hand anyway."

"What about the unions, do they ever give you any trouble?"

"Oh, The IBEW, those fuckheads would love to get their foot in the door of Kemper Wilcox. They're devious as hell but most of them are lazy and stupid. We use that against them. You see, the NLRB, that's the National Labor Relations Board, allows them to engage in what we call salting. They call it recruiting and organizing. In a sane world, it would be against the law, but well, you know the rest, we're not living in a sane world.

Charlie laughed and nodded in agreement.

"So, if someone comes in for an interview, and we have any suspicion at all that he might be union, there are some procedures we follow. First, we try to find flaws in their resume. The guys who are willing to do the salting will typically have gaps in their work history. The unions can't provide work for their people forty hours a week for months on end so they put some of them out in the field trying to infiltrate non-union shops, like ours. A guy might have a six-month period in which he was not working. When questioned about it, they all say pretty much the same thing. They were either on a, sabbatical, and I doubt many of the dumbasses even know what that means. They also have more sick relatives than the rest of us. They will often tell us that they were off taking care of their sick mother, father, aunt, or uncle, or whatever. It's all bullshit anyway. But they aren't going to tell us they were out trying to screw up merit shops."

"So, what do you do with the bastards?" Charlie said.

"Heh, heh, bastards indeed, I like the way you think, Charlie. If we can't find any way of legally denying his application, then we will put him on a job by himself, or a job with one or two good company men, and keep him isolated for as long as it takes. These folks, by evidence of them being in a union, simply do not want to work. So, they may work a few days and then quit. Sometimes we put time on a service truck with a safe guy who wants no part of his union recruiting. It costs us money but not as much as letting him bullshit our field crews into signing a union representation form. It helps our efforts that our pay and benefits are as good as or better than union levels. And we can thank your dad and Tom Wilcox for that. They made the decision many years ago to fight fire with fire and out pay the IBEW."

Before Charlie left Kemper Wilcox, he went in to see Tom Wilcox. Tom got up from his seat and reached out to shake Charlie's hand. It's good to see you again, Charlie," he said. "Some of the guys are still talking about you around here. What's on your mind?"

"I want to ask a favor of you, Tom, if you don't mind."

"Not all, Charlie, shoot."

"My dad doesn't know I'm doing this but I'd like to ask you to start calling my dad Jim, instead of Mister Kemper."

Tom chuckled. "You know, Charlie, I have tried to do that, but every time I make up my mind to do it, I get around him and just can't do it. That man made me what I am today. Everything I have I owe to Jim Kemper. Hell, he even let me marry his sister. But I'll promise you this, I will try."

"I would appreciate it. It will make him very happy, if that means anything to you. That comes right from the horse's mouth, if you don't mind me using a metaphor."

"Okay," Tom said, "it's a done deal. I'll do it. I promise."

"Thank you, Tom, it will mean a lot to him."

Charlie became an uncle in July of 1989, when his brother's wife, Shadow, gave birth to a little girl, and then again ten months later when she had a boy. They named the boy after him. Charles McKenna Kemper would surely be a blessed little boy. They determined that the boy would go by Charles, to keep from getting the two bearers of the name to be confused with the other one. Charlie decided that he was going to be the best uncle there ever was. He would be the world's greatest uncle. The honor, his "big" brother had given him was exhilarating.

Chapter 19

The Twins

Jim was sitting in the living room, reading the paper and mulling over the coming week's activities. He was vaguely aware of the two little girls playing across the room. Tea was being served and the two five-year-old girls were loudly discussing the seating arrangements. Two chairs they would occupy, of course, but the other three, as best he could tell, were for some unseen guests. The argument was about the placement of these unseen visitors. It was strange, Jim thought, how daughters changed a man. They changed the essence of a man, softened him, somehow. He wasn't sure if it was for the better or the worse, in a corporate world. But he suspected the latter, for they do cause a man to reassess the entire, Hunter-Gatherer, concept of human behavior.

When he had only sons, Jim Kemper was a hunter. One of the best. A hunter with few equals in the world of business. But now, now with these two lovely little creatures, who called him Daddy, playing on his living room floor at his feet, Jim could feel himself turning into a gatherer. A man with only sons looked at the world and said: "Lookout, world, I'm coming after you. Hide your dishes and your daughters and anything else you don't want broke."

That was Eddie Csaba's favorite phrase. Jim thought about it almost every time he thought about Eddie. But now Jim had daughters, and a man with daughters looked at the world and said: "Keep your distance, world. Come near my girls at your own risk, for I will protect them at all costs."

The wrath of a father is a terrible thing, Jim thought, *not to be taken lightly.* At five years old, one had to guard against scraped knees, dog bites, and runny noses. But one day, one day not very far off, boys would come to take his girls away. He knew the time was coming, it was the way of the world, inevitable perhaps, but not altogether pleasant to contemplate. Maybe by the time it happened, he would be ready.

"Would you care for some tea, Daddy?" Aimee extended her hand with a tiny cup in it.

"Daddy doesn't drink tea," Allison said, running over to intercept her sister's offer to their father. "He drinks coffee, tea is for sissies, that's what Charlie says, Daddy can't run a business if he drinks tea."

An argument ensued, and Jim intervened. "Girls, girls," he said, "I'll have some of both, some tea from Aimee and some coffee from Allison." He could see a pattern developing in each of his two daughters. Separate and distinct patterns that would shape and mold them and clearly mark their personalities as they grew older. It was hard to believe that they had come from the same embryo. They were as different as night and day.

In later years, as the girls grew into women and the individuals they would eventually become, Jim would be able to look back at their early lives and, in retrospect, see precisely how it had to happen. Aimee, the socialite, obsessed with her appearance and what impact she had on the world around her. Aimee, the prom queen, her Daddy's favorite, although he would never admit it. She would turn her head slightly to the side and bat her eyes at him.

"Nothing ever changes," Jim observed. "They learn these games at a tender age."

The nature of the human psyche, especially that of the female gender, would never stop baffling him. Women were born with this ability to use their beauty and their sexuality to overpower their male, opponents, and they started developing the basic skills when they were little girls. He remembered his grandfather talking about how Jim's mother had acted the same way. His daughter Aimee had turned out to be a copy of her grandmother. With no coaching and no devious, or preplanned, agenda, it had just happened. Jim Kemper would be the first and only the first, certainly not the last, male victim of Aimee Kemper's flashing eyes and seductive smile, and he would be powerless to resist her for the rest of his life.

Allison, on the other hand, was the thinker, more consumed with talking and eliciting a response from her father. She didn't seem to be aware that she was just as beautiful as her sister, they were twins after all. But Allison rarely attempted to use her charms to get attention. She rather preferred to engage others in conversation. She often donned her mother's reading glasses and pretended to be engrossed in a magazine or a book, even before she learned to read. Allison would mimic her father's mannerisms when he spoke on the phone. He would pace back and forth, stopping on occasion to write some notes on a pad he kept on the phone desk in the living room.

The years preceding the family's move to Dallas meant that Jim only saw his children on the weekends and they were starved for his attention. Aimee smothered him with her presence, fawning over him and asking for things, which he always strived to provide.

"You're going to cost me a lot of money when you grow up, Aimee," he told her, "a lot of money indeed."

"But, Daddy," she purred, "I just need lots of things."

"Allison doesn't constantly ask for stuff. Why can't you be like Allison?" The hurt look on her face made him regret what he had said. He thought she was going to start crying so he took her into his lap and put his arms around her. "I'm sorry, honey," he said. "I didn't mean it. I'm just a little tired. You make a list of everything you need, and I'll get it for you, I promise."

"Thank you, Daddy," she said and, smiling broadly, she jumped down out of the chair and skipped off into the next room. He was certain that he'd just been scammed by his own daughter, but he didn't care. Giving in to Aimee was always easier than being a strong father figure.

The move to Dallas in 1977 had less detrimental effect on the girls than it did on their brothers. They would start to school in their new home and the few friends they'd had in

Comanche would soon be forgotten for new friends in their school and neighborhood.

They would attend Armstrong Elementary School in Highland Park, one of the best schools in the country, Mattie discovered by asking around the neighborhood. The girls were very popular in school but only Allison seemed to excel at getting an education. Aimee was "boy crazy" and always seemed to have several hovering nearby. Her grades were just good enough for her to pass.

There was fierce competition between the two girls, a level of occasional malevolence almost that confounded their mother and frustrated their dad. There was always a lot of yelling which would bring Mattie, after enduring all she could stand, storming up the stairs to break up the argument.

"Aimee, did you take my hairbrush again? You know the purple one is mine!" Allison yelled as she scrambled around her room. She stormed to the bathroom door and attempted to open the door but it was locked. "Open the door, Aimee! I don't care if you're late but if you make me late, I swear—"

"Fine, fine," Aimee groaned, cutting off Allison in the middle of her threat.

The lock clicked, signifying that it was accessible. Allison entered to the smothering smell of hairspray and the amusing sight of her sister frantically brushing through the thick and stiff locks she had created.

"What in the world are you doing?" she questioned Aimee, unable to stifle her laughter.

"I'm feathering my hair," Aimee informed her, matter-of-factly, narrowing her eyes as her sister continued to snicker.

"Why?" Allison asked, nearly having to shout to break through her fit of giggles.

"So I can be pretty, like the girls on the magazines that all the boys sneak into school."

Both girls giggled, thinking about all the boys who had gotten into trouble, for toting around their newest addition of *Playboy* or *Sports Illustrated*, they had found in their brother's bedroom or their father's reading quarters. Allison continued to laugh as she examined the head of blonde, feathered, curls in front of her, "How Farrah Fawcett of you," she poked fun at Aimee, "Everyone already thinks you're pretty, though, without all of this. I mean, there's not a boy in school that doesn't follow you around like a puppy."

Aimee turned back to the mirror and smiled. "I know." She sighed, as if it were old news.

Jim would approach them more gently than his wife did. Mattie would get into shouting matches with them. "The boys get along just fine, and they sleep in the same room. Why can't you two just get along? You're sisters, for heaven's sake. Doesn't that mean anything to you?"

Allison would throw up her hands, blame her sister, and Aimee would usually start crying. Aimee cried very easily, especially when her father was around. Jim would "baby" them both. Even when they were seventeen, he still saw them as his little girls who ran to him when they were scared or disappointed or mad at each other.

They remained rivals until they were ready for college. And the prospect of being separated, either by going away to different schools or by one of them getting married and going away to begin a family—the thought of that possibility—suddenly drew them closer together. Allison had made it clear that she wanted to work in the family business. Her brother Charlie had promised her that he'd do everything he could to make that happen.

Aimee wanted to stay close to home. She was the spoiled one and the fear of being out on her own with no support system from home overwhelmed her.

At their father's suggestion, they agreed to attend SMU. They could live at home and it would not be too very different from being in high school. Jim was not surprised when Allison told him she wanted to get a business degree. It was becoming less uncommon for girls to get business degrees, and he was pleased that one of his daughters would want to join the family business.

Aimee, on the other hand, didn't know what she wanted to do with the rest of her life, other than party and sleep late in the morning. The girls had changed dramatically, not physically but emotionally, as they had gotten older. They were very different people from each other. Both girls retained their blonde hair.

But Allison had lost her curly locks. She wore her hair straight to the shoulder. Aimee was a Xerox of her mother because she had her hair cut the same way her mother did. Allison claimed she looked more like her father, but that was only true in her own mind.

Allison continued taking Spanish classes, convinced as she was that her being able to speak the language would advance her career with Kemper Enterprises. She took every opportunity to visit the office with her dad. She never forgot that Marcus Herrera had told her they were planning a venture in Mexico and that Spanish speakers would be very helpful to the company.

She would walk around the house practicing her pronunciation and speaking Spanish to everyone. "Allison," her mother told her, "I think it's wonderful that you are learning Spanish, I really do, but nobody knows what you are saying."

"Daddy knows some Spanish, Mom. He learned it in school."

"I know a little, Allison," he would often respond, "but that was a long time ago. I don't remember very much."

Once when Mattie took her to the office to visit Jim, Marcus was sitting in her dad's office speaking to Jim. Allison walked in and said, "*Como esta, Papa, este buen dia?*"

"*Muy bien, Mija, muy bien, Y tú?*" he responded.

She squealed with delight and Marcus began speaking to her in Spanish. To her father's surprise, Allison responded to him and they held a conversation in Spanish as Jim sat there amazed as they conversed comfortably and at some length.

"Wow, Allison," he said. "I had no idea you were so good at Spanish."

"She's coming along well," Marcus said. "I told her about Mexico, a few years ago, and she told me she would learn Spanish. Allison told me that she wanted to join the company when she gets out of school. I see now that she was serious."

"I had some inkling of this but I thought it was just a whim with her," Jim said. "Maybe we should schedule an interview for her."

Allison beamed with enthusiasm.

"You mean it, Daddy? You mean I can get an interview for a job?"

"Of course, I mean it, when are you available to come in and sit down with us?"

"Right now," she responded, becoming more excited.

"I suppose we could conduct an interview at this time," Jim said. "Marcus, can you sit in on this with us?"

"Of course, Jim, I'd be happy to." Marcus grabbed a chair and pulled it up the front of Jim's desk.

"All right, Miss Kemper," he said. "I see from your resume that you have no actual work experience to date, so tell me what your plans are for the future, why you want to work for Kemper Enterprises, and what you can bring to the company."

"Well, sir, my father and brother work for the company and they literally never stop talking about how great a company it is to work for. I'll be starting to SMU this coming school year. I plan to major in business administration so I can work in management and be part of a team that is growing the company. I spoke to Mister Herrera some time back, and he told me you were planning to set up an operation in Mexico. I would absolutely love to live and work in Mexico. I am almost fluent in Spanish and I plan to improve my skills in college."

Marcus smiled and nodded his head to her. "Also, I have pretty good people skills. My older brother is a published writer and, growing up, he helped me a lot with grammar, punctuation, and general letter writing skills. My mother also encouraged me to always speak proper English and I have carried that over to my Spanish, studying specifically the correct conjugation of Spanish verbs extensively."

"That's very impressive, Miss Kemper," Jim said. "Is there anything you want to ask us about the job you are applying for, or about the company in general?"

"I'd like to know what the job entails, what I would be doing, basically just everything that will be expected of me, I want to be sure that I believe I can actually do the job before I accept it. It wouldn't do either of us any good if you hire me and I fall on my face a couple of months later."

Marcus smiled at her. "Those are great answers, Miss Kemper," he said. "Aren't you going to ask how much money you will be making? Most applicants are very interested in the money."

"Money is not the primary consideration," she said, "once I know what you expect of me, we can discuss that."

"That's fair enough," Jim said. "I'd like to ask you a few questions now. If we hire you and you are in a managerial position, I'd like to know a little bit about your management technique. How would you handle your delegated work assignments with your subordinates?"

"Well, Mister Kemper, my father taught some management skills. He taught me to never belittle anyone and to always be considerate of their feelings. I would not give direct orders in a harsh manner. I won't say, 'hey, you do this, or go do that.' I would say something like, 'Clara, we have a tight deadline on this, can you get me that report out before noon? I know this is short notice but—blah, blah, blah." She emphasized the "blah, blah, blah" by motioning with her hand.

Both Jim and Marcus were nodding their heads in approval. Jim asked Allison to wait in his secretary's area while he and Marcus discussed her possibilities. She went out into the waiting area and sat down next to her mother to wait for their decision.

"We better hire this young lady, Jim," Marcus said, "before someone else beats us to her."

"I know," Jim said. "Most of that she got from Charlie, and he got it from me, but I'm really impressed that she retained it all. I was just going to tease her a bit when she first came in here, but when I saw how seriously she was about it, I went with it. I think she will fit in, don't you?"

"I have no doubt she will, Jim. I'd offer her a job if I were you."

"Okay, I agree, looks like you have another one of my children to train."

Marcus smiled and nodded his head. Jim buzzed his secretary and told her to send Allison back in.

"Well, Miss Kemper. We are prepared to offer you a part-time trainee position. You will be working every summer until you get your degree, and then you come on full time. I'll have to think about what your compensation should be, so let me get back to you on that. How does that sound?"

Allison shrieked, jumped up, ran around Jim's desk, and jumped onto his lap. "Oh, thank you, Daddy, thank you, thank you. And thank you too, Mister Herrera." She went over and hugged him.

"Call me Marcus, Allison, and you are quite welcome, but keep this in mind. You father and I did this for the company, not as a favor to you. You'll have to earn your way just like everyone else."

"I will, I will," she exclaimed. "Thank you both, thanks again." She ran out to the waiting area. "I got the job, Mother, I got the job."

"I knew you could do it, Allison. Congratulations," Mattie said.

Jim's secretary, Gina Maddox, came over and hugged her. "Welcome to Kemper Enterprises, Allison," she said, "I'm so glad you'll be working with us. Maybe you can help me keep your father in line."

"I'll do my best, Gina, thank you."

❧❧❧

Aimee Kemper finished her first year at college with a B-minus average. It was a blessing from heaven, Mattie thought. She and Jim both had worried that Aimee would flunk out, not from being incapable but rather for not trying hard enough. A B-minus was much better than they had hoped for.

One day, in her second year, Aimee was having lunch at the Hughes-Trigg Student Center when a male student walked up to her table and said, "Do you mind if I take this seat? I can't seem to find one in this crowd."

Aimee looked around the eating area, and there were hardly any other students in the room, four or five at the most. "By all means," she said, "I wouldn't want you to have to eat your lunch standing up."

He was a nice-looking boy, a bit nerdy but smart looking.

"I'm Matt Brady," he told her and reached out to shake her hand.

She extended hers and he held it for a moment and then rendered a hand shake,

Very charming, she was thinking.

"What's your name?"

"I'm Aimee Kemper," she said. "What brings you to my table, other than the packed room?"

"I've seen you here a few times before and I just thought I'd come over and talk to you and maybe meet you. Where are you from?"

"I live about a mile from here," she told him, "In Highland Park."

"No kidding."

"No kidding, I can show you my ID if you don't believe me."

"That won't be necessary, I believe you."

"So, what do you want?"

"I was hoping you might go to a mixer with me at my fraternity house this Saturday night."

"What fraternity are you in?" she asked him.

"I'm in PAD," he said.

"I don't know what that is," she said, pursing her lips to one side.

"Phi Alpha Delta," he said. "It's the pre-law fraternity."

'Oh, so you're going to be a lawyer," she responded.

"Hopefully I am, my father will be very disappointed if I don't become a lawyer. He's a lawyer in Houston, where I live."

"What kind of lawyer are you going to be," she asked him, "ambulance chasing or slip-and-fall?"

"What?" he said, with a confused look on his face.

Aimee started laughing while he stood there dumbfounded. "I'm sorry," she said, "I'm not making fun of you. It's just that my dad uses those terms anytime he talks about lawyers."

"Oh," he said, "I see, so what does your dad do?"

"He's a businessman, several businesses as a matter of fact. I'll ask my folks when I get home this afternoon. If they say okay then, yes, I'd be happy to go to the mixer, or whatever you called it, with you."

"You're in college and you still have to ask your folks if you can go on a date?"

"I don't have to but it makes them feel included, so I do it," she said. "Do you need to call your mother and ask her if it's okay if you go out with me?"

"Oh, believe me, my mother would approve of you. She'd probably be willing to pay you to go out with me. You are everything she ever wanted in a daughter."

"Well then, give me her number. I may be able to make some money on this deal."

He laughed out loud and couldn't stop chuckling over what this girl had just said to him. "Oh wow," he said, "I am so glad I worked up the courage to come over here and meet you."

They were staring at each other and Aimee knew they had made a connection. She knew that Matt Brady knew it too.

"Well then," he told her, without taking his eyes off hers, "Can I meet you here tomorrow at this same time to find out what you folks said?"

"That works for me," she said. "If I'm not here, that means they said no and you should go on with your life without me."

He turned and looked around the room in a dramatic fashion, put his hand to his chin as if contemplating some grave question.

"What are you doing?" she asked him.

"I'm looking for a place in this structure to hang myself if I walk in tomorrow and you are not here."

She smiled and then chuckled. "That's funny," she said. "I'll keep my fingers crossed."

That night Aimee told her sister, "I met a guy at school today."

Allison was studying and didn't respond to her so she repeated, "Allison, I met a guy today, a really cute guy. He
asked me to go to a mixer with him."

"What's a mixer?" Allison asked.

"It's like a party, it's at his frat house, Phi Alpha Delta."

"Daddy always said you'd marry a lawyer, or maybe a doctor. What's he like?"

"He's really cute."

"You said that. What's he like."

"He's charming, and funny. When I told him, I'd have to
ask Daddy if I could go, he pretended to be looking around for
a place to hang himself if Daddy said no."

"So, he's a bullshit artist?"

"No, he's very nice. I swear, Allison, you spend too much
time around Charlie."

"Charlie and I are going to be running the company for
Daddy one day, when he retires."

"Well, you sure do think big," Aimee said, "I have to admit, I wish I had your ambition. You got all the brains and I
got the looks, why is that?"

"We're twins, Aimee, we look just alike. I just push myself
harder than you do, that's all. You had a B-minus average last
year, and I know you didn't work very hard at it. You can do
anything you want to, you can be anything you want to be."

"I just want to be a princess," she said with a dramatic flair,
waving her right arm like she was waving to her subjects.

"Daddy's the only one who thinks you're a princess. So,
you better get ready for a letdown when you discover that the
world is not your daddy."

"Oh, I know all that, Allison. I just don't know what I want
to do or be yet."

Aimee asked Jim about going to the party with Matt Brady,
and he gave his consent on one condition. "I'd like to meet this
boy first. Have him come by the house and pick you up so I
can talk to him a bit."

"Okay, Daddy," she said, "I'm sure he won't have a problem with that. Thank you."

Matt Brady walked into the student center with a quick step in his gait, full of himself and excited about seeing the beautiful blonde-haired girl he had fallen for from across the room the first time he saw her. The place was more crowded than it had been the day before and he did not see her right away.

He continued walking around the lunch area where he could see every table, but she was not there. He was devastated and crestfallen. What kind of asshole would not let his daughter go on a date with a guy when he didn't even know him? He covered the entire room again and confirmed that she was not there. Slowly he began to deal with it by feeling sorry for himself. *The little bitch doesn't know what she's passing up. Ah, to hell with it.* He'd find another girl, a prettier one, he told himself, although he couldn't recall seeing a prettier one on the campus. He turned and walked toward the door, dejectedly. As he was about to exit the building, he heard his name being called loudly from the other side of the room.

"Matt, Matt, wait." It was Aimee and she was in a full-on sprint coming toward him. "I'm sorry," she said, as she got to him. "I'm sorry I'm late." She took his hands in hers. "My class ran over. My professor was on a tear and he held us over. I can go to the party with you."

He grabbed her and picked her up, hugging her but not kissing her. When he set her down, he tried to stifle the smile on his face. "I was going out to a Home Depot to buy some rope," he said. "Lucky for me, you're a fast runner or you'd have found me hanging from a light fixture."

She was giggling as they walked out of the building holding hands. "I'll give you my address, Daddy wants to meet you."

"I figured as much," he said. "Okay, I'll be on my best behavior."

"It's not far from here," she said, as she wrote down the address, "Go south on Preston, just past Mockingbird Lane, and turn left on Beverly then turn right on Lakeside Drive. It's the first house on the right. I'm writing all this down for you."

⟨∽∾⟩

Matt turned his car onto Lakeside drive and spotted the house. "Holy shit," he said out loud, "this family is not going to be impressed with a lawyer. They probably eat lawyers for brunch. Well, here goes nothing." He walked up to the door and pushed the doorbell.

Aimee came to the door with her father standing beside her. "Daddy, this is Matt, Matt Brady, the guy I told you about. Matt, this is my father, Jim Kemper."

"I'm happy to meet you, Sir, I appreciate your letting Aimee go out with me. Oh! And hi Aimee," he said looking at her with a pretend fearful look on his face.

"Come on in, Matt," Jim said. "Come meet the rest of the family." Matt followed him into the family room as Aimee grabbed his hand. Jim went around the room making introductions. "This is Mattie, Aimee's mother."

"I would have figured you for the sister, ma'am."

"Oh! Good job, flattery sometimes works," Mattie said, "but Aimee's sister Allison is in the kitchen. She'll be out in a minute." Mattie sized him up. He was a nice-looking kid, not extremely handsome but certainly not unattractive. His hair was black and cut like she would expect a pre-law major's hair to be cut. He was in dress pants and a long-sleeved shirt, button down. He had an easy manner and seemed to Mattie to be more or less feigning cautious nervousness. Aimee had told her about how Matt had asked if he could sit at her table because he couldn't find a seat, when to place was practically empty. It reminded her of how her husband had first approached her.

"This is my youngest son, Charlie," Jim continued. "The first one is in Maryland. This lovely young lady is my daughter-in-law, Jenny. Here comes Allison, the aforementioned sister."

"Holy cow," Matt said looking quickly at Aimee, "there are two of you. I never imagined that."

"Allison got the brains and I got the looks," Aimee said.

"But you look just alike," he said.

"She does that all the time," Allison said. "It's kind of a game we play."

"Ah, I see, well, it looks like I fell for it."

Jim beckoned for Matt to sit down and he did, as the women slowly drifted away leaving him alone with just the father and the brother."

"My daughter tells me you're a pre-law major from Houston. How did you decide to go to SMU?

"My father went to SMU, we're Methodists, and he just always wanted me to follow in his footsteps. I plan to join his law firm when I graduate and pass the Bar. I like SMU. I'm in my fourth year, then I'll have three years of law school.

"Well, here's another one who followed his old man's footsteps," Jim said, motioning toward Charlie. "He's helping me run the company. I expect he'll take over one day."

Charlie nodded and shook Matt's hand.

"What business are you in Mister Kemper?

"I own Kemper Enterprises. We do electrical and HVAC contracting, as well as building manufactured houses. I also own a dairy farm, 'Kemper Farms' west of here."

"I thought the name was familiar when Aimee told me her name. Yes, I have heard of your company. You're nationwide, aren't you?"

"Soon to be international," Charlie interjected. "We're going into Mexico and maybe Canada in a year or so."

Matt nodded and pursed his lips, appearing to be impressed with what Charlie had said.

"Now, Matt, Aimee said you were going to a mixer?"

"Yes, sir, at my frat house. It's a respectable fraternity. There won't be any drinking or drugs or any nefarious activity. I won't let anything happen to Aimee, I promise you that."

"That was my concern. I know that mixers can have a lot of unattached couples so I don't want some other guy bringing her home tonight."

"If that happens, Mister Kemper, it will be because they ganged up on me, and I'm in the emergency room."

"Ha, ha." Jim laughed. "That's the right answer, Matt. Okay, I'll let you and Aimee get on your way."

"What time do I need to have her back home?

"Since it's the first date I'd like to have her home at midnight. If this goes any further, we'll see about doing a later time. You kids have fun."

"Midnight it is, sir, thank you."

Jim and Mattie were already in bed when they heard the front door open and close. Jim looked at the clock beside his bed, straight up midnight, it told him. He listened as Aimee made her way up the stairs to her room. "That fellah said he'd have her home by midnight, and he did what he said."

"Um huh," Mattie mumbled.

When a couple of weeks had passed, and Aimee had still not become bored with her latest boyfriend. Jim and Mattie invited Matt to dinner. They figured they should get to know him just in case his and Aimee's friendship turned into something more serious. Mattie knew the look and feel of a woman in love and her daughter was beginning act and feel a lot like Mattie did when she first met Jim Kemper.

"He hasn't even kissed me yet, Mother. Do you think he doesn't like me?" Aimee asked Mattie.

"Maybe he's just being respectful, dear," Mattie said.

"But how long should it take? How long did Daddy take to kiss you?"

"Your father kissed me on the dance floor the night we met."

"See, that's what I'm talking about. Is there something wrong with me?" she asked, distraughtly.

"No, Aimee, there is nothing wrong with you, and there is nothing wrong with Matt either. Maybe he's just a bit unsure of himself."

"Maybe he's gay," Charlie yelled as he was passing by in the hall outside Aimee's room.

"Oh, stuff it, Charlie, he's not gay," Aimee yelled back.

The following Saturday, Matt picked Aimee up to take her to dinner. "Do you like Patrizio?" he asked her. "Your dad told me you guys go there quite a bit."

"It's okay," she said. She seemed to be pouting.

"What's wrong? Would you rather go somewhere else?"

"Patrizio is fine," she said, still pouting. They finished the short trip to the restaurant in silence and when they pulled into the parking lot, she asked him. "When were you planning on kissing me?"

"Tonight," he said and got out of the car, walked around to her door, opened it, and held out his hand for hers to help her out. "Right now, as a matter of fact." And he pulled her toward him and kissed her, with more passion than she had ever experienced. They stood there by his car, locked in each other's embrace, and continued with locked lips, oblivious to the world around them. He brought his left hand up and placed it on her neck, grasping some of her hair in his fingers and pulled her head back slightly. They continued, switching from one side to the other, until Aimee thought she was going to fall down, and would have, had he not held her up. It was only the shouts and cheers of some passersby that made them stop.

"Well, I had to ask, didn't I?" she said, struggling to catch her breath.

"I've been wanting to do that since I first saw you in the student center that day." he said.

"Then, why didn't you? I wouldn't have complained."

"I was afraid I was in love with you, Aimee. I had to know for sure. I waited until I was almost sure then all that was left to seal the deal was to kiss you, and now I have."

"Well?"

"Well what?" he said.

"Are you in love with me? I swear you are the most frustrating man I've ever met. You sweep me off my feet with that 'I was going to buy some rope to hang myself' line, and then you don't touch me for three weeks."

"Well, like I said, I had to be sure."

"Well, are you sure now?" she said, raising her voice.

"Yes, Aimee Kemper, I am in love with you. I think I was in love with you before I ever met you. I've been dreaming about you all my life."

"Wow that was pretty profound. I am impressed," she said, smiling at him.

"Well?" he said.

"Well what?" she responded, still smiling.

"Do you love me too?

"Maybe," she said, "let me think about it, I'll get back to you on that."

"Maybe?" he repeated. "Maybe? You better not toy with me, young lady, I do have some rope in the trunk, and there are lots of light poles in the parking lot outside."

She giggled at his playfulness. "Okay," she said, "I've thought about it, ask me again."

"I'm not so sure now. You kept me waiting for a long time. Maybe I've changed my mind."

She threw a handkerchief at him. "No, you didn't," she yelled. "Ask me again."

"Aimee, do you love me?" he said, staring into her eyes.

She said nothing but stared back into his eyes and nodded her head up and down several times.

"Well that's a relief," he said, "there's nothing sadder than unrequited love, at least that's what I read somewhere."

ﾟﾟ

Allison spent the summer of 1990 working for Marcus Hererra in the sales division. Between sales seminars, she traveled with Marcus and her brother Charlie to sales offices in other states. Jim and Marcus had determined that the best use of the boss's daughter would be as a quality-control person who would make frequent trips to the remote offices to consult with managers, check sales numbers and trends, and to just observe the operation to ensure they were maintaining the level of professionalism and fairness that Jim and Marcus had written into the company manual.

She and Charlie made one trip that summer to open a new office in Portland, Oregon. Charlie did the work that Marcus typically did and Allison did Charlie's job. "I could have done this by myself," she told him.

"Probably," he said, "but I'm not sure I'd be comfortable with you going out on your own to a strange city to set up an office. I worry about when you start doing the rounds visiting the remote locations. I know you're very capable but you're still just a girl."

"I'm a woman, Charlie, and you're a chauvinist pig. I swear I don't know how Jenny puts up with you."

"Jenny's my wife, you're my baby sister. There's a big difference. Jenny 'wants' to put up with me, you are not so thusly motivated. I can get another wife, if I have to, but I only have one baby sister—two if you count Aimee."

"Don't worry, I'll be okay. It's airport to airport and then either a drive or a cab ride to the office. I'll be there all day and then fly back out that night. If I have to stay more than one day, I'll get a hotel room nearby and get a ride or take a cab." She was thoughtful for a moment. "Two, if you count Aimee? You're an asshole, Charlie."

"I know," he said.

They finished the project and turned it over to the new manager then went to check out of the hotel room. At the front desk, Charlie told the desk clerk they were checking out and handed him the two keys.

"Two keys, sir?" he said as he looked first at Allison then at Charlie a couple of times.

"She's my sister."

"Oh yes, very good, sir," the man said.

As they walked away, Charlie put his arm around Allison's waist. "I should have planted a big wet one on you, that would have shocked the little prick."

She giggled and lay her head over on his shoulder.

On the plane ride back to DFW, Charlie told Allison his long-term plans. "Pop has told me, Allison, that he eventually wants you and me to take over the company."

"Me too? He wants me to help you run the company?" she asked, getting excited.

"With some great effort, I convinced him that you might be helpful to us, with your business degree, your command of Spanish, and your drop-dead gorgeous looks. He's going to make me VP in charge of operations. My thinking is that we can work you into the Mexico project, maybe as division manager."

"Oh, Charlie, that's like a dream come true. It's what I've always wanted."

"I know," he said, "and we're going to make it happen. I think Mom and Dad would like to take it easy for a while. This is just speculation on my part, but I think Pop wants to spend more time on the farm and Mom wants to travel some and spend more time in Maryland."

"I appreciate your being okay with my coming on board," she told him. "Some men would be too jealous to give their sisters a chance like you have given me. I appreciate it, Charlie, you're a good brother."

"We're in this together, sis. It's me and you, kid. We're going to rule the world."

∽∾∽

Aimee confided to her sister that she and Matt Brady had been "doing it" for quite some time. "I couldn't help myself," she said. "I love him and he loves me. We're going to get married and live in Houston."

"Daddy's going to lose his baby," Allison said. "How do you think that will hit him?"

"He won't be losing me, I'll be in Houston. Besides we're not going to get married until I graduate, and we'll live in an apartment here until he gets out of law school. And Daddy has you, anyway."

"Have you told Mom that you're having sex?"

"No, and I hope you won't. I know she'll be disappointed in me."

"She might figure it out. She's not stupid, you know," Allison said. "And if she does, you'd better hope she doesn't tell Daddy. I wouldn't want to be you if he finds out."

"I wouldn't either," Aimee said, and Allison laughed out loud.

In March of 1991, not long before the girls were scheduled to graduate, and about the time that Charlie came home from the Gulf War, Aimee discovered that she was pregnant. "You'd better tell Mom," Allison told her.

"I can't, Allison. I haven't told Matt yet. I don't know what to do. I'm dead."

"No, you're not," Allison said, "just go tell Matt and if he tosses you out—then you're dead. But he won't. I've seen how he treats you. He'll be happy for you, and for himself. Just go tell him. He is the father, isn't he?"

This drew a scornful look from Aimee. "Of course, he's the father. What do you think I am?"

"I'm sorry," Allison said, and she hugged Aimee. "I'm your sister. I'll always be here for you."

"Thank you, Allison," Aimee said, breaking into tears. "I love you."

"I love you too, Aimee."

Matt Brady let out a whoop, grabbed Aimee around the waist, lifted her off the ground, swung her around, and kissed her. "I'm going to be a father, is that what you're telling me?" he said to the woman he loved.

"If you want me to keep the baby, it does," she told him.

"What do you mean if I want you to keep it? Of course, I want you to keep it. I want for us to get married, right away." He kissed her again. "Did you think I was just kidding when I said I love you?"

"No," she said, "but I have to tell my parents."

"*We* have to tell your parents," Matt said. "I'll go with you. Let's do it tonight."

Aimee was noticeably nervous to her mother, but she didn't let on what it was all about. "Matt is coming over tonight to talk to you and Daddy. I'm going to be there too."

When Mattie told Jim what was about to happen, he just shrugged. "He's going to ask us to let him marry Aimee. They know we'll say yes, but it's a nice gesture, anyway."

"I hope you're right," Mattie said, "Aimee is acting very strange."

"Boys do not visit a girl's parents to ask permission to break up with her," Jim said.

Aimee led Mat into the family room, and they both sat down on the short couch. Jim and Mattie sat on the other couch across from them.

"Okay, Aimee, you called this meeting, what's on your minds?" Jim said.

Matt spoke up. "Mister Kemper, I know you have to know that I love Aimee, I think a blind man could see that." Jim nodded. Matt swallowed. "I love her, and she loves me. If you don't believe me, ask her."

Mattie stifled a smile and Jim raised his hand. "The defense will stipulate that the two of you are in love, and dare I assume you want to get married?"

"Yes, sir, we want to get married."

"Well, that's really Aimee's choice, and it looks as if she's made that choice. When do you plan on getting married, after Aimee graduates or after you finish law school?"

"No, we need to get married right away. I mean we want to get married right away."

"Oh, why the rush? There's plenty of time. It's not like you're circling the drain."

"Oh, shit," Mattie exclaimed, and Jim turned to look at her quickly. Then he understood too. "Your pregnant, aren't you, Aimee?" Mattie asked.

"Yes, Mother, I am."

Both parents were stone-faced. Had Charlie not been confined to his room for the duration on this meeting, he would have found their reaction humorous.

"Now, I know you're mad, Mister Kemper," Matt said, "but hear me out, please. I've been hoping for this, praying for this. Ever since I met Aimee I've been walking around a foot off the ground. When she told me she was going to have our baby…well, I've jumped up a foot or two. This may be a tragedy for you but this is the happiest day of my life. If you kick my ass now—oh, I'm sorry, if you beat me up tonight—this will still be the happiest day of my life. I want to spend the rest of my life with Aimee. And don't worry about her. I can take care of her. I'm going to be a lawyer. I'm going to join my dad's law firm. I'll buy us a house in Houston. And—"

"Hold on, Matt, take a breather," Jim said. "I've seen your resume. I'm okay with this. I have to admit, though, I was not expecting this news to be delivered with such fervor. You're way too happy for me to get mad at you" He stood up, shook

Matt's hand, and hugged him. "Welcome to the family, son," he said.

Aimee was elated and started hugging everyone in the room. Charlie and Jenny and Allison who had all been listening at the staircase came down and congratulated their sister and their soon-to be brother-in-law.

The wedding was held in Houston in the back yard of Matt's parent's house. John and Sylvia Brady took care of all the arrangements. Jim and Mattie felt a bit upstaged but they took it in stride. Matt and Aimee stood with the preacher on the backyard pagoda while the bridesmaids and the groom's men flanked them on the ground. The guests sat in cushioned folding chairs, in front of the pagoda.

Jim walked Aimee down the grassy aisle. "Who gives this woman to be married?" the preacher called out?"

"I do," Jim answered, "I'm her father."

Aimee was not yet showing a baby-bump, so apparently, no one in the crowd, save the Kempers, knew the situation.

Jim and Mattie visited a while with the Brady's. Mattie confessed later that they seemed very pretentious.

"They're lawyers," Jim told her, "They're supposed to be assholes."

Matt and Aimee would go to San Antonio for their honeymoon. There was not much time to waste. They had to get back to Dallas and get an apartment.

The girls would graduate in June of '91. In December, Aimee gave birth to a baby girl. They named her Matilda Ann, after Mattie, her mother. A boy would come later in 1995. They named him Matthew after his father.

"Two of my children are gone now and having families of their own. It's just sad sometimes, Jim," Mattie said, almost crying.

"Look at the bright side, Mom," Charlie told her. "That's two more off Dad's payroll."

Jim chuckled and patted his son on the shoulder.

Chapter 20

Washington

There was a band playing in the lounge of the Washington Plaza Hotel at Thomas Circle NW in Washington. Jim and Mattie were sitting at a table next to the dance floor, having drinks and talking. The singer announced that he was going to sing a John Denver song, "Today."

"I love this song, will you dance with me, James?"

"Of course, Mattie, it will be my pleasure," he said.

He held her close, as the music started, nuzzling her hair and kissing her neck. She hugged him tightly as the moved slowly to the gentle love song.

"John wrote that for us, Mattie," he whispered in her ear.

"Umm," she said. "You're a dandy all right, my darling, but not a rover, at least not as far as I know. But you can sleep in my clover anytime."

"Rover is a dog's name, I'm no rover."

They continued dancing until the song ended then they sat back down.

"I love you Mattie," he told her and reached for her hand. He took it in his, pulling her head close to his so she could hear him over the other patrons: "I loved you the first time I laid eyes on you. I've never even looked at another woman since I met you."

"I know, James," she said, hugging him tighter. "I knew the moment you sat down at my table that time in the Driftwood that we would still be together today."

"I was only hoping at that point but I sort of knew it too. I just hope you don't ever think I take you for granted. I mean, I get so caught up in the business, it takes all my time. I often forget to tell you how I feel. You gave me hope when I was in Vietnam, you gave me life, a family, and reason to live and work my ass off to succeed."

"I lived in terror almost every moment you were over there. I alternated from knowing you would come back alive, unscathed, to knowing you would not. My mother saved me through that terrible time. She took care of the boys and me. I could not have gotten through it without her. She just kept telling me that you'd be all right. How did you get through it without going insane?"

"I didn't, I went insane," he said. "The hardest time was when I got the telegram about my grandfather's death. I had hoped so much that I would get back home before he died. It breaks my heart knowing that I was probably the last thing on his mind when he passed away. Danny Carlisle can't even talk about it without breaking down. Danny looked at Grandpa almost as his savior. I thought about you and the boys a lot, usually at night, that helped but it also hurt too. I was afraid I'd get so preoccupied with you that I'd lose my focus and do something stupid, like get killed. So mostly I tried to put you out of my mind, you know, as a form of self-preservation."

"It must have been awful for you losing your friend, Eddie and the men from your crew."

"What bothers me now is that I never went to look up Eddie's family. I always said I was going to do that, and Dolan's too, but I just got caught up in life and family, and never did it. I feel like an asshole for that."

"I don't think you're an asshole, James. I'm your biggest fan."

"Well then, with that in mind, let's go upstairs and I'll show you who 'your' biggest fan is."

They finished their drinks and took the elevator to their room. Mattie went into the bathroom and came out wearing just her panties and nothing else.

Jim just smiled at her. "Damn woman," he said, "you *are* beautiful. Meet me at the bed."

They made love like it was the first time. It seemed to Jim

that it was always the first time with Mattie.

"There are two things I cannot live without, Mattie," he said.

"Only two, what might they be?"

"Air and you," he said.

"What about food, water, and Texas?"

"You're spoiling my moment. Look at me."

She turned to look at him. He put his right arm around her and his left hand grasped her hair. He kissed her long and hard and she responded with the same passion.

"Do we need to get back in bed, James?" she said.

"I love you, Mattie," he told her, "I'll always love you. You have to know that." He was in a retrospective mood, looking back over their lives together. Sometimes he couldn't believe all that had happened, what had brought him to where he was today.

"I do know it, darling, I've always known it. I love you too."

They checked out of the hotel and drove out to Annapolis to meet their new granddaughter, Lydia, and to see her folks and their son, the proud father. The baby girl was fat and sassy, she looked like both parents but a little more like her mother. Shadow was breastfeeding her daughter, which impressed Mattie and Jim with their daughter-in-law's commitment to the child and to her being a good mother.

"You've never looked more beautiful, Shadow," Mattie said, "and the baby is beyond beautiful."

"Thank you, Mattie," Shadow said. "Now I have to make Alton a boy, he wants a son."

Alton broke in. "You just take care of yourself and Lydia, we'll talk about that in due time. I'm happy enough right now. If I got any happier I couldn't stand it."

"Alton," Mattie said, "I'm worried about Mother. I hope that you and Shadow will continue to live with her so you can look after her."

"Mom, I have to tell you something," he said. "Grandpa Charles already transferred the house into our name, mine and Shadow's. I tried to talk him out of it but he insisted and so did

Grandma. I'm not sure if I did the right thing or not by taking it."

"Well I'm not surprised. Mother did mention that to me a couple of times. I think it's wonderful but your Aunt Andrea might not take it so well when she finds out she won't get the house."

"Grandpa said he took care of that with her. I don't know what he meant or what he did, but that's what he said."

"Andrea is not very stable. She married a lazy good-for-nothing man who won't work. They do drugs and just generally live a very erratic existence. You be careful if they start coming around all of a sudden. It's been years since she came to see our mother and she didn't even come to Dad's funeral. But as for the house, it couldn't be in better hands. It's a wonderful place for your kids to grow up. I grew up here and I turned out all right."

"Indeed, you did, Mom. Sometimes I just have to stop and ponder how things work out. Dad met you and ya'll have lived happily ever after. I met a girl just down the street and we will too, I know it."

"Ya'll?" she said. "Did my Yankee son just say ya'll? I guess what they say is true, you can take a boy out of Texas but you can't take Texas out of the boy." She giggled. "Wait until I tell you father that you said ya'll."

"I get laughed at all the time about my accent. Shadow copies some of the things I say in Texanese. It's cute to hear her mocking me."

"You are your father's son, I suppose. That can't be a bad thing. So, what are your plans for the future?"

"I've been offered a job at the *Washington Post*, a lot more money and free rein to write about anything I choose, not that I can't do that in Baltimore but Washington is the big-time. I was going to pass this by Dad but I haven't had a chance yet."

"Well, do it as gently as you can," Mattie said.

Alton told his dad about the offer from the *Post*. He didn't explode, as Mattie thought he might.

"Ah shit, son, *the Washington Post*? That's almost as bad as the New York Times."

"What's wrong with the *Post*, Dad? I really don't know. Grandpa Charles liked it. Tell me what you mean."

"It's a liberal organization, Alton, they always support the Democratic Party. Now, don't get me wrong, there's nothing wrong with being a Democrat, my grandfather and yours were Democrats and both were great men. But the *Washington Post* is just not conservative enough for me. They're not fair in their reporting. But listen, son, you have to make this decision. You do what is best for you and your family. If the money's good, take the job if you want it and give them your best. Just remember to keep a bar of soap in your desk and wash your hands when you leave work so you don't bring anything home with you."

Jim was smiling when he said it and Alton knew he was playing with him. Still, it was clear that his dad did not trust much of anything associated with "donkey" politics.

"Well, I already told them I'd come in for an interview. I kind of like the idea of playing in the biggest arena in the world. I mean that's what you do, isn't it?"

"Don't let me discourage you, I know you'll be good at the job. I just don't think they will let you have a free hand in choosing what to write about. I think they'll dictate to you what you have to do and you'll end up frustrated."

"Then I'll tell them to piss off and I'll quit. If they don't let me do what they said they would, then I'll quit, fair enough?"

"Yes, son, that is fair enough." Jim stood up and hugged Alton. "I love you, son," he said. "I've always been proud of you."

"I love you too, Dad."

കൈ

In the summer of '94 the National Milk Producers Federation, in association with the National Dairy Producers Conference, planned to hold their convention in Washington. It would be held at the Washington Plaza. Jim and Danny were asked to give brief talks about the establishment and building of Kemper Farms into the virtual dynasty it had become in

Texas, and surrounding states. The NMPF expressed a desire for Danny Carlisle, a pioneer in the dairy business, to tell of his rise from a basic field hand to part owner of a dairy conglomerate. Jim was asked to give his talk on the financing and cost control of dairy farms.

"The biggest problem facing the dairy industry," Jim told his fellow dairymen, "is where to put all the shit."

Alton and Shadow were visiting with the kids, so Mattie opted to stay home and not travel to Washington with Jim this trip.

"I'll be about three days but I'll be back before the kids leave," he told her.

Conventions were a boring affair unless a man liked to drink and party. Jim was now fifty-two years old, and he'd never been much for partying. He was getting too old to enjoy these things.

The first night, Danny Carlisle spoke for about an hour. It was a great talk, Jim believed, and others did as well. There was much applause for Danny's telling about how he had met Alton Kemper and how Alton had taken a chance on him and hired him to work at the dairy. Then he told them how he had come to be part owner of the business and how he and Jim Kemper, Alton's grandson, had taken it national, and how they were going to go international soon. He told them his twenty-five percent ownership of the business had made him a millionaire, a millionaire in coveralls, he added.

When Jim spoke, he went into some detail about some of the inherent problems they faced in managing an ever-expanding dairy business, not the least of which was how to handle the manure, where to put it. This drew some laughs but they listened with interest because those new to the business had most likely not even thought about that. Then he went into financing, capitalization, retention of profits, and replenishment of equipment. He mentioned that early on they had rented a fleet of trucks, rather than purchase them, in order to save initial cash outlays for equipment, insurance, and maintenance.

The last day was mainly for socializing and seeing the city. Danny flew out early that morning. He wanted to get back to the farm. Jim would leave the next day. The convention had gone well. He was glad to see Danny Carlisle so well respected by the Dairy Farmers Association. Danny made a great speech. The way he laid out his plan for exploring foreign markets and providing milk to the underprivileged in other countries was nothing short of brilliant. Jim felt that everyone there was just as impressed by his grandfather's old friend as he had been himself. Strange, he thought. He still thought of Danny as his grandfather's friend. The truth was that Danny and Jim had been almost as close for the past thirty years as Danny had been to Alton.

Jim walked into the hotel lobby bar to get a drink, more to relax for a while than to get a drink but he ordered a Scotch and water anyway. The drink was half finished when he noticed a woman walk through door of the bar. She stopped for a second, looked in his direction, and started walking toward him. Something about her was vaguely familiar, but he couldn't say what it was. She was well dressed. Expensively dressed in a black strapless evening dress that exposed tanned shoulders and arms, she drew looks as she passed by some men sitting at other tables in the bar. Her graying brown hair fell gently and flipped out just a little as it met her shoulders. She appeared to be about his age and as he watched her approach, he couldn't help but wonder why she was apparently coming to his table. He looked behind him to see if possibly she might be with someone else but the table behind him was empty.

The woman walked right up to his table and stopped. Curious eyes all over the bar watched her to see what she would do next.

"Hello, Jim," she said. "It's been a long time."

She held out her hand to him and he took it and held it for a moment. He was almost stricken mute.

"My God," he said, finally, "I don't believe my eyes. Is it really you Laura?"

"It's really me. Aren't you going to ask me to sit down?"

"Yes, yes, of course. Sit down," he said and got up to pull the chair out for her. The curious eyes all over the bar seemed satisfied with that and went back to their own business. "I don't know what to say. My god, I don't believe my eyes."

"You said that," she said, smiling at him.

The waiter came over and she ordered an Old Fashion. Jim asked for another Scotch and water. A few minutes later their drinks came.

Her smile had not changed. It was still captivating. Even after thirty years, she was still beautiful, older, of course, but so was he, for that matter. There were the inevitable lines showing in her face but it was obvious that she had taken care of herself.

"What are you doing here? I mean, what brings you to Washington?"

"I'm here with my husband for a medical convention," she said. "I spend a lot of time in my room watching television. I saw on the news that you would be here tonight. I watched your speech from in the back. You were brilliant."

"Thank you. I still get a little nervous in front of large crowds, but I'm getting the hang of it."

"If you were nervous, I'm sure no one noticed," she said. She was looking deeply into his eyes the way she had done when they were young.

He tried to avert his eyes away from hers but had difficulty in doing so. "So, you married a doctor?"

"On my third try, I did. We live in Houston. I never had any children. I guess I just can't."

"I'm sorry," he said, finally looking away from her eyes. "I can't imagine life without my kids. They're wonderful. I tried awfully hard to knock you up so you'd have to marry me."

At that, she laughed and then put her hand over her eyes. It looked to Jim as if she were about to cry. "That you did, Jim Kemper. That you did. Nobody has tried that hard since."

"It looks like you got everything that you wanted out of life," he said. He sensed that the opposite was true, and he resisted a momentary urge to be sarcastic to her, remembering the pain she had caused him so many years ago.

She looked sad but almost courageous, it seemed to him. "I no longer measure my life by the things I have, Jim. I measure my life by the things I lost somewhere along the way. Did you get everything out of life that you wanted?" she asked him.

"Not everything, Laura, but I got enough. More than enough, I guess. I got a lot more than any one man deserves."

As they talked, his mind drifted back to the three years they were together. So long ago, he thought, like in another life. He had accepted the fact years ago, that he would never see her again. Now for her to just walk into his life so unexpectedly, so suddenly. His mind was racing ahead of itself.

"Are you here alone?" she asked.

He nodded. "Mattie, my wife, stayed in Dallas this trip. She used to come with me sometimes but it's hard on her schedule and she gets bored, to be quite honest about it. My son Alton and his wife and two kids are visiting us so she stayed home."

She was staring at him again, no longer playfully as he had always remembered her, now she looked needful. Like a woman starved for love. He was saddened by the hurt he saw in her eyes. He wanted to take her in his arms again and erase the last thirty years from his memory.

"We could go to your room, Jim," she said, almost pleadingly.

He felt as if the life had just gone out of him. He was unable to speak for what seemed an eternity to him. "I can't, Laura. I'm sorry, I j—just can't," he was finally able to stammer. "My God, Laura, honey, I loved you so. I'd never loved anyone the way I loved you. You broke my heart. But it's too late now. There are others to consider."

"I know," she said. "You're still the same person I fell in love with, I see. I just had to see you again. I had to try." She stood up and extended her hand to him. He took it and in an impulsive moment kissed it. She smiled at him again. "Take care of yourself, Jim. I'm glad you're okay."

She turned and walked away. He watched her until she was through the door. He felt as if his whole life had walked out on him again.

The morning after he got back to Dallas, Jim received a call from NBC asking him to make an appearance on the Lawrence Applegate show, a nationally televised Sunday Morning news and commentary program. They wanted to schedule him for Sunday two weeks off. He was reluctant at first but finally agreed to do it.

A woman named Cindy called Jim at his office telling him that she was with NBC and she was making arrangements for his trip to New York for the *Lawrence Applegate Show*. His ticket would be waiting for him at the DFW American Airlines counter and a car would pick him up on Saturday to take him to his hotel. 'We're putting you up at the Marriott Marquis near Times Square, Mister Kemper, if that's okay. Then we'll pick you up on Sunday Morning around eight."

"That's great," he said, "I'll see you there."

Jim was up early on Sunday morning and had a quick breakfast in the hotel lobby restaurant. The NBC car arrived for him right at eight o'clock just as Cindy had promised.

They had to prepare him for the set, which meant putting makeup on him. He didn't like the idea but he knew it was necessary. He remembered how the Kennedy-Nixon debates cost Nixon the presidency because of improper preparation for the television cameras.

They had him seated before the beginning of the show and the host waited for the signal then addressed his audience. "We welcome today a very special guest, James Kemper, the nationally known business tycoon from Dallas. Welcome to New York, James," he said and stood up to shake Jim's hand. "First off, James, could you tell us a brief history of how you built a multi-million-dollar conglomerate from what most American would consider fairly austere beginnings."

"I'd be happy to, Lawrence," Jim said, "but I go by Jim, call me Jim."

Applegate nodded and smiled. "Jim it is," he said.

Jim delivered his standard rendition of his success story, which he'd committed to memory, having told it more times than he could count by now. Then the host acknowledged that he knew Jim was a pillar of the Republican Party and asked him to lay out his conservative views for the audience.

"It's pretty simple, Lawrence. Basically, it boils down to what the true role of government is supposed to be as intended by the founding fathers and the constitution. The government should defend our borders, protect us from foreign threats, and then pretty much just leave us alone. If government does everything it can possibly do to create an economic atmosphere that is conducive to the growth of private enterprise, then private enterprise will grow the economy and create jobs. Lower taxes produce more tax revenue than raising taxes ever will. So, if Democrats want to raise more revenue to fund their social programs the best thing they can do is lower people's taxes, especially taxes on small businesses. We cannot spend our way into prosperity, we have to create revenue-producing jobs."

"Thank you, Jim," Lawrence said. "Now I know you are proud to be an American, I think I read that somewhere. Can you tell me, what was the one time you can think of when you were proudest to be an American?"

"Of course, I think the proudest I've ever been to be an American and the proudest I've ever been of America was when I watched an incident that took place during the Gulf War, in which, incidentally, my son Charlie was an Abrams tank commander. But after the war was won and thousands of Iraqis were surrendering, I saw an American soldier, or Marine I'm not sure which he was, take some Iraqis prisoner. The Iraqis were on their knees, crawling toward the Americans, begging for their lives, and that American soldier had his hands out toward them and he was telling them, 'It's okay, you're okay, we're not going to hurt you.' He kept telling them over and over that he wasn't going to hurt them. I think that was the moment when I was proudest to be an American."

After a commercial break, Applegate asked Jim if he had any political ambitions. "You're a very popular man right now, any chance you might consider running president one day?"

"Lord no," Jim replied, "but you'd do well to keep an eye on my good friend Senator Jack Grantham from California, who has, incidentally, just won reelection to his third term. He's a force to be reckoned with in the next few years."

"Really," Applegate said. "I've heard of Jack Grantham but I had no idea you two were friends. How did that happen? He's a Democrat and you're a Republican."

"We served together in Vietnam," Jim told him. "My honest opinion is that Jack Grantham is probably the best man in the country to be president. I don't agree with everything he believes, and vice-versa, but he is an honest man, probably the most honest politician I know."

Jim's comment on national television caused no small stir among political pundits and news outlets. Until that time, Jack Grantham had stayed pretty much under the radar. Jack was immensely popular in California, especially in the Bay area, but relatively unknown in the wider arena. Grantham headquarters became inundated with phone calls and requests for interviews and talk show visits. Jack sidestepped it all by calling a news conference at which he made a brief statement and took no questions. "While I appreciate the praise I received from my good friend Jim Kemper from Texas, I have no plans to run for president now or at any time in the near future. My only concern is to represent the people of California to the best of my ability. That's the job I have and that's the job I intend to do."

Questions still abounded but were left unanswered and speculation began floating around about Jack's possible consideration for a presidential candidacy in the future. Nick Devoss was elated over the incident. "This is like manna from heaven," he told Jack, "but let's be subtle. We don't want to blow it, it's too early. We'll make our move in ninety-eight and then hit this country by storm. It's working just like we planned, Jack. Just keep on doing your job and spend some time in California. Your constituents are proud of you, and they want to see you a lot."

⁊⊱⊰

Jim had accepted that Alton was working for the *Washington Post*. He didn't much like it but that was his son's choice and he gave him his blessing on any endeavor he might pursue. In November of 1995, Alton called and told Jim that he was taking a leave of absence to write a book on the development of Alaska and the building of the Alcan Highway.

"Alaska," Jim said. "Why would you write a book about Alaska?"

"It's been an interest of mine for some time now," he said, "it's a fascinating place, I'm told."

"But it's so damned cold in Alaska. Why can't you at least wait until summer?"

"I want to get the feel of it in its harshest time, a better understanding of what it took for the earliest settlers who explored and developed the state. I'll go back when summer comes and get that perspective."

"And how does Shadow feel about you going to Alaska in the winter?" Jim asked him.

"She's not keen on the idea but she supports me. I really need to get another book on the market."

"Do you need money, son?" Jim asked him.

"No, Dad, it's for my ego. I'm making plenty of money. You taught me how to make and manage my money, and Shadow is working again, in Washington. Dad, she makes as much money as I do."

"Well, I hope that doesn't do any damage to your male ego."

"Not a bit," Alton said.

"Good," Jim told him. "Your mother didn't raise any male chauvinists, except for Charlie, that is." Alton laughed. "Call me some time," Jim added.

"I will, Dad, thank you."

"You're welcome, son, take care of yourself."

∽∾∽

Allison had been working in sales, under Marcus Herrera, for three years as a quality-control person. Her duties consisted of visiting the remote sales offices and doing evaluations on the performance and general professional quality of the operation. She also evaluated the managers of the individual stores and received his recommendations for pay increases and promotions. It was boring work but she turned out to be good at it. But an opportunity arose for her early in 1995. Charlie summoned her to his office along with Marcus Herrera.

"Allison," Charlie began, "you've been doing a good job. Marcus speaks highly of you and most of the managers seem to respect your business and people skills but I'm going to have to take you off your job."

"Charlie Kemper, if you fire me, I'm telling Dad. You can't fire me."

Marcus started laughing.

"Calm down, baby sister, nobody is firing you. We're starting our move into Mexico and we want you to head the division."

"Oh, my god," she yelled. "Charlie, you're an asshole to lead me on that way. I thought you were firing me."

"Come on, Allison, if I fired you, they wouldn't let me back in the house. You're being promoted."

"Oh, Charlie, I love you," she said, put her hands over her face, and started crying. "I love you too Marcus, this is a dream come true."

"It's going to be hard work, Allison," Charlie said. "We're going to Mexico City next week to meet with the government officials Marcus has been talking to for that past six months."

"Does Daddy know, I want to tell Daddy," she said with exuberance.

"He knows, Allison," Charlie said, "it was his decision but Marcus and I were on board with it. You can do the job, but just always remember that you work for Marcus and he must be in on any major decisions. Minor decisions you can make on your own."

"What's a minor decision, Charlie?" she asked.

"Which dress to wear and where to go for lunch," he said, smiling at her.

Marcus was laughing at the "sibling rivalry" that they pretended to have between them. "On that note, however, Allison," he told her. "You should dress conservatively. Mexican men can be a little rude sometimes. An attractive American girl can get some whistles and offensive remarks thrown her way in Mexico City. You brother and I will be with you. It will be a good while before you'll be able to go to Mexico alone. Usually we'll deal with representatives at the consulate in Dallas."

Allison met Charlie and Marcus at the office. Jim was going to drive them to the airport for the trip to Mexico City. She was wearing a navy-blue skirt suit with a white blouse buttoned up to her neck. "You look beautiful, darling," Jim told her. "I see you took Marcus's advice about dressing down a bit. It's perfect, the way you are dressed.

They set down at the airport in Mexico City, Sinaloa, Peñón de Los Baños, and went to the airline counter where an attaché was supposed to be waiting for them. He was, and he noticed them right away. He introduced himself as Raul Carillo and led them to a limo with a sign on the side which read, *Gobierno de Mexico Secretaría de Desarrollo Social.*

"Secretary of social development," Allison said.

The man directed them to sit in the back of the limo and then he got in with them. Two taps on the driver's window signaled him ant the car started in motion. "So, you speak Spanish, Miss? he asked Allison.

"A little, Raul, "she said, "*solo um poco.*"

"Oh, come now, Allison," Marcus said, "don't be so dismissive of your Spanish. You speak very good Spanish."

"I'm a little nervous," she said.

"Do not worry, Allison," Raul said. "The secretary is fluent in English but if you wish to converse in Spanish, he will certainly find that entertaining."

It was a half hour ride or so to the government office building of the Secretary of Social development. Raul introduced them to Secretary Senor Roberto Rios Gutierrez and told them that Allison spoke Spanish.

He began speaking to them in his language, as he looked Allison up and down, a fact that was lost on neither Charlie nor Marcus. He spoke only to Allison, at first, he made no secret of it that he was fascinated with her. "*El senor aqui,*" he said, pointing at Charlie, "*es tu esposo?*"

"*Oh, no, no, mi hermano*," she answered back. Marcus was smiling but Charlie had no clue what was going on. "Y *mi hermano no puede hablar Espanol, Con su permiso, podemos hablar in Ingles, está bien?*"

"*Si, senorita, por su puesto*, for the benefit of your brother we can speak in English."

Mister Gutierrez told them that his goal, or mission as he called it, was to eliminate poverty in Mexico through comprehensive, collectively responsible human development, achieve adequate levels of well-being with adjustment to government policies. And to improve, through social, economic and political factors, in rural and urban areas to enhance local organization, city development and housing.

It was a stock speech but he had assured Marcus, over the phone and via email, that his government was serious about this mission.

"And that's why we are here, sir," Marcus told him. "Kemper Enterprises and Kemper Industries, our manufacturing arm, can provide low cost affordable housing units to your government, deliver them out of our Dallas plant, and send specialists to teach your contractors how to construct the two-piece units together, connect the wiring and plumbing, and do the finish out, which is minimal work. My two colleagues here, are Mister Charlie Kemper, Vice-President of Operations and his sister Allison, Division Head for our Mexico Project. They will give you a comprehensive demonstration of our various size units and show you just how quickly we can make things happen."

"Let me get my assistant to come in and take notes for me, if you don't mind. I want to make sure I can remember everything you tell me."

"Don't mind at all," Charlie said.

The secretary left the room and returned with two ladies following him. One was carrying a pad and pen and the other was pushing a cart with coffee and other refreshments on it. They all partook of coffee, except Allison had some tea.

"The pastries were delicious," Marcus remarked.

Then Charlie opened the case he'd rolled in and set up his stand and started showing pictures of the different models that Kemper built. He had some scale models with which he showed the secretary how the houses were put together on site. Charlie and Allison answered dozens of questions Gutierrez had. He seemed generally interested and kept asking how this was done or how that worked. He insisted that they call him Roberto and, although it was awkward at first, they eventually did as he asked.

Two hours later, they were finished. And Roberto had apparently run out of questions.

"Your father, Jim, would be proud of you. You both did a fine job of making a presentation of your company."

"I was not aware that you know our father, Roberto," Allison said.

"Oh yes," he answered, "I met Mister Kemper and Marcus about a year ago before I came into my current job. I told them that if I got this position I wanted to pursue everything you just demonstrated to me, on behalf of my government and the Mexican people. You did a fine job. You will be hearing from me.

"Thank you, Roberto," Charlie said, and the other two reiterated that. "We appreciate the opportunity to do business with you.

"Do you have plans for dinner tonight?" Roberto asked them. They had none.

"Then don't make any plans, I will have Raul pick you up at eight for dinner on me. Where are you staying?

Marcus told him they were staying at the Gran Hotel on Avenida diez y seis de Septiembre.

"Raul knows where it his. I'll see you at dinner."

The restaurant was the Angus Butcher House. It offered up, as the review read, *Classic steakhouse fare, aged Angus cuts from porterhouse to T-bone, filet mignon, prime rib and even a folksy Mexican arrachera, plus Kobe beef if you can't make it to Japan this season.* The scantily clad hostesses told Charlie and Marcus why Roberto liked the place, given his keen eye that noticed Allison the moment she walked into his office.

Roberto arrived and they were seated. He suggested an appetizer called Tuxtla Gutierrez. "It's named after me, so I order it every time I come here," he said.

The meal was a pleasant affair. Roberto was more interested in Allison than he was his steak and Charlie decided that the presence of her brother was all that kept him from coming on to her. He made a mental note to never let his sister come to Mexico alone.

The next day they flew back to Dallas and reported to Jim the events of the trip.

"So, you found that Roberto Gutierrez has an eye for the ladies, did you?" Jim said.

"Yeah, Pop, if Marcus and I had not been there, I think he would have been all over Allison."

"He's a skirt-chaser all right. But I think he probably knows his limits."

e/ɔe/ɔ

December 6, 1995 was a date from which and by which everything in the Kemper family tree would be forever measured. The time before that date and the time after became a great open gulf that divided them from what was, and what could never be again.

Mattie was in the den of their home on Turtle Creek, working on her computer, when Emily, the housekeeper called to her. "Miss Mattie, It's Miss Shadow on the phone for you, she's crying.

Mattie went to the kitchen and picked up the phone. "What is it, darling? What's wrong?"

Shadow was sobbing and incoherent. Mattie couldn't understand anything she was trying to say. "Are you hurt, Shadow, please, honey, tell me what's wrong."

"Mattie, oh, Mattie," she stammered and yelled, "Aaah, aaah. Mattie, Alton was killed." And she continued sobbing on the phone.

Mattie gasped loudly and then gasped again. "No," she yelled, "Oh, God, no." She stumbled and knocked some pans off the counter then collapsed to the floor. Emily was sobbing and trying to comfort Mattie in any small way she could. Mattie continued yelling, "No, no. Not Alton, Oh God no, not my son." She was gasping for air.

Jenny heard the commotion and came into the kitchen. She saw Mattie on the floor and started yelling, "What's wrong, what's happened?"

Emily got up and handed Jenny the phone," Miss Shadow, Miss Shadow," she said.

Jenny picked up the phone. 'Shadow, what's wrong, what's wrong?"

Shadow was still sobbing. "Here's my mother," she sobbed into the phone.

"Hello, this is Lydia McCormack, Shadow's mother, is this Mattie?"

"No, this is Jenny, Charlie's wife, what has happened?"

"Oh, Jenny, I'm so sorry but Alton was killed in a plane crash in Alaska."

"Oh, God," Jenny moaned and dropped the phone. She then went over to Mattie and sat down beside her on the floor. Emily came back and sat down on the other side of Mattie. They just held her while all three of them continued crying.

It was at least a half hour before Mattie could get up. Jenny and Emily helped her to the couch and she lay down. Emily brought her a wet rag and put it across her eyes. Jenny tried to talk to her but she remained unresponsive except to nod her head. "Mattie, I'm going to call Charlie at the office," she said. "Is that okay?"

Mattie nodded and managed to say, "Yes, please, Jenny, thank you."

Jenny had no idea what she was going to say to Charlie but when he answered she called his name. "Charlie," she said, "I have terrible news. We just got a phone call from Shadow. Alton was killed in a plane crash in Alaska." There was no response from the other end.

Charlie just sat there, closed his eyes, and lowered his head for a moment. "How is my mother?" he asked her.

"She passed out. She's on the couch now. Emily and I are

doing what we can for her. She's not able to talk yet."

"Okay, thank you, Jenny," he said. "Do what you can for her. I'll tell Dad."

Charlie was at the Towers Project in Arlington so he had to drive to the main office in Dallas to see his dad. The drive to Dallas gave him some time to think what he was going to say. He went to Allison's office first and motioned her to follow him. She got up from her desk and went over to him. He put his arm around her and they walked to Jim's office. Allison knew something was wrong but she didn't ask.

Charlie told Jim's secretary. "Gina, we have to talk to my dad, please hold any calls or visitors."

"Of course, Charlie," Gina said.

Charlie hugged Allison before they went through the door. She was terrified of whatever it was she was about to hear, but she said nothing.

Jim looked up when they came through his door. He just stared at Charlie and felt a terrible pain in his gut. He knew bad news when he saw it, and Charlie looked like bad news. "What has happened, son?" he asked him.

"Alton was killed in a plane crash in Alaska, Dad. I got the news from Jenny at home. Shadow called and her mother told Jenny."

Allison broke down immediately and clung to Charlie, he held her up. Jim took a deep breath, put his hands over his face, and laid his head on his desk. His daughter and son stood there holding on to each other, giving him space and time to absorb it all.

Charlie drove them to the house to see how the others were doing. Jim was worried about Mattie. She was sitting up on the couch when he got home. He went over and sat down beside her, leaned over and took her in his arms, and hugged her. She remained lifeless for a short while until she realized that Jim was there with her, and she hugged him back. They hugged each other, sobbing on each other's shoulders.

"Oh, God, Jim," she said. "Our baby is gone."

"I know honey, I know," he said.

It took a couple of days for the authorities to recover the

bodies from the crash site. It was a small charter plane and just the pilot and Alton were on board. They apparently hit some foul weather somewhere near the Twin Lakes area. Jim had no clue where that was. *Damn*, he thought. If only he'd tried harder to get Alton to wait for summer before going to Alaska. If he'd asked him passionately enough, Alton might be alive now. That was all moot now because his son was not alive. He was dead, and Jim would spend the rest of his life getting over it.

The funeral was held in Annapolis on Wednesday the thirteenth. Alton would be buried next to his grandfather, Charles McKenna. Senator Grantham brought Holly and his boys to offer condolences. Jack and Holly hugged Mattie and Jim and lent as much comfort as could be on such occasions as this. Aimee McKenna, unable to walk now was in a wheel chair pushed around by Shadow. Shadow's parents also attended the funeral. Lydia held Shadow in her arms as she wept openly.

Before they left Maryland, Jim and Mattie took Shadow aside and hugged her like they didn't want to let go.

"Shadow," Jim said. "You have a home with us if you ever need it or if you just want to come for a while, please come. We need you to stay close."

"I will, Jim, I promise," she told him. "Oh, and Mattie, I'm going to put your house back in your name. I tried to get Mrs. McKenna to do it, but she refuses. It's your house, you grew up in it. It's not mine."

"No, Shadow, it is yours," Mattie said, "my parents gave it to you both, and I know Alton would want you to have it."

"I have a house down the street, I don't need two. I'm sorry, I'm going to have to defy you on this."

"Oh, honey, it's too much trouble to change the names, please don't do that."

"I'm a lawyer, I can handle it," she said, and the matter was concluded.

Aimee told her daughter, "I'll be right there beside him before too long."

And indeed, Aimee McKenna died a month later of a broken heart. She just lost the will to live.

"Will you go to the farm with me for a month, Mattie?" Jim asked "I just need to get away for a while."

"I think that's a good idea, James," she told him.

"I need you to take over for me, Charlie, just for a while, maybe a month. I'm going to the farm. You can call me with any problems or just to keep me up to speed but I just can't stay here right now."

"I understand, Pop. I know what this must be doing to you and Mom. Don't worry about anything. I'll handle it."

They drove to Comanche and then out to the farm and settled into their old room. Trent had hired a housekeeper who worked three days a week and the lady kept all the laundry done, and the house as clean as if the family was still living there. It felt good to sleep in the old room and in the same bed they'd had years ago.

Trent was up early and out to work. Danny Carlisle was now seventy-four years old and starting to slow down a bit, but only a bit. He had been teaching Trent how to run the dairy for almost twenty years. It was hard for Jim to imagine that his brother had stayed on the job that long. Living out here all alone, with no social life to speak of had to be no life for a young man, although Trent was no longer a young man, he was forty-five years old.

"Do you think Trent is gay, Danny?" Jim asked. Jim had always called his brother Trent, instead of Trenton.

"He has a woman living with him most of the time, Jim. He made her go back to Dallas when I told him you were coming."

"Well, I'll be damned, I had no idea. Are they married?"

"He claims they are, but he never said anything to me about getting married. I think they are just living together. She's very nice, name is Suzan, nice-looking gal."

"I just never paid much attention. I sort of lost track of how long he has been here. I figured he would leave at some point in time."

"I'm teaching him so he can take over for me one day when I retire"

"Are you thinking about retiring, Danny? I hope not but if you feel the need, well, you certainly deserve a rest. You've been the brains and the back bone of this farm for over thirty years now."

"I'm okay," he said. "Trent does most of my running for me so I'm good for a few more years. Oh, Jim. I've wanted to say this but it's just so hard, I can't tell you how sorry I am about Alton. He was such a good kid, and man."

"Thanks, Danny, I appreciate that. I've never known such hurt before, not in all my life."

Jim and Mattie walked around the old house like they were zombies—they didn't talk much, hugged each other occasionally, and Mattie cried a lot. They were distant, and not on purpose, it was just as if they didn't know each other anymore. When Alton died, something died in both of them. Looking at each other, at the pain on each other's face only reminded them all the more of their son who was gone. They almost could not bear to look at each other for fear of seeing the pain in themselves.

Jim went to the cemetery in town to visit his grandparents and his mother. He took along a folding chair and sat down next to his grandfather's grave. He came here often when they lived at the farm but not so much since they moved to Dallas. *There is just never enough time to do all the things you promise yourself you will do.* He sat there thinking about all that had transpired since he left his grandpa heartbroken over his decision to join the army. They lay there next to each other, Alton and Mary Kemper and Jim's mother, Allie Hargrove, joined forever in death as they were in life. There was a slight breeze blowing the leaves of grass surrounding the two graves. A whippoorwill was singing its familiar song, whip-poor-will, not too far off.

"I'm sorry, Grandpa," he muttered softly. "I'm sorry. I never understood what you went through when your son died in the war. I couldn't see your pain. I couldn't feel it until now because now I have lost a son too. I'm sorry. I'm sorry I went to Vietnam and put you through that, the worry and the torment of maybe losing another son. I just didn't know." Jim was weeping and he wiped the tears from his eyes but they kept on flowing. "Oh, Alton, my son, my son," he uttered through his sobbing. "God forgive me, this is too much to bear. I can't do this."

An hour later, he had gotten control of himself enough to permit him to drive back to the farm. "I went to see my grandpa," he told Mattie.

"I figured that's where you were," she said.

"I told him I was sorry for going to Vietnam and putting him through all that worry. But after I left, I realized that if I hadn't joined the army I would never have met you. How different my life would have been if I hadn't met you."

"I can't imagine that," Mattie said. "I don't even want to think about how it would have been. Could a person go back and take a different road and save themselves from pain like we are feeling now? Philosophically speaking, I don't believe that. Their pain would simply come from a different source. We might not have known each other and would not have lost Alton, but it would have been someone else for both of us. Life involves some pain and suffering."

"I know, Mattie, we've been so successful and so lucky, I guess I just started to take it for granted that nothing bad could ever happen. All the success and money though, won't take away the loss of a child. God, I hope I die before I lose another one."

ତ୵ତ୵ତ

The sound of men working and machinery running woke Jim up. It was the sounds of the dairy cranking up to full production, milking machines humming, and trucks being loaded. He headed out to the office to talk to Danny and Trenton. There were at least twenty people working at various tasks around the closest barn and he didn't even know how many more at the facilities across the road, over by the creek. Danny and Trenton were in the office. Danny was on the phone and Trenton was discussing some issue with a couple of the workers. The whole place was buzzing with activity.

When they were finished, Jim asked Trent about his plans for the future. "You've been working here almost twenty years, Trent. Are you satisfied with your life here?"

"I've been happy here, Jim. Danny has taught me a lot and he says I can probably take over his job when he throws in the towel, so to speak, and with him living on the property, he'd always be around for advice."

"Tell me about the woman here with you," Jim said.

"Suzan," Trent said. "We've been together ten years now. We'd planned to get married but just never did."

"What I'm trying to figure out is why I don't know about this. You're my brother and I didn't even realize until today that you've been working here almost half your life. That is unacceptable for me not to have kept better track of your career. Suzan was never here when we came down on weekends or for vacations. I asked Danny how you were doing and he always said you were working and learning and applying yourself to the job. Why did we not talk more over the years?"

"You were always busy, Jim," Trent said, "I didn't want to trouble you. I asked Danny not to mention about Suzan because I was afraid you wouldn't approve of her living here."

"I'm not a prude, Trent, and this is your home. You've taken good care of it, that's easy to see. So, the housekeeper you said you'd hired is your common-law wife?"

"She does the housework inside and I take care of the maintenance upkeep on the place."

"So, you are content living here? I mean, you don't ever have a desire to go back to Arlington?"

"I like it here, it's quiet and peaceful. Living here, where you grew up, and where your grandfather and Mom raised you, just makes it feel like home. Ever since Mom and Dad died, I just had no reason to go back.

"Well I'm sorry for pretty much ignoring you all this time. It makes me question whether or not my drive to succeed in business hasn't cost me in relationships. But, anyway, if you are okay with staying here and maybe taking over the management of the dairy, then we need to do some things. There's a good chance that Mattie and I might move back here in a few years so the first thing we need to do is build you a house."

"I can't afford a house, Jim," he said.

"It'll be the manager's quarters, I'll cut out an acre somewhere on the property, and we'll put it there. I want you and Suzan to come to Dallas in a couple of weeks, when I go back, and pick out one of our floor plans you like, and I'll have it built on your lot."

"You'd do that for me?" Trenton said.

"You're my brother, Trent, and besides, you've been a loyal and dependable employee. I've neglected you, and I want to make up for it. I want you to bring Suzan here so Mattie and I can meet her. And I want you to bring her with you when you come to Dallas to look at floor plans."

"Okay, Jim," Trent said, "thank you.

The next day, Suzan arrived. Trent had called her and told her to come back to the farm. She was a pretty girl—not an earth-shaker, Jim noted, but very nice—and she seemed to be devoted to Trent. She had decorated the house with frilly things and lots of knick-knacks. Jim now understood why he thought Trenton might be gay.

Jim and Mattie took Trent and Suzan to a plot of land that backed up to Duncan Creek. It was lined with trees on one side. "This is a good place for you house, I think," Jim said. "What do you guys think?"

They agreed.

"It's beautiful," Suzan said. "I love it."

"Then here is where it will be. I'll have a surveyor stake off an acre. We'll build a private drive, off the main road. You can walk to work, Trent, if you want to."

"Pick the four-bedroom model," Mattie suggested

"I'm thinking three bedrooms will be more than enough for us." Trent replied.

౿౿౿

Meanwhile, back in the real world, Charlie was having his problems with concrete shortages and increased costs of building material, primarily copper wire for electrical circuits. The Towers project had incurred numerous delays due to everything from rain to labor issues. The project was almost a year behind schedule. The site was so muddy most of the time that delivery truck had a hard time getting in and out. Charlie had the construction roads graded and re-graveled and had lime applied to the site to dry it up. That alleviated the problems for a while.

He called the structural trades managers together to try and light a fire under them. The steel was going up too slowly and the concrete crews were way behind schedule. "Listen, gentlemen, we just broke ground in April, and now we're approaching October. This project is supposed to be completed early in the year two-thousand. I do not intend to have people moving into this building in the next century. So, I expect the steel to be up by the spring of ninety-seven. That's March or April. Do whatever you have to do to make this happen. Let me know if you can't do this, and I'll help you look for some options."

The electrical and HVAC contracts were being done "in-house" by Kemper Wilcox Engineering. This caused great consternation with the IBEW and some of the other union contractors on the job. The case being made was that a project the size of Kemper Towers should be an all-union job. Jim had rejected that from the very beginning. Trade unions were not very popular in Texas. They were perceived as being "bullies" and offering inefficient labor that was prone to slow-downs and sabotage.

Tom Wilcox hated the unions, and Jim disliked them because Tom hated them. Tom's hatred for unions was more for the people in leadership of the unions. He did not hate the concept of a union, he hated the way they were run.

Tom's feelings about the IBEW were rooted in his experiences with them. Several years earlier, the company had contracted to do three "extended-stay" hotel projects in San Antonio. San Antonio, like Houston, was a strongly pro-union city and the city permitting office made little effort to hide that fact.

After establishing an office in the city, the Kemper-Wilcox project manager ran an ad in the local paper for electricians and helpers. Ten or twelve men answered the ad and were hired on the spot. The men turned out to be union "salts" who immediately signed cards requesting union representation for the projects. Tom was forced to sign an agreement with the union to use their labor. The first rub came when he discovered that the union would charge them $4.00 an hour per man hour for the contract. This meant that a man making $15.00 an hour would cost the company $19.00 an hour and labor burden would have to be based on that rate of pay. This charge applied to every worker for every hour he worked.

Some of the workers were good hands, Tom was told by his project manager, a man named Brandon Walker, but most of them were, not much help, as Brandon had put it.

Typically, what they had to deal with was laziness. The men were slow. One of them called it, wobbling. They would slow down and take much longer to do a job than it should have taken. Men would show up and start to work and then claim an injury and would have to be taken to the clinic. A licensed journeyman failed to show up for work one morning, thereby reducing the required journeyman to apprentice ratio, and a city electrical inspector showed up an hour later to check licenses and, finding too few licenses on the job, shut it down and sent everyone home. There was much pro-union graffiti showing up on the walls of buildings and the job foreman was continually finding cut wires and holes in sheetrock walls, for which the general contractor back-charged Kemper Wilcox.

The union contract, however, had one clause of which Tom was able to take advantage of. The clause provided that, in the event that the union could not provide the requested workers, then a contractor could hire them himself. Brandon was both crafty and quick to anger over what he considered an injustice. He knew that there were not enough journeymen or apprentices in the hall, so he put in a request for several of each. The union man told him they would try and find some but, at that time, he had none to send them. The third project was getting ready to kick off so Brandon ran another ad for electricians, but this time he had an advantage.

When he interviewed applicants, Brandon asked them if they were in the union. A couple of them told him, "You can't ask me if I'm in the union."

Under normal circumstances, they would have been correct. But in the company's current situation, Brandon was able to legally tell them that, "We already have a Union contract, I'm hiring now because they cannot provide me with the manpower I need."

Walker was able to man the third project with no union labor. He got a call from the union man who told him, "When you hire someone you need to send them to the hall so we can sign them up."

"Why would I do that?" Brandon asked the man. "These are 'my guys.' I'm not recruiting for the union."

He never heard back from the man, and they finished the job without interference from the union or the city.

The union workers involved in the construction of Kemper Towers were engaging in behavior that most grown men considered childish. They would disconnect extension cords, unscrew electrical boxes, and cut holes in air conditioning flex duct. Tensions between the non-union shops and the union workers almost caused fist fights on a couple of occasions. Charlie complained to the project managers for the offending trades but to no avail. Their response was to brush it off with, "That's what happens when you use scab labor," scab being the union term for "merit" shop—non-union.

Jim directed Charlie to contact an audio/visual company and have them install hidden cameras in various locations throughout the building. The work had to be done at night and took some ingenuity to ensure that they would be undetectable and impervious to dust. A wireless feed was connected to a twenty-four-hour recorder in the Kemper office trailer.

The payoff was not long in coming. Seven men were captured on tape cutting electrical wires and communication cables. Several others were seen on camera unplugging extension cords and committing other minor infractions which did no actual damage. Jim contacted the company lawyer and showed him the evidence, whereupon the lawyer contacted the lawyers for the several union trades whose employees were doing the damage. He sent copies of several of the tapes along with a demand letter to "cease and desist," and a list of the names of ten men, whom Jim wanted removed from the job. And at the next jobsite safety meeting, a film was shown, that had been put together from the several hidden cameras. The union lawyers also had to inform their clients that, if the vandalism did not stop completely, the film would be sent to the NLRB—National Labor Relations Board—and legal action for damages would be initiated against the unions.

By the summer of 1997 the building frame was up and the windows were being installed. Once the building was dried-in, the interior finish out would start. Three elevators were installed, a freight elevator for the lifting of material to the upper floors and two personnel elevators to get the workers to the work.

The building was fifty percent pre-sold, according to deposits already received for expected move-in by March of two-thousand. Kemper Enterprises moved its executive offices from the manufactured housing factory site and would occupy the twentieth floor in both buildings. The North Tower and the South Tower would be joined by a covered walkway between the two towers. Jim and Mattie were spending more time at the farm, and he had intimated that he might retire before too long. Charlie was reluctant to believe that his dad would actually give it all up, although losing Alton had hit him harder than anyone actually knew. After the initial shock, his mother had shown tremendous strength, more strength than her husband, and it was this strength that kept him going. But Dad just didn't seem like Dad anymore to Charlie.

The prospect of taking over the entire operation of Kemper Enterprises, without his father there all the time, both excited and intimidated Charlie. His fear of failure haunted him.

Allison and Marcus Herrera had been meeting regularly with the Mexican officials at the consulate in Dallas. The Mexican Government was ready to invest in a low-cost housing initiative in impoverished areas all over the country. Proposals were made and negotiations were proceeding. At stake was almost a billion dollars in contracts.

Jim had a packaged house sent to the farm to be erected for Trenton and Suzan to live in. He started visiting his sister Sarah more often and was spending more time at home with Mattie. He spent less time at the office and seemed content to get a brief report from Charlie every evening at dinner on how things were going.

Charlie sensed that his dream of one day running the family business was imminent.

Chapter 21

The Decision

In Late November of 1998, Senator Grantham flew into DFW airport. He rented a car and drove to the Kemper residence on Turtle Creek. Mattie Kemper let him in. They hugged and then she led him to the den where her husband was watching television. Jim got up to greet him and shook Jack's hand then pulled a chair out for him to sit in.

"This must be serious business, Jack," he said, "If it required a plane ride all the way to Dallas. Glad to see you anyway."

"It is, ol' buddy. I want to talk to you about something very important. It couldn't wait any longer."

"What is it?" Jim asked.

"I'll announce my candidacy for president next month. I wanted to tell you first."

"Well, I'm honored that you did. You've got more guts than I would have. You've really got an uphill fight on your hands."

"It will be tough, all right," Jack said. "But nothing worthwhile is ever easy. I really believe that I can make a difference. What do you think? You know I value your opinion more than anyone's."

Jim wasn't sure how to respond. He knew what was happening here, and he knew also that there could be long term consequences of what he said and did regarding the matter that Jack had just begun sharing with him. "I do believe that you are the most honest man in the race. I have no doubt about that."

"But do you think I can win?"

"You've got two major battles in this thing. You're going to have to beat Dan Murdock for the nomination, an incumbent vice president in a fairly good economy. Forget the fact that the Republicans are mainly responsible for the good economy, Murdock is going to take the credit for it, and he will get the credit for it from your party. If somehow you can do that, then you have to beat Bush in the election. I'm not sure anyone can do that."

"I have to take one battle at a time," Jack said. He was out of his seat and pacing the floor now. "Right now I have to concentrate on getting the nomination. I need your help, Jim."

"I don't understand, Jack. You know my political affiliation. What can I do?"

"You can give me your endorsement, Jim. Do you realize what a historical impact that would have, a prominent Republican like yourself endorsing a Democrat for president?"

"Do you realize what a shit storm that would stir up?" Jim said. "I'd be crucified."

"I doubt it. You're too big for them to control. Oh, they'll piss and moan about it and make threats, but in the end, they wouldn't do anything. You're too damned rich, Jim my boy, think about it," he continued. "I'm not asking this just because we are friends. You've seen my platform. You agree with almost everything I'll be trying to do. Don't you?"

"Some of it I do," Jim said. "But there are a lot of things to consider."

Mattie brought them some coffee and they stopped talking politics for a while.

Jack was wound up. Jim could see the enthusiasm and the passion that his old friend seemed to be full of. Jim wished he had some of that fire back in his belly, a cause. What he would give for a real cause at this stage of his life. He was getting tired. He hadn't had any enthusiasm or lust for life since Alton died. He wasn't sure if he'd ever bounce back or not. He was quickly running out of challenges that were worth his effort, but he was glad to see Jack so fired up. Jack might not win this thing, come election day, but the other guys would certainly know they had been in a fight.

"You're on board with my alternative energy policy. I know you are. Even with all the friends you have in the oil business, you still realize that we have to get free of our dependency on foreign oil." Jack was pacing again. "And the rapid transit systems. We have to at least look at developing new systems and improving existing ones. Look at the freeways every day, millions of cars with one person in every car. We're choking on our own fumes."

"I know, I know," Jim said "all good ideas, I agree. I'm not saying you're not right and I'm not saying you won't be successful. I'm just saying it will be tough."

"Just think about it, will you Jim? That's all I ask. Just think about it. I believe we can make this a better country. But I need help. Not money, mind you, but moral support. I need to know that my cause is just. I don't know any better way for me to know that than to have your endorsement.

"I will think about it, Jack," Jim said. "I want to discuss it with some folks I trust. I'll be in Washington two weeks from now. I'll give you an answer then. I just need to sit down with some people first and get a feel for how they are going to take this. Okay?"

"Of course, that's okay," Jack said. "I'll be back in Washington then. Get in touch with me, and we'll go to dinner. Remember, Jim, you started this whole thing with that appearance on the *Lawrence Applegate Show*. You're partly responsible.

"I'll keep that in mind," Jim said.

Jack spent the night, and the next morning he flew back to San Jose. He would be back in Washington next week in time to meet with Jim again. He knew his old friend was a businessman first and would be inclined to look at the thing from a businessman's point of view. Popular wisdom would tell him not to back Jack Grantham for president. The fallout would be too great. Their friendship would certainly stand a rejection. Jack understood the consequences that Businessman Kemper would have to consider.

He had not hesitated to put the question to him because Jack knew how critical Jim's endorsement would be to his campaign. They had to think about the country now. It was no longer about egos and personal agendas. It was no longer about trying to disrupt a presidency by impeachment for a minor sexual affair. The future of the country was at stake. Jim Kemper would see that and share his vision. Jack knew that for a fact.

It was funny, he thought. In the early years of his political career, he wanted to be president someday. He didn't really have a plan or really know what he wanted to do as president. He just wanted to *be* president. Then it all started to come together. He developed his plan and his platform. He started to believe and now he knew that he was the best person to run this country.

It was cold in Washington. Some snow had fallen but not enough to be a nuisance. The wind was brisk but it felt good on his face. Jack liked to jog around the Tidal basin alone at night. It helped him think and it was invigorating. He stopped a few minutes at the Jefferson Memorial. He liked Washington but he didn't love it. Parts of it were beautiful and other parts looked like slums. There was a pervasive aura of importance in the very air of Washington, like it was the most important place in the world. As far as he was concerned it 'was' the most important place in the world. He hoped to conquer this town.

He had a good start many of his colleagues and opponents agreed. Now in his third term as Senator he was much respected on Capitol Hill. Back home in San Jose, they thought Jack Grantham could do no wrong, at least that's what all the newspapers said, his included. He thought it only slightly unethical that his own family newspaper gave him the majority of his support in San Jose.

He jogged over to the Washington Monument and looked over to the South Lawn of the White House, remembering his first visit there. Experiencing the troubled visage of Lyndon Johnson and talking face to face with the man, Jack had decided to be president one day, it was not too unlike President

Montgomery had decided when he was sixteen that he wanted to be president, after shaking hands with JFK.

Not too many days hence, his jogging at night would come to an end. Before long he would be surrounded day and night by Secret Service Agents and his private life would be a thing of the past. It was a necessary inconvenience that he had come to accept.

Jim called him the following week. He was staying at the Wyndham Hotel on M Street. They made plans to meet that night at "Morton's of Chicago" on Prospect Street in Georgetown. It was the best steakhouse in Washington, according to Jack. Jim arrived first and waited.

The arrival of the senator from California, about whom there was much speculation, caused no small stir in the restaurant. Jack was becoming more and more recognized wherever he went, with each passing day. A few asked for autographs and Jack graciously obliged them. He was starting to enjoy the growing attention that he was getting these days. The manager of the restaurant came over and asked to have his picture taken with the senator.

Jack agreed, on the condition that his friend from Texas join them. "He's more famous than I'll ever be," Jack said.

"Don't count on it," Jim said."

The manager showed them to their table and had a complimentary bottle of wine sent over. "This is on me, Jim," Jack said, "I don't want any nosey reporters printing it in their newspapers that I'm on the take. Besides," he added. "It's not often I get to take a billionaire to dinner."

"I don't have a problem with your picking up the tab, Senator," Jim said, laughing. "What do you recommend?"

"I recommend the porterhouse," Jack said. "Listen, Morton's is famous for its menu presentation. It's worth the trip just to see it. They roll a cart out with everything imaginable on it—steaks, lobster, and other main courses selections. The house specialty is the twenty-four-ounce porterhouse."

"You must own stock in the place. You sound like their pitchman."

"Nah," Jack said, "I just like the food here."

They placed their orders and their food came. They talked as they ate. Jack was thinking about the pressure he had placed on his friend by asking him for his support in the campaign.

"Do you ever think about Vietnam, Jim?" Jack asked him. "I mean does any of it ever come back to you?"

"You mean like flashbacks?" Jim was thoughtful for a moment. "No, not really. I sometimes try to remember the good things. There were precious few of them. We lost some good friends but I came away with a friend for life. What about you?"

"Me too," Jack said. "But, you know it's the strangest thing. Last week I started thinking about those damned monkeys in the 'O' Club at Soc Trang. You remember those two monkeys? The guys fed them bourbon all the time."

"Yeah, yeah, I remember them," Jim said. "I had completely forgotten that. They sat on the shotgun above the bar. They smoked cigarettes and drank whiskey and made fun of the troops. They looked like they were mocking us. Probably were, crazy little bastards. I never would have remembered that if you hadn't brought it up."

They were both laughing now as they recalled the events of so many years ago. It was just one of the strange side shows of that time in both their lives. How intensely their lives had been forever changed by that short time in a place where everything, including life itself, especially life itself, was so cheap.

"There was a snake there, remember, Jack? A python, can't remember his name. He had a name, I know, but I can't remember it. They brought him into the bar wrapped around some guy and got him drunk. He'd slide all over the place."

"I can't remember his name either," Jack said. "I was talking to a guy the other day. I was at the airport in Denver and met a veteran, a grunt. He was wounded when his firebase was overrun in sixty-seven. I think it was after we left. What struck me most about what he said was how he dealt with the fear. When he got shot, in one firefight, he fell into a trench and just lay there. He said he watched the VC jumping over the trench as they stormed the base. As he lay there he just sort of gave up and accepted the fact that he was going to die. He knew the gooks would come back and kill him. That was when the fear left him."

"How did he manage to make it out?"

"I don't know," Jack said. "That was when I noticed he was wearing a Republican pin so I stopped talking to him."

Jim burst out laughing and others at nearby tables looked at them and smiled.

"It figures," he said.

"No, I got the guy's name and number. I told him he was invited to the White House when I win the election."

"So you really think you can win?"

"If I can get the nomination, I can win. That's why I need your endorsement. You just got everyone's attention with that interview. Now it's a hard decision you're going to have to make. Right now the eyes of the nation are more focused on James Kemper than they are on Jack Grantham. Hell, Jim, you could probably run for president now."

"No thanks," Jim said. "That's the last thing I want."

"It would be a hell of a pay-cut for you. And a lot more work," Jack said. "I don't know why anybody would want the job. I don't know why I want it so badly. I just know I do."

"Luther!" Jim shouted out, and heads turned all over the restaurant. "Luther was the name of that damned snake."

Jack slapped his knee and roared. "That's it," he said loudly, drawing more attention from the other patrons in the restaurant.

"Okay, Jack," Jim said, looking serious now, "it's time to get down to business. Let's discuss this endorsement. I'm going to catch a lot of flak about this. What is it you need from me?"

"Well, Jim, it's pretty basic, I guess, just like you said on the talk show. I don't want you to try to bullshit anyone. If you really believe that my vision for this country is the best one in the field right now, then all you have to do is say so. I don't want any financial support because I don't want anyone to say you are trying to buy the presidency. The very idea of a prominent Republican businessman supporting a Democrat for president will have a bigger impact than you can possibly imagine."

"You may be right," Jim said. "I don't know. But understand one thing. I'm not doing this just because we are friends. If I didn't believe that you are the best man for the job, I wouldn't do it, friends or not. It's not so much that I share your vision for the future, as it is that I know your character."

"I know that," Jack said, nodding his head in agreement. "And if I didn't know you believed it, I wouldn't ask you to do it."

"Okay, after you announce that you are going to enter the race, I'll sit down with my people at the Texas Republican Coalition and get their reaction. I won't waste my time trying to convince them to vote for you, and I'll assure them I'm not bankrolling you, just endorsing you. They won't like it, but I'll make it work."

"That sounds plausible, oh, by the way, Jim," Jack said. "There's one other thing."

"And what might that be?"

"If I do well in the primaries and at convention time I actually have a shot at the thing, I'd like for you to place my name in nomination."

"Good lord," Jim said. "I hope you don't expect me to vote for you too."

cつくつ

Jack's announcement that he would seek the Democratic nomination came as a surprise to most of the news media. They were pretty much resigned to the fact that Vice-President Murdock was the odds-on favorite to win the nomination, and the presidency as well. Senator Grantham's candidacy seemed, to many to be no more than an ego trip. But the news organizations in California were not seeing it that way. Jack Grantham was a "favorite son" and he stood a very good chance of carrying the state.

Nick Devoss immediately set out to establish campaign headquarters in all fifty states. There was not a short supply of volunteers, and money started pouring into the coffers as soon as Jack announced his intention to seek the presidency. Many people saw a JFK aura about him, and the comparison was not lost on Devoss, who determined to promulgate that image. Both men were US Senators, both were war heroes, and both were centrists, compared to the liberal lean of many of the leading Democratic personalities. Grantham believed in lower taxes and in expanding the private sector. Dan Murdock was pretty much universally considered to be a "tax and spend" liberal, at least in the Republican camp. It was common knowledge that he would try to run on President Montgomery's record and immense popularity.

The Grantham campaign started early on trying to portray Dan Murdock as a flip-flopper. Their biggest ally in this endeavor was Dan Murdock himself who, in May of 1999 voted in the Republican Senate to break a tie that resulted in the requirement of background check on people who bought weapons at gun shows. Grantham, while a strong proponent of Second Amendment rights, was in basic agreement with Murdock's decision to take such action regarding background checks, and he told Nick Devoss that.

"I really don't care one way or the other," Nick said, "I'm not judging him on that. For our purposes, it gives us some ammunition to use against him.

"What do you mean?" Jack asked him.

"In 1985, Murdock was a virtual poster boy for the NRA. Murdock cast some deciding votes in favor of looser gun restriction laws. Wayne LaPierre, head of the NRA, claimed they had considered making him Man of the Year. We can use this in the debate."

Jack went on the campaign trail, taking Holly with him on most junkets. They hired a nanny to stay in the Condo and take care of the boys and get them to school. Most of '99 was spent away from home. The whole family went back to their California home for the three months of summer, leaving the nanny to stay at the Washington residence while they were gone.

It felt good to be home for Holly. Washington was exciting but it wasn't home and it wasn't California. Jack was still behind in the polls but he was gaining ground and popularity with each passing day and with each campaign appearance.

Jack spent most of the month of January of 2000 traversing the state of Iowa campaigning for the Iowa caucuses which were held on January twenty-fourth. He won the Iowa caucuses by a margin of 53% to 45% over Dan Murdock. This got the attention of the news media and the Murdock campaign. Murdock then won the New Hampshire primary by 50% to 46% and alleviated some of the fear that he might be facing a legitimate challenge to his candidacy. Most Democrats had been led to believe Murdock's ascension to the White House was an entitlement and a foregone conclusion. The Delaware primary on February fifth gave Murdock a fifty-two percent to forty-five percent victory and things calmed down a bit.

On March second, the last Democratic primary debate was scheduled. Jack initially found it a bit intimidating to be going up against the vice-president of the United States, but Nick Devoss talked him down. They held some mock debates with stand-ins and with Nick reading difficult questions for Jack to answer. "Listen, Jack," he said. I know Dan Murdock, he's no Bill Montgomery, and he sure as hell is no Jack Grantham. Murdock is as phony as the proverbial three-dollar bill. I guarantee you he is as afraid of you as you are of him. He was not expecting to have any opposition in this campaign and now he has a legitimate challenger."

Both men readied themselves as the moderator made some initial remarks and laid out some guidelines, then he commenced the debate.

"A coin toss has determined that the first question goes to Senator Grantham," said the host of the debate, Bernard Show. "Many Americans were very happy to hear Senator McCain condemn the Christian far-right leadership for their derisive effects on American politics. Would you each be willing to echo what the senator said about that and even take it a step farther?"

Jack cleared his throat. "Let me say to you I think that we have a country where there is freedom of religion, and I think there should be freedom of religion. I don't agree with the notion that the far right has gone too far on social issues. I think these folks are as sincere and serious about their beliefs as are people on the other side of the political aisle. Have they tried to dominate this country with their political viewpoint? Of course, they have, but so have we. The key in that debate is to meet a happy medium. As a United States Senator, I have always tried to see both sides of any issue. Religion will always be a part of politics, whether by its presence or lack thereof. We cannot legislate a person's moral stance and his personal beliefs out of the public dialogue."

Dan Murdock shook his head. "You know, I thought that Senator McCain's speech made a very powerful point, but I think his speech illustrated that the Republican Party today is in the midst of an identity crisis. They are trying to figure out who they are. And frankly, he was introduced by Gary Bauer for that speech. Both he and Governor Bush are for taking away a woman's right to choose. Neither had the guts to speak out against the confederate flag flying above the state capitol building in South Carolina. Both are in the hip pocket of the NRA so I agreed with the speech, as far as it went."

"I keep hearing that the Republicans are trying to take away a woman's right to choose," Jack argued. "I have not heard any Republican, in public service, make that statement. There are some on the right who would like to see Roe v. Wade overturned, granted, but I have not seen any movement, at the national level, toward that end. As for the Confederate flag flying above the capitol building in South Carolina, I certainly can see the offense that has been taken by the African American community. I think that is a virtual poke in their eye, and I would support any effort to change that. And on another note—"

Shaw cut him off. "Your time is up, Senator."

"Just one quick comment, Bernard, this is important," Jack said. "The vice-president made a comment about being in the hip pocket of the NRA. In 1985 Mister Murdock was so friendly with the NRA that Wayne LaPierre considered naming him Man of the Year. I find that to be a bit hypocritical."

"Would you like to response to that, Mister Murdock?" Shaw asked.

Murdock nodded. "Yes, I would. My earlier views reflected the perspective of a congressman from a rural part of the South where guns did not really present a threat to public safety but rather were predominantly a source of recreation."

"I just believe that people who live in cities have the same constitutional right to protect themselves from threats against their homes and their person as do rural folks," Jack argued. "I don't have a different policy for Los Angeles than I do in the Santa Clara Valley. And one additional comment—as a young representative of a conservative Tennessee district, Murdock opposed putting serial numbers on guns so they could be traced, and voted to cut the budget of the Bureau of Alcohol Tobacco and Firearms which negatively affected its ability to do its job."

"Mister Murdock, you have spoken out about Pat Robertson and Jerry Falwell, neither of whom, I think it fair to say, were likely to support either of you anyway," Shaw commented. "And both of you have met with Reverend Al Sharpton, a person who has repeatedly used very inflammatory language about whites and other ethnic groups. Now, I'm asking, if the Republican candidates have an obligation to forcefully, unambiguously condemn extremists on their side, don't you have an obligation to be equally forthright in condemning such language by people who tend to be more on the Democratic side of things?"

"Well, I do condemn the language that he used," Murdock retorted. "I think that in America, we believe in redemption and the capacity of all of our people to transcend limitations that they have made evident in their lives in the past. I did not meet with Reverend Sharpton publicly, I met with him privately. And I talked with him about some of the concerns that I have. I will not violate the privacy of that conversation, but these subjects were discussed. And I will point you toward a couple of facts. Number one, he received something like, I think, one hundred thirty-one thousand votes in the last New York City election. He is undeniably a person to whom some people in the city look as a spokesperson. And you know, there is a racial divide in the way people in different races perceive certain events. I would not be so quick to completely dismiss what he has to say about some of these issues."

Shaw turned to Jack. "Senator?"

"Yes, I went to the House of Justice in Harlem last summer for a community meeting that Reverend Sharpton invited me to attend," Jack said. "The last time a primary candidate for president had a large public meeting in Harlem was Robert Kennedy in 1968. I went, in order to hear the concerns firsthand of the six hundred people that came to share them with me. I believe that was a legitimate thing to do. I don't agree with everything Reverend Sharpton has said or done, but I do share the vice-president's concern for the needs of the people whom Mister Sharpton represents."

"Vice President Murdock, the next question is for you," Shaw announced.

"Okay."

"My question, is in your life, what mistake have you learned the most from?"

Murdock laughed. "Claiming that I can leap tall buildings with a single bound. No—"

Laughter.

"—I think that early in my career in public service, I fell prey to what a lot people who get into the workforce, and get excited about their work, do. And they get drawn into it so much that they don't balance their lives enough by enriching their life with joy and fun and family interaction, and as I got a little bit older, I came to understand the overriding importance of balancing work and home and finding time for yourself. You've got to make time for your spouse, your kids, and yourself."

"Senator?" Shaw asked, turning to Jack again.

"Well, I wish you'd called on me first because that would have been my answer. When I came back from Vietnam, I went to work for my father-in-law at his newspaper, and I plunged myself into the job, working long hours and not spending enough time with my family. Likewise, when I got into politics that became my pursuit and I continued to neglect my family. I've learned to take more time off and tend to the most important things in my life."

"Senator Grantham, the next question is for you. You're challenging a sitting vice-president in what is considered to be a very successful administration and in a robust economy. What is your strategy for winning the Democratic nomination for president?"

"I won Iowa and was competitive in New Hampshire. We're coming up on 'Super Tuesday,' a contest in eleven states. I expect to carry the West Coast states and the Southern states and remain competitive in some of the others that the vice-president is expected to win.

"What about Ohio?" Shaw asked. "Many believe that Ohio is the key to winning primaries just as it is in winning a presidential election.

"I'll win Ohio."

Murdock sighed and shook his head.

"You seem confident about that," Shaw remarked.

"Our internal polling gives us the indication that we will carry Ohio."

"I think that one thing that most of us running for president agree on, is that we prefer to get questions about substance rather than process," Murdock interjected. "I respect your question, but I'd prefer to address questions about the issues facing the American people rather than about the process."

"I have no problem with that question," Jack said.

"Gentlemen, our allotted time is up," Shaw announced. "I'd like to give both of you an opportunity to express any closing remarks you might have. Mister Vice-President, you may go first.

"Thank you, Bernard, and my thanks to CNN for hosting this debate. Let me say that I believe that there are many purposes in a presidential campaign. One that tends to dominate is to give the American people an opportunity to choose who will lead this country for the next four years. But the purpose of a campaign is also for us to define who we are as a people and as a nation. And we need to have an ennobling, educating, revealing discussion about all the challenges that we face, review some of the proposed solutions. We've been doing that in this campaign. And I believe very deeply that once this dialogue is over with, those who agree with the common values that we have expressed are going to want to see them enacted in the general election. I intend to continue the great work that President Montgomery and I have been engaged in for last eight years."

"While I agree that we are indeed in an era or prosperity," Jack said, "we must realize that prosperity, like fame, can be fleeting and it's going to take more than talk to continue the current trend. There are many pitfalls that can impede our progress. We cannot let government be one of those impediments. We must continue to encourage and enact legislation to help the private sector do what the private sector does best—create jobs and increase the tax base. With no intended disrespect for the vice-president, I have to remind the American people that Dan Murdock is not Bill Montgomery. They should not consider this next election to be a Montgomery third term."

❧❦❧

Two days after the debate, just prior to the "Super Tuesday" primary vote, Jim Kemper appeared on Fox News' *O'Reilly Factor*. O'Reilly asked him, some probing questions. The exchange went like this:

"Mister Kemper, you're a businessman and a quite successful one I understand, but there are some rumors going around that you might endorse a Democrat, California Senator Jack Grantham for president," O'Reilly asked. "What say you?"

"I have endorsed him for president," Jim confessed. "Jack is an old friend, we go way back. And I believe him to be an honest and capable candidate for the office."

"Isn't it risky for you, a Republican, to endorse a Democrat—for anything?" O'Reilly asked.

Jim shook his head. "It's not unprecedented. I can't think of any who have endorsed a Democrat for president but there have been some who sided with senators and congressmen in the opposition party. My endorsement of Jack Grantham is not an endorsement of his politics and certainly not of that ideology. It's an endorsement of the man himself."

"This has got to have caused some concern among your fellow Republicans," O'Reilly pointed out.

"I won't deny that my decision has not been well received, but I am not a political person and my support for Jack Grantham is not politically motivated. My business associations are, of course, primarily with more conservative individuals but socially I lean more to the center. In 1968, I hired a woman to run a chain of feed and supply stores for me and one of my top managers is Hispanic. I take seriously Doctor Martin Luther King's dictum that we should judge a person, not by the color of his skin but by the content of his character. I have been successful in business by adhering to sound business principles and fair dealings with people."

"Have you made any financial contributions to the campaign?" O'Reilly asked.

"I have not. When Senator Grantham asked for my endorsement several years ago, he made it clear that he was not after my money. I have not at this time made any contributions to either political campaign."

"I've heard that you have a great dislike for Dan Murdock, is that true?" O'Reilly asked.

"I have no inherent dislike for the vice president. I've never even met him. My feeling is that he is simply not friendly enough to big business for my purposes."

"What about the Bushes, what dealings have you had with them?" O'Reilly wanted to know.

"I've met President Bush and the governor. I have great respect for both men. If Governor Bush wins the Republican nomination, I will most likely support him financially."

"Well, Mister Kemper, you're an interesting man. Your success in business is well documented and you spoke the truth when you said you are not a politician because you didn't give me any spin at all. You would not go very far in politics giving straight answers to tough questions. Thank you for coming."

"Thank you for inviting me."

♥♪♥

In the "Super Tuesday" primaries, Jack won five states to Murdock's six. As he'd predicted in the last debate, Jack carried California, Georgia, Missouri, and Ohio. Surprisingly he also won Maryland albeit by a margin of only one percentage point.

The score card thusly reflected:
California: Grantham 66% Murdock 33%
Connecticut: Murdock 55% Grantham 42%
Georgia: Grantham 57% Murdock 43%
Missouri: Grantham 55% Murdock 43.5%
Rhode Island: Murdock 56% Grantham 40%
Massachusetts: Murdock 59% Grantham 37%
Maryland: Grantham 48% Murdock 47%
Maine: Murdock 47% Grantham 41%
Ohio: Grantham 54% Murdock 44%
New York: Murdock 65% Grantham 33%
Vermont: Murdock 54% Grantham 43%

The significance of the big wins in California, Georgia, Missouri, and Ohio and the close win in Maryland was not lost on the Murdock-friendly media. The sting was also felt within the inner circles of the Murdock campaign. Some were starting to panic, and others were suggesting that, "We need to find some dirt on this guy."

"Come on, guys," Murdock said, "he's a medal of honor winner. How will it look if we start floating negative rumors about him? That could hurt us more than it does him."

"No one is so clean that he hasn't fucked up at least once," the campaign coordinator said. "If we don't find something, you can bet your ass that Karl Rove will. And that may be after we have lost the nomination. Grantham has 'movie star' looks, there has to be a broad in his past somewhere."

"Then let Karl Rove find her, I won't. And I'm not going to lose the nomination."

᷒᷒᷒

Jim received a call from Able Hansen of Hansen Trust which was the major financial institution for Kemper Enterprises. He wanted Jim to come to a meeting with Fred Wheeling, President of the TCRB—Texas Coalition of Republican Businessmen—and several other members. Jim agreed to come to the Hansen Trust office. There were five others in attendance, including Ed's VP, Roger Bolling.

Abel Hansen spoke first. "Jim, I'm sure you are aware of why we asked you here today. Fred, Fred Wheeling, is concerned about your endorsing a Democrat for president. Frankly, I share his concerns. Can you give us any hope that this will not have long-term repercussions?"

"What long term repercussions are you worried about, Abel?" Jim asked him.

"Fred is asking me to pull our financing from the Kemper Towers Project and from your international projects in Mexico and Canada."

"Well, Abel, you and I had a meeting before I announced my intention to endorse Jack Grantham. I didn't have any illusions that you would be on board with it, but I thought I made it clear why I decided to do it."

Fred Wheeling spoke up and told Jim, "Some very powerful people in the national party are pretty steamed up over this. They just don't understand why a top Republican would go to bat for a Democrat. It's like a betrayal to us."

"I'm not going to bat for him, Fred. I mean I'm not out campaigning for Jack. Let me explain this again for the benefit of those of you who have not heard my explanation. Now, I know that most of you know that Senator Grantham and I served in the same attack helicopter company in Vietnam. Jack was my squadron chief. When I came home, Jack was there at the airport in San Francisco with my wife and two boys. He had brought them there from Maryland, where they were staying with her parents, so they could be there when I got off the plane. Now I was twenty-five years-old and Jack was twenty-six. He confided in me that he intended to run for president one day. I thought he was just blowing smoke but I soon discovered that he was serious. He worked toward that goal from 1967 until now, and here he is on the verge of winning the Democratic nomination against the sitting vice-president. I told him that day I came home that, if he followed through with his plan, I would help him any way I could. It was a promise made to a friend who saved my life in combat. He has not asked for any money, only my endorsement. I had no political affiliations back then when I made that promise. I kept that promise. If you pull your financing, it will have a negative effect, I won't deny that. I could stay in business but I can't finance the international operations "in house," and I'd most likely have to cancel the new office building. A lot of people will lose their jobs and a lot of companies might go under."

"I'm just getting a lot of pressure to take some punitive action against you over this," Wheeling said.

"Is this coming from the Bush campaign, Fred?" Jim asked.

"I'm not at liberty to say, Jim, but my job might be one of those lost that you were referring to. I'm telling you straight up, people are pissed."

"Well, I sure as hell can't revoke my endorsement now. The toothpaste is out of the tube," Jim said. "You folks do what you think you have to do. My business will survive, regardless. I hold no animosity toward any of you, I understand your concerns, but what is done is done. My friendship with Jack Grantham transcends politics."

Jim and Mattie flew to Maryland to see Shadow and the two grandkids, Lydia, and Charlie. Lydia Marie Kemper was eleven-years-old and Charlie was ten. Lydia was a beautiful girl.

"How could she not be beautiful?" Jim said. "She looks just like you, Shadow."

"She's a good girl, and Charlie is…well, a boy. I love them both so much. I only wish Alton could be here to watch them grow up with me."

"I do too, darling," Mattie said. "We worry about you every day. I'm so glad you are living in yours and Alton's house close to your parents."

"I love this house, it keeps me in touch with Alton, but it's your house, Mattie. I stayed here just because it is so close to my folks, but I had the title put back in your name."

"I didn't want that, Shadow. If you don't feel comfortable with it then put it in the kid's name or let me just will it to them. I want you and them to have it. I don't intend to ever come back here, except to see you when we can. Jim and I think of you as one of our daughters. We'd love to have you come and live with us but I know your job and your life is here."

"It is," Shadow, said, "as long as my parents are alive. I have good job in Washington and I thought about buying a condo there but I just can't leave Alton." She started crying and Mattie went over and hugged her.

"Shadow, we are planning to leave Dallas and move back to the farm," Jim told her. "We'd love to have you come there with the kids when you get a vacation and spend some time with us."

"When are, you moving?"

"Looks like September," Jim said. "Charlie is pretty much running the business and I am frankly getting tired."

"I will bring the kids and stay with you on my next vacation, I promise," Shadow said. "I'd love to do that and the kids would like it too."

"That would be wonderful," Mattie said, "we'll look forward to it, now Jim wants to say something to you."

Shadow turned toward Jim.

"Shadow, this is not easy for me to say but I have to say it. I know that eventually you will want to remarry. Mattie and I certainly do not expect you to become an old maid. My gosh, honey, you're a beautiful woman. You cannot tell me that men are not offering themselves to you. We want you to be happy and, if remarrying is something you decide to do, then we will certainly not stand in your way. You were a better wife to our son than any woman could ever have been. You two grew up together. I think you're the only girl he ever kissed."

Shadow laughed. "I hope so," she said. "He was the love of my life. I won't ever find another boy like Alton."

"Just don't dry up and blow away in the belief that your love and loyalty for Alton prevents you from marrying again. Don't deprive some young man of the joy he'll get when he introduces you as his wife."

Thank you both. I love you and I don't know right now which direction my life will go. My kids are my main concern but, should I meet the right decent man who wants to marry me, I'll call you guys first to ask permission—deal?"

"It's a deal, Shadow," they both said, laughing.

Until the Texas Primary on March 12, the two candidates had been running neck and neck. Grantham carried Texas and leaped ahead by a sufficient number of delegates that even Murdock's wins in Pennsylvania and Wisconsin could not close the gap. It was clear that Jack would run the table and take North Carolina, Indiana, Nebraska, and New Mexico. Murdock closed out the campaign winning West Virginia and Kentucky.

What was thought impossible became the reality. Senator Grantham ended up with 52% of the allotted delegates, 1,836 in all, while Vice President Murdock won 1,694 total delegates, Strangely, enough the total popular vote wound up with Grantham wining by less than a percentage point.

The Democratic Convention would be held in Los Angeles, at the Staples Center, from August fourteenth to August seventeenth. The nominating process would take place on the fourteenth.

Jim flew to Washington to discuss the speech he would give, placing Jack's name in nomination. It had come to this, Jim was thinking. A promise made over thirty years ago, that was never expected to materialize, and a subsequent reaffirming of that promise in 1998 was now a debt of honor on which he could not renege.

"I'm going to focus on our friendship and your incredible journey to get to where you are today, I won't get into ideology, lest I risk being ridden out of the convention hall on a rail. I want to tell the story of how you met LBJ at the White House and decided to become president one day."

"That's good, Jim, I understand your reticence over this, but I think what you are doing will be good for our country. If you, a Republican, can do this for a Democrat, then maybe the American people can commence on a new path to cooperation and mutual understanding," Jack said.

Nick Devoss thanked Jim and shook his hand. "I know this is not easy for you, Jim, but I really appreciate it. I've been waiting for this day for twenty-nine years. I started working for this guy in seventy-one and I knew we would get to this point one day. Your friend is going to be the President of the United States, Jim, ain't that a boot in the ass?

"It is, Nick," Jim responded.

Jack motioned to Jim and asked him to step outside the office for a moment. "Let's go the cafeteria down the hall and get a cup of coffee. I want to tell you something."

They got their coffee and found an isolated table.

"What's on your mind, Jack?" Jim asked.

Jack appeared to be in deep thought. "This is going to be hard, Jim, but I have to tell you. Damn, I just don't know how to do this."

Now Jim was more than curious. He was concerned over what might be that difficult for Jack to share with him. "Just tell me, Jack, whatever it is, it won't leave this table."

"I had an affair, Jim, many years ago, it was only a one-time deal but it happened, and I've been carrying the guilt around with me for many years now."

To Jack's surprise, Jim made no reaction at all. "Is there any chance it could come up in the election?"

"I don't know. I hope not, obviously. She promised she would never say anything and, so far, she has not. She may have more character than I do."

"How did it happen, Jack, did you fall for her or what? I know you are not a serial skirt chaser, like some prominent politicians I could name, but won't. What caused it?"

"She was a woman who worked at the newspaper, very attractive naturally. She came to my hotel room in Sacramento when I was in the state senate. It just happened. She stood up and took her clothes off in front of me and came over and sat across my lap. I couldn't tell her no. I mean I literally could not resist her. As soon as her skirt hit the floor my dick started doing my reasoning for me."

"Yeah, that'll happen," Jim said. "Well, Jack, my advice is to not worry about it. She's remained silent all this time. Chances are she meant what she said about never going public."

"I just hope you don't think less of me because of this, Jim. I just had to get it off my chest. There *is* no one else I could ever tell this to besides you."

"Six years ago, I was at the milk producer's convention in Washington. I had gone into the bar to get a drink, and the woman I was in love with in college just walked up to my table and wanted me to take her to my room. I had not seen her in almost thirty years. I told her I couldn't do it, but it was one of the hardest things I ever had to do. Let's just hope the Republicans don't get wind of your past indiscretion."

"Thanks, Jim," Jack said. "I'll see you next in Los Angeles."

୧୬୧୬

August 16 2000:

The Staples Center was packed, as was typical of the quadrennial foolishness known as a national political convention. Thousands of people engaging in a four-day party, only slightly seriously described as an event of great importance, was not Jim's cup of tea. He thought they were a waste of time and money. Were it up to him, the business would be concluded as soon as the final delegate count came in. Four days of polyunsaturated bullshit, no matter which party Democrat or Republican, was a piss-poor commentary on the greatness of the American political process, in Jim's opinion.

But here he was and in just a short while it would be finished and he would get out of here and go home to the civilized world. The lights dimmed and an announcer began speaking. "Please welcome to the arena, nationally and internationally known Texas business tycoon James Earl Kemper who will place into nomination the name of Senator Jack Grantham for the presidency of the United States."

Cheers filled the auditorium. Jim wasn't sure if they were for him or for Jack. He assumed they were for Jack. He walked out to the podium and grasped each side of the stand. He carried no notes.

"Thirty-three years ago, I came home from Vietnam, after my tour of duty. When I got off the plane, there was a man waiting there who had made arrangements to bring my wife and two boys to San Francisco to be there for me. That man was my platoon leader in the three hundred thirty-sixth attack helicopter company based at Soc Trang, Vietnam. I would probably not be standing here before you tonight had not that man committed many selfless acts of valor and courage. Under heavy enemy fire, fraught with extreme peril, he saved my life. He saved many other lives of men in our platoon as well as several members of the United States Special Forces, the Green Berets. For those acts of valor and courage, this man was awarded the Congressional Medal of Honor by President Lyndon Johnson in the White House Rose Garden. In San Francisco that man took me and my family to his own home and gave me the opportunity to get reacquainted with my wife and oldest son, Alton, and to meet my youngest son, Charlie, for the first time. That same man was there to offer me what solace could be offered when my son, Alton, died in a plane crash in 1995.

"During that time we spent together in San Francisco after I came home, this man confided to me that his trip to White House in 1967, in which he had personal conversation with the president, had convinced him that an honest and forthright man could accomplish so much more for the American people than the standard fare of career politician which are so abundant it seems in our national arena. That man told me that he was going to run for president one day, and he asked me that when that day came if I would support him and help him if I had any way to do so. He was twenty-six years old at the time, I was twenty-five.

"I told him that, when that day came, I would indeed endorse him and even place his name in nomination at his party convention, if he so desired. Well, here I am. I would now like to place into nomination for the Presidency of the United States of America, my best friend and the greatest American I have ever known, Senator John Fulton Grantham,"

The crowd went wild, and the cheering seemed as if it would not end. Jack came strolling onto the stage with Holly on one arm and Mattie Kemper on the other. They met and shook hands, everybody hugged each other, and Jack waved and held his hand up with Jim's hand in his. The women hugged and then the men hugged both women again, and then again. Jim wanted them to tell the crowd to shut the hell up, but they never did. Finally, the Grantham and the Kempers walked off the stage.

On the plane ride, back to Dallas, Mattie told Jim that she overheard some conversation backstage. "Some folks seemed upset that you didn't say, 'and the next president of the United States,' after you nominated Jack."

"There was a reason why I didn't say that, Mattie."

"Oh, and what was the reason?"

"I don't think he can beat George Bush."

"And yet you delivered that great speech, and it was a great speech, Jim. I was so proud of you. I'd pee on myself if I had to speak in front of that many people, I really would."

"Then let's be sure you never have to do it, we can't have you peeing on yourself."

Jack picked Missouri Congressman Dick Gephardt as his running mate. It was less than three months until the election and things were heating up in both camps.

In late October, the *National Enquirer* ran an unconfirmed story that Jack Grantham had an affair with a campaign staffer when he was a California State Senator. According to the magazine, the woman had told her immediate supervisor at the

San Jose Examiner, another woman about the alleged affair. The Grantham campaign denied the charge and labeled it as desperate muckraking from the Bush Campaign. Liberal news media, being reluctant to pursue rumors of wrongdoing by Democrats, especially ones involving affairs of the heart, or some other errant body part, let the story drop. It would have no effect on the election.

Jim and Mattie would watch it on television.

Chapter 22

The Wrens Return

October 2000:

A year had passed since Jim made the decision to move back to the old place. He still had no regrets about it but he was surprised by how well Mattie had accepted the idea. He had been ready for a fight, had even prepared a speech for her stating all the reasons he thought it would be best for them. In the end, she offered little resistance.

He was tired of the rat race, the politics of business and the constant in-fighting and the jockeying for position that some felt they must do to achieve their goals. He was saddened by the fact that a man, regardless of who he was or how much money he had or didn't have, could not do what he knew in his heart was right without jeopardizing long-time friendships and business relations. It was a superficial world, and he had too much power and influence over it. He had become insulated from it all. Money was certainly a great insulator from the petty games of life.

He was thankful for that but then he had never "played the game" as others did. If one simply refused, as a matter of principal, to join in the rat race could he not exercise that option or did he have to quit the game altogether? He didn't know. Maybe it was easy to say if you're the lead rat. He had seen so many others fail some of them many times, often losing everything and he wondered how they could allow that to happen. A few simple concepts and principles, if adhered to, could prevent failure. Never try to scam anyone, be honest always, above all else shoot people straight. And do what you say you will do. Have a good product that people need and don't try to sell them something they don't need. He had always tried to stick to those tenets.

Perhaps there were times over the years, he couldn't remember now, didn't want to remember, when he had strayed from the path. But always right there in the deep recesses of his mind was the memory of his mother and his grandfather and even his stepfather. Their gentle words would lift him up and remind him of how he should be conducting himself. He could never get very far away from that, not now, not ever. Those flash-in-the-pan fast talkers and bullshit artists who came along and set the world on fire for a few months, or even a few years, never lasted. The first thing they did was buy an expensive car and a boat and then start running around on their wives and then before long they were broke.

So many people violated the one rule of business that must not be violated. Simply put, they spent more money than they made. It seemed too simple to mean anything, something everybody should know but did not. If you spent more than you made, then it really didn't matter how honest or dishonest you were, you wouldn't last very long.

Inside the house, Mattie and Aimee were still unpacking and arranging things. The movers had left, and it was quiet again. He was happy that Aimee had driven up from Houston to help her mother with the settling in. Since Aimee was here, his wife would be busy with her and would leave him alone. He could relax for a while.

He put his feet up on the porch rail and kicked back in the chair and looked out over the old place. It was different now. The old buildings were all gone and cow barns and silos and all the other facilities necessary to a modern dairy farm now took up most of Grandpa's farm. The windmill still stood although it been almost completely rebuilt, the one remaining memento of his grandfather's legacy. He could not allow it to be torn down. As long as that windmill was here Grandpa Alton was still on this land. And Jim could feel his presence in the breeze that gently caressed his face now. It was not all that far from the big house in Dallas but it was a world apart.

Jim shifted in his chair and leaned back a little farther. He watched a hawk making slow lazy circles in the afternoon sky and was reminded of the magic shot that Alton Kemper had made. He might go down to the square this Saturday and see if any old-timers still hung out there. He looked forward to sitting on the square and just talking to whoever happened to be there.

It occurred to him that maybe none of the old men sat on the square anymore like they did when he was a boy. All the older men were gone now, all of Grandpa's old friends. Homer Sudbury was dead now, and so was John Beaty and Kinnie Sullivan, *My God*, Jim thought, *Kinnie has been dead for twenty years now*. Perhaps no one did that any more. He hoped that was not the case. Comanche had not changed much in the past forty years, as far as he could tell. It would probably would be the same forty years from now. No, there would be somebody on the Square to talk to, he was sure of that, probably no one who would remember the day Grandpa knocked old Leland Trumble on his ass but he was certain there would be somebody to carry on casual conversation with.

Aimee's boy Matt was playing around in the yard, trying to work his way close to his grandfather without being too obvious. Jim watched him scurrying about, using a stick for a rifle and making gunshot sounds as he wreaked havoc on some make-believe enemy.

"Things sure don't change much," he mumbled to himself. He wondered if this boy would ever have to go off and fight in some damned war and maybe get killed for no good reason. God he hoped not. It had been thirty-three years since Eddie Csaba died in Vietnam, and Dolan too. Jim still thought about them almost every day.

He wondered if their folks were still alive. If they were, then the war was not over for them. All he had left of Dolan and Csaba were the two pencil and paper engravings that he made at the Vietnam Veteran's Memorial in Washington. Aimee had framed them for him and hung them on the wall in his office. It was a sad legacy for a man, his name etched on a wall along with all the others who died for no damned good reason. It was little comfort to their families. He could not allow this boy to go off and die for the policy decisions of whatever administration happened to be in power at a given time. He simply could not let that happen. He wouldn't allow it. He'd pull strings if he had to. That might not be right but he didn't care. They weren't going to take his grandson to use for cannon fodder.

Listen to yourself, he thought. Like he could stop it. Could Grandpa stop him from going to Vietnam? No. He wasn't able to stop Jim's dad from going off to war after Pearl Harbor. Jim had not worried that much when Charlie went to the Gulf War, although Mattie had fretted day and night until their son came home. But that wasn't much of a war, not really, not like Vietnam. He shouldn't say that. For the men on the line, it was as much of a war as any war could be. For the ones who were killed, for their families, it was just as tragic as any other war. *It was our best war, our greatest victory*, he supposed, *if you used kill ratio as the determining factor*. Well, at least now he knew what the old folks who stay behind had to go through when their sons went off to war. It was bad enough when it was a boy but now the sick bastards were trying to send girls into combat. *We simply cannot allow that to happen*, he thought. There was something wrong with America, something very wrong, indeed and he was convinced that changes needed to be made. Real changes, not just rhetoric and false promises. He had lost the energy and, the want to, to get involved in any more great projects but he could support those who had not.

Jack Grantham had the Democratic nomination for president, and Jim was glad now, that he had helped make that happen. Even if all the predicted repercussions, over his role in that, actually did come about, he still did not regret the part he had played in it.

He laughed out loud when he heard some news reporter saying that "the senator from California could not have gotten as far as he had, had it not been for the support of his lifelong friend James Earl Kemper, the well-known Texas billionaire."

What bullshit. They didn't know Jack Grantham very well. They didn't know the man who had charged over that dike in Vietnam, in the face of certain death, to defend his buddies and help rescue wounded men, they didn't know him the way Jim knew him. Sure, he had followed right behind but that was because he was less afraid of dying than he was of letting his friend know how scared he was.

No, whatever help that Jim Kemper might have lent to the Grantham campaign was strictly supplementary. He really believed that. Jack, if he could win, could straighten the country out. Even some of his "oddball" ideas were starting to gain popularity. Jim could never have imagined a more unlikely scenario than his old friend on the verge of winning the presidency. It might not happen but it sure made one hell of a story.

His grandson was playing right near the porch now, right up under Jim's feet. He was raking the stick along the railings, back and forth and back again.

"Stop that," Jim said and the boy stopped and looked at him. "What is your name, boy?" He asked, a slight smile slowly breaking across his face.

"You know my name, Granddad, I'm Matthew Brady."

"I've heard that name before, Matthew Brady. You wouldn't be the famous Civil War photographer, now would you?"

"I don't think so," the boy responded.

"No, of course you wouldn't, you're not old enough. How old are you, boy?"

"I'm five, Granddad," he answered.

"Listen, Matt, we have to knock off this Granddad stuff. From now on I want you to call me Grandpa. Okay?"

"Mother said I should call you Granddad because it shows more respect."

"Well, I know your mother quite well, and I know she is a very proper woman, but I am the oldest member of this family, and I get to be in charge. So, I would consider it a personal favor from you if you would call me Grandpa. I will speak to your mother about it. It's very important to me. Is that okay with you?"

"Sure, Grandpa," the boy said with a shrug and the matter was concluded.

Over to the northwest across Duncan creek some clouds were starting to form and it looked like they would get some rain. There was a storm brewing all right and not just over Kemper Farms but across the whole nation. The coming election would usher in a new century and maybe a whole new direction that the country would take. Jim really hoped that things would get better for all Americans. He owed this country a lot.

"Let's take a walk, Matt. I'll tell your mother we're going to the creek."

Matt took his grandfather's hand and followed along, stopping here and there to pick up a rock to toss into the water. They came to a particular spot on the creek bank and Jim told him to sit down and then sat down beside him.

"You see this place here, Matt? It was right here on this spot that, many years ago, your great grandfather, my father, asked my mother to marry him. She was your great grandmother and they lived here for a long time."

"Where are they now?" He asked.

"You wouldn't remember them Matt, they died before you were born. They were happy here though. Someone in your family has lived on this land for over seventy years, ever since my grandfather got it, way back, and someday you may live here too."

"But we live in Houston, Grandpa," Matt said, confused.

"I know you do, but this can be your summer home. I'll be here all the time now. You'll come and see me, won't you?"

The boy looked up at him, squinting. "Mother says I'm very fortunate to have you for a grandfather."

Very fortunate, Jim thought, laughing to himself. The boy was indeed his mother's son and she had taught him to speak properly. "No, sir" he said. "I'm the lucky one, Matt. I've got you for a grandson. I'm the luckiest man in the world."

Matt smiled at him, not altogether sure just what his grandfather was talking about but, nonetheless, happy to be the center of the older man's attention.

"Look, Matt," Jim said, pointing at the side of the creek, "snake doctors, see the snake doctors?"

"What's a snake doctor?" Matt said.

"It's an insect, a dragon fly, I think. They call them mosquito hawks sometimes. I don't know what they're really called, but in Texas we always called them snake doctors because they hang around snakes a lot and land on the snakes' backs. They don't carry doctor's bags, though."

Matt giggled and threw a rock at the little insects, scattering them momentarily. They then returned to the mud on the creek bank. A clap of thunder reminded Jim that there was rain approaching.

"Come on, Matt," he said. "We'd better get back to the house before the rain sets in. Come on, up you go, on my shoulders." He lifted him up and told him to hang on tight and then started to run for the house. Matt whooped and yelled and wrapped his hands around his grandfather's head.

"You can run fast, Grandpa."

"You mean for an old man?" Jim said.

"Yeah," Matt said, giggling.

The rain was starting to come down when they got back and Jim sent Matt inside and he stayed a while on the porch watching the lightning dancing off the tree line across the South pasture, some of the hands were still closing up the barns and trying to get inside so they could stay dry and Jim waved to them and they acknowledged him.

He was grateful for the opportunities he'd had. Few men in this life were as fortunate as he had been and, looking back on it, he didn't really know why things had turned out the way they did. He was probably more surprised than anyone. Mattie had never doubted him, not for a moment, neither had his mother. Mother had always been his biggest fan, all those years he'd spent so much time away from home, the long hours, and the endless business trips without his family had taken a toll on him, but Mattie had never complained. She had

kept his home and his children intact and they had turned out
wonderfully. She had been his strength when their son Alton
was killed. Though she suffered as much as he did, she seemed
to bear it better than her "unconquerable" husband had. It was
Alton's death that had made him decide to come home, and he
was sure that it had weighed heavily in Mattie's agreement to
give up her mansion and move to the country.

"I go where you go, James Kemper," she had told him.
"You should know that by now."

He went inside and sat down at the kitchen table and Mattie
poured him a cup of coffee. He added some cream and swirled
the spoon around to mix it. His face was staring back at him
from the front of the *Time Magazine* that Aimee had brought
for him to see. *Man Of The Year, 2000*. They talked about his
business prowess, how he always seemed to be in the right
place at the right time. What a crock of shit. A lot of luck and
some real good people on his team was the truth of the matter.

His companies directly employed just over twenty-
thousand people now and, indirectly, many thousands more.
But that was not what had created such a furor over him by the
news media. All those bastards were interested in was the fact
that he had "jumped ship" and was supporting a Democrat for
president. That was all they wanted to talk about, a "big time"
Republican abandoning his party to get on the liberal band
wagon. On talk shows and news programs they were speculating about all the reasons for Kemper's decision, the possibilities that now existed because of it. "The Republican Party"
had finally started to crumble and it was just a matter of time
until the Democrats controlled the country completely again.

What the stupid sons-of-bitches didn't understand was that
his decision had nothing to do with the Democrats or the Republicans. They were too busy congratulating themselves to
realize that Senator Grantham was the *only* Democrat that Jim
Kemper would even sit down to coffee with. As far as he was
concerned, there hadn't been a "morally decent" Democrat
since Jimmy Carter, and there had *never* been a good Democratic president, except maybe for Harry Truman. Anyway, he
had lost his train of thought.

The rain was pouring down now, drenching the farm. Good, he thought, they needed it.

Ah, this farm. He loved it so, this farm was his greatest love, and his greatest accomplishment, his greatest accomplishment by far, and his old friend Danny Carlisle had done most of that. It had been Jim's plan for the dairy and his decision to put Danny in charge of the business that had started it all, but Danny had certainly lived up to the confidence Jim had placed in him.

Quiet, unassuming Danny, was as close to Grandpa as anyone Jim had ever seen. Danny looked as comfortable in a business suit as he did in overalls and was just as engaging in conversation on the Comanche square as he was at the state department in Washington. Danny had turned out to be a good friend as well as an invaluable business partner. These were the things that mattered most in life, the kind of person a man turned out to be and who his real friends were. Yes, that was what was most important. Jim was convinced that he would not have turned out any different had he not been successful, even if he had been dirt poor. There was no way of knowing for sure but he had been blessed with the finest family any man had ever had and nothing could ever change that. A man's roots, and not his money, determined what he was truly made of.

His wife's voice broke his concentration. She was calling to him from the living room, her hand, with the thumb and pinkie extended and held up to her head, told him there was a telephone call for him.

"Hey, Pop, how's it goin'?"

It was Charlie in Dallas, that cocky manner of his, both endearing and irritating at the same time, made Jim smile to himself. "Just fine, son," he said. "We're getting settled in just fine. Your sister, Aimee, came to help your mom and it's like a hen house around here. Don't quote me on that. How is it there?"

"Better than I had expected. Allison and I met with the big shots at Hansen Trust, even old Warren Hansen himself and Abel too, of course, were there, and I don't see any problems.

They just got their asses up on their shoulders over all this political stuff. We're going to be able to smooth everything over.
I had to blow a little smoke you know where, but the bottom
line is those bastards know how much money you've made for
them over the years. They don't really care one way or the
other who's in the White House. I had them convinced that if
Jack Grantham is elected president they'll have a friend in
Washington because of Jim Kemper. Let's face it, Pop, they're
all a bunch of kiss asses. In the end, they'll do what we tell
them to, don't worry about the Towers Project. I'll get that
back on track right away."

"That's good news, Charlie, the best possible news. Thank
you, son, thanks very much."

"Nothin' to it, but I gotta tell you, Pop, you would have
been proud of Allison. My little sister doesn't take a back seat
to anyone. She told old man Hansen that if he pulled the financing for Kemper Enterprises, then she would get Washington and Mexico City involved because it would destroy the
Mexican low-priced housing project. She said she would create an international incident that would seriously endanger
Hansen Trust's standing with the US Government.

"Can she do that? I mean, does she have that much pull
with the Mexican Government?"

"I don't know, she seemed to think so, it sounded good."

"I guess you were right about putting Allison in charge of
the Mexico Division, Charlie. I'm really glad it worked for all
of us."

"She was great, Dad, those old boys aren't used to having a
woman talk to them like a construction worker, especially one
that looks like Allison."

"That's my girl," Jim said.

"Anyway," Charlie said, "you just stay on vacation as long
as you like. We've got it under control."

"It would appear so, but I may not be on vacation. I might
just call it quits."

"I don't think you mean that," Charlie said, more seriously
now. "I know you don't mean that, Pop. You're just feeling
bad because of all the pressure lately. You'll get that fire back

in your belly and, when you do I'll have your desk dusted off. It's one thing to run things for a little while and it's fun to throw my weight around, but I'm not ready to take over yet. Besides, this house is too big for us. What do I do with the house, Pop?"

"The house is yours, son, yours and Jenny's and Allison's. Allison will eventually get married and move out I imagine. It's all yours, Charlie. That's the way I want it to be."

"Okay, Pop," he said, "but I'm not ready for you to be gone yet. You're my rock. You do what you want to do for a while and come back when you're ready, don't worry about a thing. Relax, Dad, you've earned it."

He had barely hung up with Charlie when the phone rang again. "Jim? This is Tom Wilcox." Tom had finally stopped calling Jim, Mister, after Charlie talked to him that time.

"Yes, Tom, how are you?"

"Just fine, sir. I just wanted to tell you, Jim, that no matter what happens with the Towers project, or anything else, I will always support any decision you make. You've been more than fair with me for as long as we've known each other, I wouldn't be where I am today if it weren't for you. So, don't worry about anything you do hurting me or my business, nothing you do could ever hurt me."

Jim sensed that Tom was on the verge of tears. "I appreciate that, Tom," Jim said. "Everything is going to be okay. I just spoke to Charlie and he assures me that the project will be back on track directly. Now I want you to go back to work just like nothing ever happened. Help Charlie out as much as you can. He's capable and confident but he's young. It helps to know you have a friend here and there."

"Yes, sir, I'll do that," Tom said. "Thank you."

"And, Tom, please tell Sarah I love her and that Trent will be taking over the dairy one day."

"Will do, Jim," he said.

Well, well, Jim thought. *Even Alton could not have written a more intriguing work of fiction than the Kemper family saga.* Charlie had stepped in and taken over when the need and opportunity had arisen. Jim was a little surprised but he knew he should not be. Charlie was always stronger than Alton in business matters but he'd had to live in the shadow of his older brother. He was a rebel, all right, but one with vision. And Allison, damn! He was proud of her. What greater certification for a man's life than to have his daughter follow in his footsteps.

He remembered seeing a video, during the Gulf War. There was this top sergeant whose daughter was an officer in the army. It was common for a boy to aspire to be like his father but when a daughter did it, well, it was just that much more special.

He looked out the window at the rain that had now started to fall. A summer storm, it would quickly blow over. His mind wandered back over the years. They had all passed so quickly. He wished Grandpa was here to see how things had turned out. He would be happy to know that the dairy was not only still working but was the biggest dairy corporation in Texas and was branching out to more and more states, and other countries too, thanks to Danny, with each day that passed.

Grandpa's dream had come true after all. A vicarious dream, lived out through his grandson, but in the end the dream had come true. Perhaps his son Alton would have written about it if he'd lived. Jim would have loved that, Grandpa too, a history of the Kemper family, told by its very own family Historian. That wouldn't happen now. He missed Alton so much it hurt him, physically. He knew he would never get over losing his son.

Mattie was in the kitchen doing some dishes and he watched her for a moment. She was still a beautiful woman. Even at fifty-six, she was still beautiful. She turned heads where ever she went. Just like his mother had done. It was a wonder those two hadn't kept him in fistfights all the time.

Mattie was a treasure. She always knew the right thing to say, it seemed. One of the first things she did, when they started moving in, was take a long look out at the farm, now bustling with activity, and tell him. "Your grandfather is still alive here. He's alive in you, and he walks this farm just as surely as you do. As long as there are Kempers here, Grandpa Alton will be alive.

God, he thought, the Kemper men were blessed with great women, wonderful, beautiful women—mothers, wives, and daughters, and two daughters-in law. Sweet, wonderful, and beautiful Shadow McCormick, Alton's, and theirs, a gift from heaven. She still called him and Mattie on the phone from time to time, and they met in Washington as often as they could. Shadow and Mattie had gotten him through the tragedy and kept him from literally dying from a broken heart. Perhaps that was the secret to their great success. And Jenny Benson, probably the only girl who could have lived with and kept Charlie under control. They'd had an up and down relationship but somehow, it worked. He walked up behind Mattie and encircled her with his arms.

Thank you," he said.

"What for?" she asked.

"I don't know, everything I guess, for the kids, for moving back here, for being in California when I came back from Vietnam. But most of all for dancing with me that time at The Driftwood in Annapolis. You could have laughed me out the door."

"Oh, that? I did that on a dare."

"You did it on a dare on a dare?"

"Yes, Cindy Newsome said I was afraid to dance with a soldier. I showed her, didn't I?"

"Are you telling me that the entire Kemper family tree owes its existence to a dare?"

"Life sure takes some strange twists, doesn't it?" she said.

"Yes, it does, some strange twists indeed. Anyway, I guess what I was trying to say is, I love you."

"Well, that is good to know after all this time. And I love you too, but I think you know that."

"I know," he said. "And isn't it wonderful being able to take each other for granted?"

"Don't push your luck, soldier," she said.

He laughed and let go of her then walked back out on the porch. The rain was letting up and the sun was trying to force its way past the slowly dissipating clouds. It was calm now and the air smelled fresh and sweet. He loved the way the world smelled after a rain, like it was brand new.

Jim walked into his bedroom, pulled a locked metal box from the top of his closet, opened it up, took something out of it, and put it in his pocket. Then he relocked the box and put it back in the closet and walked out to the porch.

"Come here, Matt," Jim called to the boy, "I want to give you something."

"What is it, Grandpa?" he asked.

Jim took the watch out of his pocket and handed it to Matt. "This is for you, Matt," he said, my grandfather gave me this watch when I was five years old and I want you to have it. It's one of the finest watches in the world. It's a railroad watch."

The boy looked at the watch and rubbed his thumb across the face. "But I can't tell time, Grandpa."

"I know, that's okay, you will one day. But for now I want you to give it to your mother to keep for you. And one day I want you to give it to your grandson." The boy looked confused but nevertheless, stuck the watch in his pocket. "Go give it to you mother to keep for you, Matt," he said, and the boy went back into the house to find his mother. He was quickly back on the porch and, watching something in the yard, he tugged on his grandfather's pant leg.

"Look, Grandpa, some birds are trying to get into the bird house."

Jim hadn't noticed Matt standing next to him until the boy spoke. Now he was pointing to the little bird house that Danny Carlisle had put up years ago.

"I see, Matt. No birds have ever lived in that bird house. What do you know about that?"

"What kind of birds are they?" Matt asked

"I don't know, they look like—" Tears filled Jim's eyes and a lump came up in his throat, and he thought for a moment that he would cry out with joy. He knew if he did that his grandson would think he was crazy. He almost could not contain himself. Then a warm, peaceful feeling came over him and he understood. "They're wrens, Matt, house wrens. They used to live here a long time ago. Now they've come back. They've come back because we've come back. The Kempers have come home, and Grandpa's house wrens have come home too."

Jim retrieved a ladder and a hammer from the tool shed and started taking a vent out the soffit of the house. As he hacked away at the metal vent the little boy stood watching, wide eyed, wondering what going on.

"What are you doing, Grandpa?" he asked.

"I'm taking the vent out so the wrens can get into the eave of the house. We'll get some bird seed and put up in there and coax them back. They used to live in the eave of the old house and, with a little coaxing, they'll move in here."

"Why don't you just hang the bird house on the corner of your house?"

"What, what did you say, Matt?"

"The birds have already moved into the little house, why don't you just move it over here?"

Out of the mouths of babes, Jim thought. It made sense to Matt so he guessed it made sense to him too.

The birdhouse was soon hanging from the eave, and the wrens were busying themselves making a home of it. Jim wondered how he would explain to Mattie about the mangled vent in the soffit. He would cross that bridge later. He had the rest of his life to explain things to Mattie.

He picked up his grandson and lifted him up to the relocated bird house to watch the wrens. "I love you Matt," he said, and squeezed the boy lovingly.

"I love you too, Grandpa." Matt said, giggling, not knowing what had brought on this day's attention from his grandfather but not caring either. He was just content to be as close to the old man as he could be. "I love you too."

"Come on Matt, let's go into the house and see if Grandma has some hot biscuits and sugar syrup, okay?"

"What's sugar syrup?" the boy asked, puzzled.

"That's something my grandmother made for me a long, long time ago. I forgot that you had never heard of sugar syrup. I'll bet your grandmother doesn't know how to make it either. That's okay, we'll make do."

Jim Kemper had become his grandfather. He looked back out over the farm, now washed in beams of sunlight breaking through the clouds. It was a beautiful place. The most beautiful place on earth, he thought, and it was a beautiful day. "Yes, sir, it has really turned out to be a beautiful day."

End of Story

Author's note

Many of the people, places, and events in this story are real, but some of it I just made up out of thin air. Some of the real people I knew, many I did not. Some of the events were based on my own experiences, many were based on the experiences of people I knew and know.

The little farm in the story was an actual working farm just a few miles north of Comanche, Texas, and about two miles east of Mount Pleasant Baptist Church. I first visited that farm when I was five years old. The man who owned the farm and behind whom I followed along, running to keep up, as he walked his plowed fields, was my paternal grandfather. The woman, who made biscuits and sugar syrup for me, and for my many cousins, was our grandmother.

The little birds were real, they lived in the eave of my grandfather's house. On my last visit to the farm, many, many, years ago now, the buildings were all gone. The house, the smoke house and the barn had been torn down to make room for some other purpose. The windmill was still there and it was still pumping water.

I have lived to be of sufficient age to have known and loved those of my family who came before me, and I have been fortunate enough to have lived long enough to know and love those whom I will leave behind. The story did not end, it continues on today.

This book was twelve years in the making, a triumph of part-time labor.

Credits and Acknowledgements

Chapter 1: Jess Leroy Sprouse (the author's paternal grandfather) who was the inspiration for the character of Alton Kemper.

Chapters 9,10,11,12: Jack E. Grimmer (the Author's cousin/brother) on whose personal experiences, as a Helicopter pilot in Vietnam, the experiences of Jim Kemper in Vietnam are based. Grimmer also acted as advisor on the Vietnam chapters of the book.

Chapter 10: Bobby Sullivan Swaim (the author's cousin) for use of her father's name (Kinnie Sullivan) and persona as a character in the book.

Chapters 10,14: Pat Beaty Atwood for use of her father's name (John Beaty) and persona as a character in the book.

Chapter 11: George Burton from Somerset, Kentucky (who served at Soc Trang with the 336th Assault Helicopter Company).

Credits and Acknowledgements

Chapter 1: Jess Leroy Sprouse (the author's paternal grandfather) who was the inspiration for the character of Alton Kemper.

Chapters 9,10,11,12: Jack E. Grimmer (the Author's cousin/brother) on whose personal experiences, as a Helicopter pilot in Vietnam, the experiences of Jim Kemper in Vietnam are based. Grimmer also acted as advisor on the Vietnam chapters of the book.

Chapter 10: Bobby Sullivan Swaim (the author's cousin) for use of her father's name (Kinnie Sullivan) and persona as a character in the book.

Chapters 10,14: Pat Beaty Atwood for use of her father's name (John Beaty) and persona as a character in the book.

Chapter 11: George Burton from Somerset, Kentucky (who served at Soc Trang with the 336th Assault Helicopter Company).

About the Author

Jack Sprouse is from Dallas, Texas, although he now lives in Lewisville, a few miles north of Dallas. He studied American History at Texas Tech, in Lubbock, and his fields of greatest historical interest are the American Civil War and World War II. He served in the United States Navy as a crewmember on an ASW (anti-submarine-warfare) patrol aircraft. Writing fiction is his passion.

Sprouse just loves making stuff up (his mom used to punish him for doing that when he was a kid). He has written two books of historical fiction: *Adventures in Time Book I: The American Civil War* and *Adventures in Time Book II: The American West*—these are both Walter Mitty type stories in which he places himself back in time as a war correspondent following historical events and interviewing the major players in those events; two books of original poetry, *The Quiet Place* and *Dreams of a Forgotten Man*—both books contain approximately fifty original poems on various subjects: Life, love, friendship, relationships, war, conflict, tragedy; and several novels: *The House Wren*, a saga of a fictional Texas family; *On Neptune Wings*, a love story set in the 1960s against the backdrop of a US Navy Patrol Squadron; *Magnolia Road,* an improbable love story between a girl from Vermont and a rancher from Colorado. She is purposeful and dedicated to her chosen calling in life; and *Clare*, about a twenty-four-year-old woman who faces life with quiet confidence and inner turmoil; experiencing love, hurt, uncertainty, sexual harassment in the workplace, and tragedy. He is currently working on several ideas for new books.